Anne Baker trained as a nurse at Birkenhead General Hospital, but after her marriage went to live first in Libya and then in Nigeria. She eventually returned to her native Birkenhead where she worked as a Health Visitor for over ten years. She now lives with her husband in Merseyside. Anne Baker's other Merseyside sagas are all available from Headline and have been widely praised:

'A stirring tale of romance and passion, poverty and ambition' *Liverpool Echo*

'Highly observant writing style . . . a compelling book that you just don't want to put down' *Southport Visiter*

'A gentle tale with all the right ingredients for a heartwarming novel' *Huddersfield Daily Examiner*

'A heartwarming saga' *Woman's Weekly*

'A truly compelling and sentimental story and rich in language and descriptive prose' *Newcastle Upon Tyne Evening Chronicle*

Also by Anne Baker

Like Father, Like Daughter
Paradise Parade
Legacy of Sins
Nobody's Child
Merseyside Girls
Moonlight on the Mersey
A Mersey Duet
Mersey Maids
A Liverpool Lullaby
With a Little Luck
The Price of Love
Liverpool Lies
Echoes Across the Mersey

A Glimpse of the Mersey

Anne Baker

HEADLINE

First published in 2001
by HEADLINE BOOK PUBLISHING

First published in paperback in 2001
by HEADLINE BOOK PUBLISHING

10 9 8 7 6 5 4 3 2 1

ISBN 0 7472 6777 4

Printed and bound in Great Britain by
Mackays of Chatham plc, Chatham, Kent

Typeset by CBS, Martlesham Heath, Ipswich, Suffolk

HEADLINE BOOK PUBLISHING
A division of Hodder Headline
338 Euston Road
London NW1 3BH

www.headline.co.uk
www.hodderheadline.com

A Glimpse of the Mersey

Chapter One

March 1919

Daisy Corkill always listened for the tap of Brenda's high heels when it was time for her to come home from work. Tonight, she was later than usual and the fish shop over which they lived had closed. Daisy sensed Brenda's excitement the moment she came running upstairs.

'Wonderful news.' Brenda laughed as she threw her coat on her bed and swept into the living room, where Uncle Ern was setting out plates of fried herring and mashed potatoes on the table. 'Lots to tell you.'

'What is it then?' Auntie Glad demanded as she pulled out a chair to sit down.

Brenda was all smiles as she twisted the emerald ring on her engagement finger. She was the younger of Auntie Glad's two daughters and worked in a dress shop. Before she sat down, Brenda fastened on a green apron to protect the smart black skirt and white blouse she was required to wear for work.

Daisy sat down opposite her and felt suddenly breathless with hope. 'You haven't broken it off?'

'No, silly.' A playful foot pushed against Daisy's knee. 'Gilbert and me, we've fixed our wedding day.' She laughed with joy. 'Been down to the church. It's

1

to be the last Thursday in June.'

Daisy gasped. She wanted Brenda to be happy, of course she did, but she was apprehensive. Brenda didn't often bring Gilbert home, Daisy hardly knew him but she certainly hadn't taken to him.

Brenda Maddocks was no relation but Daisy had grown up wishing she really was her big sister. It was some comfort that most of the people she came in contact with, customers and neighbouring shopkeepers, assumed she was. Not having blood relatives of her own, Daisy longed for them above everything else.

Countless times, as Brenda had powdered her nose in the dressing-table mirror they shared, Daisy had crowded behind her seeking some likeness in their faces, hoping to prove she was related, if only distantly. She wished she was more like Brenda.

Brenda was well-groomed and elegant, with lovely dark hair and soft luminous eyes. Daisy had never seen herself as anything but plain. She thought her nose too big and her chin too square. Diffident blue eyes stared back at her from a rather large face framed by two brown plaits of enormous thickness that reached below her waist.

Uncle Ern leapt from his chair to kiss his daughter and wish her well. Brenda had been engaged to Gilbert Fox for two years, so it wasn't totally unexpected.

'I'm pleased you've set the day.' Auntie Glad, a big-boned woman with a florid complexion, retrieved a herring bone from her mouth. She was always a little dour but like the rest of them, she doted on Brenda. 'And not before time. Wouldn't like you to be left on the shelf.' At twenty-six, Brenda was ten years older than Daisy and had been engaged four times before.

Uncle Ern chuckled. He was a gentle person, with a shock

of white hair and a grey walrus moustache. 'We always thought you'd be married at eighteen. Snapped up quickly. A good-looking girl like you.'

Daisy told herself that if Brenda was determined to marry Gilbert Fox, there was nothing more she could do to stop her. The wedding would be lovely, Brenda would make sure it was done in great style.

'Can I be your bridesmaid?' she asked. 'Do let me. I'd love that.'

Brenda pulled a face. 'I've already agreed to three child bridesmaids. Relatives of the groom.'

'Three's plenty.' Auntie Glad was straight-lipped. 'Think of the cost.' Daisy's hopes sank.

Brenda laughed again. 'No cost to us. Gil's family will be fitting them out.'

'I didn't know Gil had relatives like that,' Uncle Ern said.

'Neither did I. It just happens they'll be here on a visit from Canada. Distant relatives of his mother, she thought it would be a good idea.'

'Please,' Daisy pleaded. 'I've never been a bridesmaid.'

Brenda's dark eyes met hers. She smiled in the way that made Daisy feel she was Brenda's nearest and dearest.

'If you want to be the only grown-up bridesmaid, I can borrow a dress for you from Mrs Fanshaw. She's already offered it.' Brenda's boss had become Mrs Fanshaw in the early years of the war, and still had all her wedding finery.

'Yes please. I'd love that,' Daisy breathed.

Auntie Glad put in, 'What about our Ruth? She's your real sister. What if she wants to be a bridesmaid too?'

Daisy felt that as another jab to remind her she didn't really belong here.

'Ruth can if she wants.' Brenda's smile was warm and seemed only for Daisy. 'The more the merrier. She won't expect me to buy a dress for her.'

Ruth had left home when she was twenty to train as a nurse but she often came to see the family when she had time off. She was now working as a midwifery sister at Grange Mount Hospital.

There was a large framed photograph of her on the parlour mantelpiece, wearing her uniform dress and apron and large fluttering folds of starched muslin over her head. Three years older than Brenda, she wasn't nearly so pretty. She resembled Uncle Ern, with a rather plump face and benign expression, and as befitted a nurse, she was kind and caring.

Daisy had never seen Ruth in uniform. When she came home she was always fashionably dressed. She was a customer at the shop where Brenda worked and had the benefit of her expertise. Daisy liked her, impossible not to, but she didn't feel as close to her as she did to Brenda. She didn't know her so well; Ruth was more self-contained, a little introverted. Nowadays she seemed almost a visitor in the house.

When they'd finished eating, Uncle Ern pushed two half-crowns into Daisy's hand.

'Nip down to the Queen Vic for me. See if you can get a bottle of port. We'll all drink to our Brenda's health and happiness. British Ruby Port, that's what your Auntie Glad likes.'

'I'm going out, Dad. Gil's calling for me in half an hour and I've got to get ready.'

'Time for a quick one, love. Anyway, your mam and I will enjoy it.'

The only coat Daisy owned was the one she wore in the shop and Brenda wouldn't allow her to bring that up to their bedroom because it smelled of fish. She pulled her mackintosh round her and ran down Market Street to the pub. Nothing was too much trouble if it was for Brenda. She enchanted them all, nobody could do enough for her.

When she got back and tried to give the one and six change to Uncle Ern, he said, 'Put it towards the coat you want, love. You're a good girl and you've been saving for it a long time.'

'This gives me enough. I'll be able to buy it now.' Daisy felt almost as happy as Brenda. 'Auntie Glad, can I call in Brenda's shop tomorrow morning and get it?'

'As long as you don't stay there half the morning.'

'I'll watch out for you.' Brenda winked at her.

'Only after you'd done all the deliveries, mind,' Auntie Glad added.

The next morning was bright but frosty. All the way up Market Street Daisy stood on the pedals of the delivery bike to make the wheels turn faster. It was huge and heavy and had a great metal fitment on the back and an even bigger one on the front that held carrier baskets. Daisy had been very keen to learn to ride it, a bike was a desirable object, even one such as this. To start with, she'd barely been able to hold it upright when it was stacked high front and rear with bags of fish and vegetables. So that the girls could make the deliveries, it had a ladies' crossbar; beneath that the red and gold lettering read: G.G. Sampson, Fish Monger and Green Grocer, Market Street. Brenda had been very keen to teach her to ride it so she could help with the deliveries.

'I wanted a fairy cycle,' Brenda told her. 'This was what I got.'

Daisy had mastered it by the time she was ten and now went soaring round the streets. She felt like singing, delivering orders was her favourite job, but today she'd hoped to finish as quickly as possible to give herself time to choose a coat. Just as she was setting out on this round which she'd left until last, Uncle Ern had rushed out to say he'd made up another three orders to be delivered in town.

She was throwing every ounce of energy into pedalling and was breathless by the time she propped the bike upright against the kerb outside the premises owned by Gilbert Fox's family. It did have kick-down legs so it could stand upright, but they were so stiff Daisy still found them difficult to use.

The first thing she did was to look across the road to the clothes shop where Brenda worked. It surprised her to see the red coat she'd fancied still in the window. Brenda had promised to put it away for her so nobody else could buy it. Still, it hadn't been sold. Daisy had seen it on the day the sale had started. A price tag of thirty-five shillings swung from the belt.

With a shiver of excitement, she lifted the bags of greengroceries from the bike's basket. She'd always thought the Fox business rather odd. The shop that fronted the big building was a dairy, there were churns of milk standing along one wall and they ran a milk round every morning. There was also a discreet brass plate beside the door that read: Z.A. Fox and Sons, Funeral Directors.

She'd heard that customers for that service were led through to another room furnished with a desk and comfortable armchairs, and once she'd peeped through the small window but an aspidistra in a copper pot almost blocked the view inside. She knew hire cars could be ordered there too.

She was taking the bags to the door alongside the dairy to ring the bell when she heard the scrape of bike brakes and the jangle as another bike touched hers. She saw hers wobble but it didn't fall.

The rider leapt off and kicked his pedal against the kerb

to prop it upright. He wore a smart pepper and salt tweed jacket and seemed in an even greater hurry than she was. Gilbert Fox chose that moment to rush out of the dairy to talk to him. Brenda's fiancé was a handsome man of thirty-three with a lot of wavy dark hair and a waxed moustache. Daisy had heard Uncle Ern say he was rather a ladies' man; she thought so too.

She rang the house bell again, then let her eyes linger on the scarlet wool coat, believing its bright colour would transform the drabness of all her other clothes. The house door was opened by a stout woman, wiping her hands on her apron.

'Morning, Mrs Bagshott.' Daisy had been delivering orders even before she'd left school and knew the cook general employed by the Fox family. 'Your weekly order from Sampson's.' She put the bags into her arms and turned to go.

'Er, wait a minute till I check this stuff over. Last week you didn't bring the leeks I ordered.'

'There's leeks there today. And the cod and two pairs of bloaters. Isle of Man, the best.' Usually Daisy carried the groceries into the kitchen for her. 'I want to make a call across the road.' She nodded towards the clothes shop. She'd been waiting for this chance for days and she wasn't going to put it off any longer. 'I'll knock again when I'm finished over there.'

'See you do then.'

Daisy let a pony and trap pass before running across. The clothes shop door pinged open and the warmth enveloped her, bringing the scent of new cloth. She filled her lungs with a shiver of pleasure. Brenda came out from the back room.

'I've come for the red coat,' Daisy gulped. 'You said

you'd take it out of the window for me.' She felt for the thirty-five shillings she'd saved from her wages. It was safely in her pocket, tied up in her handkerchief.

'I put it away for you.'

'No, it's still here. This is the one.'

Brenda was frowning. 'That coat won't fit you. Not your size. Much too big.' Daisy saw her eyes travel over her slight figure.

She was wearing her working clothes and in here they made her feel shabby. Old boots and gaiters that reached to just below her knee with a skirt that barely covered the tops of them so she could ride the delivery bike. Once all these clothes had been Brenda's; Daisy rarely had new ones. She felt deflated.

'Too big?' She peered into the window. From this side she could see some of the width of the red coat had been pinned back to give it a more attractive line when viewed from the street.

'Much too big. Bust size forty.'

Daisy could feel a ball of disappointment growing in her throat. The coat looked so smart. She'd imagined herself wearing it, suddenly transformed from a drab sparrow to a swan. She hadn't thought about its size. In desperation, she said, 'Can I try it on?'

Brenda sighed. 'I know it won't fit you,' but she started to unpin the coat from the model in the window. 'By the way,' she looked up with a dazzling smile, 'Mrs Fanshaw is bringing her wedding dress down for me this afternoon.'

'What about . . . ?'

'Yes, and the bridesmaid's dress for you.'

Daisy felt another swirl of pleasure.

Through the plate glass, she could see Gilbert Fox still

out on the pavement. He was waving his arms about angrily, and seemed to be arguing with the man who'd parked his bike behind hers.

At last Brenda was holding the red coat out and sliding Daisy's arms into the sleeves. It had a beautiful scarlet silk lining but felt light and slack, not body hugging and warm as she'd anticipated.

They were standing side by side in front of the big mirror. Daisy studied their reflection and wished as always that she was more like Brenda. The truth was, Brenda was beautiful and would look good in sackcloth, while the red coat she'd hankered for hung garish and shapeless on her slight frame and her oversized plaits dwarfed everything else. She could see disappointment in every line of her body.

Both Brenda and Auntie Glad told her that it was high time she wore her strong wiry hair up. She'd tried to fix it on top of her head but it wouldn't stay there for more than half an hour. There was just too much of it.

'Like I said,' Brenda was still frowning, 'this coat's much too big for you. Mrs Fanshaw should never have ordered it. It's too bright a colour for the large woman it would fit. You'd see her coming a hundred yards away. That's why it's in the sale at this price.'

Daisy was biting her lip in indecision.

'Why don't you try the one I put away for you?' Brenda fetched it from the back room.

'That isn't red.'

'A reddish rust. I thought this was the one you meant. It's your size.'

'It's more a brown.'

'More practical, Daisy. You could get tired of a bright colour and it's a wool bouclé. A good warm coat.'

Daisy felt the red coat being lifted off her shoulders and

her arms fed into the sleeves of the brown bouclé. She thought the colour rather drab.

'Fits well.' Brenda's hands smoothed the material over her shoulders. Daisy shook her head, she wanted something brighter, more attractive.

'There are other coats that will fit you. Try this blue and grey tweed.'

Moments later, the belt of the blue tweed was being pulled tight round her waist. Strong hands turned her round so she could see herself in the mirror. It was marginally better, but tweed was very down-to-earth.

'It suits you.' There was enthusiasm in Brenda's voice.

Daisy's eye caught the price tag. She was shocked. 'I can't afford three guineas.'

'I get discount. Mrs Fanshaw needn't know it isn't for me. That would bring it down to two guineas.'

The shop door pinged again and she said, 'The coats on this rail are all reduced. See if there's anything here you like,' and went to greet the newcomer.

Gilbert Fox came into the shop. He looked pleased with himself as though he'd won the argument he'd been having outside. Daisy thought he was about to throw his arms round Brenda but she caught at one of them and led him into the back room. Daisy could hear lowered voices and delicious little laughs from behind the half-closed door as she felt for another coat to try on.

She needed a coat badly and she daren't stay long or she'd be in trouble with Auntie Glad when she got back. She had only the navy blue melton, a hand-me-down from Ruth, that she was wearing. It was warm but shabby and she'd had to wear it to work since the beginning of the winter. Now it was none too clean where the apron she wore in the shop didn't cover it.

She tried on a fawn coat. Not bad, but nothing compared with the red. She fidgeted with the collar trying to make up her mind. It wasn't what she really wanted, but it would do. Better to buy here where Brenda could give her discount than try somewhere else.

She could hear the rise and fall of Gilbert's voice from the back room. Across the road, the door to his dairy flew open and the man she'd seen talking to him earlier came racing out. He was followed by Ellis Fox, Gilbert's younger brother, who was trying to catch him.

Daisy's attention was riveted, she held her breath. Something extraordinary was going on. The man grabbed for his bike in such a hurry that he knocked hers again. This time it crashed to the pavement.

Her heart missed a beat. She'd be in trouble if it was scratched. She was feverishly unbuttoning the fawn coat when she saw Gilbert's mother come to the shop door and shout.

When the significance of what she was watching sank in, Daisy couldn't move a muscle. Then, feeling half wild with panic she rushed to the back room and threw open the door.

'Brenda, Gilbert, come quick. I think your shop's being robbed.'

They were all across the road in seconds, all shouting at once. Ellis was coming back slowly, out of breath and limping slightly. He looked very down. He'd fought in the trenches and had only just returned home. She thought he looked very different to Gilbert, not like a brother at all. She'd heard Brenda say he was eleven years younger, more serious and lacking all Gilbert's polish.

'He got away, I couldn't stop him. He's taken what was in the till.'

'Stolen?'

'The takings – got clear away with them.'

Daisy followed the others into the shop. Everybody was talking at once in a fever of outrage and excitement. Mrs Fox, a small woman who wore black ankle-length skirts, was now sitting in the corner with her apron over her head.

'Are you all right, Mam?' Ellis asked her.

The apron was lowered, her face twisted with pain. 'He pushed me over.'

'You fell against the churn, there,' he said sympathetically. 'I heard shouting and—'

Hard and heavy thudding on the ceiling silenced them all.

Gilbert looked up. 'It's Father!'

Ellis said, 'He'll want to know what's happening. All the shouting.'

'Go and tell him.'

'I want to phone the police straight away.'

'No! No, don't do that.' Gilbert was breathing heavily. 'Not necessary.'

'Course it is.' Ellis hesitated, looking nonplussed. 'What hope do we have of getting our money back if we don't?'

'We've got to report it,' his mother insisted. 'We can't let that fellow get away with this.'

'No, hang on a minute.' Gilbert was holding up his hands.

'Don't be silly,' his mother retorted. 'The sooner we let the police know, the better chance they'll have of catching him. Get on the phone to them, Ellis.'

Daisy was watching. Without another word, Ellis went down the passage at the back to the office. Then she turned to stare at Gilbert. She couldn't believe this.

'You knew him, didn't you?' She knew she sounded suspicious.

He said hotly, 'I didn't even see him.'

'You did, it was the man you were talking to. In the pepper and salt tweed jacket. Out there on the pavement, before you came across to the dress shop.' She turned to Brenda. 'We saw them talking, didn't we?'

Brenda looked blank.

Gilbert said, 'It wasn't him.'

'It was. He left his bike right behind mine.'

'No, that fellow pedalled away. I watched him go. This was someone different. Quite different.'

Daisy recoiled, her heart pounding. It was not just Gilbert's words that shocked her, she could feel the tension and anger behind them. And his confidence was making her doubt what she'd seen. She hesitated, trying to think back. No, she wasn't mistaken. She'd seen the man come out of the dairy and mount his bike. He was wearing that unusual jacket. Gilbert was acting very strangely. She was beginning to think there was something very odd going on.

As Ellis returned, saying, 'The police are on the way,' there was another burst of hammering on the ceiling.

Gilbert tried to push Brenda towards the stairs. 'Go up and tell Dad what's happened.'

'I can't, I've got to get back to the shop. I've left it unlocked. Don't want the same thing to happen there, do I? I'd get the sack.'

As Daisy watched her run back across the road, an old man's voice shouted from the stairs, 'What's going on down there?'

'Go and help him,' Mrs Fox implored. 'I'm afraid he'll fall.' It was Ellis who ran up to him. Daisy hadn't seen old Mr Fox for a long time, he'd had a stroke last year and didn't often come downstairs now.

'What's going on?' In his formal dark suit and waistcoat he looked like an undertaker. His face was cadaverous, thin with greyish cheeks. He collapsed heavily on to a chair and glowered up at Gilbert.

His wife said, 'A man came in and stole money from the till.'

'Did he . . .' Mr Fox was breathless. 'Did he threaten you?'

'He knocked me flying. He was in such a hurry to get away.'

Ellis looked decidedly ruffled. 'He came in and started talking to me. About our undertaking business. I thought he wanted to arrange a funeral, but when I asked, he said no. He wanted to speak to you, Dad. Said it was a personal matter. I explained that you hadn't been well for some time and he said Mam would do. I could hear her in the kitchen so I called her in.'

'Who was he?'

'I don't know.' Mrs Fox started to sob.

'What did he say to you?' Gilbert demanded.

His mother was shaking with sobs. 'Some long story. About the old days, when his family used to work here. I couldn't make head nor tail of it. Oh deary me.'

'Ellis?'

'I didn't listen. I was taking an empty churn out to the back. I was just rolling in a full one when I heard Mam scream. The fellow leapt suddenly at the till and scooped out all we'd taken this morning. I tried to stop him when I realised what he was up to. He just shoved past us both, knocked Mam flying and was gone before I could stop him.'

Ellis looked white and shaken, but seemed concerned for his mother. 'You need to lie down, Mam. This has shaken you up. Are you hurt? Come on, I'll take you upstairs and get Ruby to make you a cup of tea.'

'What about the police?'

'I'll bring them up to talk to you.'

'I could do with a cup of tea too,' his father grunted and tried to lift his bulk from the chair.

Daisy took a deep shaky breath, it had all happened so quickly. Her head was in a whirl and her knees felt weak.

She looked up to find Gilbert's pale green eyes staring at her; they were full of aggression. 'You'd better go,' he said roughly.

'Won't the police want to talk to me? I saw the man outside.'

'No.'

'I had a really good look at him. Hadn't I better wait?'

'No.' His hand shot out with the speed of a viper's tongue to fasten on her wrist; his fingers bit painfully into her flesh. 'We can tell them all they need to know. Go on now.' There was raw anger in his face. 'We're all a bit upset here and this has nothing to do with you.' He propelled her towards the door.

Daisy was affronted. Not many people wanted to hear what she thought, but in this case she'd seen more of what had happened than anyone else. She'd never seen Gilbert like this before, all tensed up with fury. And why had he tried to tell her she was wrong about that man? It rather looked as though he wanted the robbery kept quiet and that could only mean . . .

She went out into the cold frosty air and shivered. Then went slowly across to Brenda's shop. She'd left in such a hurry she hadn't put her own coat on.

Brenda said, 'I had to put it in the back room. It stinks of fish.'

'That's why I need another.'

'Look, I could give you that green one of mine.'

'I want a new one Brenda, but I daren't stay longer now.

Auntie Glad will be mad with me for being away this long. I've got more deliveries to do.'

When she picked up her delivery bike, she found a bad scratch along the side of the deep carrier on the front. Spitting on her handkerchief and rubbing at it didn't help. Some of the paint had come off. She was afraid Auntie Glad would be cross about that too. The red coat had turned out to be a big disappointment. It had been a bad morning.

She rushed back to the fish shop. In the yard behind she loaded another round into the large panniers on her bike. Her stomach was still churning as she set about delivering them as quickly as possible. She was afraid Brenda could be making a big mistake in marrying Gilbert Fox. He'd been quite nasty.

Chapter Two

Daisy pedalled back as fast as she could. From the far end of Market Street, she could see the big double shop with boxes of fruit and vegetables spilling outside on the pavement. She went round the back to the yard, put away the bike, tied her apron on over her coat and went to serve. The shop was full of customers.

'Where've you been until now?' Auntie Glad demanded. 'I knew you'd hang around Brenda's shop for hours if I said you could go. You take advantage. You knew we were busy.'

Daisy explained about the theft. Her mind still whirled as she let the details spill out.

'Hardly believable.' Auntie Glad, her mouth round with shock, stopped blaming her. 'Fox's robbed like that!' The fish shop customers waiting to be served listened with rapt attention too.

'In broad daylight?'

'At half ten in the morning? With people about?'

'The nerve of it!'

But as far as Daisy was concerned, the worst part was that Gilbert had wanted to brush it away as though it was of no importance. He'd refused to admit he'd spoken to the thief and he'd shown such rage at her. She'd felt threatened and his aggressive green eyes had scared her. If he could be like that to her, how would he treat Brenda? She tried to explain it to Uncle Ern, but he didn't think there was anything sinister in what Gilbert had done.

'He believes it was a different person, luv. That's all.'

Old Willie, their shop assistant for the last twelve years, pushed his fingers under his cap to scratch his head. 'We ought to be careful. Would you know this fellow again? He could come here.'

When Auntie Glad closed the shop at dinner time, she emptied her tills and took the money upstairs.

'You never know who's waiting to snatch your takings,' she told Daisy.

After dinner, Uncle Ern put a lick of black paint over the scratch on the bike, saying, 'Got to keep it smart if we can. It reflects on the business.'

That afternoon, there were only two topics of conversation in the shop, the theft at Fox's and Brenda's wedding.

Mrs Mack, who'd sold their fruit and vegetables for the past decade, said, 'Brenda will make a lovely bride. Marrying in white, is she? And you a bridesmaid?'

Auntie Glad acted as though she'd personally seen the theft and told everybody she felt involved because Brenda was going to marry into the family. She asked Daisy if the Foxes were upset.

'The old people, yes very. Gilbert . . . I don't understand him.'

'Wait till Brenda comes home, she'll tell us more.'

'She doesn't know any more,' Daisy said impatiently. 'She saw less of what happened than I did. She was in the back room with Gilbert at the time.'

'The police will be down to talk to you. They'll be on to that man, he won't get away with this.'

Daisy herself expected the police to come to hear her

version of what had happened. When they didn't, she began to think that Gilbert was going to succeed in hushing it up. He hadn't wanted the police called in the first place. It seemed he didn't want the thief caught, but that didn't make sense. He'd surely want his money back if he could get it.

Daisy had to recount her story several times. For her the theft itself became a distraction. Auntie Glad's conversation switched continually from the theft to the wedding, and in the end Daisy made herself think instead of the bridesmaid's dress she would wear. She didn't even know what colour it was yet. She fancied blue satin.

It was getting on towards closing time, Auntie Glad was growing irritable and the afternoon had turned cold and wintry. The double doors of the shop on Market Street stood wide open whatever the weather.

'Get a move on, Daisy. You've done nothing but daydream all afternoon.'

That brought her back with a bump. She shivered. Her feet were freezing though she wore strong boots and thick socks over her stockings. Auntie Glad was tossing finnan haddock on the scales for one of the last customers of the day when an angry woman rushed in under the shop lights and without waiting for her turn at the counter announced to them all, 'I should have more sense than to buy from you. We couldn't have that cod for our dinner, it was after half twelve when your daughter delivered it. She was late coming again.'

Daisy quaked, she knew she was in trouble. 'I'm sorry,' she said though she'd apologised at the time. It was the theft at Fox's that had made her late. Auntie Glad was bristling with annoyance.

'She's not my daughter,' she snapped, and the cherries

on her shabby felt hat bounced with emphasis.

The words cut into Daisy. She hated to hear her say such things, especially in that tone of voice. It sounded as though Auntie Glad wanted to disown her altogether. She was saying a lot more; a lengthy apology to the customer.

Daisy couldn't listen, she wanted to hide. She had often pondered on the turn of fate that had put her in this fish shop. She remembered as a toddler being tied to the stand on the other side of the shop where fruit was displayed. She'd lived with the Maddocks family all her life though she was not related to them.

Auntie Glad turned on her. 'You've got to learn to jump to it. I knew if I said you could go to Brenda's shop for that coat—'

'I didn't get a coat. There wasn't time. It was the robbery that made me late.'

'You're always in a daydream, mooning on about some lord or earl coming round to claim you as his daughter. You've got to keep your mind in the real world, on what needs doing, or you'll be no use here.'

Daisy found that hurtful. She hadn't had those daydreams since she was eight years old. She prided herself on having a practical streak. She reckoned she worked hard.

In Daisy's opinion, Auntie Glad didn't suit her name, she was never glad about anything. She was a rather bitter person with deep ruts of dissatisfaction running from her nose to the corners of her mouth.

Brenda had inherited her mother's brown eyes; hers could be challenging too. But Auntie Glad's eyes were hard and cold and no longer beautiful and she had the beginnings of a dark moustache on her upper lip. She ordered and demanded instead of pleading and cajoling as Brenda did, and always she seemed angry. She never gave an inch to anybody else.

Sampson now, that was a name that did suit her. As a child, Daisy had asked why the name Sampson was over their shop when their name was Maddocks.

'Sampson was Auntie Glad's name before she was married,' Uncle Ern had explained. 'The business belonged to her father, she inherited it when he died.'

For Daisy that threw a new light on Auntie Glad. She was strong, very strong, stronger than Uncle Ern. The lines of power ran through the women in the Maddocks family. It was Auntie Glad who tended the shop counter all day. Uncle Ern who cooked meals and saw to the fire upstairs. Of course, he had to be in the wholesale fish market by four o'clock in the morning to buy their stock and then he had to do the same for their fruit and vegetables and bring everything back to the shop.

Daisy was glad to see an old man coming in and went to serve him.

'Three herrings, please.'

'Fine fat herrings today, sir.' They were the last on the tray, thank goodness. Herrings were the most icy and slippery of fish. Her numb fingers could no longer grip them.

It was getting dark. When the old man left, Daisy started collecting up the enamel trays that were empty and taking them out to be washed. Mrs Mack was already sorting through the vegetables that remained. Auntie Glad expected wilting greens to be marked down or discarded every night. It was their way of hinting that it was time to shut up shop, but they only did that when Auntie Glad gave the word. If customers kept coming in, they could be open at ten o'clock at night, and sometimes were on light summer evenings.

Auntie Glad gave a gusty sigh. 'Might as well close. Won't

21

be many more customers tonight. Daisy, get this fish put away.'

'Don't let her upset you,' whispered old Willie as he carried in the sacks of potatoes and crates of vegetables that were set outside on the pavement.

Daisy packed the fresh fish that hadn't been sold back into boxes and carried it out to the ice box in the back yard. A cart delivered blocks of ice every day, though they hardly needed it this weather. Only the smoked fish, kippers and bloaters stayed in the shop overnight.

Auntie Glad shut the doors, put the closed sign against the glass and turned her attention to the tills.

'Get a bucket of hot water to wash this slab down, Daisy, and when Willie and Mrs Mack are ready to go, be sure to lock up after them.'

'Yes, Auntie Glad.' It was what Daisy always did.

'I'll take the cash upstairs to count, too cold down here.'

Daisy went out to the wash house in the yard and ran the tap. In the mirror over the sink her nose looked red and her face pinched. She wore a rubber apron under a cloth one, both tied over the old coat, with a thick cardigan underneath for warmth. Her clothes gave her the shape of a sack of potatoes. She flung off the woolly hat she wore pulled down over her ears; she particularly hated that.

Pushing up her sleeves, she put her hands into the bucket of hot water. After the first pain, it was bliss to feel her fingers thawing out. She would have liked to splash hot water on her face but the only towel often had fish scales sticking to it. Her last job at closing time was to wash the trays on which the fish had been displayed and scrub the cutting blocks and knives. This was better than standing about waiting for customers to come in and signalled the end of the working day. Daisy had worked in the shop since she left school on her fourteenth birthday.

'We kept you at school right to the last minute,' Auntie Glad had assured her more than once, 'though we could have taken you out to help in the shop before then.'

She was now paid seven shillings a week and her keep, to serve in the shop, sweep up, lift sacks of potatoes about and deliver orders round the neighbourhood. In addition she was paid a commission of a penny in the pound on the money she collected. Some customers liked to pay when she delivered their orders and on some weeks she could earn as much as half-a-crown that way. She considered it good money.

In the shop, she was treated exactly like Mrs Mack and Willie, the two assistants. It was what she expected. Upstairs in the rooms above the shop, Auntie Glad didn't always treat her as family.

Daisy scrubbed hard at the cutting blocks. She couldn't get Auntie Glad's words out of her mind. She minded very much that she had no blood relations. Everybody else had brothers and sisters and cousins and uncles and aunts but she had only the Maddockses. She was filled with longing; she must have had parents but Auntie Glad refused to tell her much about them.

'You've been at me ever since you were six years old, asking everlasting questions.' She would mimic Daisy's voice. 'Why is my name Corkill when yours is Maddocks? Where is my mam and dad? Why aren't I with them?'

When Daisy was twelve she asked Auntie Glad if she was her mother's sister. She knew a girl at school who lived with her aunt.

'No, I'm not, I'm no relation. I just got landed with you. I wish you'd stop poking into what's long gone, it's unhealthy.'

'If you'd just tell me,' Daisy pleaded. 'I'd know then and be satisfied, wouldn't I? What is the secret?'

On days when Auntie Glad was in a better mood, she'd say, 'We've given you a good home, looked after you, fed and clothed you. Just be glad you've got us and show some gratitude.'

Daisy tried. Auntie Glad could be right about providing a good home. There was always plenty to eat. Most of what went on the table was bought at wholesale prices to sell in the shop, but was all the better for that. They had the pick of fresh vegetables and fresh fish and ate salads all through the summer. Auntie Glad told her to help herself to the fruit in the shop when she wanted it. 'No point in taking it upstairs to put in a bowl. Just spoils if it isn't eaten quickly.' Daisy knew she meant the apples or oranges. She was not allowed to touch the expensive hothouse grapes.

But however good her home, she couldn't help wondering what her roots were and why Auntie Glad's face became a stone wall when she asked. It made her feel different and alone and insecure.

The shop was cleaned and made ready for the next day. Willie and Mrs Mack had gone. Daisy had been listening out for some time. Brenda was due home and she hoped she'd bring the wedding finery Mrs Fanshaw had offered to lend her.

At last she heard Brenda's high heels tapping up the back yard. She was carrying two large boxes. Daisy felt a shiver of anticipation as she locked up behind her.

'I've got them. The wedding dress is absolutely beautiful. I've tried it on already.' Brenda went shooting past her through the shop and upstairs to their bedroom.

Daisy ripped off her aprons and coat and followed her. 'What's my dress like?'

'Very nice.' Brenda was taking the lid off the box.

Daisy stared down at the folds of pink taffeta. 'Lift it out for me. I don't want to touch it, not until I've washed my hands properly.'

Brenda did so, shaking the folds out. It wasn't at all what Daisy had seen in her mind's eye but . . . She gasped. 'It's lovely. I'm going to wash.'

When she returned to her bedroom, Brenda was changing into the ivory satin bridal gown.

'It's magnificent,' Daisy told her. 'You'll look beautiful in it.'

'It needs taking in. Mrs Fanshaw must have been quite plump. I'll do it after tea. It was high fashion when she had it and very expensive.' Brenda twirled round in it.

Daisy threw off her jumper and skirt, while Brenda examined the pink taffeta she'd spread out on the bed. 'It's beautifully made. This would have been very expensive too.' She helped to lower it over Daisy's head and pull the long skirt down.

'It feels a bit tight! Very tight.' Daisy was fighting disappointment. It was quite a struggle to get into it.

Brenda was apologetic. 'I didn't realise it was made for a thirteen-year-old. Not until today, but you're so thin, I thought it would probably fit.'

'A thirteen-year-old? Oh no! It's for a child?' Daisy thought her figure quite womanly now.

'Mrs Fanshaw had two bridesmaids but the other one was only ten at the time.'

Daisy felt as though her ribs were being squeezed in when Brenda buttoned up the back of the bodice, and the skirt was gripping her round the waist with the strength of a boa constrictor.

'It's a bit short,' Brenda said. 'But there's a good hem, you could let it down.'

'Can I let it out? I can hardly breathe.'

'There's nothing extra on the side seams, I've already looked. No.'

'Move the buttons back half an inch,' Auntie Glad suggested, when they paraded in front of her. 'We can't think of getting you a new dress, not with the war just over and everything scarce.'

Back in the bedroom, Brenda tried on her veil and headdress.

'I'll need to get myself some shoes, Mrs Fanshaw takes two sizes larger than I do.'

Daisy turned anxiously in front of their mirror. 'I feel as though I'm bulging out of this dress.'

'Not a bulge anywhere,' Brenda assured her. 'It makes you look beanpole thin and taller.'

Daisy said sadly, 'I love the shawl neckline and it's a pretty dress but it doesn't fit and I don't think pink suits me.'

Brenda's voice was suddenly sharper. 'You should be used to wearing other people's things.'

'I am.' She'd always been dressed in clothes that had belonged to Brenda and Ruth.

'The dress looks fine.' Brenda lost patience with her. 'You don't have to be a bridesmaid if you don't want to wear it. I'm the bride and if I'm not having a new gown, I don't see why you should.'

'Of course I'll wear it.' Daisy wasn't going to miss out on the chance to be a bridesmaid.

Brenda relented. 'I'll do your hair for you on the day. Put it up for you so you can wear this hat.' She held it out, turning it slowly.

Daisy gasped with delight, it was of fine straw with pink velvet flowers round the brim. 'That's lovely.'

'Tea's ready,' Aunt Glad called. 'Get those gladrags off and come and eat it.'

'What is for tea?' Brenda called back.

'Finnan haddock.'

'Not again!' Brenda wrinkled her nose in distaste.

As they sat down at the table Auntie Glad said, 'I hope it won't be too much of a rush. There's a lot to do for a wedding. To get everything ready.'

Brenda smiled. 'I bet all mothers say that. There'll be plenty of time. It's going to be a quiet affair. Just the two families and a few friends.'

'The wedding breakfast . . .'

'We'll have it here, of course,' Brenda said. 'That's what you want, isn't it? I'll do most of the work beforehand.'

Throughout the meal, Daisy thought of the hat. She ate quickly, impatient to return to the pink taffeta dress to move the buttons back on the bodice. Auntie Glad expected her to wash up first; she rushed through that.

Brenda brought her wedding gown into the living room and laid it out across the table. 'I've tacked in bigger darts to make it fit.' She did alterations in the shop and knew exactly how to go about it. 'I haven't time to finish it tonight,' she mourned. 'I'll have to get ready. Gilbert will be here in a minute, we're going out. Would you do it for me, Mam? Be a darling.'

Auntie Glad grunted. 'I'm tired. Can't you do it at the shop?'

'I don't want to be seen doing work for myself while Mrs Fanshaw's around.'

'But you already have – the darts.'

'She went out so I knew I'd be safe. You can sit quietly

by the fire and do it. I'd ask Daisy but your sewing is much neater than hers. It isn't as though the dress is mine.'

'You've got months yet, Brenda. Plenty of time for that.'

Brenda went to her bedroom to get ready. She changed into her new green blouse and decided to wear her green felt hat with it. She couldn't be bothered changing her skirt tonight and, anyway, they were only going to the pictures, Gil would hardly notice what she wore.

She perched on the side of their double bed so she could see her reflection in the dressing-table mirror and went to work with her powder puff. Was that the beginning of crow's feet round her eyes? She pressed more powder into the creases. Daisy was lying across the bed they shared, her big eyes watching every move she made.

She said, 'There's another powder puff in that drawer. Can I have it?'

Brenda opened it to have a look and threw it to her. 'It needs a wash.'

'Thanks very much.' Daisy caught it deftly and applied it to her own nose straightaway.

Poor Daisy, nobody stirred Brenda's sympathy more. She was so grateful for anything and so good-natured. Too good-natured for her own good. She rarely thought of herself.

'Brenda?'

'What?'

'It's definitely Gilbert then?'

'Yes, I wouldn't be fixing the date of the wedding otherwise, would I?'

'I'm a bit bothered about . . . Is he up to something?'

'What d'you mean?' Brenda knew her voice was sharp.

'He knew the man who stole that money.'

'He said he didn't, Daisy.' She could see Daisy pursing

her lips trying not to say too much, afraid of upsetting her. She could read Daisy like a book.

'Are you sure he's . . . You know, above board? Do you trust him? Trust is very important. You must if you're going to marry him.'

Brenda clucked impatiently. 'I know it's important but trust isn't the most important thing. You'd trust my mum, wouldn't you?'

'Ye-es.' Daisy sounded undecided.

'I'd trust my mam anywhere and so should you. She'd always want to do the best for us, but I wouldn't want to throw in my lot with her. I'd have a terrible life. That's what you have to think of, Daisy, when you choose a husband. What sort of life you're going to have with him.'

'You think you'll have a good life with Gilbert?'

'Definitely. Don't you think he's handsome? He took me to the pictures to see Rudolph Valentino and I'd swear he looks quite like him. He has the same athletic body, the same face almost, and eyes that smoulder at me across a table.' She took out her comb and started on her hair. 'He thinks he's more like Douglas Fairbanks because he's got a moustache like his. But it's not just looks, Daisy, he's a Fox too. I'll be marrying into a family with a good business.'

'I know that. I deliver fish there every week. Twice, some weeks. But I'm sorry you gave Charlie the push. I grew quite fond of him. Get your rings out, Brenda. Let's look at them again.'

Brenda laughed and took the four ring boxes out of her dressing-table drawer and opened them up. 'I'm not going to add another to this collection.'

Daisy reached across for a hoop of three diamonds. 'I like this one best.'

'Charlie gave me that.' Mam had belittled it by saying,

'Diamond chippings,' in a disgusted voice.

'The opal is pretty too.'

'Arnold Smith.' Mam had been equally firm about the opal. The moment she saw it she'd said, 'Unlucky. Nothing will ever come of him.' She'd been right about Arnold. He'd been killed in France six months later.

Brenda swallowed hard. She might have married Arnold, he'd been a lovely person.

'You don't wear any of them any more.'

With one quick movement Brenda tipped all four rings onto the bed in front of Daisy. 'Definitely Gil. I've made up my mind.'

Daisy tried on the deep blue sapphire; easily the biggest and most impressive stone, but Mam had said it wasn't real, just glass.

'Gil turned on me this morning, was quite nasty. He grabbed at my wrist, you can see the bruises. I don't think I like him very much.'

Brenda smiled at her. 'You don't have to. I like him and that's what counts.'

'Don't you love him?'

'Course I do, silly.'

As far as Brenda was concerned, the best thing about Gil was that he liked having a good time and set out to give her one too. He was generous. He believed in buying the best seats when he took her to theatres and cinemas and he always bought her a programme and chocolates. He knew where they could go for a nice meal too. He made her feel pampered, driving her round in the Dodge, leaping out to open the passenger door for her. Of course, she knew the car belonged to the family business and was not his personal property.

'Acts like your chauffeur,' her mother had hooted when

she saw him opening the passenger door for her to get in. 'Well-trained to do car hire.'

Even so, Gil made her feel valued and she certainly felt as though she was going up in the world. She'd already turned down three suitors for being either too poor, too mean or too thrifty; reluctant to provide little treats and presents, unable to relax and have fun. By comparison, Gilbert treated her like a princess and of course there was the family business behind him. She'd decided she was unlikely to do better. Anyway, she was getting on a bit. Twenty-six, it was time she made her choice and settled down.

Gil had a polish about him, but she hadn't leapt at the chance to marry him when he'd first asked her. There was always a downside. She really didn't like him being an undertaker. It gave her the shivers to think of that. Burying the dead was a real turn-off.

When the doorbell rang through the upstairs rooms, Brenda said, 'That'll be Gil now. Be an angel, Daisy, go and tell him I'll be ready in a minute.'

Daisy ran down. Gilbert Fox was on the shop doorstep when she opened the door. It had scared her to see his eyes bulging with fury this morning, and she was nervous of seeing him now. Gilbert didn't seem pleased to see her either.

'Isn't Brenda ready yet?'

'Not quite, you'd better come in for a moment.' She closed the door behind him and couldn't resist asking, 'How did you get on with the police? Have they any idea . . . ?'

His jaw tightened. 'They aren't very interested,' he said coldly.

Daisy recoiled, her distrust of him surfacing again. She was very conscious of his heavy step on the stairs behind her as she led him up to the living room.

'I'm thrilled Brenda's let me set the day.' He was all smiles again to Auntie Glad. 'She's taken some persuading. My parents are delighted too. They've been saying for ages it's high time I found a wife and settled down.'

Daisy had heard Brenda brag about Gilbert, she thought him quite a catch. His family had standing in the district, and was thought to be socially above the Maddockses. Daisy had heard it said that the Fox business had been established for over a hundred years. But not everybody approved of Gilbert himself because he'd managed to avoid fighting for his country in the war. As the eldest son, he'd pleaded a need to stay in Birkenhead and run the family business, though his father had been well at that time and quite capable of doing it.

Brenda had contradicted that. Gilbert had told her he'd had to go before a tribunal to get permission to stay home after he'd received his conscription papers, and it wasn't true that his father had been well. He'd lost his health years ago. Gilbert was really needed at home to keep the business running.

At the beginning of the war there had been six Fox brothers, but there had been no question of the other five avoiding conscription. They all went to fight but only Ellis the youngest had returned. Daisy felt drawn to him. Sometimes when she delivered fish to his home, he'd smile at her and say a few words but he'd never given any sign that he knew she was connected to Gilbert's fiancée.

Auntie Glad made the same mistake that Daisy had by asking Gilbert, 'Have the police caught that thief? Daisy told us all about it. She saw it all.'

'Aren't you all upset?' Uncle Ern added. 'Mid-morning, wasn't it? Not usually the time thieves choose. They wait till late afternoon when the till is likely to have more in it.'

Daisy saw immediately that Gilbert didn't like their questions, he didn't want to talk about it.

'No. We didn't lose much. It's not worth bothering about.'

'Even so, it's a loss,' Uncle Ern persisted. 'I don't suppose your father's pleased.'

'I'd be bothering if anything was stolen from my shop,' Auntie Glad retorted sharply. 'You can't have customers coming in and raiding the till. The cheek of it.'

Chapter Three

As soon as Gilbert and Brenda had clattered downstairs, Daisy settled down to move the buttons back on the pink taffeta. When she tried the dress on again she found that though the bodice was not yet comfortable she had enough room to breathe. But there was nothing she could do to let out the waistline and the patent fasteners in the placket kept popping open under the strain.

'Hooks and eyes,' Auntie Glad recommended. 'Just sew two on. They'll keep the fasteners together.'

Daisy did and put it on again. 'It's hard to fasten up.'

Auntie Glad tugged hard on the material. 'Pull your stomach in. There you are, I've done it.'

Daisy took a tentative breath. 'It still feels very tight. A real grip.'

'It looks all right. I wouldn't worry about how it feels, it's only for one afternoon, after all.' Auntie Glad settled back in her chair and wheedled, 'Look, Daisy, now you've finished your own dress, sew Brenda's for her, there's a good girl. You can sew very nicely when you try.'

Daisy changed back into her jumper and skirt, feeling rebellious. Auntie Glad was putting on her. She would have liked to read her book. Instead, she sat at the living-room table where the lovely ivory satin gown had been spread out, and started to stitch in the darts, making her stitches as small and neat as she could. If it was for Brenda, no trouble was too great. That's how it had always been.

She thought of Brenda as she stitched. Most Sunday mornings she took tea and toast to her in bed, and Daisy never ever mentioned the crumbs she could feel through her nightdress the following night. As a toddler she remembered trailing round behind Brenda. She'd mothered her, treating her like a living doll one moment, ordering her to fetch and carry for her the next. She'd been Brenda's willing slave and it seemed she still was. Daisy wished again she had someone of her very own.

Her mind went back to her own parents. She'd always been very curious about them. Countless times, usually in bed before they went to sleep, she'd talked to Brenda about how she'd come to live with the Maddockses.

Brenda had whispered, 'I remember your mother living with us. Rosa, her name was.'

'Rosa? A pretty name. What was she like?'

'I liked her. She was supposed to keep an eye on me and Ruth in the school holidays.'

'But what did she look like?'

'She was tall and . . . I remember her wearing a blue dress.'

'Did she look like me?' Daisy couldn't hide her eagerness for any fact at all.

'Not specially. She had dark hair. She helped in the house, did a bit of cooking and that. Helped set up the fish in the mornings and clear up at night, but I don't think she served in the shop.'

'Why not?' Everybody was pressed into service when the shop was busy. Daisy had been from an early age.

'How do I know?' Brenda was losing patience.

'What happened to her?'

'It was sudden. She was all right in the morning before we went to school. When we came home, she'd gone. We never saw her again.'

That night, Daisy had held hard on to Brenda's nightdress. Her mother had gone away and not taken her?

'Didn't you ask where she'd gone?'

'Yes, Dad said she'd had an accident. I thought she'd gone to hospital, but he told us later that she'd died.'

Daisy's heart turned over. 'Died, just like that?' She ached inside and out with a longing that wouldn't go away. Over the years the longing had grown and multiplied until it was burgeoning out of control and colouring her whole life.

It was always there at the back of her mind. When she wasn't setting out fish on the counter, adding up three and a half pounds of herrings at twopence a pound, or giggling at Brenda's gossip, her mind was casting round for some explanation of who she was. What her roots and origins had been and how she'd come to be here in this fish shop.

She told herself that if only she could find out the facts it would settle her, give her peace, but the sense of loss remained. Her longing grew, feeding on the minute particles that Brenda conveyed, gnawing away inside her ever more strongly. She felt driven by it.

Daisy knew Brenda had told her all she could, because Brenda had been only ten years old when she was born. So deep was her need she was prepared to risk Auntie Glad's displeasure. She couldn't understand why she refused to talk about Rosa. However much she asked, further knowledge was denied her. Auntie Glad said it was bad for her to know these things, unnecessary. Unhealthy, the way she went on about it.

Daisy knew it was essential. She'd never get this longing

out of her system until she knew all the facts, however trite and ordinary they turned out to be. She just had to know.

She kept on trying to find out more. A good time was when they were finishing tea and able to relax after the rush of the day. She targeted Uncle Ern, sensing he was more likely to tell her.

'Poor thing,' he said. 'Your mother was just a slip of a girl herself.'

'How did you come to know her?' Daisy had asked. 'What was she like? She lived here with us, didn't she? Which room did she sleep in?'

'Up in the attic.'

'Don't you be going up there messing everything up.' Auntie Glad turned on her. 'Do you hear me?' For Daisy this was nothing new. For her, the attics had always been forbidden territory.

It didn't stop her creeping up for a look round when Auntie Glad and Uncle Ern went down to the shop to rearrange things one Sunday afternoon. The attics felt freezing cold and smelled dank, but it looked as though people had once used them as bedrooms. Now they were stuffed tight with unwanted furniture and ancient domestic bric-a-brac all covered with dust and grime.

She was glad to get back to the warmth of the living-room range and didn't want to think of her mother sleeping in such a miserable place.

It did nothing to cure her curiosity though. A few days later, after tea again, Daisy was asking about her father. 'Tell me about him, Uncle Ern.'

'He was a sailor. Deep sea, he used to go off for a couple of years at a time. West Africa to America or something like that.'

'When will he be back?'

'He won't,' Auntie Glad had put in. 'His ship foundered in a storm and sank. With the loss of all lives.'

'I can't believe . . . When was this?'

'You were still just a baby. Off the West African coast, it was.' She must have seen the doubt Daisy felt because she added, 'I'm not making this up.'

'A sailing ship. There were still a lot of them about in those days,' Uncle Ern had tried to explain. 'They were quite small.'

Daisy's throat had been tight. 'How awful . . . What poor Rosa must have felt.'

Auntie Glad had said in a vicious voice, 'A fitting end for him, that's what I think.'

Daisy had been horrified. 'How can you say such a thing?'

'No more than what he deserved. After what he did.'

That didn't stop Daisy's questions for long. There were still a thousand things she wanted to know about her parents. On the following evenings she'd asked, 'What did my father do?' But Uncle Ern wouldn't be drawn to add more.

It was Brenda who'd said, 'You and your mam were sort of lodgers here. Your father paid our mam to look after you both.'

'Until he was killed,' Auntie Glad had added tartly. 'We haven't had a penny since. Nothing towards your keep. We got stuck with you.'

'I made her keep you,' Brenda had whispered. 'And Dad. We wanted you here.'

'Shut up, Brenda.' Her mother turned on her.

That had gone through Daisy. She'd always felt that as far as Auntie Glad was concerned, she was only here on sufferance.

'What did my mother die of?'

'An accident, we've told you.'

'But what sort of an accident?'

'Banged her head in a bad fall.'

'What, here in this house?'

Uncle Ern had looked at Auntie Glad as though he wasn't quite sure.

'No, outside,' Glad said. 'Give over, Daisy.'

While she'd been still at school, Daisy had helped in the shop on Saturdays and during her holidays. From the age of ten she'd been sent out to make deliveries round the neighbourhood. She loved being out where Auntie Glad couldn't keep an eye on her, it gave her a wonderful sense of freedom. She loved riding the bike and feeling the wind blow through her hair.

One day, in some long-ago school holiday, she'd been sent to deliver fish up in the North End and had seen the big cemetery at Flaybrick Hill. She'd gone in to look for her mother's grave and had started reading the inscriptions on the gravestones. It was such a big place she soon realised she'd set herself an impossible task. She didn't even know for sure that her mother had been buried here. She'd told Brenda about it that night in bed.

'You poor love.' Brenda was always quick to give supportive hugs. 'You want to find it that bad?'

'Yes.' Daisy could think of nothing else.

'But it won't tell you anything you don't know already.'

'It'll tell me where she is now. She's my mother.'

'I expect there are records. Of who's buried where . . . You could ask somebody.'

'Will you come with me? Help me?'

Brenda had been reluctant, but Daisy had persuaded her to go with her one sunny Sunday afternoon. It was a longish walk and they were glad of the shade cast by the tall trees when they reached the cemetery.

'It's enormous,' Brenda had said as they walked round the wall to the gates. 'I didn't realise it was this big. We'll have to ask.'

Daisy had held on to her hand, glad Brenda was ten years older. She was grown up by that time, twenty-three years old and she knew how to smile so that people wanted to do things for her.

They'd walked up towards the two chapels of rest. That day, there'd been quite a lot of people about. A priest had been coming towards them, she'd asked him for help. Brenda knew how to charm people.

'Rosa Corkill?'

'My mother,' Daisy had gulped. 'We want to find her grave.'

He'd smiled down at her sympathetically. 'I've just been speaking to the man in charge here, he'll know how to go about it.'

He'd led the way into the vestry and handed them on to an elderly man wearing his Sunday best. He'd asked, 'When was your mother buried? We'll need the date.'

Brenda was frowning, trying to work it out. 'You were born in December nineteen hundred and two. So it would be nineteen oh four.'

'You don't know which month?'

'The weather was hot, so it would be summer.'

'I was nineteen months old,' Daisy had put in. 'Uncle Ern told me that.'

'June then, possibly.'

Daisy had stood first on one foot and then on the other, willing him to find her mother's name in the registers he was consulting. It had taken him some time.

'Yes, here we are,' he'd said at last, and written a grave number down for Brenda.

He'd started pointing out the way they must go to find it, but Brenda's helpless smile made him offer to show her. It was quite some distance and even he had difficulty in locating it. The number was missing from the grave itself but he eventually worked it out.

Daisy had looked at the strip of ground covered with rough grass and burst into tears. It was unmarked and even the mound seemed to be levelling out.

Brenda had held her tight. 'Perhaps Mam was right. Perhaps it isn't good for you to know these things.'

'It looks as though nobody cares,' Daisy had sobbed. 'Even if the other graves don't have headstones, they do have flowers.' She jerked out of Brenda's arms and knelt to pull the rye grass out in tufts.

'We can find you some flowers,' their guide had told them. 'We had two big funerals late yesterday afternoon, and there were more flowers and wreaths than would fit round the graves. Usually we send them down to the Borough Hospital but they haven't gone yet.'

'That's kind of you,' Brenda had said. 'Daisy would appreciate that.'

They'd walked back to the chapels of rest with him. He found Daisy a bunch of pink carnations and a big jam jar and showed them where they could get water. Even the second time, it hadn't been easy to find the grave. Only when they saw the grass Daisy had pulled up were they sure.

'I shouldn't have brought you,' Brenda had said. 'It is upsetting.'

'I want to know these things.' Daisy had been dry-eyed by then. 'Come and help me weed this properly. I want to make it neat and tidy.'

When she'd been satisfied it was the best they could do,

Daisy had set the flowers on it. 'Now she'll know I care about her.'

'Let's go home.'

'I wonder if my father's grave is somewhere here.'

'No.' Brenda had taken her hand firmly. 'He died at sea, remember? Let's go home and don't tell Mam what we've been doing. If she asks, say we went to the park.'

Daisy had been back quite often. She kept the grave free of grass and when they had flowers in the shop during the summer, she sometimes bought a bunch to take with her.

She sighed and paused for a short rest before starting to sew the last of the darts. She'd always felt close to Brenda. As a child she'd spent all day looking forward to the time when Brenda would come home from work and be with her. Daisy could still remember the searing disappointment when she'd come home to eat and then got up from the table to get herself ready to go out again.

Even now Daisy liked to lie on the bed they shared and watch Brenda change into a different dress, comb out her dark silky hair and pin it back on top of her head.

Of course Brenda was beautiful. Everything about her was beautiful. She had a slim figure, a pretty face and a lovely smile. Shapely legs and neat ankles too; even her hands were beautiful, with long elegant nails.

Daisy couldn't help but notice that people wanted to speak to her. Customers made a beeline to be served by her if she was in the shop. She drew people to her. They liked her, even loved her at sight. How lucky Brenda was to have two parents and a sister, and now she was going to have a husband as well. She must feel enveloped in love.

Daisy wished she had what Brenda had. Life was different for plain girls; nobody noticed her in that way, nobody bent over backwards to please her.

Brenda always knew exactly what she wanted and went after it with single-minded determination. Daisy had always given in to her whims. It was only recently she'd realised almost everybody else did the same.

Uncle Ern gave a little snore from the bedchair pulled up against the range. He always wanted to please his daughter. Brenda's brown eyes could melt with gratitude when any of them did.

It must be wonderful, Daisy thought, to have such an effect. And it wasn't just her looks, there was a lovely warmth about Brenda. She had an endearing way of offering little confidences; of throwing her arms round people and smiling up into their faces. It had taken Daisy many years to realise that her manner could change. If Brenda wanted her company she would be sweet-natured; if she didn't, Brenda could be less than nice. And Brenda could say nasty things about everybody, even Uncle Ern. Daisy had noticed that if she didn't get what she wanted, she could turn quite cold.

Daisy was finishing off, trimming her threads, when she heard Auntie Glad give a guttural snore. Brenda was her favourite too, there was no doubt about that. All the same, Auntie Glad knew how to say no to her. Nobody else did.

Daisy was tired now and her shoulders ached, but the wedding dress was finished and ready for Brenda to try on once more. She took it to their bedroom, put it on a hanger and ran her hands over the beautiful satin. It seemed almost disloyal to think it, but could Brenda be just a touch selfish?

Brenda was late coming home. Daisy had been in bed for some time when she heard her creeping upstairs, and the flickering candle came into the room.

She yawned. 'I've done your dress.'

'You've done it, Daisy? Finished it? Thanks ever so. That's lovely. I must try it on.'

Daisy watched through sleep-glazed eyes. Brenda looked an angel in the dim light.

'It feels fine. A good fit now. How does it look?' Brenda lit Daisy's candle to double the amount of light so she could judge for herself.

'You look a dream. Beautiful.'

Brenda added her veil to get the whole effect. Then she swooped to kiss Daisy's cheek.

'You're very kind. This is marvellous, it just needs a press to be ready for the big day.'

She smiled dreamily at Daisy, blew out her candle and floated round wraith-like to blow out her own and get into the bed on the other side.

Daisy had been feeling drowsy until Brenda cuddled close for warmth and put her cold feet on her. That roused her a little and the threat from Gilbert seemed to grow in the darkness.

'Brenda,' she whispered. Brenda sounded half asleep already, she was breathing deeply.

'What?'

'I'm worried. About Gilbert.'

'What's that?'

'I know I saw him talking to the man who robbed his till.'

'Mistaken. Says you're mistaken.'

'I'm not.'

She thought Brenda had dropped off but after a pause she grunted, 'Must be.'

Daisy yawned. It seemed everybody believed she was more likely to make mistakes than Gilbert was. And everybody thought him a great catch for a husband. It seemed a heavy weight on her chest.

'He scares me.' She couldn't come right out and say he was a liar to Brenda. 'I'm afraid he won't treat you well. I much preferred Charlie.'

'Charlie used to keep caramels in his pocket to give you.'

'Or Peter.' He'd teased her unmercifully.

Brenda gave a sleepy chuckle. 'It's me who's going to marry him, not you.'

Daisy wished she'd take her warnings seriously.

At breakfast the next morning, Brenda looked up from her porridge.

'Daisy, you didn't get your coat. Why don't you come in again today and I'll help you choose. Really help you. Yesterday when you came, me and Gil still had a hundred and one things to agree about our wedding. My head was full of that and I did nothing for you. Today, it'll be different, I promise.'

Daisy nodded. 'I will. I've got to get one.'

Later on that morning, as she pushed the door of the clothes shop open, a lone customer was just leaving.

'Right,' Brenda said. 'We've got the shop to ourselves this morning.' She set about picking out all the coats in Daisy's size and putting them side by side for her to choose.

To Daisy the smell of new cloth was wonderful. 'You are lucky to be working in a shop like this.'

'You could too, if you want it that badly. I had to fight to get away from Mam and her fish. I've told you what to do.'

Daisy tried the coats on one after the other, and decided she particularly liked a stylish blue one. She tried it on for the second time. It fitted beautifully, and she'd almost made up her mind to have it when Brenda said, 'I know what we'll do. Since you've set your mind on red . . .'

'Scarlet.'

'Yes, scarlet. I think this coat is made in that colour too.' She went to the back room to look through the catalogues there. 'Yes, pillar-box red. That's scarlet, isn't it?'

Daisy nodded. She felt her cup was brimming over.

'I'll order it specially for you. It won't be at sale price, because it'll be a new order.'

'I won't be able to afford it,' Daisy wailed. The price was three pounds ten shillings.

Brenda patted her hand. 'Don't worry, I'll buy it for you and get the discount. I want you to have a coat that you really like.'

When Daisy saw it in pillar-box red, she thought it a dream. And Brenda took her thirty-five shillings and said she'd pay the rest because Daisy did so many things for her.

Daisy chided herself for thinking Brenda was selfish. Really, she was the most wonderful sister in the world. Couldn't be better.

As the months went by, Daisy knew that Uncle Ern and Auntie Glad were finding the preparations for the wedding exhausting, they were taking up every spare moment they had. Brenda was making lists of things she thought ought to be done, but she expected others to do most of the work.

'Daisy, I want you to move the boxes of cauliflowers and cabbages stacked on the stairs. They take up half of every step. How will people get up?'

Daisy went up and down many times a day and hardly noticed. When she went to do it, she found sacks of carrots and onions there too. She tidied up the stockroom behind the shop and made space to stack everything neatly in there. Then she cleared the wooden crates from the back yard and washed it down.

To please Brenda, Uncle Ern had planted nasturtiums in the dusty soil of the narrow borders. They were coming into flower now and would look lovely on the big day.

Brenda said, 'If the wedding breakfast is to be held here we must have everything looking its best, mustn't we? I don't want the Foxes to think our home is shabby. The whole house needs a thorough spring-clean and tidy-up.'

They had a parlour, a living room with a kitchen range where they cooked, and a scullery with a sink where they washed up.

'The living room needs painting and papering,' Brenda decided. 'A lick of whitewash in the scullery is all that's needed and the parlour isn't too bad.'

'It's hardly used,' Daisy pointed out. It meant lighting another fire if it was. The living room was always warm because the range had to be lit in order to cook.

'It'll be used on the big day.'

They talked about it for a few days, and then Uncle Ern, who couldn't do enough for his daughter, said, 'It does need it, she's right.'

'I'll try and find some wallpaper,' Auntie Glad agreed.

'Plain wallpaper,' Brenda suggested. 'Pale in colour with perhaps a faint stripe. With cream paintwork.'

'Brown would be a more practical colour,' Aunt Glad returned. 'We need something that won't show the dirt.'

That night Brenda's sister Ruth came to spend the night with them. Round the table over high tea, Ruth agreed that the house needed to be redecorated.

'I'm having a week's holiday in May. I'll come and help paper the living room then,' she offered.

Brenda and Ruth had their heads together all evening discussing plans. Daisy watched them, telling herself she must not be envious. Of course Brenda wanted to give all her attention to Ruth, she didn't see her often and she was her real sister.

When it was time to go to bed, Ruth went to the bedroom with Brenda. Once, all three of them had shared the same double bed but now that Daisy had grown up and they were all used to more space, Brenda thought it too much of a squash.

Daisy got an eiderdown and some pillows from the wardrobe, kept specially for occasions like this. As she put down the back of the bedchair in the living room, she told herself firmly there were compensations. It was lovely on a winter's night to snuggle down here where she could see the glow from the dying embers in the range. It could be very cosy. Even tonight in early spring it was nice, but she found it hurtful that Brenda had turned her out of her bed. Ruth had said it wasn't necessary but Auntie Glad wouldn't hear of her sleeping in the bedchair.

Despite Ruth's offer of help, Uncle Ern started to paint and paper a few days before her holiday began.

He said, 'It causes such chaos moving the furniture out and it's worse when there are five of us here. You can give me a hand, Daisy.'

Auntie Glad had gone out alone to buy the paint and wallpaper without saying anything to Brenda. On Monday they whitewashed the scullery and had the meat safe and kitchen cabinet back the same night. It was cold meat for tea as it always was on Mondays, and it wasn't too difficult to cope with all the pots and pans in the living room.

The next day they crammed as much of the living-room furniture into the parlour as they could, while still leaving room to sit round the table for meals. Ruth came home that day and stripped down for work, with her hair bound up in a scarf and one of her mother's pinafores covering her dress.

Daisy worked with her and Uncle Ern when she could be spared from the shop. Ruth worked alone on Friday and Saturday when the shop was too busy to spare either Daisy or Uncle Ern.

It was late afternoon on the fifth day, Daisy was still busy sponging dried flecks of wallpaper paste off the newly painted woodwork when she heard the flurry downstairs.

'Brenda's home,' Uncle Ern said, straightening his back with a grunt. 'She'll be pleased with this. Looks a treat if I say it myself.'

They'd just finished. Daisy stood back to survey the effect. She felt tired and messy and had brown paint all over her fingers.

'I love the wallpaper, it's so fresh and pretty.' And for once the smell of fish that drifted up from the shop had been banished by the smell of new paint.

Brenda came running upstairs full of bounce and energy to stand in the middle of the room. 'You've finished? Good.'

'Looks nice, doesn't it?' her father asked, pulling on his moustache.

Brenda's well-groomed dark head turned slowly as she looked round. 'A bit busy, isn't it?' The new wallpaper had pink cabbage roses trailing over a green trellis. 'They had some rolls of very nice wallpaper in—'

'Your mother liked this paper. Said it was the best she could find.'

The Great War had ended only months earlier and British industry hadn't yet turned round from making guns and armaments. There were still shortages in the shops.

'Not my taste, Dad. Neither is the dark paint. But at least the place is clean.'

Uncle Ern was put out. 'After all the work we've done.

Daisy and Ruth and me – we've been slaving for days on this.'

'You should have done it last year, Dad. It needed doing.'

He sighed. 'It's a huge job and I've got more than enough to do in the shop.'

Daisy hadn't found it hard to do the extra work but she thought Uncle Ern was showing signs of strain.

Chapter Four

Gilbert Fox hummed a tune as he towelled himself dry after his weekly bath. This morning he was booked to drive Miss Cornwell to the law courts at Chester. She was a regular he enjoyed having in the back of the Dodge. He wrapped a towel round his waist, flung the other round his shoulders and crossed the passage to his bedroom.

He knew he had problems, Ellis was needling him in a way he hadn't expected, but he didn't want to think about Ellis. Not this morning.

He towelled hard at his hair until his head buzzed, but nothing could rub away his feelings of resentment. For years he'd been running the business himself, and now Ellis was back and trying to elbow himself into a position of power by finding fault with everything he was doing.

He met the gaze of his own green eyes in his wardrobe mirror. He didn't look worried or anxious about what Ellis would dig out. Nothing showed. He looked his usual self. His body pleased him. At thirty-three he had a broad chest with only a little hair on it, muscular arms and a flat stomach.

He dropped one towel and turned sideways. Straight strong legs too. He studied his reflection for signs of weakness or ageing and could honestly find none. He took a deep breath, straightened his back and drew in his stomach. If anything, the years were improving him, broadening his shoulders.

His face didn't show his years either; firm olive skin without lines and he had a head of glossy hair. He took his nail scissors from his dressing-table drawer and carefully trimmed his moustache, taking plenty of time over it.

Gilbert sighed, and reached in his wardrobe for his dumbbells. He liked to do a few excises each morning to keep his body in trim. Reflected in the mirror, he watched as his muscles flexed and relaxed smoothly.

He'd kept his wits about him when the war had started. He wasn't swept off his feet by Kitchener pointing a finger at him from the hoardings, saying King and Country needed him. He'd been quite sure there'd be nothing in that for him. He'd stayed where he was, running the milk round and the shop. Much the easiest option.

Much the best option, he'd discovered when his brothers were conscripted to fight in the trenches. He'd congratulated himself then on avoiding all that, especially when the newspapers started to print long lists of those who'd lost their lives in battle. Soon the first terrible telegram was delivered to his home, to tell them Walter was dead, and, one by one, three more of his brothers had been killed. That made him freeze inside, knowing that it would probably have been his fate if he'd not fought to stay at home.

He'd been sent three white feathers. The first had upset him, but it was better to be thought a coward and be alive than be a dead hero like his brothers. Feathers hurt nobody. He didn't care what other people thought.

His dad had always talked him down and made him bend to his wishes. He didn't want the sort of life his parents had had. They thought that to have enough food on the table and somewhere to sleep at night was all anybody needed. They were prepared to work hard and long for just the bare necessities.

Gilbert wanted much more, he craved the good things in life. He wanted to go out and enjoy himself. A few drinks on a Saturday night, perhaps supper out too, followed by the last house at the Argyle Music Hall. Wine, women and song more or less summed up what he wanted, but he preferred beer to wine. He liked male company too, he was gregarious and had lots of cronies. He liked to play and watch games of every sort.

His father kept him working hard and he had a grasp of iron on the company takings. Gilbert thought him mean, he provided him with less than he needed to buy the things he craved.

He didn't think of himself as dishonest. He was a Fox, he'd been brought up to have respect for the law, but he was forced to help himself occasionally from the till. Just a few shillings now and then before the takings were cashed up for the day. What he took was unlikely to be missed. It was only what a more generous father would have given him. It was his due.

His father revered the business. 'We Foxes have earned our living from it for several generations. We've lived well, never had to hire ourselves out to others. We've been very fortunate to have it.'

It was what Gilbert had heard from the neighbours and even from the boys he'd known at school. While others had had empty bellies and holes in their boots, or in some cases no boots at all, the Fox brothers had always been warmly clad and well fed. Yes, others were envious of their family business.

The Foxes had all been brought up to expect the comforts of life to come to them without too much effort.

Ellis Fox woke up sweating, his sheets were rumpled and

damp. Even now, half awake, the terrible images of war would not be banished from his mind. His finger still nursed the trigger of his Lee Enfield, his ears ached from the boom boom of the big guns.

He pulled himself up the bed and looked round at his own familiar bedroom. It was quiet and peaceful in the grey light of morning, but he was not finding the peace he'd expected here.

During the long years he'd fought in the trenches of the Somme and at Ypres, amidst all the horrors he'd dreamed and longed and looked forward to being back here. His own little bedroom, overlooking Camden Yard, had seemed then to be the safest, most peaceful place on earth.

He'd been injured three times and altogether had spent over ten months of those years in hospital. He'd come here twice to convalesce and have home leave. The peace of this room had built up his strength so he was able to face life in the front line again.

Now, when he was home for good, the peace he'd always found here had gone. Almost every night, nightmares racked him; terrible nightmares that put him back in the trenches where he was facing a German onslaught.

Ellis threw back the blankets, there was no point in lying here any longer. He started to dress but a pain shot up his leg when he put his weight on it. His most recent injury, a shrapnel wound, had occurred just two weeks before the end of the war.

He limped down to the warmth of the kitchen, looking about him at every step. Nothing had changed in this house during the war. The same tables and chairs were in exactly the same places; the wallpaper was just a little more faded and the paint a little shabbier, but oh how the people had changed in that time.

He remembered the house ringing with the happy shouts of his brothers; Esmond who'd been killed in the fighting at Gallipoli, Walter who'd died of his injuries in Flanders, and Frank and Nick who'd been killed in France. It seemed impossible that he'd managed to survive at all.

There was the pain of seeing his father reduced to a hulk of his former self. Once he'd been upright and strong and had masterminded every aspect of the business. He still tried to control things, insisting on taking decisions and tried to hold tight to the purse strings, but Ellis didn't think he knew half of what was going on.

He could remember his mother, baking wonderful bread and cakes, singing as she went about her household chores. She didn't sing any more. She lived on her memories of the sons she'd lost. Didn't bake any more either, she left all the cooking and most of the household management to Ruby Bagshott. There was another woman, Ida, who came in three mornings a week to help with the heavy work. Mam spent her days looking after Dad now.

The kitchen was warm and welcoming. Yellow flames were licking round the kettle, but Ruby had already put a pot of tea on the table. Ellis poured himself a cup while she filled a bowl with hot porridge to put in front of him. Ruby hadn't changed at all, she didn't even look much older.

Gilbert came down and pulled out the chair next to his. 'Good morning, Ruby.'

Ellis looked up. His brother nodded in his direction and his lips tightened into something that might be thought a smile.

Ellis spooned up his porridge, remembering a younger Gilbert, the eldest brother who'd always appeared to be an adult and in charge of things. While Ellis was still at school, Gilbert had got him out of bed very early and taken him out to learn how to do the milk round. Dropped him off just in time to snatch a bite of breakfast and get himself to his classroom. Gilbert had shown him how to muck out the stable and feed the horses and then told him to get on with it. Ellis had loved the work and had revered Gilbert.

When Ellis had left school to start full-time work in the business, it was Gilbert who'd told him which jobs needed doing and made sure he did them properly. He'd looked up to Gilbert, admired the way he went about his work with his shoulders back, so confident in all he did. He remembered Walter complaining about Gil's high-handedness, and knew his other brothers were sometimes at loggerheads with him.

Even at that age, Ellis had felt the competition between his brothers. They all knew the business wouldn't support six sons and that only the two keenest and most able would be able to work in it. He thought they were all striving for the privilege. Ellis had always hoped that one of them would be him.

While he'd been in the trenches, it had been a comfort to know Gilbert was here helping to keep it running. He'd thought he still had much to learn from him. It was only when he'd come back from France, ill and drained, that he began to think Gil wasn't giving the business the care and attention it needed. Gil was spending a lot of time down at the Queen Vic with his cronies and the cronies were in and out of Camden Yard all the time playing table tennis with Gil on the table he'd set up in one of the old buildings.

Soon, the feeling began to niggle at Ellis that the business was not being run as efficiently as it could be. He wanted to play a full part in the running of it. The problem was, he remembered so little of the jobs that had to be done. He was more used to handling guns and fighting men. He'd been promoted to staff sergeant, which wasn't bad for a 21-year-old. Of course, to Gilbert he was still the baby of the family. There were eleven years between them, but after the life and rapid death of the trenches, nobody could feel young any more.

Ruby had set two breakfast trays for his parents. Now that Dad was finding the stairs difficult, they had their breakfast upstairs. She lifted one and headed for the door.

'Let me help you,' Ellis said and followed with the other.

'Should you with your bad leg? I could manage.'

Ellis didn't miss the glance her old eyes cast at his healthy brother. She seemed to think help from him would be more appropriate, but she probably knew he wouldn't offer it.

Their house was a vast warren of rooms on four floors. With the business taking up so much of the ground floor, only the kitchen and a formal dining room they rarely used was down there. The living room was on the first floor with the main bedrooms.

After propping his father up comfortably on pillows so he could eat his breakfast, Ellis had a few words with his mother before going down to the kitchen again. Gilbert had gone. The shop was reached through the labyrinth of narrow passages. There were no customers; the ginger-haired assistant was polishing the counter.

'A bit slack this morning, Enid?'

'Gone quiet now but I've sold nearly a whole churnful of milk.'

Ellis went on to the office and found his brother at the larger of the two desks there, working at figures in a register.

'I need you to explain the accounts system to me, Gil,' he said. 'It looks complicated.'

'Right, but I'm a bit pushed for time now. I have to go out. You serve in the shop today. Enid's there, she'll explain how to go about it.'

That annoyed Ellis but he didn't let it show. 'I've served in the shop for the past week. Enid's been great, told me everything I need to know. I feel I've got the hang of what goes on in there. It isn't busy this morning, she's managing perfectly well on her own.'

'Well, you could wash down the cars . . .'

'I've been meaning to talk to you about the shop.' It had worried Ellis. 'We advertise that we're selling milk from TB tested herds, but not all of it is. We had two churns from Brancote Farm delivered yesterday and their herd isn't tested at all. I asked specially.'

Ellis saw his brother's face stiffen. 'You would,' he said sharply. 'But the customers don't ask. I don't think they care, and anyway they'll never know whether it is or it isn't.'

'They'll know if they become ill with bovine TB. If the only milk they buy is from us, they could sue us.'

'With all the shortages caused by the war, they're glad to get milk at all. You weren't here. You don't know how bad it was. We had customers queuing outside for hours.'

'There's no queues here now. Milk and eggs are easier to come by, aren't they?'

'A little, I suppose. Things are getting back to normal.'

Ellis tried to sound firm. 'Well, I think we should keep untested milk separate and sell it a bit cheaper. Either that or we take down the notice that says our milk is from TB tested herds.'

'Don't interfere, Ellis. You don't realise how hard it is to make a profit in the dairy now.'

'What's that got to do with it?'

'We can't reduce our prices. Dairy produce is more readily available and customers are going elsewhere. We ought to modernise, bottle the milk instead of selling it loose.'

'Bottle by hand you mean? Buy bottles and crates and take on a man to do it?'

'I hear the Co-op is planning to set up a huge bottling and pasteurisation plant at Swan Hill. Pasteurised milk is thought to be safer than TB tested. We'll be left behind if we don't do something.'

Ellis pulled out a chair and sat down. He hadn't realised they had big problems like this.

'We couldn't do anything like that, it would cost a fortune to set up. We don't sell enough milk to make it profitable.' His brother's angry eyes stared up at him. 'You know that, Gil.'

'Only too well. The dairy won't be profitable for very much longer. We've got to do something drastic. The war held everything up. Nobody needed to modernise anything then with the shortages, but now . . .'

Ellis was trying to think. 'We could try buying milk that's already bottled. Have you asked?'

'Yes,' he barked. 'I'm not wet behind the ears, you know. I've been working here all my life. Nobody wants to wholesale it to us. They'd rather squeeze us out of business.'

Ellis sighed. 'I still think the TB tested sign should come down.'

'Leave things to me. We've got to hang on to anything that gives us an edge.'

'For God's sake. It isn't honest.'

'You're insufferable,' Gil said, slamming the drawers of his desk shut and locking them. 'I've got to go out, I've got work to do.'

Ellis didn't move until he'd heard Gil drive out of the yard, then he went into the shop and took down the TB tested sign. He hid it in the stable under a pile of hay where he knew Gil wouldn't find it.

* * *

Gilbert felt riled. Ellis was full of confidence, he didn't seem to have self-doubts like any normal person. His attitude had been clearly judgemental. Ellis had put him on the wrong foot, made him over-defensive, had got the better of him; Ellis had ruined his morning.

He mustn't think of Ellis, not today. The Dodge throbbed powerfully on its way to Hamilton Square to pick up Miss Cornwell. It was two minutes to ten when he rang the doorbell and told her parlourmaid that he was waiting to take her. He stood ready to swing open the car door as she approached.

The glimpse of her life intrigued him. Her home was a large stone Georgian terrace house in the smartest square in town. He knew she lived with her parents, he drove them too but only to local destinations. Her father settled the bill monthly. A taxi all the way to Chester was a luxury. She could easily take the train, Hamilton Square Station was just round the corner.

She was coming quickly down the front steps, swinging a briefcase. She was young, though not particularly good-looking.

'Good morning, Mr Fox.' She had a friendly and bubbly manner.

'Good morning, Miss Cornwell.'

She climbed in and beamed at him from the back seat. 'A lovely morning.'

He swung the door shut reluctantly, he'd like to talk to her, get to know her better. This was the only time he wished the Dodge didn't have the glass partition cutting him off from his passengers. But the Cornwells stipulated the Dodge rather than the old Austin in which he might have scraped an acquaintance.

He was instructed to take her to the law courts but he didn't know what she did there. He could see her in his mirror opening her briefcase and studying the papers within. She belonged to a social class he couldn't aspire to.

He drove along the New Chester Road wondering how old she was. He usually spent the journey fantasising about what might be possible if only his circumstances were a little different. She had a slim figure and looked as though she enjoyed sport. Tennis perhaps? He played occasionally in the park but he'd never seen her there. She didn't belong to the Table Tennis Club either. He believed they'd have a lot in common if only he could get to know her.

Gilbert had always enjoyed sport. In his youth he'd loved football and had attracted all the neighbourhood lads into Camden Yard to kick a ball round with him. They'd chalked goalposts on the inside of the gate. His father had objected to them crashing their ball continuously against it, so old Cuthbert Corkill had made him real goalposts and even provided a net to contain their goals. It was smaller than the real thing, which was all to the good. If he could kick goals into that, it made it easier on a real football field.

He'd never seen eye to eye with his father. However much he tried, he couldn't please him. Dad had taken him aside more than once to say in his heavy manner, 'As the firstborn Gilbert, you have a big advantage. I'll take you into the business if that's what you want. There won't be room in it for all your brothers. Some will have to find other ways of earning their living.'

At fourteen Gilbert hadn't had the slightest desire to get up early to go out on the milk round. He'd wanted to fill his life with sport, be a great sportsman, but he didn't know how to go about fulfilling his ambitions. It had been easier to tell Dad he wanted to work in the business and fall in with his plans.

Gilbert smiled into the mirror. His greatest pleasure had been to go to Tranmere Rovers and watch a real football match. At fifteen, he'd dreamed of being good enough to join their team.

'Damn stupid idea,' his father had grunted. 'You've got a living to earn. Give over knocking that ball about and unload the hay from that cart. Do something useful.'

Gilbert remembered the surge of resentment he'd felt then. Anybody could unload hay; it took skill to score goals and control a football. That was what he was good at and where his interest lay.

'If I practise hard, I might get taken on.' He'd been so eager in those days. 'They pay a wage.'

His father had rounded on him scornfully. 'A wage! I'm offering you more than that, a share in a good business. You've got to learn which way your bread's buttered.'

Gilbert had thought of the business as something he could fall back on if all else failed. It wasn't what he wanted to do with his life.

'But if I am good enough to be taken on—'

'Fat lot of good that will do you. They'll only want you to play for a year or two. Only while you're young. It won't last.'

After the dressing-down from his father he couldn't be seen playing with a football in Camden Yard, but he didn't give up his football. He inveigled his way into the fraternity at Rover's Football Club and was able to practise with their second and third teams. He always gave his father reason to believe he was doing something else at the time. Gilbert knew his game was improving, but he'd never forget the thrill of being picked to play in their second team. He tingled with triumph for a week, but Saturday afternoons were a difficult time for him to get away, he was needed in the shop. His father raged at him when he found out what he was doing.

'Saturday's a busy day here. If you're going to work for us, that's the day we need you most. Make up your mind which way you want it. If you're going to spend most of your time kicking a ball about, there's no point in pretending you want to work here.'

'Don't be too hard on him,' his mother had put in on his behalf. She always supported him. He was her firstborn and easily the best looking.

'I've been too damn soft,' his father had sworn. 'Walter puts more effort into the business than he does. I'd have thought Gil would've had more sense than this. Wasting his time kicking balls about.' He'd swung back on him, his face working with anger. 'Don't you know balls are playthings? You're eighteen, it's time you learned to work for your living. You've got to grow up.'

After that, Gil had concentrated on table tennis. For some years they'd had an old table in one of the disused buildings, on which all his brothers played. To his father that made it an acceptable pastime. Gilbert could beat them all with one hand tied behind his back. To find partners who could give him a decent game he joined the Table Tennis Club in Dacre Street. Soon he could see himself as one of their best players. He still played regularly.

He'd reached Chester, it was journey's end. He pulled into the kerb and leapt out to open the door for his passenger.

'Thank you, Mr Fox,' Miss Cornwell said and flashed a smile in his direction. 'See you next week as usual.' He watched her run up the steps before getting back into the car. He had no idea how she travelled back to Birkenhead and was curious about her reason for coming. He wished he was only required to work on one day a week.

On the return journey, Gil's thoughts were all on his own position. He'd seen his father's stroke as a major crisis. He'd wanted him off his back but suddenly everything became his responsibility. Not only was he left to run the business on his own, but his mother looked to him for support.

In all the years he'd worked in the business he'd done only what his father had told him to do; usually the physical jobs. Although he'd always been interested in what the business earned, he'd learned nothing about how the books were kept. His father told him what the earnings amounted to but it made little difference to him, he'd been paid a weekly wage. Dad had moaned at him from time to time. He wasn't showing enough interest; he was too keen to get out and play his stupid ball games. 'Stay in tonight,' he'd say from time to time, 'and I'll explain the profit and loss account to you. You ought to understand our accounting system.' Or he'd want to talk about something even more boring.

Once his father had had his stroke and was no longer able to explain things clearly, Gilbert regretted that he hadn't made the effort to listen. When he'd got into a mess, he'd turned to Cuthbert Corkill instead, though he'd been too proud to ask about minor matters. He didn't want Cuthbert to think he was stupid for not grasping such details after working in the business all these years. And even now, Dad still tried to keep a firm grasp on the takings.

Gilbert believed the problems weren't all of his making. Wartime conditions had brought many changes. Everybody admitted that. It made running the business more difficult. Everything was in short supply and rationing was an added burden. Some customers would always pay over the odds to get more than their share and Gilbert managed to keep their earnings up that way.

He was taking a bigger interest in what the business was earning now he had the responsibility of running it, and it didn't seem all that much.

When the war had started, Cuthbert Corkill, his father's friend and partner, was already a widower and almost eighty. He was still running the carpentry shop that made coffins for the business. He'd had to take on more carpenters to help him; there were now four of them, all old men. The Corkill family had never been as big as theirs. Ralph, Cuthbert's only son, was older than Gilbert and had gone to fight in France. Cuthbert had lived in dread of hearing of his end, but it seemed that the Foxes had all the losses and, like Ellis, Ralph had appeared to have a charmed life.

Things were even harder when at the end of 1916 Cuthbert Corkill died. If Gilbert had wanted to know any fact or decide on anything difficult, he'd always been able to talk it over with him first.

His parents were very upset at Cuthbert's funeral. They'd been the main mourners and had provided their best funeral for him. Ralph, of course, could not get home.

Gilbert knew Cuthbert had been a partner in their business and had drawn a share of the profit they made. His demise meant that Ralph and Ellis were the only two people standing between him and a much increased share of the profit he was earning. And their chance of surviving the war in the front line seemed slim. Gilbert began to think he could end up with a bigger share of the business than he'd ever dared to hope.

In the three years since his father's stroke, Gilbert had found his feet and now saw himself as the head of the family and in charge of its affairs. Dad still wanted to take charge of the daily takings but less often now was he able to count them himself. It was becoming easier now to limit his father's influence on what he did. Gil expected to have things done his way and felt entitled to the biggest share of what the business earned.

At the end of the war, he'd been surprised to find Ellis had been spared. He'd welcomed him home, and like the rest of the family he'd been shocked to see him looking so ill. They all feared Ellis would never recover completely. Gilbert thought of his young brother as just a kid, who when he regained some of his strength would lend a hand in the shop or the stable.

But within weeks Ellis was hanging about the office asking searching questions and trying to ferret into everything. He seemed to think it was his duty to learn all he could about running the business.

'I'll be able to give you a hand,' he'd said. 'When I figure out how everything works.'

Gilbert felt threatened and tried to tell him it wasn't necessary. He was afraid Ellis was out to cause a big shake-up in the way things were being done. He began to resent his interference.

Chapter Five

Ellis had been home for several months, he was feeling stronger and knew he was getting over both his injury and his illness. His leg was much better, he could walk on it without it aching. He was beginning to enjoy working in the yard, looking after the horses. He'd have liked to do the milk round again, but Charlie Chalker was being paid to do all that and he didn't want him to feel pushed out. He understood better than most just how hurtful that could be.

He meandered from the yard to the shop and back again. The shop was quiet and there was nothing going on in the yard. He wanted a definite job to do, something he could get his teeth into.

What interested him most was their car hire business, he'd have liked to drive the cars himself but that was Gilbert's first choice of work too. Gil only allowed him to drive when he was already booked to drive the other car. Ellis drifted into the office and saw Gil was entering figures into a ledger.

'How profitable are the taxis?' he asked him.

'You leave the cars to me.' Gilbert's pale green eyes flashed an angry warning, challenging him to ask for a bigger share of that work. Ellis knew he wouldn't be allowed to know how much business they had or how profitable it was.

Gil was making it clear he wanted to be in overall charge

and Ellis was to play second fiddle. His manner was arrogant and Ellis didn't like being ordered about, Dad had told him the business was to be shared fifty fifty between them.

Ellis wanted to sort out in his own mind how the different parts of this business functioned. He'd worked in it before he'd been conscripted into the army, but he'd been little more than a boy. He'd done whatever he'd been told to do. He hadn't questioned where exactly the money was made or dared ask how much. None of them had; two other brothers had been working in the business before the war, and Dad had talked of trying to expand it. None of them had known anything about how the business had been built up or what had driven their forebears to start up in the first place. They'd all accepted things as they were.

'There's a funeral at midday on Wednesday.' Gil looked up. 'I arranged it yesterday. I thought you were going to do more of that but goodness knows where you were when the message came through.'

Ellis felt Gil was pushing him to spend most of his time on their funeral service, but he was preventing him seeing the figures relating even to that.

'I'll be driving the Austin then?'

'No, better if you take Black Bess in the carriage. You handle horses well. I've booked Mr Cummins to drive the Austin.' For years, Mr Cummins had been called in on occasions like this when they had need of an extra driver. 'It's going to be a big do. The hearse, a carriage and two cars.'

Ellis was looking through the paperwork for the funeral when Gil left. It was for a man of thirty-five who was leaving a widow and five children.

Ellis felt he'd had a sickener of death. It was not just his brothers who'd been killed but many of his friends. Bill Hood had been shot by a sniper's bullet. Derek Conolly and Buzz Birkett had copped it in a savage German offensive. He'd hardly dared to make a special friend during the last year of the war. The grief and horror when they were killed was almost more than he could bear.

Since he'd come home, he'd attended every funeral the business had organised in one capacity or another. He didn't care for it, sometimes the feeling of death was overwhelming. But there was one thing he could contribute: what he'd been through had given him compassion when it came to dealing with others who'd been bereaved.

Enid knocked on the office door. 'I've shown a Mrs Delsey in to the funeral parlour. She's asking for Mr Gilbert but he's out at the moment. Will you have a word with her?'

'Of course.' Ellis got to his feet and gathered up the ledgers. He recognised the name, this was the widow for whom Gil had arranged the funeral on Wednesday. He went to see what she wanted.

Mrs Delsey was sitting on the edge of her chair. She was painfully thin with a paper-white face and over-bright frightened eyes. Ellis thought their funeral parlour a quiet tranquil room, but the woman was very much on edge. Clinging to her brown coat was a girl of about ten in a shabby red dress and torn cardigan. Ellis pulled out another chair for the girl, but she tightened her grip on her mother's coat and wouldn't move from her side.

'What can I do for you, Mrs Delsey?'

'I had to come.' She sniffed into a crumpled handkerchief. 'It'll all be too much. I want to stop it now.'

'This is about your husband's funeral?'

'Yes. I worried myself sick all night. I'll never be able to pay for all those cars and carriages. I'd like to give Bert a good show but we can't afford it. Goodness knows what we'll live on from now on. Bert won't care if he doesn't have horses with black feathers on their heads, he'd rather the kids had something in their bellies.'

'Of course he would,' Ellis agreed. Clearly the woman had very little money. 'No plumes then. We can change anything you want.'

She burst into tears. 'The man who came to our house yesterday . . . He said – do him proud. Have a good show and he could put on the best, but I can't pay for anything like that.'

There was no mistaking the note of desperation in her voice. The child silently put an arm round her mother's shoulders. Ellis bowed his head in disgust at what Gil had done.

'I'm glad you've come in to see me. Let's start at the beginning. You don't want two cars as well as the carriage? The big limousine provides seats for six, the smaller car three more. Then the carriage will take six or even eight if they're children.'

'No limousines, we only live two streets away from the church anyway. We can all walk.'

She wept silently. Ellis was filled with anger at Gil. He'd talked her into this; he should have had more sense. The poor woman was very upset and he had to get things right this time. Ellis left her for a moment to ask Ruby to make some tea.

When he returned, he said, 'The only essential is to transport your husband to the church and the cemetery. We have a hearse that can be pulled by hand, but it would need six men to do it with any ease. Do you have men in your family who could do that?'

She nodded. 'Yes, but . . . Not a handcart? I want it to be . . .'

'Dignified? It will be. You can have the horse to draw it if you prefer, it is the same hearse we use. I have a picture of it here.'

'Yes, he showed me that yesterday. I'll not have the horse, thank you. I have a father and several uncles.'

'Right.' Ellis amended the records. 'Are you happy with the coffin? Oak with brass inserts; hand-engraved with white satin lining?' His heart sank, it was their most expensive model.

She gulped. 'I know you have cheaper ones. Mr Gilbert said that would be much the nicest but . . .'

'Yes, the problem is that he would have measured your husband and the coffin will be being made up now – if it isn't already finished.'

Ruby arrived with a tray with three cups of tea on it. 'Stay with them for a moment,' Ellis told her. 'I'll just pop over to the carpentry shop and see how far on they are with the coffin.'

He was furious with Gilbert. This was no way to treat a poor woman who had just lost her husband. He'd talked her into having the biggest show they could put on. Not many could think clearly when they'd just lost a spouse and even fewer would have the guts to come down the next day and alter the arrangements.

The coffin just needed the lining putting in, but Mr Delsey had been of average size and they could use it for someone else. The engraved nameplate was ready but not yet fixed in place. He took it back to show her.

He got out their brochures and pointed to a more economical coffin. 'It'll be tomorrow morning now before we can bring it to your house.'

'That's fine. You've been very kind. I'm sorry to trouble you like this . . .'

Ellis changed the coffin and cancelled Mr Cummins. He was cancelling the two ornate wreaths they'd ordered on her behalf from the florist when Gilbert returned and heard what he was doing.

'I ordered those floral tributes, what are you cancelling them for?'

'Mrs Delsey's been in.' Ellis could hardly control his anger. 'She's decided on a simple bunch of flowers and I told her where she could buy them more cheaply than from us.'

'You're a damn fool. We'll not get any commission that way.'

'No, Gil, we won't.' Ellis met his brother's smouldering eyes. This was confrontation.

'The time I spent with her yesterday! That's all wasted. How can we hope to make a living out of this?'

'I've spent a lot more time this morning changing most of your arrangements and trying to calm her down. She was very distressed. You can't run a funeral service this way. You must do what the bereaved want, not push our most expensive items on them.'

'We'll go bankrupt if you push the cheapest,' Gil retorted. 'You've got to learn where we get the greatest profit and sell them that.'

'And what if they can't pay? That doesn't do either of us any good. Do you never think of the turmoil our clients are going through?'

'Clearly you're more suited to undertaking,' Gilbert told him. 'Here's another one for you. Enid's just given it to me. Exmouth Street, the name's Wills. Step on it, you won't want to keep the widow waiting.'

Ellis thought that particularly unfeeling. He walked to Exmouth Street. It wasn't far and he needed to clear his head. On his return he felt a little better but he knew he had to straighten things out with his brother, even though he didn't trust him to be fair either with him or their customers.

He found Gil working in the office.

'Look,' he said, sitting down at the small desk opposite him. 'We've got to work together, let's have everything open and above board and see if we can get on better than this.'

'Very sensible,' but the green eyes were still challenging him.

'I'm ready to start at the bottom and do the lowliest jobs, I know you have more experience . . .'

'But you still changed everything I did. That funeral, you undid my morning's work.'

Ellis sighed. 'We have different ways, Gil.'

'You need to adapt, you aren't in the army now. You've a lot to learn.'

'I know that.'

Ellis had been making a point of keeping his eyes open. There was a new bill on Gil's desk. He turned it round to read it. It was for five pounds in respect of a load of hay for the horses.

He asked, 'How much do they get through in a year?'

'Too much.' Gil swung the bill back to face him.

'The business has more problems than I thought. Especially the dairy.'

Gil gave a grunt.

'I'd like to see the accounts relating to it. Two heads are better than one. Perhaps I can see some way of saving expense or making a bit more profit.'

Gil snorted with derision.

Ellis lost his patience. 'Where d'you keep the balance sheets for all our ventures? I'd like to see all the recent ones.'

'They'll take some reading through.'

'I want to get a picture of what's profitable and what isn't and how everything works together.'

'I'll look them out for you sometime,' Gil said, but shortly afterwards he locked everything up and went out again.

Ellis felt he was being shut out. He was asking questions which were not being answered. He'd asked Gil for keys to the office filing cabinets, but they were not forthcoming. He was beginning to feel Gil didn't want him in the business. It was almost as though he resented his presence. It looked as though Gil would rather he'd been killed in France like their brothers.

Gil fumed, he'd had to get out of the office before he blew up at Ellis. He couldn't stand any more of his 'holier than thou' drivel. The lad was a fool, he was getting him down; working with him wasn't going to be easy, but nothing was easy any more.

Even Brenda was giving him problems. Gilbert strode upstairs and flung himself down on his bed. There was no peace anywhere, nothing was going right for him. He lay back on his pillows reflecting that Brenda wanted things her way and was showing great determination to have them. He felt manipulated. She knew he was like putty in her hands because he loved her and wanted to marry her. She was using her power to the full.

On his twenty-fifth birthday his mother had begun hinting it was time he found himself a wife and settled down. He couldn't have agreed more. In the years before that he'd been very much attracted to Stella Thorpe and wanted no other. As far as he was concerned, he'd have been happy to marry her just as soon as it could be arranged.

It was Stella who was undecided and, because of her, the affair had been off and on for years. He'd never doubted that she'd eventually agree. She'd been the only girl who could beat him at table tennis. They'd played together a lot, she'd been bubbly and good-humoured and great company. It had come as an enormous shock when she'd rejected him for another. It had hurt his pride. He still ached when he thought of her, and he missed her company too.

That had been just before the war started. Gilbert had always liked women; in his youth they'd thronged round him, but then when he'd been left high and dry by Stella and wanted to attract another, those who took his fancy didn't want him.

Until he met Brenda, that is. When he'd first seen her going in and out of the ladies' clothes shop opposite, he'd felt such a tug of attraction. He'd spent hours at the dairy window trying to catch a glimpse of her as she went about her work. He thought he'd never seen anyone quite so beautiful, he'd only to look into her eyes to feel full of love. He'd wanted to protect her, look after her always.

Brenda had never been easy. He'd lost no time asking her to marry him but she, too, had been undecided. He'd never felt confident about keeping her. From the beginning he'd been afraid she'd say no and be off with another.

He wanted many things from life; more money and more power in his family and greater freedom to run the business, but most of all he wanted Brenda. He felt very much in love with her. If he could persuade a stunning girl like her to be his wife, it would restore his self-esteem, allow him to forget Stella's rejection. All would be well with his world again.

When Brenda had agreed to set the date for their wedding, he'd been overjoyed. He'd expected her to move into his home. His mother wanted him to marry, she needed help to run the house. There was plenty of room.

'Move in with you?' Brenda's handsome brows had shot

up. 'I don't want that. I'm not going to live with your mother. I won't have time to wait on her.'

'She wouldn't expect you to.' Gilbert was indignant. Surely a dutiful wife would expect to do a little about the house?

'She would. No daughters of her own. A daughter-in-law is the next best thing. No, I'll stay well clear of that. And I've had enough of living over a shop. Wouldn't you prefer a proper house?'

'I couldn't afford a house. Not for a long time.'

'I want to carry on with my job.'

He'd tried to laugh that off. 'There'll be no need for you to go out to work.' Fox wives never did. 'There'll be plenty you can do in our business.'

'Milk and eggs? The clothes shop is more my sort of work. It's what I'm good at, what I like.'

It had taken him a month of bargaining about that. 'You keep on your job then, but come and live with me. There's a good home all set up, it makes sense. And the dress shop's right opposite. What could be more convenient?'

'Your mother . . .'

'We could explain about your job needing all your attention. She'd understand that. She's lived close to a business all her life.'

'That's another thing I don't fancy. You being an undertaker.'

'Brenda! It's a good steady trade. With all the flu we've had this year, we've more work than we can cope with. We're very busy at the moment.'

'Burying the dead! It's a hateful trade. I wouldn't want to tell people I was the wife of an undertaker, and as for living over that business, it makes my toes curl up in agony; it's cringe-making, depressing.'

Brenda hadn't yet suggested that he should live over the fish shop, but he was afraid she might. He didn't relish the thought of that.

Daisy knew Brenda had big ideas about where she wanted to live. Brenda had told her about the lovely houses she and Gil had looked round with a view to renting. Real houses further out of town in the better parts of Oxton and Claughton, not just rooms, and definitely not over a shop. Brenda had even bigger ideas about buying their own business.

In bed one night after they'd blown the candle out, Daisy heard all about it.

'I'm so disappointed, Gilbert's digging his feet in. He says we'll have to save up before we get a place of our own. He's been virtually running his family's business since his father had that stroke. I'm sure he could afford it really. We saw such a beautiful house in St Andrew's Road, I quite set my mind on it. I really thought he had too.'

'Perhaps when you've had time to save, in a year or two . . .'

Brenda snorted with disgust. 'That's exactly what he says. But would it ever happen? Once he gets me into Camden Street, there'd be no escape.' She tossed over, taking most of the bedclothes with her. It seemed she was settling down to sleep.

'Good night,' Daisy whispered.

Brenda was in a prickly mood for days and then one evening she came home in a very bad mood indeed.

At the tea table her father asked, 'What's the matter, Brenda? I can see you're upset.'

'I've told Gil I'm going to break it off. He's being impossible, dictatorial. I can't possibly fall in with his whims.'

Daisy felt a wave of relief.

Brenda said angrily, 'Do you know what? Gil really expects me to move in with his family.'

After a stunned silence her father said, 'It would be very convenient for you. With you working in the clothes shop right across the street.'

'That's another thing, he thinks it's a wife's duty to stay at home and take care of him. And the housekeeping, of course. He thought I'd want to move in with his parents and do that.' She tossed her head defiantly. 'I've told him no, definitely no.'

'You're going to be left on the shelf,' Auntie Glad thundered. 'You're too fussy. Lots of girls would jump at the chance. You'll get a good home there.'

'Their house is very nice,' Daisy assured her.

'It's not that. His father's an invalid and his mother does nothing but sit about all day. She'd have me waiting hand and foot on both of them.'

Daisy couldn't imagine Brenda waiting on anybody. 'Surely they wouldn't expect you to? Anyway, they have help in the house. Mrs Bagshott sees to almost everything. She's a proper cook general.'

'Mrs Fox is the sort who'd want a lady's maid too,' Brenda retorted. 'I'm not cut out for that sort of thing.'

'So you've changed your mind? You're not going to marry Gilbert Fox?' her father asked.

'Well, we'll have to see,' she said slowly. Daisy understood that this was Brenda's way of negotiating. She wanted marriage on her terms.

Two days later, she announced that after the wedding her new husband would be moving in with the Maddockses. There was another shocked silence.

'Here?' Auntie Glad asked. 'Well, we don't want to lose

our Brenda, do we, Dad? The place wouldn't seem like home without her.'

'It won't be for long,' Brenda told them. 'I definitely want us to have a place of our own and Gil's promised we'll get it as soon as we can.'

'Oh, you'll not be staying permanently then?'

'No, absolutely not. I'll come back to see you and you can come and visit me.'

'We'll miss you.'

'You'll still have Daisy.'

'Yes,' Aunt Glad agreed but the look she cast in Daisy's direction told her she couldn't possibly take Brenda's place in the family.

A new double bed was ordered to accommodate the newly-weds. It was to be put up in the bedroom Daisy had shared with Brenda for as long as she could remember.

'Where am I going to sleep?' she asked, having visions of spending every night on the bedchair in the parlour.

'You'll have to clear the clutter from the attic and move the old bed up there,' Brenda told her.

Daisy wasn't sure she'd be allowed up there, and anyway, she didn't care for the idea.

She turned to Auntie Glad. 'Will that be all right?'

'Of course,' Uncle Ern said. 'There's nowhere else.'

Ruth happened to be at home that evening. Daisy noticed she was staring white-faced at her mother.

'There's nowhere else,' Auntie Glad repeated fiercely.

'I'm going up to look,' Daisy stood up.

Ruth jerked to her feet. 'I'll come with you.' She rushed up ahead and threw open both the doors that opened on to the landing. There were two rooms, they were both big, but the front one was really huge.

'Goodness!' Ruth shrank back. 'The state of them. It's

years since anyone came up here.' The dust, cobwebs, old furniture and general clutter was off-putting.

'Which room are you going to use?' she asked. Daisy thought both looked near derelict. She'd thought the parlour airless and unused, but up here it was ten times worse.

'It'll have to be this one,' Ruth decided for her. 'The other is vast, and it's full of old furniture and other rubbish.'

There was a rusting iron bedstead with a thin mattress showing greyish black flock through holes in the cover.

'Who used to sleep up here?' Daisy asked. She thought she knew.

Ruth seemed tight lipped. 'Families used to be bigger in the old days, and there's only two bedrooms downstairs.'

'My mother used to sleep here, didn't she?'

Ruth's usually gentle eyes shot to hers. Daisy thought she saw panic there.

'What's the matter, Ruth?'

'Mam told me not to talk to you about your mother.'

'Why not, for heaven's sake?'

'It upsets you.'

'It upsets me more to hear that. I just want to know about her. What's wrong with that?'

'Nothing, Daisy.' Ruth was three years older than Brenda and must remember more.

'Anyway, Uncle Ern told me this was her room.'

'Yes, I felt sorry for her. She had so much to do.'

'More than Auntie Glad?'

'She had you to look after. A baby makes a lot of work, washing and feeding. You used to wake her in the night so she never had a decent night's rest.'

'Did I? Didn't she like me?'

'Oh yes, she hated leaving you to attend to anything else. She'd have sat and nursed you all the time if she could. She was supposed to be a sort of lodger but Mam treated her like a maid. I think she wanted to do a bit to help.'

Daisy could feel the tension sparking out of Ruth. 'Here, Daisy, give me a hand with this window.'

Together they forced it up. 'There's no sash cord on this side,' Daisy said.

'Must have broken.'

'Someone's taken it right out.' They had to prop it open.

'Probably meant to put another in. What a mess,' Ruth said, looking at her grimy fingers. 'It'll be cold up here too.'

Daisy didn't mind that. Except when Ruth came home to spend the night here, she'd have the attic to herself. She thought that after all, she would like to sleep in the room her mother had used.

Auntie Glad came up to look round. 'I'll get you some distemper to clean up the walls. White, I think, it's cheaper than coloured, but there's no hurry. You won't have time to do it until after the wedding.'

The next morning Daisy had to go out to deliver the orders and serve in the shop. At dinner time, Ruth told her she'd washed down the window and the walls, and had walked down to the market and bought a new window cord and six pounds of distemper.

'Mam said white, so that's what I got. Probably the wisest choice, it'll lighten the room.'

'It's going to look lovely, thank you. What did it cost?' Daisy had spent all her savings on the coat.

'Forget it,' Uncle Ern said. 'You don't have to pay for that.'

Ruth said, 'I saw some nice lino in the market, Mam. It wouldn't hurt to get a new piece. What's up there is worn out.'

'Not now,' Auntie Glad barked. 'Not with all the expense

of the wedding. When wc're over that, perhaps. Nobody will see what's up there. Daisy can take her time painting it now.'

Daisy felt that for Auntie Glad she didn't count.

It was a busy day in the shop and Daisy worked there all day. By the evening Ruth, helped by Uncle Ern, had spread white distemper over the walls and ceiling of the attic.

'It took three coats.' Ruth seemed more relaxed now. 'We put it all over the skirting boards too, to clean them up.' They'd threaded in the new cord for the window and the glass gleamed. Ruth had even polished the deal chest and scrubbed the lino though it hadn't much pattern left on it.

'You've washed the curtains too,' Daisy marvelled. They were fluttering in the breeze.

'You won't need nets to the window up here. Too high for anyone to see in.'

Daisy was very grateful. 'Thank you for doing all this for me,' she said to Ruth. 'It's a lovely light room now. I can see right down to the river.'

'The buildings in Price Street are in the way. It's all chimney pots.'

'Look, if you stand here, there's a slit between them. I can just see a glimpse of it.'

Auntie Glad came up to inspect the room. 'It looks lovely, really clean. You can rely on it being totally hygienic if Ruth's done it.'

Later, when they were having tea downstairs, Glad said, 'I hope you're grateful, Daisy. Our Ruth's put a lot of effort into that room for you, and she gave up her day off to do it.'

'I'm very grateful, Ruth. Grateful to you all.'

Ruth seemed more her old self again. 'There's just the bed to take up now.'

'I'll help Daisy with that,' Brenda said. 'Or we could do it now and sleep there tonight. Then we could repaper the bedroom down here before we put the new bed up.'

'Hold on, Brenda,' Auntie Glad said sharply. 'We've all had enough of decorating, thank you.'

'You haven't done any.'

'Neither have you. I've got my business to run and all this painting and papering causes chaos up here.'

'But if Gil's coming to live here—'

'If it isn't good enough for him, he can paper it himself,' Auntie Glad retorted. 'It isn't too bad, we did it at the beginning of the war.'

Ruth went back to the hospital that night, she was on duty the next morning. Brenda helped Daisy collapse the old bed and carry it up. By the time they'd put it together again and made it up, Brenda said, 'What a job, I'm ready to get into this now.'

Daisy felt exhausted. She undressed and was rubbing Vaseline into her chapped hands when she noticed Brenda was filing at a well-manicured nail.

'I wish I had a job like yours. Cold fish and muddy veg are hard on the hands.'

'Do what I did,' she advised. 'Get out. Escape from it. This is a terrible place to work.'

'It's different for you. Auntie Glad thinks I should repay her for bringing me up.'

'She told me that, and Ruth too. You have to look out for yourself when you're growing up. Ruth and me, we'd still be selling kippers if we'd listened to Mam. What a life, eh?'

Daisy had expected to be asleep as soon as her head touched the pillows. Instead, the fluttering curtains and the strange light room were keeping her awake. Brenda was awake too.

'Listen, Daisy, you've got to go after what you want. I hated working for Mam; she's a hard taskmaster. I don't know how you stand it. We're all entitled to get the best from life we can, even you. Go out and find yourself a job you want to do. That's what I did. Mam can't stop you.'

Daisy knew she didn't have that sort of strength. The thought of having to confront Auntie Glad with that news made her shudder. Besides, there was Uncle Ern to think of, he wouldn't want her to go either. He'd called her Little Daisy for years. Even now when she was almost as tall as he was, it still slipped out sometimes. She'd seen hurt in his gentle eyes when Brenda pressed him too hard. She didn't want to do that to him.

She said, 'I suppose I ought to be grateful for what Auntie Glad's given me.'

Brenda hooted with derision. 'She's had her money's worth out of you. Didn't you help unload the vegetables from the carts before going to school every morning? And sweep up and wash the slab down every night when the shop closed? And didn't you spend the school holidays helping with the Easter rush? And at Christmas and all through the summer holidays when Charlie and Mrs Mack took their week off? You remind her of that.'

Daisy knew she couldn't. Not yet anyway. She tried to count her blessings. She had Brenda who meant everything to her: it had taken her many years to understand the cruel fact that she wanted more from Brenda than she was willing to give.

Daisy reminded herself she also had Uncle Ern. She thought of him with great affection and warmth. He was always kind and gentle, but he was like that to everybody and she wasn't all in all to him either. He had two daughters of his own and Daisy couldn't doubt he loved them dearly. He also had Auntie Glad and they seemed to live in harmony for the most part. He came in for less of her cutting tongue than anybody else so she must love him.

Daisy found Auntie Glad hard to live with. Her tongue was a hurtful whiplash always flicking at her, robbing her of confidence and security. Auntie Glad was deliberately withholding knowledge from her that she thought vital to her happiness. She was a force Daisy couldn't come to terms with.

For a start, Daisy felt she received too much correction. Auntie Glad was impossible to please. 'I'm training you up, teaching you a trade, so that you'll be able to manage this shop,' she told her by way of explanation.

Next year, Daisy was to go with Uncle Ern to the wholesale market every time he went. She'd been once or twice already just to see what it was like and didn't care for getting up in the middle of the night. He would teach her what she must buy, but she was too young at the moment to have the responsibility of buying the stock.

First she must learn to fillet and steak large fish and gut them all. And never ask a customer if she wanted her fish gutted, the word to use was clean. Daisy must recognise what was fresh and what was not and understand how to price everything from potatoes to shrimps.

'One day, when I'm old and grey,' Auntie Glad told her, 'I'll be able to rely on you to run this business for me.'

To Daisy it seemed a long way off although Auntie Glad was already grey. She could see her own future stretching ahead, a whole lifetime of fruit and fish in the Maddockses'shop. And it wasn't the future she would have chosen for herself.

Uncle Ern was frying plaice for tea and all the family was upstairs with the table set in readiness. Daisy knew the moment Brenda came into the room, face all smiles, dark eyes alight with excitement, that something had pleased her. Something important, delight was shining out of her.

'Such good news,' Brenda laughed outright. 'Gil won't be coming to live here when we're married after all.'

It was only a week since Brenda's bedroom had been spring-cleaned and her new bed made up with new linen and new blankets. Auntie Glad's florid complexion deepened to dusky crimson as she shot her a ferocious look.

'Isn't this place good enough for him? After all we've done? All that work up in the attic for nothing. All that expense too. I don't know what our Ruth's going to say.'

It took Daisy a moment to recover. 'Not coming? I thought you were against living with his family?'

'I not going to, I told you that. No, Gilbert has bought the clothes shop for me.'

Uncle Ern came to the scullery door. 'Good lord! Bought you a business?'

'Yes. You know I love clothes and that shop suits me down to the ground.'

'Just like that, he's bought the dress shop, the one you work in?'

'Gil agreed we should buy a business of our own. We always intended that. The good thing is, we can live over it. A home of our very own. Not a house yet, but that will come in time. And it's right opposite the dairy, what could be more convenient for him?'

That dumbfounded them all. After a moment's silence to assimilate it, her mother said, 'I didn't know the shop was on the market.'

'Mrs Fanshaw is expecting again. She said it was getting too much for her now she has a family. She was glad to sell it with so little hassle.'

'To you?'

'Well, I asked Gil to get it for me. He paid, of course, he'd saved enough. It's something I can do. I've more or less been running it for the last few years, after all.'

'Have you looked at the books?' Her mother's voice was like a foghorn.

'Yes, Gil's gone through everything. Of course he has.'

'You're sure he hasn't paid too much? You should have let me and Dad look at it first.'

'Gil knows what he's doing, Mam. It's making a profit, always has, but I'm sure I could earn more from it.'

Daisy smiled as she went to help Uncle Ern dish up. It seemed Brenda had the same effect on Gilbert Fox as she had on her own family.

Chapter Six

The following week, Daisy was at home sitting down with the rest of the family to their evening meal.

'Guess what?' Brenda's handsome eyes went round the table as she forked cod's roe into her mouth.

'What?' Auntie Glad was inclined to be irritable by this time of the day.

'You're all invited to tea at the Foxes' next Sunday. Mrs Fox thinks she ought to get to know us better since we're to be related by marriage.'

Auntie Glad looked sour. 'She just wants to show us they've got more than we have.'

'Oh, come off it, Mam. She's only being friendly. Anyway, it's right that she should. You ought to get to know them better.'

Auntie Glad sniffed.

'Gilbert will invite you officially when he calls for me. For heaven's sake be nice to him.'

'Course we will, love,' her father said.

Daisy asked, 'Will Ellis be there?'

'Yes, the whole family will.'

When the time came for Gilbert to call for Brenda, it fell to Daisy's lot as usual to bring him up to their living room. She wished she had some of his confident swagger.

91

'Brenda has told you?' he asked from the doorway. My mam and dad want you to come for tea next Sunday. Five o'clock, if that's all right with you?'

'How kind.' Auntie Glad smiled from him to Brenda. 'Thank your mother very much. Very nice of her to ask us. Five o'clock is lovely.'

'Looking forward to it.' Uncle Ern beamed his enthusiasm.

On the day they were going, Brenda got changed to go out with Gilbert straight after Sunday dinner. It was the one day of the week when they had their main meal in the middle of the day.

'I thought you'd be taking us.' Auntie Glad was offended.

'You can find the way. It's not far. Anyway, Daisy can show you, she goes there often enough.'

'To introduce us, you can't just—'

'Gil and I don't get much time to be together, Mam. Sunday's the only day. I'll be there, see you at five.'

Daisy felt almost as smart as Brenda in her new red coat as she led them to the house door in Camden Street and rang the bell.

'It's a huge place they have,' Auntie Glad said looking up at four storeys of blackened brickwork. There were a lot of sash windows, typical of the Victorian period; those on the first floor were larger than those above.

'You'd think our Brenda would want to live here.'

Daisy indicated. 'That's their dairy.'

'I can see that.'

'Almost all the ground floor is given over to their business.'

The sign over the dairy window read: Z.A. Fox and Sons, Purveyor of Fresh Dairy Produce. The window had a large cardboard cow in the middle and was full of advertisements for eggs at 1/6d per dozen, and fresh farm butter at 1/5d a pound.

'Thought they were undertakers too,' Auntie Glad sniffed.

'And car hire,' Uncle Ern said.

'Funny mixture of trades, to my mind.'

'There's a brass plate there near the shop door.' Daisy lowered her voice as though afraid the Foxes might hear themselves being discussed.

'Z.A. Fox and Sons, Funeral Directors.' Auntie Glad was standing with feet apart peering at it. 'You'd have thought they'd have something bigger. Something to let people know. Just looks like a dairy to me. And not all that high class.'

'Shh.' Daisy rang the doorbell again. Heavy footsteps came slowly in answer.

'Good afternoon.' This was not the Mrs Bagshott Daisy knew. She was wearing a frilly white muslin cap and apron and her long black dress almost reached the floor. She gave no sign that she recognised Daisy. 'Do come in. This way, if you please.'

They were heading upstairs instead of to the kitchen. This was new ground for Daisy. She thought the handrails on one side and the rope to hold on to on the other very smart. So was the fawn stair carpet with a red stripe going up each side. At home they had lino on the stairs.

She could hear Auntie Glad breathing hard as she climbed behind her and knew she'd be taking in every detail, including the fancy plates hanging on the wall just out of reach.

'Mr and Mrs Maddocks and Miss Maddocks,' Mrs Bagshott intoned when she threw open the door.

Daisy saw Brenda sitting with the whole Fox family. They all got to their feet except old Mr Fox.

'You'll have to . . . have to excuse me,' he wheezed.

Gilbert made the introductions. Daisy sat down on the brown leather settee next to Gilbert's mother. It felt cold and slippery and the atmosphere strained and formal. Mrs Fox was a small bent woman who moved slowly and appeared much older than Auntie Glad. 'And you're Brenda's little sister?'

'Not exactly.' Daisy felt uncomfortable. At home Auntie Glad was always pointing out that she wasn't a relative at all. She was afraid Auntie Glad would disapprove of her if she allowed the Foxes to assume she was. 'Auntie Glad and Uncle Ern brought me up, but I'm not a relation really.'

'The next best thing.' Uncle Ern was trying to sound hearty.

Daisy could see Auntie Glad eyeing the fine carpet square with brown lino surround and the three big windows looking out into Camden Street. It was a fine big room. At one end was an oval table surrounded with mahogany chairs, already set with the tea things.

'And my name isn't Maddocks as Mrs Bagshott said. It's Corkill.' Daisy felt she ought to correct that too. Auntie Glad might not like her claiming to be a Maddocks.

'Corkill?' Gilbert's cheeks seemed to be losing their colour. 'I didn't know that.' He turned to Brenda. 'You didn't tell me.'

She shrugged. 'Didn't I? Is it important? I think of Daisy as my little sister. Names don't seem to come into it. Not at home when we're together.'

Dora Fox tightened her black silk shawl round her bent shoulders. She was stick thin with sharp elbows and a style of dressing that went back to the turn of the century. She, too, wore a long black dress that almost swept the floor, but whereas Mrs Bagshott's was of serviceable barathea, Mrs Fox's was of silk and had a lot of fancy ruching down the front.

She asked, 'We've had close connections with a family of that name for many years. Are you related to those Corkills?'

'No,' Gilbert said quickly.

It surprised Daisy that he seemed so concerned. 'I don't think I have any relatives,' she confirmed.

'Not a common name. We knew the family very well, didn't we, Albert?' Dora Fox stroked her lank grey hair; it was drawn back into a bun worn on the nape of her neck.

'Business partners of my husband's family for generations . . .'

'Employees, Mam, I think we decided,' Gil put in.

Daisy was pleased when Ellis turned on his brother. 'I'm sure you're wrong about that.'

Their father was dozing in his chair; Ellis woke him up by addressing him directly. 'Dad, you remember the Corkill family, don't you?'

Mr Fox's eyes looked blank for a moment, then he was trying to pull himself upright in his chair. 'Who? Corkill? Yes, of course. Cuthbert Corkill, good friend.'

Then he recounted haltingly, with frequent breaks, some long-ago anecdote that threw no further light on the point.

'Anyway,' Mrs Fox went on, 'I think the Corkills were related too. Distantly, of course. Enoch Corkill and his son Cuthbert worked in the carpentry shop on our yard sixty years ago, used to make the—'

'Not now, Mam,' Gilbert put in. 'I don't think Brenda's parents are interested in what happened sixty years ago. It's what's happening in the business today that counts. And the future, of course.'

'I've never known anyone else with the name of Corkill,' Daisy said. 'Perhaps after all they are . . .'

'No,' Auntie Glad barked and started to talk about the

cold weather. When they all moved to sit up at the table to eat, Daisy stayed close to Mrs Fox, hoping to hear more.

'You come and sit next to me, ' Gil ordered, and she found herself between him and Ellis instead. That didn't displease her, she thought Ellis looked much more approachable than his brother but he didn't say much. Most of the time he seemed lost in thought, and the conversation was general, if all about the forthcoming wedding.

Daisy ate sponge cake and thought how marvellous it would be if it turned out she was related to the Corkill family who had lived in Camden Yard.

When the meal was over and they got up from the table, she was careful to sit down next to Mrs Fox again. She kept her voice low when she spoke to her, she didn't want Gilbert to break in on this.

'I'm so interested in what you were saying. About the Corkill family who had the carpentry shop. Do go on. Did you say Cuthbert Corkill was his name?'

'Yes. When I married Albert and came to live here, Cuthbert was quite an old man. Well, I thought so then. He was probably twenty-five or thirty years older than us. Such a help to Albert when his father died and he was left to run the business.'

'Tell me about his family. He was married?'

'Yes, he married quite late in life. Alice was a dear, but she wasn't strong. Dead within ten years. Poor Cuthbert was heartbroken.'

'They had children?' This was what Daisy really wanted to know.

'Just one son, Ralph. A few years older than our Gil. A lovely boy.'

'So he's still alive?'

Dora Fox sighed. 'No, I don't think so. He was a Kitchener

volunteer right at the beginning of the war. I know he went to France, he used to write to his father regularly. It was only after Cuthbert died that we heard Ralph was missing.'

'Missing presumed killed,' Gilbert put in. 'You saw his name printed in the *Echo*. You showed it to me.'

'That's right. During the war, every paper carried these long lists printed inside black borders.'

'When would that be?' Ellis wanted to know.

'In the summer . . . It must have been 1917. We heard nothing after that, but he must have been killed, he'd have surely come back otherwise.'

Daisy sighed too. She'd hoped to hear of a Corkill daughter called Rosa. Daisy knew she must have relatives somewhere; Rosa must have had a family. Searching for them seemed a near impossible task and this hadn't got her any closer to finding them.

Gil came over. 'It would be nice, Mother, if you offered a glass of sherry to your guests before they went. Come, let me help you.'

Daisy couldn't help feeling he'd only suggested sherry to stop them talking about the Corkills. He seemed more than strange; taking such action to keep hidden the things that others wanted to talk about. And why should he? His behaviour made no sense at all to her. He was a very strange man, rather scary. Brenda seemed happy enough with him now but . . .

Ellis couldn't take his eyes off Daisy. He'd heard Gil and Brenda talking about her. Gil had said, 'very plain and only sixteen.' She hadn't sounded interesting.

When he saw her come into their living room, he changed his mind, though she looked younger than she was. She had impressive hair. He'd never seen so much of it on one head.

Such thick crinkly plaits that seemed to dwarf her.

He knew straightaway he'd seen her before. It took him a few moments to remember that she'd been in the shop on the day the till had been robbed. Gil had said she was delivering fish for their dinner. Her grey wool dress was even more familiar. He'd seen Brenda wearing that quite recently. He half smiled to himself; like him, she was low in the family pecking order.

Looking at her now he decided she wasn't a chocolate-box beauty like Brenda but her face was full of movement and life. He could almost see what she was thinking. She'd lit up with interest when his mother mentioned the Corkill family. He could see she wanted to hear more about them. Perhaps she wanted to be related to them. He could understand that too, Brenda's mother kept trying to disown her.

It struck a chord and set him thinking of Cuthbert Corkill. For an instant he could almost smell the freshly-cut wood shavings that had been ankle deep in the carpentry shop. He remembered Cuthbert's son Ralph working there too. But not very well, he hadn't been there long.

Daisy was nervous, a bit on edge, but she was hanging on to every word about the Corkill family they knew, and willing him to go on talking about them. Her avid interest in the family awakened Ellis's. He wanted to find out more to please her.

He noticed her fingernails were bitten down to the quick.

Gilbert said, 'Anyway, what does it matter? It's all history, the Corkills have all passed away now.'

Ellis knew he could find out definitely by looking through their old account books. They'd be somewhere in the office, or possibly Dad had them in his room. They'd be here somewhere and he knew he'd have to get his hands on them.

* * *

As Gilbert saw Brenda's parents out, he had the feeling he was sinking deeper and deeper into the mire and he didn't know what he could do about it. He wasn't sure he'd said the right things, it had all been off the top of his head and he wasn't as good at that as he'd like to be.

He tried to tell himself it didn't matter. That he'd tied it all up legally. He honestly hadn't known that Daisy was a Corkill. It had come as a nasty shock, and it had scared him to hear her digging for information about the Corkills, with Ellis and Mam doing their best to help. It would have been better if he'd let them get on with it. They'd be able to do it every time they met, and he couldn't stop them meeting. By trying to put them off, he'd given Ellis some clues. Easy to see he'd picked up on them too, and he had the tenacity of a terrier once he got going.

Brenda wanted Gil to take her for a drive. For once he wasn't keen, but to please her he headed the Dodge towards Hoylake.

He could guess where Daisy might fit into the family. He'd have preferred to search out Bernard Corkill, he could tell him whether he was right or wrong, but he couldn't talk to Bernard while Brenda was with him. The less she knew about his troubles the better.

Gil told himself that perhaps it was better this way. The last thing he wanted was to find out he was right. He'd only been trying to help a friend and here he was caught up in complication after complication.

'Why didn't you tell me Daisy's name was Corkill?' he asked Brenda.

It was only when she snapped, 'What d'you keep asking me that for? What difference does her name make?' that he realised it was the third time he'd said it. He had to keep his mouth shut, but he felt sick every time he thought of Daisy. He'd seen her many times but it had never occurred to him . . . He'd thought she was just Brenda's little sister. Now he was almost sure . . . He'd ask Bernard next time he saw him.

Gilbert had always known the other branch of the Corkill family, and understood very clearly why nobody else did. Bernard was the proverbial black sheep. He had itchy fingers; couldn't keep them off other people's property and had been in trouble with the law more than once.

Cuthbert Corkill had considered his brother James to have been very unfortunate. There had been no room in the business for him but he'd entered the church and by doing so they thought he'd done well for himself. Then he'd married beneath him and both his children had taken after his wife's family. He'd cast them off. Cuthbert and his family hadn't wanted to know them either.

When Cuthbert died, Gil knew Ralph would inherit his share of their business. It was only when he heard Ralph was missing, presumed killed in France, that he gave it any thought at all.

Fortune then seemed to be smiling on Gil. He still drank with Bernard but never once mentioned the Corkill estate. He knew Bernard would be mightily interested in that, though he hadn't bothered to come to Cuthbert's funeral.

The evenings were lighter now and when he parked on Hoylake Promenade the dark was gathering across the Irish Sea and Liverpool Bay. It was a chilly evening and there was nobody much about. They both moved to the back seat where they had plenty of room for a necking session.

For an hour he was able to forget his problems. Brenda knew how to arouse him and give a man a good time. He felt more relaxed afterwards until she spoilt it by suggesting they had a week's honeymoon in Torquay.

'I'd love to, Brenda, but we can't afford it. Not with everything else. Perhaps next summer we could go for a holiday.'

'By then I'll have the shop to look after and it'll be harder to get away,' she mourned.

Brenda had big ideas about what he could afford, big ideas about everything, and she set about trying to persuade him. She even had him thinking of ways in which he could get a little extra money. After all, it was their honeymoon.

But then Gil remembered it was the search for extra funds that had brought his present trouble and for once reason prevailed. Besides, Torquay didn't particularly appeal to him. Brenda was not in a very good mood when he dropped her off outside the fish shop and that upset him again. He came home to find all his family in bed and the place in darkness. Once in bed himself, all his problems crowded in on him again and he couldn't sleep.

Damn Bernard Corkill! If he'd known he was going to cause him all this trouble he wouldn't have had anything to do with him.

Damn all the Corkills. Daisy had made things a hundred times worse. Rotten luck to have her hanging about the shop on that day, and that she should notice so much. It had shocked him when she'd accused him of knowing the thief; worse, she'd gone on saying it.

Such a stupid thing for Bernard to do, snatch a few pounds from their till. It had churned everybody up. Mam and Ellis had made a fuss and had insisted on calling the police.

Bernard Corkill was not exactly one of his cronies but he'd known him all his life. He was a family connection and he drank with him occasionally in the Queen Vic, a pub down at the bottom of Market Street. Recently, he'd even come round to play an occasional game of table tennis with him.

Damn Bernard for causing all this bother, he had no self-control at all. Bernard had shouted and hurled insults at him that day and the last thing he'd wanted was for Bernard to give his side of the story to the police. And all this had come about because he'd gone out of his way to help him when he needed it. Gilbert simmered with fury as he thought of that awful night. It had been in February, a week before Ellis came home from hospital.

He'd gone out to lock the gates of Camden Yard as he did every night. He'd been later than usual and it was already dark. He had just looked up and down the street and thought it deserted when Bernard came out of the shadow cast by the high wall and was near enough to touch. It had made him jump.

'For pity's sake help me.' Bernard's anxious fingers had gripped his wrist. He'd looked scared stiff, his face had been running with sweat and splattered with spots of something. It couldn't be blood surely? It was all over his clothes too!

'What's happened?' Gil pulled him inside the yard before throwing the bolts across the high gate.

'It all went wrong.' There was a tremor in Bernard's voice.

'What did?' He'd felt the hairs on the back of his neck stand up as cold terror washed over him. 'What have you done?'

'Tried to take a car.' For the first time, Gil saw the cranking handle he carried. 'It was parked almost outside the Gaiety Theatre. Oh God! We thought they'd gone into the first house. Thought we'd have plenty of time. The engine was still warm, it started the first pull I gave it. Then this woman came rushing at me, screaming and yelling. Alf was keeping watch, but he didn't see her. No warning at all.'

Gil could feel himself stiffening. 'What's all this splattered over you? Not her blood?'

He could see Bernard shaking, he could hardly speak. 'It could be.'

'What did you do?'

'Not me, it was Alf. He had a penknife, drew it on her.'

'For God's sake! All you had to do was to run for it.'

'I didn't know he had a knife and the woman had her driver with her. A great bear of a man. He had me on the ground before I knew where I was.'

Gil had begun to feel desperate himself. 'Is she all right? I mean, he didn't kill her, did he?'

'How do I know?' It was a wail of agony. 'When I managed to break free I ran off. I wanted to get away from all that.'

In the dim light from the kitchen window, Gil watched him moisten his lips.

'They got Alf. Some lads, passersby, held on to him. I'll have to get some clean clothes. You've got to help me. I can't be seen like this.'

That was more than obvious. He'd had to take a deep breath. 'This is nothing to do with me. Why come here? You could land me in it. I don't need your troubles. Not this sort.'

'I've done favours for you, haven't I, in the past?'

He had, once the war was over; Gil had wanted a better car than the old Austin his father had bought in 1911. It had done valiant service as a hire car for all that time but it was breaking down more often now. He'd thought a smarter and more reliable car would be good for the business, but good cars were very difficult to get hold of.

After a long afternoon spent trying to plug a petrol leak in the Austin, Gil had held forth about it to Bernard over a couple of pints in the Queen Vic. He'd known the Dodge Bernard had offered him a few weeks later was stolen. It was almost new, he could see his face in the polished black paintwork and the brass lamps were very smart. The price Bernard asked had been reasonable. Gil put it through the books as a car of 1913, when in fact it had first gone on the road in February this year. Bernard could fix false paperwork so well that nobody would suspect. And he guaranteed there was no danger of questions being asked. The car had been brought up from London, the number plates changed and false documents provided. Gil loved the car from the moment he saw it and it was a treat to drive.

'Who else have I got to turn to? We're related and you're my friend! Please . . . Some clean clothes.'

Gil had given in. 'You'll have to wash that gore off your face. Come up to my room. My parents are in, but they don't usually come out of the living room until they're going to bed. Keep your mouth shut. As long as they don't hear us talking, they'll think it's just me walking about. Oh, and we'll have to be careful passing the kitchen, Ruby's probably still pottering about in there.'

Gil had led the way in through the back door and let it bang shut behind them both. It was dark in the passage, except for a strip of light showing under the kitchen door. He'd taken Bernard by the hand and led him upstairs to his bedroom. With that door carefully closed, he'd switched on the light.

'Christ!'

Gil hadn't meant to say anything. He was shocked now he could see Bernard clearly. He was well and truly splattered with dried blood all up the side of his neck, his face and into his hair.

He'd dropped his voice to a whisper. 'Where's your cap?'

Bernard's eyes had flared with fear. 'It fell off, lost it. It's all right, there's nothing in it to prove it's mine.'

Gil had felt fluttery with panic himself, it was catching. He mouthed, 'You need a bath. Strip off. Don't worry, my parents will think it's me. So long as they don't see you.'

He'd crossed the passage to the bathroom and turned the taps on over the tub, leaving the door open so he could monitor the living-room door. Ruby usually went up to her bedroom about this time of night, so he needed to keep an eye open for her too. He'd wondered then what he'd let himself in for, it could be big trouble.

When he returned to his bedroom, Bernard was wearing only his long johns; blood had soaked through his trousers, staining them.

'Get those off too.' Gil's mouth was dry. He went back for a towel and flung it at Bernard. 'Wash your hair. Get all that blood off before you dry. Don't leave smears on the towel, OK? Lock the door and don't be long. Mam and Dad will want to use the bathroom before they go to bed. I'll give you ten minutes and if the coast's clear, I'll tap once on the door.'

Gil waited in his room, leaving the door open. He needed to know what was going on in the house. He'd have to intercept Mam if he saw her heading towards the bathroom. He felt sick and his stomach was churning with fear.

He heard Ruby's slow heavy step on the stairs. He made himself go to his bedroom door to see her.

'Good night, Mr Gil.' She was taking a cup of steaming cocoa up with her. At least she couldn't see into his room. Not from the stairs.

'Good night,' he said. That should be the last he'd see of her tonight. She went up to her attic room and switched off the lights on the stairs.

He retreated to his bedroom and looked at the heap of clothes belonging to Bernard. His vest looked all right, he could put that back on. But he'd have to burn everything else. His trousers had been soaked; good wool twill too, Bernard was a dandy dresser. Gil rolled everything up in Bernard's shirt which had been badly smeared too, and went quickly down to the kitchen.

Ruby had just backed up the fire in the range with slack to keep it in all night. Using the poker, Gil drove the garments one at a time into the middle of the fire where it was red and covered them up with hot coals. Then, to be on the safe side, he piled on more slack.

Would cloth make a strange smell as it burned? He was afraid it would. He opened the kitchen window slightly then crept back upstairs. Now he had to find something else for Bernard to wear but there was no point in giving him his best things.

Bernard was a good bit taller than he was. Gil had some brown corduroys that were a bit long for him; they'd do him. The fawn shirt was beginning to fray round the collar but all Gil's underwear was new, he didn't want to part with it but he'd have to.

Would Bernard be ready yet? When Gil looked at his alarm clock, he could hardly believe he'd spent only seven minutes in the bathroom. He heard water swishing vigorously and felt himself sweating. His nerves were really on edge. He had to get Bernard out of this house before anyone saw him.

Never before had anyone come in to take a bath and he didn't know how he'd explain it to his mother if she should come out of the living room now. He tore off the shirt he'd been wearing all day and put on a clean one; combed his hair and put on a tie.

Surely Bernard would be ready by now? He crept out onto the landing. The living-room door was still closed. He

106

tapped gently on the bathroom door and heard the bolt being withdrawn.

Thank goodness! Bernard streaked into his bedroom.

'Get dressed,' Gil mouthed, pointing at the clothes he'd spread out on his bed. 'Whatever you do, don't come out, don't even open the door. I'll come back for you when it's safe.'

He checked the bathroom first, opened the window to let the steam out. The towel was wet but not smeared. Then he went to the living room and said, 'I think I'll go down to the pub for an hour. I'll lock up when I come home.'

His mother looked up, stifling a yawn. 'It's very late to go out, dear.'

'It's only just gone nine.'

'I think it's our bedtime. Your daddy's had a nap in the chair already.'

'Can I give you a hand, Dad?'

'Yes, you can take him to the bathroom.'

At the door, his father straightened up. 'Have you had a bath?'

'Yes.'

'You'll – catch your death of cold. Going out – after a bath. Ugh, close the window, will you?'

His mother went down to the kitchen to make a bedtime drink. It was what she usually did. Gil followed her down, worried about the burning clothes.

'Funny smell in here.' His mother sniffed suspiciously. 'Ruby's burning something.'

'Floor cloth or something,' he muttered. It wasn't too bad, his mother had a real nose for bad smells.

'D'you want a cup of tea, Gil?'

'No thanks, I'm going out in a minute.'

He heard the lavatory flush upstairs. 'I'll just help Dad undress first.'

'I can manage that if you want to go.'

'No, no.'

He wasn't usually so obliging, but he couldn't take Bernard out of his room until he'd got both his parents out of the way. He went back to his father who couldn't be hurried. He'd got his shoelaces in knots.

'You're being very kind tonight,' his mother remarked, which almost panicked him. To Gil it seemed an age before they were both safely settled in their bedroom.

At last! He pulled Bernard downstairs after him. Out on the pavement, he took deep breaths of cold air. Such a relief to get him out of the house.

'Thank you.' Bernard had had trouble keeping up with him. 'Let's go to the Queen Vic.'

'That's where we're going.'

'I'll buy you a drink.'

'I'll die if I don't get one soon.'

'Thanks for lending me these clothes. You've been great.'

'I want them back, mind.'

'Of course. I feel better now I've had time to calm down.'

'I wish I felt better.' It had been a long time since Gil had felt so agitated.

'Would you do me one more favour?'

'You're pushing your luck. I feel I've done enough for you.'

'Just one last thing.'

'What d'you want?'

'I might need an alibi.'

'Oh my God!'

'For between six and eight this evening.'

'At six I was having my tea. I can't say otherwise. Both

my parents sat down with me, Ruby served it. I can't alter that.'

'What time did you get up from the table?'

'I don't know, not exactly, it would be about half past, I suppose.'

'Right, if you're asked, will you say that?' Bernard had stared at him with such intensity. 'It must have been around seven when we were doing the car. Seven till half past, that's the time I'll need to have covered. Can I say I came round to your place and we had a yack and then a game of table tennis in the back?'

'I suppose that would be OK. I was in the office by myself after tea, I did some work.' Gilbert suddenly realised how much this meant to Bernard. It could keep him out of prison. 'I'm not doing this for nothing, mind.'

'Course not. I'll pay you, do you a favour, whatever you want.'

'Fifty pounds. In cash.'

'Good God, Gil, I haven't got that sort of money.'

'How much have you got?'

'I could pay you five now. Maybe another fifteen later. Here we are. Forget that for the moment, I'll see you're all right. Let's chat up the barmaid while she draws our pints. I want her to remember us. Pretend nothing's happened, Gil. It hasn't to you, I don't know why you're so knotted up.'

With a pint in him, Gilbert had begun to feel more his normal self. Twenty pounds was a lot of money to him, but now he'd had time to think, he knew the one favour he could ask of Bernard that would give him more. He'd ask him to forgo making any claim on his Uncle Cuthbert's estate. It probably hadn't occurred to him to do so. Right then, he'd see making a promise like that as the easy way out. Gil thought of all that blood. That showed how desperately Bernard needed an alibi.

There were other acquaintances of theirs in the pub; Bernard told them they'd had a game of table tennis to work up a thirst before coming down. Gil marvelled at how well Bernard kept his head. If such a terrible thing had happened to him, he knew he wouldn't be so calm.

He'd seen no harm in giving him an alibi, he understood Bernard might occasionally steal a car locally and drive it down to London for sale there. He was a petty thief but he certainly wouldn't draw a knife on anybody. It had been his accomplice who'd knifed the woman. He'd got into bad company, that was Bernard's trouble.

A few days later, Gilbert had been shocked when Enid had run down the passage to the office to say there was a policeman in the shop asking for him. That had made his heart thud, but he'd followed her back to the dairy and brought the officer with him to the office. He didn't want anybody else to hear what he was going to say.

The police officer had been rather pedantic as he'd read from his notebook. Did he know Bernard Corkill? Had he seen him on Wednesday last?

Gilbert knew he must not appear nervous. He kept telling himself to stay calm, but he hadn't been. His mind felt splintered, but he'd told the story that Bernard had asked of him.

He'd found out from the police officer that Bernard had been arrested and the woman who had been knifed had since died of her injuries. The charge would be one of manslaughter or even murder, and that had set his heart racing again.

He was asked to go down to the police station and make a statement under oath. That had frightened the living daylights out of him but he'd done it and told the same story to two other policemen. It had taken days to get all that out of his mind.

It was some days before Gilbert saw Bernard again. Then quite unexpectedly he turned up at the Queen Vic just before closing time. There were dark shadows under his anxious eyes, he didn't look too good.

'I was arrested,' Bernard told him as he walked up Market Street with him. 'There were witnesses and my name was given by a passerby as the second man. The alibi you gave got me off. The barman at the Queen Vic told me the police had been in asking about me.'

'I did you a great favour then.'

'They got Alf, he's been charged with murder.'

Gil felt sweat break out on his forehead. 'Surely he'll say you were there too?'

'Alf knows how to keep his mouth shut, and he owes me a few favours.'

'He'll need to owe you a lot. My God! He could hang.'

'It wouldn't save his own neck to tell on me, would it? I've told him I'll look after his wife and kids.'

Gil had scarcely been able to get his breath. He'd perjured himself on Bernard's behalf. What if that should come out too? Could he go to prison for perjury? He was afraid the answer could be yes. He'd been unable to sleep for nights after that.

He'd told Bernard to stay away from the shop and the yard. The last thing Gil wanted was for his parents to recognise him. He didn't think it was very likely because it was years since Bernard's father had thrown him out, and he hadn't been in the habit of visiting his relatives even before that time. But Bernard made him nervous and Ellis had come home by then and was making him nervous too. Gil wanted to feel safe.

He was very cross indeed when Bernard cycled down one morning to ask him for money.

'Just a little, to tide Alf's family over.'

'I've done more than enough for you,' Gil had spat at him. 'Stay clear of me and my family.'

'I've got to have it. Got to keep Alf sweet. You know what he can do.'

With hindsight, Gil wished he'd given him what was in the till that morning. It would have caused so much less turmoil all round.

Chapter Seven

In the week before the wedding there was a frenzy of cooking, which Daisy enjoyed. The wedding cake had long been iced and decorated, but there were hams to boil, herrings to souse, and pastries and cakes to bake. Brenda had talked of having a whole dressed salmon and a lobster with the salad, but when it came to the point Auntie Glad said no.

'Yes of course we can get lobster at wholesale prices but they still cost too much. What's the point in paying out to feed the family as though they're all princes?' Auntie Glad was the only person who didn't bow to Brenda's wishes. 'Anyway, there's more flavour in soused herrings than there is in lobster. They're overrated and can be tough too.'

'I wouldn't know,' Brenda retorted. 'When have I tasted lobster? I hate soused herrings. We're always having them and I think they're common.'

To placate Brenda, Uncle Ern bought shrimps the day before the wedding and he and Daisy spent hours shelling them and then potting and sealing them under melted butter.

Mrs Fox's Canadian relatives had no sooner started their holiday than one of the child bridesmaids went down with measles. Brenda was on edge because the two remaining ones were sisters of the patient and it was possible they too might succumb before the big day.

'Such a shame,' she mourned. 'Elsie looked so pretty in her satin dress.'

'Two little ones will be plenty,' her mother said briskly. They'd been invited to meet them before the wedding but had only stayed an hour. 'You'll have to keep your eye on them, Daisy, they'll be up to all sorts of mischief. Colonial children have no discipline.'

The wedding had to take place on a Thursday afternoon because that was early closing day in Birkenhead and the only time those working in shops could attend a wedding. Auntie Glad had decided the wedding party would walk together to the church on the corner of Hamilton Square; it was only a few hundred yards from the shop.

'Walk on my wedding day?' Brenda laughed. 'No fear, it could rain.'

'Walk is what I did when I married your dad.'

'Gilbert knows I can't walk in my long satin dress. It's got a train, Mam. It would drag on the pavement and get dirty. He's offered me the choice of the carriage or the limousine.'

When she was out doing her morning deliveries, Daisy had often seen their milk float out in the streets with its four milk churns pulled by the grey pony. She knew the same horse also pulled the hearse and at other times the carriage. She'd seen their other black horse and knew they also had two fine motor cars that could be hired.

'Which are you having?' Daisy wanted to know.

'Their best limousine, of course. It's an American Dodge, with a landaulette body.'

'What's that mean?' her mother sniffed.

'In fine weather, half the roof at the rear can be unlatched and folded back on itself. It's made of waterproof black mackintosh with some soft material inside. It's very stately and Gil says the royal family have a similar one. There's a glass panel to cut off the driver and a tube so passengers can speak to him from the back seat.'

Auntie Glad's mouth twisted. 'You won't have time to say a lot on a drive as short as that.'

'No,' Brenda smiled. 'There's a bit of a problem too. Mr Cummins who drives for them is ill in hospital. It means Ellis will have to be the driver as well as the best man. Gil doesn't trust anyone else to drive the motor cars.'

'But there is another man,' Daisy said.

'Yes, Charlie Chalker who does the milk round. He drives the carriage and the hearse. He's sixty now and Gil says he's too old to learn to drive a car. He couldn't trust him with it; he's always worked with horses.'

Daisy said, 'If it would make things easier to have the carriage, why don't you?'

'I want the best on my wedding day. The car is much more eye-catching. Lovely high roof and straight back and it's got running boards. Much easier to get in and out of it in my long gown and train. It doesn't rock like the carriage. I shall feel like a queen in it.'

It was nine o'clock at night, Ellis was leafing through the *Evening Echo* and feeling at a loose end. He craved basic information about his family's business. What he wanted to do was study the company balance sheets. Gil had taken Brenda to the pictures. His father was dozing in his chair and had been all evening. Suddenly his mother laid aside her magazine.

'Your dad would be better in bed, wouldn't he? I'll make his hot milk. I think I'll have an early night too.'

Ellis was losing patience with Gil. He'd asked him for details about many aspects of their business and been fobbed off. He felt he was banging his head against a brick wall. The only way Ellis could think of to get things moving was to work through his father. He'd put off doing that because Dad wasn't at all well. It went against the grain to bother him and it upset his mother. Dad was growing less able to help himself now and was too heavy for his mother to manage by herself. Ellis had taken over that job.

His opportunity came when he helped Dad to his bedroom and lowered him down to sit on the edge of his bed.

'Dad,' he said as he untied his shoelaces, 'I could do with a set of office keys of my own. I'm always having to ask Gil for things. Can I borrow yours and have another set cut?'

That made his father's pale eyes stare down into his. Ellis feared that he, too, was about to refuse, but he was only trying to pull his damaged thought processes together. He pulled a cumbersome ring of keys from his trouser pocket.

'No need . . . to cut a whole new set. Got spares to some. Look . . . in the little drawer over there. On the dressing table.' He was unfastening the buttons on his waistcoat. 'Extra keys . . . to the desks. They're there.'

Ellis gathered them all up in a rush of triumph. As soon as he'd got Dad into his nightshirt, he rushed down to the office to find out what keys he had. He unlocked the door. There wasn't another big key like that, he'd need to have one cut.

What he really wanted was to get into the filing cabinets. Good, he had a spare to this one. Straightaway he opened the bottom drawer. In a file marked 'Legal Affairs' he found some very old papers, copies of several wills. They went back generations; his grandfather's was here and so was his own father's.

He took it out and sat at one of the desks to study it. Dad

had left everything to his mother in trust for her lifetime and then it was to be divided in equal shares between his sons. Ellis pushed his straight hair back from his forehead. There was only him and Gil left now, so that was clear enough. Gil was not to be favoured in any way over him.

He started a key ring of his own and made a list of those he needed to have cut. In the morning, he'd go straight out and get them. Now he could get into the filing cabinets, he wanted to know whether the Corkill family had been partners or employees. Gil was adamant that they'd been employees but Ellis wasn't sure he believed him.

He knew which drawer the accounts were filed in. It was packed tight with documents that went back years. Really, the very old ones should be parcelled up and put out of the way. He took out a whole armful of files before locking up, pleased that he could now see anything he wanted. Then he took the stairs to his bedroom two at a time, keen to get into bed and start reading.

He felt a quickening of interest when he saw from the balance sheet for 1914 that Cuthbert Corkill had been a partner. The profits had been split sixty forty between the Foxes and the Corkills. Not quite equal partners, but partners all the same.

Yet Gilbert was doing his best to convince him and the Maddockses that they'd been employees. Why would he do that? Ellis felt his suspicions multiply. Had this something to do with Daisy? Gilbert had not at first realised her name was Corkill and when he had, the fact had upset him. Pointless to say the Corkills weren't partners when the fact could be so easily proved by looking at the accounts. Ellis shivered. What had Gil done? He'd guess it was illegal. Gil had guilt written all over him.

Ellis reached for the accounts for 1917. He couldn't

believe his eyes. There was no mention of any split in the net profit and no mention of any Corkill. Nor, as far as he could see, was there any split-up of profit for subsequent years.

Was this what Gil had tried to prevent him finding out? That he'd taken the Corkill assets into the business, when he had no legal right to do so? If so, it was fraud and as a family member he felt involved.

It hadn't taken Ellis long to decide Gil wasn't managing the business well and to think he could improve on what Gil was doing. It was a bigger and altogether more shocking step to believe he wasn't honest in his business practice.

Ellis lay back against his pillows and tried to think. His head felt full of feathers as he tried to remember what he knew of the Corkill family. He remembered Ralph leaving to join up in 1914, how they'd all patted him on the back and thought him a hero. Later, his mother had written to say Cuthbert had died of a heart attack. That must have been late in 1916; Ellis had been in France himself by then.

Had there been other members of the Corkill family? Had Cuthbert had a wife in 1916? Ellis thought not, but he wasn't sure; by then the Corkills no longer lived in the cottage in Camden Yard. He wished he knew exactly when Ralph had died.

Ellis went through the accounts for the years 1916 and 1917 with a fine-tooth comb. Perhaps he was wrong and the Corkill family had been bought out. He searched but could find no sign that they had.

He felt as though there was a weight on his chest. Gil had done this by sleight of hand. That's what he'd been trying to hide. That's why he kept everything locked up and wouldn't give him the key. He knew the truth would be obvious from the accounts.

Ellis felt suddenly sick. Surely Gil wouldn't do such a thing? And what about Dad? Did he know? Ellis tried to remember exactly when Dad had had his stroke. Had that happened before Cuthbert's death? No, but certainly before the accounts would have been drawn up for that year.

He shot out of bed, pushed his feet into his slippers and pulled a jacket over his pyjamas to pad down to the office again. He wanted to know now what the Corkill family had put into the business and when they'd done it.

He rummaged through the files and spread out those for the early years of the century on the desk. There was no doubt the Corkills were being paid a share of the profits, but he couldn't find what he was looking for; his head was spinning with a thousand details and he was getting cold. He could do no more tonight, he was too tired and could hardly see straight.

Ellis was sorting the papers he'd been looking at back into date order when he heard a door slam. He straightened up with a jerk and felt the blood rush to his cheeks. He'd forgotten Gil was still out. His footsteps were coming down the passage. No doubt he'd seen the office light on. He was sorting frantically when the door creaked open.

'Oh, it's you!' Gil's face was ugly and twisting. 'I've caught you, have I? Spying on me?'

'Spying? What makes you say that?' Ellis was trying to be calm and firm but felt neither. 'Anything that happens here is as much my business as yours, you know that as well as I do. Why pretend otherwise? You hope I'm going to be satisfied with a few crumbs?'

'Don't be silly.'

'You're taking over all you can. Why did you say the Corkills were employees when they were our partners? You've taken over their assets – whatever they were.'

'They hadn't much . . .'

'Don't be daft, they owned part of this business. Did Cuthbert leave a will? Did you get probate?'

'Cuthbert left everything to Ralph, but he's dead too. Killed in the war. He didn't have time to make a will.'

'So you took over everything they owned and said nothing?'

'Of course not.'

'You've cheated on this, haven't you? I feel implicated because my share of this business is going to be equal to yours. I can't believe what you've done. I'm shocked, horrified even.'

'Don't be a bloody fool, Ellis.'

'If it's fraud, you could go to prison.'

'The Corkill family died out, I tell you. We are the only relatives left.'

'What d'you mean? We aren't relatives. Not blood relatives.'

'Yes, Dad's family was related to them by marriage. Honest.'

'I've never heard that before.'

'Ask him. Ask Mam. They'll tell you. You're barking up the wrong tree.'

Ellis found that hard to believe. Besides, there must be some reason why Gil didn't want him to peruse the accounts. He'd gone to great lengths to prevent him doing it, and he'd been livid when he'd found him here.

'If there is a relative, if someone does try to claim—'

'There isn't, I tell you. There's no one else.'

'Why say Cuthbert Corkill wasn't a partner? The proof is here in our own documents. We paid a proportion of the profits to him every year and there's no trace we ever bought his share from him. A claimant could point that out.'

Gil's face was red and angry. 'We should destroy all those documents. We aren't a public company, there's no law that says we have to keep them. We could refuse to have them scrutinised. They are for our own use and for tax purposes.'

Ellis shuddered. 'How d'you know there aren't other members of the Corkill family?'

'I just know there aren't.'

'What about Daisy?'

'Her? Don't go putting ideas into her head. She has no family, you heard her say that yourself.'

'You should have applied for probate, done it properly.'

'You know nothing about it. You can't get probate if there's no will.'

Ellis paused. Gil was right, he didn't really know what should have been done. 'You should have done it legally.' He was turning away in disgust. 'This way is cheating.'

'It was done legally. How many times do I have to tell you?'

'Was it? You're trying to hide something, I know that. You're greedy, you want all you can get for yourself. Not totally honest . . .'

'Shut up.'

He half saw Gil's fist shoot out. It caught him on the nose and the pain was excruciating. Ellis staggered back against the filing cabinet while his head sang in agony. By the time he'd recovered enough to wipe away the nose bleed, Gil had gone.

He slid onto the chair by the desk and stayed still for ten minutes until his head cleared. Then slowly and methodically he put away all the papers he'd got out and locked up again. He felt utterly weary as he pulled himself upstairs to bed, put out the light and lay aching against his pillows for what seemed hours. Was Daisy related to the Corkills? The thought that she might be had seemed to scare Gil.

Ellis was up early the following morning. His nose felt sore and there was faint bruising under one eye. Nobody seemed to notice except Gil. When his mother got up, he asked her if the Corkill family had been related to them.

His mother said, 'I think Dad's family was related by marriage.'

'How exactly?'

Her face screwed up. 'I don't know. A generation or so back. You'd better ask him.'

Ellis took his father's breakfast porridge up to his room and settled him against his pillows to eat.

'Yes,' Dad agreed. 'Related. Distantly but definitely related.'

'How?'

Dad frowned up at him, trying to explain. 'By marriage. Cuthbert's father . . . I think . . . he married a Fox.'

'So it was all right for us to take over the carpentry business – Cuthbert's business. I see from the accounts we did . . .'

His father stared up at him. 'Legal. Quite legal. Got solicitor . . . Letters of administration. Advertised . . . For other relatives in the paper. Quite legal.' Slowly he spooned up his breakfast.

Ellis felt he'd made a fool of himself, showing so much suspicion of his brother. Perhaps he'd deserved that biff on the nose. Except that . . . Gil was trying to hide something. He hadn't wanted him to have the keys to the office. He'd done his best to avoid letting him see the accounts.

Ruth arrived home the night before the wedding to help with the preparations. She'd decided not to be a bridesmaid. She'd said, 'I'd rather get myself a really smart outfit I can wear afterwards for best.'

She'd brought it with her. Daisy and Auntie Glad admired the green costume as she took it out of its wrappings and hung it up in their wardrobe.

Their old bedroom looked bare. Brenda's new bed had been removed to the flat over the clothes shop and the bedchair had taken its place. Ruth elected to sleep on that.

'It can stay here tomorrow,' Brenda said. 'It takes up too much space in the living room.' They would be twenty-seven in all.

Daisy was pleased Brenda would spend her last night in the attic bedroom with her, but they were both so busy getting things ready and washing their hair, they were too sleepy to talk by the time they got into bed.

The next day being Brenda's big day, ordinary routine was banished. It was a lovely sunny morning. For Daisy, the whole atmosphere had changed. There was an air of excitement in the house. She took Brenda's breakfast up to her in bed, but she had to get up shortly afterwards to help Ruth make the salads and carve the ham. Daisy had to do her deliveries as usual but she spent less time serving in the shop. She helped move furniture about, ran up and down to the attic with wet cloths and polish and brought down small chairs and stools so that those who wanted to could sit down.

Uncle Ern closed the shop early to give everybody time to get ready for the three o'clock wedding. There was very little fish left over and that was carefully stowed in the ice box out in the yard. For once, Mrs Mack and Willie were left to sweep out and close the shop.

Dinner today was a sandwich and a cup of tea. All attention was focused on the wedding breakfast. Daisy spread a white starched cloth on the living-room table and laid out the plates. There were salads of vegetables and fruit, plates of ham and tongue, sherry trifle, jellies and fancy cakes. Uncle Ern said the spread looked magnificent. Guests would have to help themselves because there wouldn't be room for everybody to sit round the table.

Then for Daisy it was a rush to change into her bridesmaid dress. She needed Auntie Glad's help to close the placket at the waist and it gripped her hard.

Brenda had promised to put Daisy's hair up for her but she was panicking about being ready in time herself. Daisy combed out her fat brown pigtails and let her hair fall loose from an Alice band. It reached to her waist. There was far too much of it to pile on her head. She looked at herself in the mirror and thought she looked thirteen again.

Auntie Glad objected when she saw her, but by then Ellis Fox was waiting outside in the car to take them to the church and they had to go.

'It would have been just as easy to walk,' Auntie Glad complained. 'Only a few paces, and that poor lad has to keep going backwards and forwards to get us all there.'

Daisy loved riding in the car and knew Brenda wanted to do things in grand style. She said nothing. She could feel herself shivering with excitement as she waited with the two child bridesmaids in the church porch for the bride to be ferried in.

Uncle Ern was sweating as he helped Brenda out of the car. His suit was of wool alpaca and bought little more than a year ago for the funeral of a fish wholesaler. Auntie Glad said it was ridiculous to think of buying another lighter one, that he'd never get the wear out of them. Brenda looked ethereal behind her veil. The organist was playing softly. Auntie Glad had damned that as another unnecessary extravagance.

They had to wait a few moments for Ellis. Daisy noticed his limp as he went down the aisle to stand by the groom. When the organ burst forth she was marshalling the two toddlers to follow the bride and trying to prevent them tugging on her train.

Gilbert Fox stood with a very straight back in a smart new suit and took his vows in a clearly audible voice. Daisy shivered; he was joined to Brenda and it was too late for her to change her mind now.

It was some comfort to see him look at his bride with love in his eyes, and Auntie Glad said afterwards that Brenda couldn't have asked for more and that it was all very romantic. Daisy hoped Brenda would be happy but she was filled with foreboding. How could she be happy with him?

When they went out into the street again, a small crowd had gathered to see the bride. The sun sparkled while the photographer took pictures and the guests threw confetti. Brenda looked really lovely with her veil thrown back.

Auntie Glad sent Daisy and Ruth hurrying home on foot to get the place unlocked and be ready to serve the sherry.

'Dad and I'll follow. Ridiculous to wait around for a car when it's such a short distance.'

Ruth sniffed hard as she opened up. 'I can smell fish in here again.'

'I've been smelling it since the weather turned warmer.'

'A pity when there's often such a lovely tang of apples at the back of the shop, so sharp and fresh.'

The wedding party was close on their heels. Brenda and Gilbert beamed happily.

'Watch out for Ellis, would you?' Gil hissed at Daisy. 'He's gone back to the church for Father. He'll need help to get him up these steep stairs.'

Daisy ran down as soon as she heard the car outside and

brought up Mrs Fox to sit in a chair in the parlour. Ellis said his father was too heavy for her so she asked Uncle Ern to help him.

As Brenda had instructed, Daisy handed round a tray of sherry. Her dress was feeling tighter by the minute; as though her waist was being pulled in by a rough length of rope.

Within a short time she couldn't believe the noise that came from their packed living room. The cider cup and cask of ale caused raised voices and jolly laughter to mingle with the music from the gramophone that Gil had brought round. Occasionally, Canadian accents predominated.

Daisy wasn't used to parties. She couldn't remember being invited to any and Aunt Glad had never given a real party before. Sometimes on a Sunday they had neighbours who kept the ironmongery shop in to tea, but never had the house been filled like this.

Daisy didn't know all of them. She asked Ruth, 'Who is the lady wearing a royal blue dress and hat? That one with the dangling tassels down one side of her face?

'That's Auntie Hilda, Mam's younger sister.'

'But I've never seen her before.'

'She doesn't have much to do with us these days.'

Auntie Hilda took another glass of cider cup from the tray Daisy held out to her.

'Is this the girl?' she asked Auntie Glad. Daisy could feel cold eyes assessing her. 'You should have shown that hussy the door. I don't know why you had to take her offspring in. Did you never stop to think what an embarrassment it would be for me?'

'Ern wanted it.'

'You should have said no.'

Daisy hardly knew what to make of this, but she understood well enough that it all referred to her. Uncle Ern came up and took a glass of ale from her tray as Brenda's laugh tinkled happily round the room.

'Your turn next,' he smiled at Daisy.

'What a hope.' Auntie Hilda cackled into the sudden silence, her face flushed from the cider cup. 'She's an ugly duckling if ever there was one. And who'd want to marry anyone with her background?'

Daisy couldn't get her breath. She looked round, every eye in the room seemed to be on her. Pitying eyes. She rushed to the scullery knotting with hurt to have heard that said so publicly. She had to get away from them. The worst part was she was afraid it might be true. She had no boyfriends; they didn't seem to notice her.

She'd lost touch with most of the girls she'd known at school, but she knew they all would have wanted what Brenda had. She did herself; perhaps because she had no real relatives Daisy wanted it more desperately than most. She longed to have a husband who would love her and a large family of her own. To have as well the security of a business to support them would be wonderful. She'd have liked to be pretty like Brenda too, but she knew some things were impossible.

She was wiping her eyes on a tea towel when she heard the door open behind her. Every muscle in her body stiffened. The door closed again softly. Somebody had joined her in the tiny confines of the scullery.

'You mustn't let things like that upset you.' The voice was masculine, she didn't recognise it and had to turn to see who it was. Through a shimmer of tears she found it was Ellis Fox! The last person she would have wanted to hear that, or to see her looking like this. The tears started again. He pushed a handkerchief into her hand.

'It was a cruel thing to say. The cider cup talking. She

didn't mean it. You're no ugly duckling.'

'Not like Brenda, though,' Daisy choked. 'Not pretty like her.'

'No, especially when you're down in the dumps like this, but you've got a lovely smile. You're attractive when you're happy.'

'D'you think so?'

'Yes. You'll have the fellows flocking round wanting to marry you when you're a bit older.'

'I'm sixteen,' she said with a touch of indignation. She looked up at him and could feel a smile tugging at her lips. 'How old are you?'

'Twenty-two.'

'I haven't seen you about much, not like Gilbert.'

'I've been away fighting in France since I was nineteen.'

Ellis didn't resemble his brother in any way. He was not so tall and of a wiry build, being rather underweight. He had a lot of straight brown hair and his eyes had a haunted look about them. He didn't look well.

'I was fighting in the trenches and unlucky enough to get a shrapnel wound in my leg in the last week of the war. Then I caught the flu that's sweeping through Europe, but I'm over all that now.'

Ruth came in to get another tray of ale. 'Go and get something to eat,' she told Daisy. 'Before it all goes.'

Daisy took Ellis to the table and together they heaped food onto their plates. As she led him to the chairs she'd left out on the landing, the only possible place left to sit down, Daisy felt she couldn't eat until she'd loosened the waist of her dress. Surreptitiously she eased the hooks out of the eyes and the press studs burst open. It was such a relief to breathe freely again, and as she happened to be sitting with the placket facing the wall, nobody need notice. She pulled thick strands of her hair round to hide it.

She decided this was the best part of the wedding. Ellis Fox had taken the trouble to seek her out and try to comfort her. She wondered if she could count him as a boyfriend after this? He was lovely, much nicer than his brother. He seemed trustworthy and didn't have Gil's high opinion of himself.

Chapter Eight

For Daisy, the day after the wedding seemed flat. Because everybody wanted fish for their dinner on Fridays, it was their busiest day in the shop and she was out delivering all morning. It was a rush to get it all done in time.

'Get this room back to normal,' Auntie Glad fussed as soon as they'd eaten dinner. 'There'll be no comfort here until we do.'

The furniture in the living room and parlour had all been rearranged for yesterday's party. Daisy helped Uncle Ern put things back where they belonged. She'd have liked the bedchair to stay in the downstairs bedroom for Ruth to use when she came home. That way, they could have a bedroom each.

'I want it here by the range.' Uncle Ern pulled at his walrus moustache. 'It's the most comfortable chair in the house.' He usually had a ten-minute nap on it after his dinner every day. 'Do you want to bring your bed back downstairs?'

'No, I love my new attic bedroom.' Daisy hadn't expected to feel instantly at home there but she did. It was almost as though she belonged, and with Brenda gone she was looking forward to having it to herself.

She had to make several journeys up to the attic to return the chairs and stools she'd brought down. She decided she could do with another chair in her room and took the best one there. She turned in the doorway to appraise the effect. Apart from the double brass bedstead, it was furnished with a deal wardrobe and a chest of drawers. She already had one chair beside the bed on which she put her candle, but she thought a little table or a bedside cabinet would be better and there might be one amongst the jumble in the other attic.

The shop was opening again then and she had to serve there all afternoon. It wasn't until tea had been eaten and cleared away that she was able to look in the big attic.

She couldn't see anything very clearly. Although there were three windows they hadn't been cleaned in years and were coated with grime. The place smelled dusty and airless. A low chest with two drawers caught her eye; she had to lift away a lot of odds and ends before she could reach it.

As soon as she tried to move it, dust flew up, making her cough. She went down to the scullery for a damp cloth and some polish. When she'd cleaned it, she pulled out both drawers and carried the chest to her room. She was pleased with it, it looked exactly right beside her bed.

She went back to turn out the drawers; the bottom one was full of old clothes, petticoats and nightdresses that smelled of damp and decay. She tipped them out and wiped it clean.

She hardly knew what to make of the contents of the top drawer; there were several scarves and handkerchiefs, and a pair of leather gloves now stiff and hard. Half hidden, she found a tin box with a picture of Queen Victoria as a young girl on the lid. Inside was quite a pretty necklace. She held it up against the dim light, wondering if it was coloured glass or amber. There was also an opal ring that looked bigger and better than the one Brenda had. Daisy felt as though she'd found a treasure trove. Why didn't Auntie Glad wear the ring? She was sure it was real gold.

There was a pile of darned stockings, not very nice; she tossed them out on the pile of petticoats. Underneath, face down, was a faded sepia photograph which she took to the window to study. A couple walking along what seemed to be a pier smiled out at her. Yes, it was New Brighton pier, she could see the Mersey estuary behind them and in the distance the docks on the Liverpool side of the river. It was a holiday snapshot, the photographer's name was stamped on the back. She wondered if the couple were relations of Auntie Glad or Uncle Ern.

The man wore a straw boater at a jaunty angle and the girl the flowing skirts of the turn of the century. Daisy would have guessed they were father and daughter except that they were holding hands and their bodies arced together. They looked so happy like that, they had to be lovers.

Losing interest in them, Daisy carried on with her job, searching systematically through the contents of the top drawer, tossing out what she didn't want. She came across a small mirror in a wooden frame that would be very useful, and then a prayer book.

She flicked it open and there written on the fly leaf in large youthful script was the name Rosa Corkill. She froze, her stomach churning. Until that moment it hadn't occurred to her that she might be looking through her mother's belongings. She stood staring down at them for ages, while her heart thumped away like a steam hammer.

She didn't know how long it took her to recover enough to snatch up her mother's precious belongings and clatter downstairs to the living room. Auntie Glad was dozing beside the range. Uncle Ern was reading his newspaper.

'Is this my mother?' Daisy held up the photograph. 'I found it in the big attic.' There was a shocked silence, then

Auntie Glad, her face working with fury, pulled herself up with a jerk.

'How many times have I told you? You've no business to go searching through my things.'

'But they aren't yours! This prayer book belonged to my mother. Why shouldn't I have it? Why shouldn't I know all about her? I've asked and asked but you never tell me anything.'

'Don't speak to me like that,' Auntie Glad thundered. 'I won't have it from you.'

'Is this her? In this picture? Why won't you talk about her?'

'Give me those things.'

'No, I want them. They aren't yours.' Daisy swept everything up in her arms and ran back to her room in the attic, slamming the door behind her. She couldn't stop the tears pouring out as she spilled the treasures out on her bed and threw herself down beside them.

It was cruel of Auntie Glad to pretend she didn't know the first thing about Rosa and to stop her having these things. Daisy was shaking with tears and didn't hear the door open.

'Daisy, love.' Uncle Ern was breathing heavily after climbing the stairs. 'I was afraid you'd be upset.' The bedsprings creaked as sat down beside her and put an arm round her shoulders, just as he used to when she'd fallen and hurt her knees as a little girl.

She turned to him and sobbed against his jacket. 'I don't understand. Why shouldn't I know? She's my mother and nobody wants to tell me anything about her. It's as though you're all trying to pretend she never existed.'

'She existed, Daisy. I've wanted to tell you for a long time. I know you've been asking . . .'

'Why didn't you then?'

'Glad was against it.'

'But why? I don't understand why.'

'You're old enough to understand now. Rosa wasn't married and when she was having you, her father didn't want her at home. She came to live here for a time with us.'

Daisy could feel her heart racing again. Not married! That was the worst possible sin any girl could commit, to have a baby before being married. Auntie Glad had drummed into her that it must be avoided at all costs. It didn't happen to good girls. Men must not be allowed to kiss or cuddle.

In bed, Brenda had said her mother had been just the same with her and Ruth. She was paranoid about it, but all the same it could only lead to trouble to find oneself in that position. And it had happened to her mother!

It made her feel foolish that she hadn't realised that before. She'd felt once or twice that Brenda had been on the point of saying something important but had changed her mind. Not married! Uncle Ern was telling her the real facts at last.

'You understand now why Auntie Glad doesn't want to keep all this fresh in your mind. In anybody's mind. It was considered a terrible disgrace.'

Daisy could hardly get the words out. 'Didn't my father want to marry Rosa?'

'That was the big . . . difficulty. You know Auntie Hilda, Glad's sister?'

'Yes, we hardly see her but she came to the wedding.' Daisy sighed. 'I don't think she liked me. Seemed to hate me on sight.'

'She said too much. That was nasty, in front of everybody like that. Especially after all these years. None of it was ever your fault.' Uncle Ern's arm tightened round her shoulders. 'Your father was her husband.'

Daisy tried to take this in. 'Auntie Hilda's husband?' That made her feel worse.

'Perhaps you can understand now how she feels.'

'He preferred my mother to her?' Daisy could understand that. Hilda wasn't physically attractive and, even worse, she was bitter and twisted. 'At the wedding yesterday, she took her spite out on me and I couldn't understand why.'

'He fell in love with Rosa.'

'What was his name?'

'Harry Grainger. He was my brother-in-law and we'd been good friends up till then. I was really fond of him. Rosa desperately needed a roof over her head, you see. He'd put her in an impossible position. He asked me to help.'

Daisy blew her nose. Uncle Ern would help anybody, he was that sort. 'Auntie Glad said his ship went down in a storm and he was drowned.'

'Yes, he was a sailor and used to work on the Irish ferries, but after the row with Hilda he went deep sea.'

'What's deep sea?'

'The ship does long voyages, only rarely comes to a British port. Not popular with most sailors.'

'What happened to Auntie Hilda?'

'Nothing happened to her. Harry told me he'd left her. Her version of the story is that she didn't want him in the same house. She told him to clear out. You can see the trouble it caused. It wasn't just a family row, it spread fast. Customers were talking about it in the shop; soon it was all over town, a huge scandal. Harry was sixteen years older than Rosa. He should have known better.'

Daisy tried to visualise these two people as parents. It was impossible . . . Not at all what she'd imagined.

'And I'd agreed to have Rosa here, which didn't make it any easier for us.'

'But didn't he want to stay with my mother?'

'I'm sure he did. Rosa had letters from him regularly. She said he was sorry he'd signed up for such a long voyage and that he meant to set up house with her as soon as the ship docked in Liverpool. I think at the time he was overwhelmed by the trouble he'd caused. He didn't have a lot of money and Hilda claimed their savings for herself. A long trip must have seemed the only way out.'

'It was cruel of Rosa's parents. To turn her out of their home. I would have thought her mother, my grandmother – surely she'd have wanted to help her?'

'Rosa's mother died before she grew up. Her father was vicar of St Luke's . . .'

'A vicar?'

'You can see how difficult it would be for him. He had to think of his parishioners. They'd count Rosa as a fallen woman.'

'But she was his daughter. I'd have thought he'd put her above his flock.'

'The scandal, it devastated him. In his position it would be hard to take.'

'St Luke's Church? I'd like to go and see him. He's my grandfather.'

'Rosa told me he moved to Essex shortly afterwards. I don't know exactly where. He wanted to get away from the scandal too. We've heard nothing of him since Rosa died.'

'Oh! Did she have any brothers or sisters?'

'I believe she had a brother, but I didn't know the Corkill family, Daisy. I can't tell you anything about him.'

'He'd be my uncle.'

'Yes.'

'It seems I did have relatives once but I don't suppose they'll be easy to find now.' Daisy dried her eyes. 'Thank you for telling me.' She sighed heavily. 'But I still don't understand why Auntie Glad was so against me knowing about my mother.'

'We had a hard time in the shop. Customers stopped buying from us. We lost business and it took years to get it back. We couldn't ask Rosa to serve in the shop. She worked down there when it was closed, setting up and cleaning out. People didn't want to speak to her.'

'That's awful. It must have made her feel terrible.'

'It did. And there were other reasons . . . because of you girls. Ruth and Brenda were growing up then. Glad didn't want the same thing to happen to them and she was afraid it might. It was such a disgrace, you see. She didn't want any hint of that attached to them.'

'But . . .'

'She was protecting all three of you. As she saw it, it was best put behind us and forgotten. Hilda was not well pleased with us for taking Rosa in. She looked upon that as betrayal by her sister. We haven't seen much of her since.'

'Did Hilda have any children? They'd be half sisters or brothers, wouldn't they?' Daisy didn't feel she'd want to know them now.

'She had no children. That was another thing she was unhappy about. She'd wanted a family for years and it didn't come. But for Rosa, well, you came on the scene far too quickly.'

'I brought nothing but trouble to her,' Daisy said sadly.

'She loved you, however much trouble you brought.'

'My parents, dead and gone so quickly, before I knew them. It's a comfort to know you were kind to my mother, Uncle Ern. And knowing she slept here in this same attic before me. It felt good from the first night.' She stopped as another thought came to her. 'How did my mother die?'

She let the words 'my mother' roll on her tongue.

Uncle Ern blew his breath out through his teeth. 'It was an accident. A terrible accident. Just a bang on her head. One minute she was right as rain and the next lying dead.'

'She just bumped her head?'

'Yes, we heard the bump and we heard you crying. You were lying beside her on the . . .'

'Where? What did she bump her head on?'

'Er . . . out in the yard at the back. She was lying near the, er, ice box.'

'She wasn't attacked?'

'No, no. It was an accident. We got her to hospital but she died later that day.'

Daisy felt overwhelmed. She'd ached to know these facts but now she did she felt utterly exhausted; totally drained. She should have guessed it would be something like this. She counted herself very unlucky to lose her mother in such a simple accident. Poor Rosa, her luck had been out from the beginning.

When she heard Uncle Ern close her door and go downstairs, Daisy put her head down on her pillow and closed her eyes. She felt she could rest now. At least she knew what had happened. It explained why she had no uncles and aunts or brothers and sisters. Poor Mother, she'd had such a sad and unhappy life.

Ernest Maddocks went stiffly down to the living room feeling depressed. He was cold and his rheumatism was playing him up. He'd known for years that Daisy was determined to learn all she could about her mother. 'Don't tell her, whatever you do,' Glad had insisted. He'd put it off time and time again, knowing it wouldn't be easy, but it had been painfully awful. He'd had to tell her enough to satisfy her curiosity.

He had to stop her asking and asking, it was going through him and getting on Glad's nerves.

To see Daisy's raw emotion had brought tears to his eyes. He hadn't really understood the depth of her need. He'd done his best, he could say that, and it had brought such a wave of tenderness, he had a lump in his throat now.

He'd been fond of Rosa and her ending had brought such grief and guilt and loss. He and Glad were not over it, after all these years.

The only sound in the living room was Glad's soft snore and the dropping of hot coals in the range. Ern sank down on to his bedchair and closed his eyes, wanting to shut out from his mind what he'd just done.

Talking about Rosa brought it all back with dreadful clarity. He'd had one heart-stopping moment up there with Daisy when he'd felt such a compulsion to unburden himself, to tell her the whole pitiful story. It might have brought him relief from the gnawing guilt that he should have done more for Rosa, but it would have added to Daisy's distress. Better this way.

Poor little Daisy, he didn't know what he could do to help her, but he wanted to. She'd lasted longer in the shop than Brenda had. She took a pride in the work. He liked to see her laughing with Willie, and listening to Mrs Mack's gossip. What would he do without her now? He was half afraid he'd lose Daisy. Working with wet fish was not a young girl's dream.

'The likes of her can't afford dreams,' Glad had grunted. 'She'll stay, she needs a home. Such a plain girl, she's not likely to get married.'

But Daisy always had a smile and her face shone with intelligence. He couldn't see that she was plain, but at his age perhaps youth had an attraction of its own.

He was feeling down and weary. At sixty-one he'd be glad to retire from all this. Getting up to go to the wholesalers at four in the morning on three days a week was a bit much for a man of his age. Especially with the burden of Rosa's end still heavy on his conscience.

Daisy woke up at midnight to find her room bright with moonlight. She was cold because she'd gone to sleep on top of her slippery pink eiderdown. All was quiet in the house and in the streets outside. She got undressed quickly and closed her curtains before getting into bed.

She'd thought it would be a comfort to know all about her mother, but to find she was illegitimate was somehow quite shocking. She could understand Auntie Glad's reason for absolute secrecy. Nobody would want it known that there was such a thing in the family. It didn't make Daisy value herself more highly.

Because she'd slept for over four hours already, she found it difficult to get back to sleep and, anyway, her mind was working overtime on her mother's sad history. Uncle Ern had told her many things she hadn't known before and she'd been so sure that it would satisfy her curiosity. She'd expected to have peace from the everlasting yearning to know, but already her mind was beavering away at the accident which had caused Rosa to lose her life. Uncle Ern had been vague about that. Daisy wanted to know more. And then there was Rosa's father, her own grandfather. He could still be alive. He hadn't been kind to Rosa in her time of need, but so great was Daisy's need for blood relatives that she was prepared to overlook that.

As she helped Uncle Ern to set out the fish on the counter the next morning, she asked him about both.

He said, 'You never give up, do you?' They talked of

Rosa's accident but Daisy learned nothing new.

On Saturday morning, Daisy had no order to deliver to Fox's dairy, but there were several in Camden Street close by. As she cycled slowly past she noticed several customers waiting in the dairy. She could see Ellis, together with the red-haired woman who served there.

She delivered an order round the corner in Price Street and came back. Outside on the pavement again, she hesitated. She wanted to go in and talk to Ellis but was nervous about it. She paused to watch him. He'd been sympathetic when she'd been upset at the wedding. She felt a need to talk to him. She wanted to tell him what she'd found out about her mother. The shop was emptying, was less busy now.

Go on, she urged herself, you know him well enough.

A customer came out with a jug brimming with creamy milk and stood holding the door open for her. She took a deep breath and went in.

'Hello, Daisy.' Ellis came to meet her, took her hand in his.

'I had an order . . . close by . . . I wanted to tell you . . .'

'I'm glad you've called in.' He was pleased, a smile was lighting up his face. 'Enid can manage on her own for a bit. Come in here, where we can talk.'

He led the way to a rather bare and formal room with a polished desk and a shiny floor. It was dominated by a religious picture on one wall. Daisy looked round and sat on the chair he indicated. The only other furnishings, apart from the telephone, were a few leatherbound books and a vase of fresh flowers.

'I hope you don't mind, coming in here . . .' Ellis's eager manner had gone, he seemed uneasy now.

'No, no.'

'This is what we call the funeral parlour.'

She found his dark eyes hypnotic. 'I guessed that. You arrange things here?'

'Sometimes, but usually we go to the house of the bereaved. It doesn't make you uncomfortable? Brenda hates anything to do with . . .'

Daisy shook her head. 'No, no.'

'It's always quiet in here, tranquil. I think it must be the subdued light.' There were heavy net curtains at the window.

Ellis was not as handsome as Gilbert, and his expression seemed always serious. He listened carefully to what she'd learned from Uncle Ern last night; of how she'd asked and asked about her mother, and now suddenly she knew everything.

'Nobody understands how I feel. Everybody has relatives but me. I feel better about it now I know.'

'They didn't want to upset you, Daisy.'

'They feel anything like that has to be kept quiet. Hushed up. A scandal is bad for business. But once I was old enough to understand, they should have told me.'

He said, 'I can understand now why your Auntie Hilda . . .'

'Brenda's Auntie Hilda.'

'I can understand why she was so nasty to you, but it was wrong of her. You mustn't let things like that worry you, Daisy. You must put them right out of your mind.'

'I can't do that. I need to *know*. The problem is the more I know, the greater my need becomes to know more.'

'I wish I could help you.'

'There must be some other way. Not just asking Auntie Glad and Uncle Ern, I mean.'

'What d'you want to know?'

'I'd like to find out more about my grandfather. Uncle

Ern said they'd never known him. Never seen him. And I don't understand about my mother's accident. I feel Uncle Ern's being cagey about that. Not telling me exactly what happened.'

'Brenda or Ruth?'

'He said they were at school. They don't know either.'

'I'm sorry, Daisy. Can't help there.'

She could hear a strange clatter and rumble. 'What's that noise?'

'It's Dolly bringing the milk float in after the morning round. Come and have a look round our place.'

Daisy felt a stab of guilt. 'I'd love to . . .' Saturday was not as desperately busy as Friday but there were other orders waiting back at the shop for her to deliver. 'I can't stay long, I'll get into trouble if I do.'

He led her along a narrow passage. 'This is our office.'

Daisy looked into the big room. Two desks covered with ledgers and papers. A telephone on the wall and a big clock.

'And this is our yard. Camden Yard.'

She'd known there was a yard at the back. The narrow entry into it was next to the shop in Camden Street, but there was little to be seen from there except the high solid gates. 'I'd no idea your premises were this big.'

'Once, years ago, there were several businesses sharing this yard, and the owners lived here too. You can see the little cottages over there, though they've fallen into disrepair now and there were more that were pulled down to make room for the cars. There were rooms over the workshops too.'

Daisy let her eyes go round the yard. 'So this is where the Corkills lived and worked? Your mother talked about them. It made me wonder if they were related to my mother.'

'It's possible.' His eyes were sympathetic, Daisy warmed

to him. 'Everybody had big families in the old days. Many sons left home to find work elsewhere. This was the Corkills' carpentry shop.'

'It still is, isn't it?'

'Yes, but in Enoch Corkill's day it made furniture and gates as well. Today the shop makes only coffins.'

'When you say the name Corkill like that, it makes me think that perhaps, just perhaps, I am related. You probably think I'm being silly.'

'No.' He smiled. 'We all have things we take to heart.'

Daisy looked at the buildings which went all round the yard; there were stables and haylofts, some were open garages now. She could see the cars lined up under cover. The carriage was ready to go out, and Black Bess was already between the shafts.

Charlie Chalker was releasing Dolly, the grey pony, from the shafts of the float.

'She'll have to go out again with the hearse straightaway,' Ellis called to Charlie.

'I'll just give her a quick drink and a nosebag.' Charlie was leading her towards the water trough where she drank deeply. Daisy followed Ellis over and together they patted Dolly's rump.

'She's getting old now.' He smiled at her. 'Been here for as long as I can remember. But it's not a bad thing for a horse that has to pull a hearse. She moves it at a stately pace. Especially when she's been out with the milk float since five o'clock in the morning. The last thing we want is a high-stepping pony that wants to break into a canter.'

Charlie started to brush her down. 'Got to tidy her up a bit first.' Then with a nosebag over her head, he was backing her towards the shafts of their hearse.

'It's little old-fashioned now, I'm afraid,' Ellis said. 'I'm trying to persuade Father to get a motor hearse but in its day this was thought to be a very handsome vehicle.'

Daisy had seen it out in the streets many times. It was in effect a large box on wheels, just big enough to take a coffin.

'It was made by Cuthbert Corkill many years ago. Father says he put some of his finest work into it.'

There was etched glass let into the sides all round so the coffin could be seen. The roof was trimmed with an edging of wrought iron which served to keep the flowers and wreaths from slipping off.

'It can be pulled either by hand or by a horse. Most of the funerals in Grandpa's time were walking funerals. In Father's too, families hadn't the money to spend on a big show when there was a death. Things have changed, especially since the war. The extravagant funerals of the rich are being copied by the poor. Nowadays almost all our clients want Dolly to pull the hearse.'

He stood staring down at Daisy for a moment. 'Do you mind me holding forth like this about undertaking?'

'No, Ellis. I told you.'

He grimaced. 'I'm glad. It usually puts girls off. Lots of people don't want to think such a business exists. Not until they need us anyway. They want to turn their backs on everything to do with death. The lads I knew at school, those I knew in the army, they made jokes about undertakers.'

'You find it embarrassing?'

'On a social level, yes.'

'So is selling fish.'

He smiled. 'When we were kids, Gil and I would have given anything to have Dad in fish. No business could be more embarrassing than this. What the other kids said used to make our skin crawl.'

'But not now, not when they order . . . ?'

'No, no, it's different when they want to use our service. They're often upset themselves, of course. Having a death in the family can be a very difficult time. What people want then is to be treated with kindness and sympathy.'

Daisy didn't doubt that Ellis would provide that. He was the sympathetic sort. She said, 'Perhaps we've all had more than our fill of death with the war.'

Chapter Nine

Auntie Glad had invited the bridal couple to come to the fish shop for their tea on Sunday afternoon. 'You won't have any food in, you won't want to be bothered shopping, not this Saturday.'

Gilbert and Brenda had spent their three-night honeymoon in a boarding house in New Brighton. Brenda already had the keys of the clothes shop, together with those of the flat above. She'd arranged for the shop to be run by Mrs Fanshaw until she came back to take it over for good on Monday morning.

Daisy had set the table with their best cloth. For Sunday tea, Auntie Glad always provided salad with a slice of cold roast meat cut from the remains of the joint they'd had for dinner. Meat was a rare treat in her house.

Daisy could see Gil adored Brenda, they kept smiling at each other and he addressed all his remarks to her. They were sitting side by side at the table; he kept putting his knife down to stroke her hand. Rosa's sad story was in Daisy's mind and she couldn't help but think how much more fortunate Brenda was. She had such bounty, her cup must be brimming over.

'We've had a lovely lazy time.' Brenda had eyes only for her new husband. 'But we came back early this morning to get our flat straight. It needed a lot of cleaning, the Fanshaws haven't lived there since their first son was born and he's turned three now.'

'You're straight now?' Auntie Glad wanted to know.

'We've got it clean, but we need lots more furniture and things. You must walk up with us after tea and see it.'

'You'll find a lot of useful stuff up in the attic here,' her mother said. 'You can take anything you want.'

After tea, while Daisy was washing up, Brenda took Gil up to the attic. They were back down within five minutes.

'Nothing up there that I'd want, Mam. I want my house to be nice.'

'If you're short of chairs, those we brought down for your wedding were—'

'We're not that short. Gil's parents are giving us some things. Antiques, aren't they, love?'

Auntie Glad sounded a little frosty. 'You asked for money for your wedding present and that's what you got. And we've given you a lot from here; underblankets and sheets and those cups and saucers with lilies on.'

Brenda looked a little ashamed of herself. 'Of course you have, Mam. You've been very generous.'

Daisy and Uncle Ern led the way briskly up Market Street. She was looking forward to seeing Brenda's new home.

The rooms above the clothes shop were light and airy. There was a big parlour overlooking the street, and an even bigger living kitchen overlooking the back yard. The new bed was erected and made up in one of the two bedrooms and they had a bathroom with a washbowl. The lavatory was out in the yard, just like their own.

Ruth came round as soon as she was off duty, which meant there were no longer enough chairs for them all to sit down. Gilbert took Uncle Ern across the road to get the sofa they'd been promised for the parlour. Ellis helped them carry it over. Daisy sat on it and found it hard to believe they were giving away such a lovely piece of furniture; green velvet and not a mark on it. Ellis sat down next to her while Brenda made them all another cup of tea.

Uncle Ern turned to Ellis and said, 'How's business? These are hard times for most, but between the dairy and your funeral service, you'll be all right?'

'Yes, all right.'

Auntie Glad was interested in any sort of business. 'There's a lot of small firms doing funerals these days.'

'After the Co-op, we're the biggest, and we've been established the longest.' Daisy heard the pride in Ellis's voice.

'There's enough business for you all?'

'More than enough with this flu epidemic still raging.' Ellis went on to enlarge. 'Back in the old days only the rich had elaborate funerals. They'd hire mutes, professional mourners, you know, and carry a feather board of black ostrich feathers with plumes of them on each horse's head as well as on the hearse itself.'

Daisy was fascinated because Ellis was being drawn out. He didn't often hold forth in company.

'Since the turn of the century the poor have wanted funerals like that too. People feel terrible grief and want to show it. Those living round here haven't much money but they want to give their loved ones the best send-off they can when the time comes. It's a way of showing their friends and neighbours how much they valued the deceased and—'

'Stop it.' Brenda turned on Ellis, wrinkling her pretty nose. 'Stop it, I hate to think of funerals and all that goes with them.'

'Someone has to,' her mother told her sharply. 'We'll all

need the service sooner or later.'

It pleased Daisy that Auntie Glad was supporting Ellis. She felt she was getting to know him now and she very much liked what she saw. His eyes kept coming back to meet hers. She hoped that perhaps he liked her.

Friday came round again and Fridays were always busy for Daisy. She was out delivering fish and vegetables all morning. The Convent of the Little Sisters of the Poor ordered so much, it took up a journey in itself. It was one of her favourite calls; she was curious about life in the convent but was allowed to see little of it.

The nun who answered her tug on the huge doorbell always took her into a whitewashed anteroom which was bare except for a couple of hard chairs, a large scrubbed table and a crucifix on the wall. There wasn't much daylight and it smelled like a church.

Then, always, the nun summoned the sister in charge of domestic affairs with a tug on a different bell. The atmosphere was calm and tranquil, Daisy felt both nuns beamed kindness and goodwill at her. Her delivery was checked over on the table with great thoroughness and the money counted out and given to her before she left.

Outside again, the fresh morning sunlight was dazzling. She was about to mount her heavy delivery bike for the ride back to the shop when she was passed by another cyclist. She was taken by surprise and hardly able to believe her eyes.

The man was wearing a jacket of pepper and salt tweed the colour of wet sand. It had big patch pockets that stuck out – poacher's pockets, they called them – and the waist was marked with two rows of sewing to look like a belt.

Only once before had she seen a jacket like that.

She was tingling all over as she leapt on her bike and pedalled hard to keep him in view. He was wearing a fawn cap. An ordinary cap, there were hundreds like it, but she was almost sure it was the same one he'd been wearing the day he'd stolen money from Fox's Dairy.

He was going fast on a business-like bike, black and big and in good condition. She'd noticed that when it had knocked against hers. He turned into Conway Street, and she had to put on another spurt to keep up. It wasn't easy, her heavy delivery bike wasn't made for speed but adrenaline was pumping through her now. There was a lot of traffic here, motorbikes with sidecars and heavy drays pulled by four horses on their way from the docks. She narrowly missed a motor car and the driver hooted at her, making her heart jump into her mouth.

She was cycling faster than she ever had before, she mustn't lose sight of him. They were heading down Conway Street into town. She shot past the end of Adelphi Street feeling she had wings on her feet. She should have turned there to go back to the fish shop. There were still five loads waiting for her to deliver, Auntie Glad was going to be cross with her, but she didn't care. This was important to Ellis. If Gil didn't care that money had been stolen from his till, Ellis certainly did.

She followed as the cyclist pulled out to overtake a brewer's dray and a rag and bone man's cart. They were instantly overtaken by a charabanc; Daisy felt her bike move in its slipstream and had that awful feeling of travelling at a speed she could barely control.

For the first time she asked herself what she should do when she discovered where he was heading. They were crossing a busy part of town. Was he going to buy something in one of the shops? Should she challenge him if she caught up? She shuddered at the thought of confronting him. She'd wait for him if he went into a shop. Eventually, he must lead her to where he lived. Then if she could get his address . . .

But he didn't turn into Argyle Street as she'd half expected, he went straight across it. Daisy began to think he might be going straight home. She was puffed and couldn't go at this speed for very much longer, but he was slowing down. He'd never once turned his head, he couldn't know he was being followed.

She braked, not wanting to be too close. They were heading up Henry Street, it looked as though he lived here. The New Theatre Royal backed on to it. On the other side was a long terrace of small houses; women were gossiping on their front doorsteps, children were playing hopscotch. He was riding straight on and drawing close to the end of the road. At the last minute he turned his bike into a back entry.

Daisy dismounted, hot with disappointment. She couldn't follow him there. He'd be bound to see her, there wouldn't be anybody else about. A handcart piled high with furniture was pushed past her. A small boy rolled his hoop along the pavement, but she couldn't lose him now. She propped her bike against the yard wall of the end house and crept forward to take a look.

His bike was bumping over the setts some way down. Yes, he lived here, he was swinging his leg over and cruising to a halt. He dismounted and wheeled his bike to a back door that had once been painted red. She heard it grate against the concrete of the yard as he pushed it open. She held her breath; he must live in that house. As he pushed his bike inside she caught a side view of his face and knew this was the right man. Then he was gone and the back gate grated shut behind him.

She stood shivering for a moment, unable to take her gaze from the door. She had to know what number he'd gone into. It took courage to venture closer; she made herself run as softly as she could between the two high brick walls with solid wooden doors set into them. Most had a number painted on, but she hadn't been able to see from the end of the entry. She could see now; it was number twenty-seven.

The moment she saw that she turned and fled, wanting to put as much distance as she could between herself and that place. Her knees were shaking as she mounted her bike again. She felt better when she reached the end of the street and made all haste to get back to the fish shop. Uncle Ern was in the yard when she pushed the bike in.

'You're running late this morning,' he said as he loaded the orders into the basket in front and strapped a box onto the carrier behind. 'St Lawrence's Presbytery and Park Street. Get a move on, love.'

Daisy did. She'd recovered now. She knew she'd have fish to take to the dairy this morning; she could wait until then to see Ellis.

Daisy still felt excited when she propped the pedal of her bike against the pavement outside Fox's Dairy. She could see Gil in the shop but there was no sign of Ellis. When Mrs Bagshott, their cook general, opened the door, Daisy carried their order into the kitchen for her.

'Five pounds of potatoes, two of carrots and two of onions, some spring greens.' Mrs Bagshott, stout and breathless, was checking over what she'd brought.

'Is Ellis at home?' Daisy asked. 'I'd like a word with him.'

'Ellis? The lad'll be out the back if he isn't in the shop.'

Eventually, when Mrs Bagshott was satisfied that everything she'd ordered had come, she opened a door at the back and shouted for him.

'Yes?' Daisy saw Ellis's head come round a door across the yard. 'Hello, Daisy.' He was coming to meet her with a broad smile on his face. 'I was thinking about you. Wondering if I'd see you when you brought the order, or whether I'd have to call in at the fish shop.'

Daisy couldn't wait to tell him. 'I saw that man again,' she said as soon as the house door closed behind Mrs Bagshott. 'The one in the pepper and salt jacket. I know where he lives. You could go round there and face him.'

She told him exactly what had happened. Ellis was trying to wipe black paint off his fingers. 'You're sure it's the same man?'

'Certain.'

'Then I think we should go to the police and tell them. They can do what's needed.' He looked up and smiled. 'I don't think I want to face him myself. He might turn nasty.'

Daisy hesitated. 'I won't be able to come with you now. I've still got orders to deliver. I could go in the dinner hour, after we've eaten.'

'That's better for me too. I'll call for you at the fish shop. It's on the way.'

All the way back to the shop, her mind was on what Ellis had said about wanting to see her again. She wished she'd asked him what he meant. But he had been pleased to see her, she hugged that exciting thought to her.

'I think we're going to nail the thief,' Daisy told Auntie Glad over the fried cod, and she was allowed to leave before the washing up was done.

She walked with Ellis to the main police station in

Brandon Street. Now his leg had recovered, he had a long loping stride. He had to slow down to keep pace with her and he talked nonstop about the theft. She wanted to hold on to his arm but was afraid he might think her forward. The other matter was still going round in her head. She had to ask.

'You said you were thinking of coming to see me,' she blurted out. 'Why?'

He turned to her and took her arm. It was almost an automatic gesture and made her wonder what she'd been fussing about.

'I wondered if you'd like to come out with me? To the pictures or something.'

'I'd love to.' Daisy felt a warmth spreading through her. That must mean he felt the same way about her! She smiled up at him delighted. 'Nothing I'd like better.'

'There's *Hearts of the World* on at the Electric Pavilion. That'll be good, Lilian Gish is in it and her sister Dorothy, but it's a war story. If you've had enough of war, Tarzan is on at the Queen's Hall in *Tarzan of the Apes.*'

'Either.' She just wanted to be with him. 'They both sound good.'

'Here we are, this is the place.' He held the door open for her.

Daisy had never been inside the police station before. The atmosphere seemed oppressive, it made her shudder.

'A visit here's enough to keep anybody on the straight and narrow,' she whispered.

Ellis explained to the officer on reception duty why they'd come. Daisy was glad to have him with her.

The officer was looking through the record books to find the case they referred to. Daisy had the feeling he was failing to find it. 'It should be here.'

They were led to an inner room starkly furnished that

was even more forbidding than the entrance hall. Daisy sat on the edge of a hard, cold chair. Ellis looked as nervous as she was. At last, another police officer came in to talk to them. Ellis had to tell the story over again.

'Let me just see . . .' The police officer leapt to his feet and left them. He returned a few minutes later to spread an open file on the table, his perplexed frown gone.

'I remember it now. The case has been closed, that's why we couldn't find the documents.'

'Closed?' Ellis was surprised. 'You've caught the man who did it?'

'No. Mrs Dora Fox, that's your mother? She was brought in here last Friday, by a Mr Gilbert Fox.'

'That's my brother.'

'Yes, they both said they didn't want us to proceed.'

Ellis was frowning. 'And that's the end of the matter?'

'Your mother was the person who lodged the complaint in the first place, so yes, if she wishes to withdraw, if she isn't willing to testify . . .'

'But what reason did she give?'

'She doesn't have to give a reason. If she withdraws . . .'

'She must have said why she changed her mind.'

'Your brother said there'd been some mistake. The man was owed some money, it wasn't theft. Your mother's signed this document, it confirms that she doesn't want to proceed.'

The form was pushed in front of them. Daisy saw the police officer put his finger against the scrawling signature.

'It is your mother's?'

'Yes, no doubt about that.'

'So that's it as far as we're concerned. The case is closed.'

'Thank you.' Ellis leapt to his feet and hurried Daisy outside into the sunshine. She could see he was furious.

'Gil went behind my back. I bet he talked Mam into

signing that form. Neither of them said anything to me. They knew I wouldn't like it.'

'Gil knows the man,' Daisy said. 'I know he does. He almost bit my head off when I said that to him.'

'You said it more than once.' Ellis gave her a wry smile. He was striding out at a rapid pace, Daisy was having trouble keeping up.

'It's true, I'm certain of it.'

'What are we going to do now?'

'I've got to get back to the shop,' Daisy said. 'I'm needed behind the counter.'

Ellis's eyes looked into hers. 'Why would they want to withdraw? He stole that money, they were as shocked as I was at the time. I'm going to have this out with Gil. He's hiding something from me. And Mam's in on this.'

'Don't be too hard on her.'

'I'll have to be hard on Gil. He'll walk all over me if I'm not.' Ellis's face was grim. 'We aren't on good terms, always arguing.'

'What about?'

'We don't see eye to eye about anything, Daisy, and we're trying to run the business between us. Dad holds the purse strings and thinks he makes all the decisions, but he can't do anything about the day-to-day running of it. Not any more.

'While I've been away fighting a war, Gil's been getting his feet under the table. He's a lot older than me, he's had more experience and he doesn't allow me any say at all. It's Ellis do this and Ellis do that.

'I'd like to take responsibility for part of the business and run it by myself. I have to stand my ground all the time, if I don't I'm sure Gil would push me out.'

'He's your brother!' Daisy felt shocked.

'You think blood relatives are wonderful because you haven't got any. Believe me, they can be hell. Staying on good terms with Gil isn't easy. Not when we're together all the time, living and working. It's no holds barred when it comes to a row, I can tell you. Neither of us is prepared to back down. I'm not looking forward to doing it, but I'm going to make a fuss.'

They had come at a great pace past all the shops on Market Street. Daisy slowed down; the fish shop was at the end of this block. She could see it was full of customers.

'See you again, Daisy,' he said as they drew level with the shop, and went striding on towards the dairy.

Daisy was busy all afternoon. She had plenty to think about. Plenty to regret too. Ellis had been so angry he'd quite forgotten about taking her to the pictures. They hadn't fixed the night or what they were going to see. But he had suggested it, to think of that was lovely.

Ellis strode home simmering with rage, he was determined to get to the bottom of this. He'd thought he'd sorted Gilbert out, but he hadn't. He should have known there was more behind the theft from the dairy till than Gil was prepared to admit. He'd been very secretive about that and Ellis still didn't understand why. But to go to the police and get Mam to sign that she didn't want them to proceed with the case and say nothing whatsoever to him? That really drove home that Gil was trying to conceal something.

He was in the shop when Ellis went in.

'Come to the office,' Ellis said, trying to keep his anger from showing. They weren't busy. 'Enid can look after the shop.'

His brother looked up. 'Thank goodness you're back. I

was getting worried, there's a job for you—'

'Come to the office first,' Ellis barked out.

'What for?' Gilbert didn't like to be asked to do anything.

'I want to talk to you. We can't have a row here in the shop.'

Gil chortled. 'We can't have a row anywhere, we haven't time right now.' But he followed Ellis down the passage towards the office. Gil picked up the two chauffeur's caps they kept there and handed one to him, together with a slip of paper.

Ellis was careful to close the office door. 'Tell me one thing first. Why don't you want the man who stole from our till to be prosecuted?'

He couldn't believe Gil was trying to laugh it off, but he was.

'Six pounds is all he got. Is it worth making a fuss? What can six pounds get you?'

Ellis thundered, 'Are you asking me what it would buy? That's hardly the point. Why should he be allowed to get away with anything? You must have a reason. You wouldn't go to all this trouble otherwise.'

'Bad for business to prosecute, to go to court. That sort of thing.'

'I can't see why. Daisy was right, wasn't she? You do know the man who did it.'

'No,' he denied. 'If you must know, he's a rogue, a con man, just trying it on. Trying to get me to give him money.'

'And how did he hope to do that?'

'Said he was Ralph Corkill and part of our business belonged to him.'

Ellis was choking back his fury. 'I thought you said there were no more Corkills.'

'But he wasn't Ralph.'

Ellis took a deep breath and paused. It was a long time since he'd seen Ralph but he was not the man he'd chased from the shop.

Gil said smoothly, 'I'd know Ralph anywhere, so would you. It wasn't him. Anyway, I saw his name in the paper. He was reported missing, killed on the Somme. The family's died out.'

Ellis tried to calm down and think. Was Gil telling the truth about this? He was such a twister, it was hard to believe anything he said.

'This fellow is an imposter trying to get himself a bit of extra cash. I told him to push off before I set the police on him.'

'But he didn't push off, did he? He put his hand in our till.'

'I called his bluff so he snatched what he could. A spur of the moment stunt. He didn't get much so what's the point in worrying about it? You wouldn't believe his story, would you? Not now I've explained it.'

Ellis was afraid he would not. For once it sounded as though Gilbert was telling the truth. And yet . . .

'Why all the secrecy? What are you trying to hide?'

'Nothing.'

'If he wasn't Ralph Corkill, who was he? He must have known Ralph . . . or of him . . . or us. He knows something about our business.' Ellis tried to think. 'Are you sure he said Ralph? It wasn't some other Corkill?'

'For heaven's sake, stop going on about it. All this was over and done with ages ago. There isn't time now. Take the Austin and get down to the Central Hotel. A Mr Henry Geraghy wants to be taken to Rhyl. I said you'd be there at two o'clock. That's more important. I've got to take somebody to Wrexham.'

'What a mess you're stirring up.'

'Get a move on, for heaven's sake,' Gil said irritably. 'Goodbye.'

Ellis sighed as he studied the directions his brother had given him. Then he put on his chauffeur's cap and picked up the keys of the Austin and went to do the job.

Chapter Ten

The afternoon was well advanced when Ellis returned home and he'd had time to calm down. The Dodge was not back, which meant his brother wasn't either. Enid was in the shop, everything was ticking over nicely. Ellis went to the office, pleased to have the best part of an hour to read through more of the accounts files.

He was convinced there was something here Gil didn't want him to know about. If Gil was not trying to hide what had happened to the Corkill carpentry shop, then there must be something else.

To get a clear picture, he started studying the accounts from the year 1910. It surprised him to find their net profit had fallen a little in recent years, though Ellis knew the war years had brought greater prosperity to almost everybody else. He finished reading through the figures for last year and could see nothing that Gil would particularly want to hide from him. He even asked himself if he was barking up the wrong tree again.

He reached for the books in which they entered the figures that would go to make this year's accounts, and was leafing through when he found what he was looking for. It hit him with the force of an enemy bullet.

There was a debit of five hundred pounds in respect of the freehold premises at No. 5 Camden Street, consisting of a shop with living accommodation above. Ellis could feel his hackles rising. He'd been home before the date on which that money had been paid over, yet he'd heard no whisper of such a transaction. He'd also heard Brenda speaking of the shop as hers.

He began searching for a further amount. Gilbert must have paid more for the goodwill and fittings, as well as the stock on hand, but Ellis could find no further debit from their account. Brenda might have paid that herself, or it had come from Gilbert's personal account.

Ellis felt thoroughly stirred up. He'd seen the credit balance in their capital account and had wanted to suggest they buy more motor vehicles, a hearse particularly. In this day and age they must get a motor hearse. It wasn't right to spend their capital on something for Brenda. He rushed outside to see if the Dodge was back. It wasn't. A pity, because he was in just the mood to let fly at Gil.

Enid came down the passage to ask him if she could close the shop. While she locked up, Ellis cashed up and took the money from the till back to the office. He had to open the safe to put it in, and while it was open he looked through the deeds of their property which were kept there. He took out the documents relating to the clothes shop. As he'd half expected, the freehold of the property had been registered in the joint names of Gilbert and Brenda.

He could hear Ruby calling down the passage to tell him tea was ready. He locked the office and went upstairs feeling almost too angry to eat.

A meat tea always used to be the main meal of the day and the whole family used to sit round the big table in the dining room next to the kitchen. These days, the meal was taken in the living room upstairs because his father was finding the stairs difficult. It hardly seemed a family meal when there were just the three of them.

Tonight, his mother had gone to lie down with a bad headache and Ruby was taking her something up on a tray, so it was just himself and Dad. Ellis tried not to show his agitation, but he was not prepared to allow Gilbert to take such liberties with the firm's funds. He had no right to buy property like that without so much as a word. Ellis considered he was entitled to be consulted before the money was spent. Besides, the business needed that capital.

He wondered if his father knew. He rather thought not.

'Have we had a good day?' Dad always wanted to know what the business takings were. Gil insisted on cashing up himself, he didn't like Ellis doing it but tonight he hadn't been here.

'Better than usual.' Ellis told him the amount. 'And there's still the fare Gil's earned this afternoon to add in.'

'Good. Everything's going well.'

'No, Dad. There's a few things bothering me. I know you've had to leave a lot to Gil these last few years, but I don't agree with all he's doing. And he's trying to keep things from me. Treats me like a junior employee.'

'Just his manner. He's got used – to being left to . . . work on his own. He knows . . . when me and your mam go, it's to be shared. Between the two of you.'

Ellis was determined not to be put off. 'I'd like us all to get round a table and talk. There are things I want you and Gil to explain to me.'

'What . . . what sort of things?' His father's watery eyes locked onto his. Ellis wasn't going to be drawn on that now. He wanted to know if his father knew Gilbert had used company funds to buy property for himself, or that Gil had taken Mam down to the police station to withdraw charges against the man who'd stolen from their till. There were things going on he didn't like.

Ellis said, 'It's a long story and we're all tired now. Tomorrow morning?'

'Not too early.'

'Elevenish? Here?'

His father sighed. 'I'll see how I feel. Easier in the office – if you want us to go through the records.'

'That's fine. Thanks Dad.'

That night, Ellis was plagued by nightmares. He was back in France and the enemy were putting up a huge barrage of fire. He was scared stiff. They all were, but like him they were trying not to show it as they rammed shells into their big guns and fired back throughout the long exhausting hours. It was just before dawn when they saw the enemy streaking across no man's land and breaking into their trenches. A German soldier was coming straight for him with his bayonet at the ready, and worst of all, as the Hun came closer Ellis saw he had Gil's face.

Ellis heard his own scream as he woke up. It left him shivering with fear while the sweat poured off his forehead. He was afraid he was going mad.

Having got his father to agree to a discussion, he felt he should be more relaxed but he could hardly sit still. During all those terrible years in the trenches he'd looked forward to coming home. This wasn't what he'd expected. Gil's hostility made him nervous but he had to stand up to him. This morning, Ellis needed to tell him about the meeting and get him to come, but there was no sign of him coming to work.

It was after ten when he first saw his brother in the yard. He rushed out to have a word.

Gil frowned. 'A meeting? What for? I've got things to do.'

'We're supposed to be partners. If we're to work together, I've got to know what's going on. There's things we have to sort out.'

'But I can't see—'

'Be there, Gil. I'm not prepared to put up with what you're doing. I want everything out in the open.' If Gil managed to sideline him now, he'd be doing it for ever more. Ellis saw it as a struggle for power too. 'By the way,' he added, 'I didn't write yesterday's takings in the cash account book.'

Gil was glowering at him. 'You didn't have to cash up. I came to do it when I got back.'

'You were not here so I did it. Left a pencil note as to how much was in the till. You'll need to add the fare you earned in the afternoon.'

He saw his brother's lips straighten. 'Right. I will.'

Ellis felt he'd scored something of a victory when he had his parents and Gil sitting in the office with him.

Gil scowled at him. 'So what's bothering you? Is it something new, or have I heard it all before?'

'You've heard most of it before, but I want to get something done. Let's start with the dairy.'

'Go on then.'

'You say it needs major changes. Modernisation.'

Gil said irritably, 'Everything's changing. Almost every other dairy is selling milk in bottles. Customers like it. We're losing trade.'

'Then what can we do about it?' Ellis asked. 'What d'you think, Dad?'

Dad's head was in his hands. 'Still making a profit,' he gasped.

'Only just,' Ellis retorted, 'as far as I can judge. We're all working for very little. Dolly's over twenty years old and getting past it.'

'There's Black Bess.'

'But Charlie's due for retirement.'

Gil said quickly, 'He doesn't want to stop working.'

'He's over seventy. He can't go on much longer, starting work at five in the mornings. We ought to consider what changes have to be made.'

Ellis didn't miss the sour look Gil gave him when he was forced to open up the ledgers for the current year to go through the figures. They compared them with previous years.

'Falling off,' his father grunted. Ellis knew it was losing profitability and had been over the last years of the war. Gil must surely know that too.

'Are you sure we can't buy in bottled milk? Wholesale, I mean.'

'When the big new dairy at Swan Hill goes into production it's possible that we will,' Gilbert spat irritably. 'But it will cost more and we'd have to transport it from Prenton ourselves. I can't see that proving any more profitable.'

'Have you thought of anything we could do?' Ellis asked.

'Plenty,' his brother flared. 'We could manufacture condensed milk. Sales of that are going up. It can be kept in the larder, never goes sour, lots of people prefer it and we have the milk supply.'

'But the cost,' Ellis gasped.

'Or we could set up a bottling plant here. We have room for anything we want to do.'

Ellis said faintly, 'We should work out some figures – for both if you wish.'

'I've done it. A bottling plant would not be wildly expensive provided we don't want to pasteurise, but we'd need to employ another man to do it. I don't think it's worth it. It's not ideas I'm short of, Ellis.'

'Are you suggesting we close the dairy down?'

'No,' his father protested. 'No.'

His mother said sadly, 'Been a dairy here since . . . since eighteen forty-two. It was the first venture for Zachary Fox.'

'I'm against closing the shop,' Gilbert said. 'It's an open door for customers for our other services.'

'We need to compare all the figures, think it through—'

'I have,' Gil blustered.

'And come to a decision. Nothing has changed here since the turn of the century.'

'The war—'

'It needs to change now.' Ellis knew they all agreed with that. There was a long pause.

'Right,' said Gil. 'We'll compare the costs and think about it. That's it then?' He was getting to his feet.

'No, it isn't, I haven't finished,' Ellis snapped. 'We need a bigger sign outside advertising the funeral service.'

Gil said through his teeth, 'Everybody knows we do funerals.'

'Some may not. Newcomers to the district.'

'I'm not for it. You have to be discreet about that sort of thing. That nice brass plate is fine. We get plenty of custom.' Gil was getting to his feet again.

'I've not finished yet,' Ellis said, tight-lipped. 'About the theft from our till. I'd like to know, Mam, why you went to the police and told them you didn't want to proceed.'

He saw Mam's eyes twitch nervously to his father and then to Gil. There was dead silence.

Ellis added, 'You all know about this but me.'

He could see his father sweating. 'I didn't,' he choked.

'Better to drop it,' Gil said harshly in an aside to Ellis. 'Better for Mam. You don't realise what a strain it can be standing up in a witness box. No point in Mam going through all that. It was only six pounds we lost.'

Ellis gritted his teeth. Gil had managed to put him on the wrong foot again. Making out he'd done it for Mam's sake.

'Why didn't you tell me what you were going to do? You did it behind my back.'

'You weren't yourself when it happened, Ellis. Not at all well, getting the flu before you'd recovered from that wound.'

'We aren't talking about when it happened. You did this last week. Why didn't you tell me and Dad?'

Mam put a hand on his arm. 'Gil said you'd take it to heart. Get upset.'

'I was trying to save pain and upset all round,' Gil glowered at him.

'What upsets me is that you hide things from me. I don't want to be kept in cotton wool.'

'Neither do I,' their father grunted.

Gil took a deep breath. 'How did you find out?'

'I know where the man lives. I went to the police to tell them, so they could prosecute. They told me you'd been round and asked them to drop the case.'

Gilbert's mouth was round with shock. His voice grated. 'How did you find out where he lived?'

'Daisy was out delivering orders and saw him. She followed him home.'

'Daisy Corkill? That girl?' Gil's lip curled with contempt. 'Causing more trouble.'

'She seems a nice enough girl,' his mother protested.

'I wish she'd keep her nose out of our affairs. You shouldn't encourage her, Ellis. I've had enough of this, I'm going.' He was on his feet again.

Ellis said firmly, 'I still haven't finished. There's something else I'd like you to explain, Gil. I see the freehold of the shop and living accommodation ·at number five Camden Street has been bought and registered in your name. Well, yours and Brenda's. But the business paid for it. Did you feel I wasn't up to hearing about that either?' He saw the crimson colour run up Gil's cheeks, his eyes were anxious.

'Did you know about this, Mam? Or you, Dad?'

'Brenda's shop?' His mother swung accusing eyes on Gil. 'You said you were buying it. You said with your savings.'

'It was with my own savings.'

Ellis couldn't believe what he was hearing. That was an out and out lie. He put his finger under the entry and pushed the ledger across the desk.

'Here, Dad. The money for the freehold, five hundred pounds is debited to the firm's account. The capital account. You've used the firm's money, Gil. To buy an asset for yourself and your wife. It isn't on.'

'You didn't tell us that.' His mother was shocked.

'I did ask for a loan. That's all it is, a loan,' Gil blustered.

'Don't remember . . .' his father sounded breathless, 'any talk – of a loan.'

'We talked about buying more motor vehicles, didn't we Albert?' Dora Fox was upset. 'Hadn't we earmarked the money for that?'

'It's just a loan, I tell you.' Gilbert was getting angry.

Ellis was almost enjoying seeing Gilbert squirm. 'If it was a loan, there should be a note of the agreement and the terms of repayment. I can't see that you've repaid anything yet.'

'It was only a couple of weeks ago. I shall.'

'I make it nearer a couple of months,' Ellis said and quoted the dates.

'Taking advan-tage.' His father looked agitated.

Gilbert had gone white.

'Not been able to – look after things properly. Not recently.'

Ellis was beginning to feel light-headed. 'It seems the only thing we can do now, Gil, is to draw up a loan agreement for you. You have no objection to standard commercial terms? I don't see any reason to feather-bed you after this. Besides, the firm is going to need the money.'

His father was almost too angry to get the words out, his face was suffused with colour. 'Gil, I'm horrified, appalled . . . Haven't we – spoken to you before – about this sort of thing?'

His mother was staring at him accusingly. 'You promised you wouldn't, ever again.'

'Damn it, I've said it was a loan, haven't I?'

'I've tried – to be a – good father to you. Tried to – treat you all alike. God knows I've tried . . .'

It was only then Ellis noticed that his father was struggling for breath. 'Dad, are you all right?' His face was suddenly grey and pinched.

They could hardly catch his words. 'Feel terrible. Can't see . . .'

'Oh my God!' his mother breathed. 'Albert? What's the matter?' He didn't answer. He was sliding down in his chair and seemed in a state of near collapse. 'Is he having another stroke?'

Ellis felt paralysed, the strength was draining from his legs. 'Surely not.'

'Phone for the doctor, quick.' His mother was agitated, there were tears in her eyes. Ellis unhooked the instrument from the wall and did so. 'Tell him it's urgent.'

He and Gil half carried their father upstairs while Mam ran ahead to turn the eiderdown back. Since his first stroke

Dad had been paralysed down his left side and unable to help himself much. Now he was a dead weight between them.

'This is probably going to kill him,' Gil hissed savagely. 'And it's all your fault. Making all that fuss, causing such turmoil.'

'You helped yourself to the firm's money.'

'It was a loan, I tell you. I've been busy with the wedding and everything.'

'Nonsense, Gil,' his mother turned on him angrily. 'You've had months since your wedding. You kept quiet about this and hoped nobody would notice. Don't try and blame Ellis for upsetting your father. It's always you who do that.'

Ellis was blaming himself. He'd brought this row to a head. He'd seen that Dad was blaming himself for not keeping a tighter rein on Gil.

They put their father to lie on the bed. Ellis untied his shoes and loosened his tie. He undid the buttons on his jacket, but they'd have had to roll him over to take it off. Mam always saw that he was dressed as neatly as he would have been had he been able to dress himself.

Gil was looking desperate. 'I said nothing because I was trying to shield you, Mam. I've done my best not to upset either of you. Not to bother Dad at all, or you either. I know you can't cope with trouble now.'

'Don't be silly, it wouldn't have upset us if you'd have said you wanted a loan. But you knew Dad would probably say no, that the business needed the money.'

'I've got to go, Mam,' Gil said when they'd covered him up. 'I've got a fare to take to the station, he's catching the London train.'

Ellis looked from his mother's face, creased with worry, to his father who was now breathing noisily. 'I'll just make sure everything is all right downstairs,' he said.

Enid was coping in the shop. Charlie was back from the milk round and washing out the churns. There was nothing Ellis had to do until the funeral booked for two o'clock this afternoon. Both he and Gil would have to drive the cars then.

He told Ruby what had happened and asked her to make some tea for his mother and to show the doctor up when he came. He tiptoed upstairs again. Mam was sitting by the bed holding his father's limp hand.

'How is he?' he whispered. 'Is there any change?' Ellis felt heavy with guilt that he'd caused such a catastrophe. He pulled a chair to the other side of the bed and sat down feeling totally useless. He couldn't reach his father from here. The only sounds were the rasp of his laboured breathing, and the alarm clock with two brass bells on top ticking away the slow minutes.

Ellis wished the doctor would come. His wife had said he'd gone out on his rounds but she'd try to reach him with a message. It could take a long time for him to get here.

Ruby brought in a pot of tea and three cups on a tray.

'Not for Father,' he said as she began to fill the cups. Dad seemed deeply unconscious now and there was an ominous rattle in his throat. His mother ignored the tea when it was put beside her. She seemed oblivious to everything.

Ellis found himself watching the rise and fall of his father's chest. Breathing seemed to take an ever increasing effort. Was the interval between each breath growing, or was his mind playing tricks? He was waiting, watching and listening for the next breath.

His father's chest rose once more and fell. It was followed by a soft and gentle sigh. The terrible rattle in his throat went through Ellis. He waited again, willing him to take another breath. It didn't come.

'Oh God!' He shot a nervous look at his mother who was still holding Dad's hand and staring into space.

'I think he's gone, Mam.'

She turned to look at him, but didn't seem to understand.

'He's gone,' he said more sharply. 'Oh God, he's gone.'

Her frightened eyes focused on him then. 'Are you . . . are you sure?'

Ellis had seen enough of the dead and the dying to be sure.

'How do you know?' She was agitated now, fluttering her hands. 'Shouldn't we feel for his pulse or something?'

He shook his head and his mother burst into tears. He got up and put his arms round her in a hug of comfort. They'd never been a family for hugs and kisses. He felt stiff and ill at ease doing it now. Her body felt like a bag of bones, there was so little flesh on her. She put her head down on his shoulder.

'I'm sorry, Mam. I'm so sorry. I shouldn't have argued with Gil. I shouldn't have made him lose his temper.'

She clung to him for an age, only pulling away when they heard the doctor's step on the stairs. Ellis felt stricken, his mouth was dry and there was a huge ball in his throat. He felt for his cup. The tea was cold and he could hardly swallow. This was worse than when Hood his best friend had been killed in the trenches.

The doctor listened for a heartbeat; he was making sympathetic murmurs. Ellis knew there was nothing he could do, nothing anyone could do.

Ellis went to the stable, took out Dolly's curry comb and set to work on her coat.

'I've given her a good going over,' Charlie told him.

Dolly's coat was already shining but for Ellis, grooming her was soothing, a form of therapy.

'Your father was a fine man,' Charlie murmured. 'A good boss, we'll all miss him.'

Ruby came out to tell him dinner was ready. He fetched his mother down to the table, but neither of them could eat.

The daily routine ground on but there was an unreal quality about everything. Gil came in and Ellis told him the worst had happened.

'He died and I wasn't here?' For once, he thought Gil might cry too.

Ellis said gently, 'I don't think Dad would have known. He didn't say anything, even to Mam.'

Suddenly his brother was blazing with anger. 'It was all your fault, I blame you. If you hadn't gone at me this morning, and got Dad there to listen, it needn't have happened.'

'Dad was upset because you'd taken the money, Gil. He and Mam were shocked at that. The rest of us would never treat company money as our own. That's what caused it.'

Ellis went to his room without another word. He couldn't fight any more. He just had enough time to pull himself together and change into his dark suit before the funeral arranged for two o'clock. He went down to the yard and found Gil was already there similarly attired, waiting in the Dodge. Even he must have sympathy for the bereaved today.

Ellis got into the Austin and drove off behind his brother. They always gave Charlie a head start but hoped to catch up with him before he reached the house. Ellis could see Black Bess now, her coat freshly brushed and decorated with black ostrich feathers, between the shafts of the little hearse.

When Ellis returned home Ruby was putting fresh sheets

on the double bed his parents had slept in all their married lives.

'Mrs O'Reilly has been in to wash and lay out your father,' she told him. Every street had a woman who provided such a service to the dead. 'We've moved him to Walter's old room.'

Ellis peeped in. Dad was wearing his best suit and what looked like new shoes now. A white sheet was draped at the window and two vases of flowers had been arranged beside him. Mam was still sitting by his bed.

He sat next to her and asked what she wanted him to do about the funeral. His mother understood all the possible variations.

'Let's have the best for your dad,' she told him. 'He'd expect that.' Ellis went down to the funeral parlour and set about making the arrangements.

At teatime, Ellis persuaded his mother to eat the meal Ruby was bringing to the living-room table. Again neither of them had any appetite. He and Mam were going to rattle round this big house now. Her tears were more or less under control but he was only too conscious of the empty chair at the head of the table.

His mother was trying to cut her lamb chop. 'This morning you said you blamed yourself. You mustn't, Ellis, I don't want that.'

'I upset Dad.'

'A long time ago, the doctor warned us both he could have another stroke at any time. His blood pressure was sky high.'

The only sound was the scratching of knives and forks against plates, but Ellis couldn't swallow.

His mother sniffed. 'Albert hated being paralysed, he'd

always been so active. He hated being dependent on the rest of us. He said often enough it would have been better if the first stroke had carried him off, that he felt only half alive anyway. It so frustrated him that he couldn't do things. Don't upset yourself, Ellis. He wouldn't want that.'

'It's hard not to be upset. When I see how you feel . . .'

She said quietly, 'I shall miss him of course, but for your dad . . .'

'We'll all miss him, Mam.'

'We'd been married for thirty-three years. I leaned on him, I don't know how I'll manage without him.'

'You still have me and Gil. I'll do my best.'

'I know, love. My comfort is . . . that for him . . . Well, it isn't a bad thing. He was no longer getting much pleasure from life.'

Ellis got up from his chair and stepped forward with his arms outstretched, but his mother put up her hand.

'It would only make me cry again.' She was biting her lip. 'And I've done more than enough of that already.'

Ellis went back to the office, choking with emotion but relieved that Mam didn't blame him.

Chapter Eleven

Daisy was clearing the table after tea when Brenda came round.

'What's the matter?' Auntie Glad demanded as soon as she saw her. It was written on her solemn face that something was.

'Mr Fox had another stroke and died this morning. So sudden, out of the blue. Isn't it awful?'

As she listened to the details Brenda was recounting, Daisy felt so sorry for Ellis. He'd be very upset. Her first thought was to go round to see him but she didn't know whether she should. She was afraid she might be intruding on family grief.

'The funeral's on Thursday afternoon, so we can all go. I want you to come too.'

'I've only got a red coat,' Daisy said.

'Doesn't matter about you going,' Glad told her pointedly. 'They won't expect it.'

'I want to.' She wanted to be near Ellis whatever the occasion.

Brenda sighed. 'Ruth might lend you her navy gaberdine if you ask her.'

'Her uniform mac?'

'Who's to know that if you wear my navy hat with it? The one with violets. It would go well and navy's right for someone young.' Brenda wrinkled her nose. 'I shall have to have full mourning, he was my father-in-law.'

'Daisy, make another cup of tea for our Brenda.' Auntie Glad counted herself hospitable. All visitors were offered tea.

An hour later, Brenda was on her way out. Daisy went downstairs with her to put the bolt back on the shop door. When she opened it, Ellis was on the step, his arm just lifting to reach the bell.

'What are you doing here?' Brenda wanted to know.

He ignored her. His dark eyes sought Daisy's. He seemed shy. 'I came to see if you'd come for a walk with me.'

Daisy felt such a surge of joy. He did need her. 'I'd love to. I'll just get my coat and tell Auntie Glad I'm going out.'

She raced up to her attic room and ran the powder puff she'd begged from Brenda over her nose. She wanted to look her best. She snatched her new red coat from the wardrobe regretting that she hadn't managed to buy a red hat to go with it. She crammed her brown one on her head and raced down to the living-room door.

'I'm going out,' she announced. 'For a walk.'

'You haven't washed up yet.' Auntie Glad was indignant.

'I'll do it when I come back.' She added proudly, 'Ellis Fox has called for me.' When Brenda was going out with Gilbert, household chores did not have first call on her time.

Ellis was standing in the shop doorway looking uncomfortable. 'I hope you don't mind me coming like this. I had to see you.'

'No, no.' She noticed for the first time that it was beginning to drizzle and Ellis wore a mackintosh. She felt a stab of anxiety for her new coat. 'I'll have to get an umbrella.' She ran back to borrow Uncle Ern's big one from the hall stand on the landing. Ellis took it from her, opened it and held it protectively over her. The need to stay close made it seem right to take his arm.

'Brenda came to tell us about your father. I'm so sorry. You must have had a dreadful day.'

'I have. I've felt quite strange ever since. Sort of light-headed.'

'Brenda said the same. Auntie Glad said it was shock.'

'I'm better this evening. More myself. Mam's devastated, she's gone to bed. With Dad gone, I feel so alone. Silly, isn't it, with Mam there?'

They tramped round Hamilton Square and down towards the ferries. It was a bleak damp evening and the drizzle was being carried on a chill wind from the river. Daisy hardly noticed it, she wanted to comfort Ellis.

'A cup of tea?' he suggested. 'We can get one in the Refreshment Rooms if we go down to Woodside Station.'

Daisy felt awash with tea but she wasn't going to refuse anything that would prolong this outing. She had to visit the Ladies before she could face it. There were few people about in the railway station, it was beginning to get dark. The café was almost empty too, but it was warm and the tea urns hissed comfortingly.

Ellis looked sad. He talked about the family meeting that had led to his father's death.

'Gil has a talent for seeing what he does in a favourable light.' Ellis sighed. 'He blames me.'

'If someone has to be blamed, then clearly your father was upset because Gil had used your firm's account to buy property for Brenda.' Daisy frowned. 'I'm sure she thought it was Gil's own money – I'm certain she did.'

'No point in blaming anyone, but Dad's gone now.'

Daisy felt such sympathy for him as the silence dragged on.

Ellis put his teacup down. 'Before the war when I was growing up, Dad seemed like the Rock of Gibraltar. Always there, someone I could rely on whatever happened. He was a support for the whole family and I don't mean just in the financial sense.'

'You sound as though you had a happy childhood, but then you grew up in a big family.'

'Very happy. Idyllic. There were six of us, all boys. Not that Gilbert ever seemed anything but grown up to me. He'd left school and was working for Dad before I even started.

'Nick was only eleven months older than me and we were great pals. We played about in the hayloft, rode the horses round the yard, and when Dad turned his back we used to take them out and ride round the park. Pretend we were great toffs. Dad didn't like us doing that, he thought the horses should rest when they weren't out with the milk or doing a funeral. Everything was for the good of the business, you see. We were brought up knowing that it had to make a profit. We all looked forward to working in it when we grew up, it was all great fun. Until the war.' Ellis sighed.

'The house seems so quiet without my brothers. Nick and I shared a bedroom, I miss him most of all. It's a house of ghosts, sometimes I can feel them there.'

'Does that scare you? Ghosts?'

'No, mine are friendly ghosts. I feel they're trying to help me through this difficult time, but I need more concrete help. I shall miss Dad, I relied on him, needed his support even though I knew he was too ill to give it. You see, Mam has always relied on others and Gil is always fighting me. Not just fighting, he's got me down on the canvas at the moment. I don't feel safe with him around. I need someone of my own. Someone to lean on. Someone I can trust. I thought of you. I hope you don't mind?'

Daisy was flattered. 'I want to help you.' She'd always wanted a father and Ellis had just lost his. 'But I don't know how.'

'To be with you helps. You calm me.'

She put her hand over his on the table and felt moved almost to tears herself. They sat for an hour over two cups of tea and two rock cakes. Daisy told him about her life in the fish shop and why she felt she didn't belong there.

They got up to go as the London train came in and suddenly the station was thronging with people who slowed their progress. A young woman in a blue coat ran past them to greet a man coming through the barrier. He put down his overnight bag to take her into his arms.

Daisy felt Ellis's arms go round her and pull her close. The next moment his lips were pressing on hers. She trembled, taken by surprise.

He lifted his face three inches from hers and smiled. 'If it's all right for them, it's all right for us. I've been wanting to do this all evening. I need somebody to cling to, I've had a terrible time.' He put his head down on her shoulder. 'But I shouldn't be doing it. Not the right time. Too sudden, you'll think I'm using you. Perhaps I am.'

Daisy cuddled closer, so filled with joy she wanted to cry. 'I've been wanting this for months. Nothing sudden about it. Not as far as I'm concerned.'

He looked up and smiled. 'Oh Daisy! I haven't said what I really mean. I think I'm falling in love with you.'

They walked slowly back to the fish shop. The drizzle had stopped, there was no further need for the umbrella, but Daisy clung tightly to his arm. She felt she was walking on air but couldn't help wondering if it was wrong of her to feel like this. It should be a time of great sadness. It was for Ellis, he was very upset at losing his father.

On the doorstep he kissed her again and told her again he loved her.

'The next few days are going to be difficult,' he murmured. 'There'll be people coming to pay their last respects to Dad and Mam's taking it hard and the work still has to be done. I mightn't be able to see you, but I'll be thinking of you. It'll help a lot . . . to know how you feel about me. I'll be in touch, Daisy.'

She crept upstairs to the living room. Uncle Ern had gone to bed.

'You're late.' Auntie Glad shot upright in her chair. 'That lad shouldn't keep you out like this, you're only sixteen. Does he know that?'

'Yes, I've told him. You've done the washing-up?'

'Uncle Ern did it for you. Get yourself to bed now and don't make a habit of this.'

Daisy giggled as she climbed into bed, for her sleep was miles away. Never had she felt so alive, she was in raptures. She could scarcely believe that Ellis was as eager for her as she was for him, perhaps even more so. Everything for her had suddenly come right.

Daisy hardly knew what she was doing the next day. Her head whirled whenever she thought of Ellis. He'd said he loved her and that made her feel on top of the world. She wanted to sing. Her life was taking a new and very exciting turn, but she couldn't forget her search for relatives.

Although last night they hadn't mentioned the man who'd robbed the dairy, he'd been in the back of Daisy's mind since she'd left the police station. Gil had told Ellis the man had pretended to be a Corkill. Daisy thought this a complete change of story on Gil's part. To her, he'd sworn black's white that he didn't know him. She'd known all along that that was a lie, because she'd seen them talking together. It made her think there must be more she could find out.

Ellis said this man must know something of their business and of the family of the same name who'd lived in Camden Yard. He could be a Corkill. It seemed a logical step to ask him if he was related to them or to her mother. She'd intended to ask Ellis to go with her to Henry Street but after his father's sudden death, she didn't think she should bother him with this.

When she saw Uncle Ern making up two orders for her to deliver in Argyle Street this morning, she decided to go round on her own. Henry Street, where the man lived, was only a stone's throw from Argyle Street. There seemed no reason why she couldn't just knock on the door and speak to him herself.

At last she was off on the bike. Tuesdays were not busy. She could afford to spend ten minutes this morning after she'd made the deliveries.

It was easier, she found, to make up her mind to call on the man than it was to carry it out. She could remember only too well the rapid ride in his wake and how nervous she'd felt in Henry Street when he'd pushed his bike into number twenty-seven. Yet she'd had no intention of speaking to him then. Just to follow him had scared her. Even Ellis had seemed reluctant to face him about the theft. Daisy primed herself not to mention that; all she wanted was to find out if they were related.

Her heart was thumping even more wildly now as she pedalled slowly up Henry Street. Long terraces of smoke-blackened Victorian houses opened straight off the street. Her heart was in her mouth.

She'd go to the front door today. She was counting the numbers and could see the house now, it looked shabby and rundown. On each side of it, the doorsteps had been holystoned but not here. When she drew level, she couldn't bring herself to stop and pedalled slowly past.

Daisy told herself she was a fool to shillyshally like this. She was going to do it. What was the point in wondering and hoping and then doing nothing? She could settle this now, one way or the other. She turned her bike round and rode back; balanced the pedal against the pavement and knocked on the front door. She made herself stand there, fighting the instinct to flee.

Being rather a damp morning, there were fewer people about than when she'd come last time. Just a few children playing hopscotch on the pavement further down the street.

Daisy lifted the knocker and banged it purposefully. Moments later, the greyish net curtain at the window twitched, and then a stout woman in a dirty apron opened the door a few inches. 'Yes?'

'Is there a Mr Corkill living here?' Daisy took a shuddering breath. 'I'd like to see him.'

'I'd like to see 'im too.' The door opened wider and the woman folded fat arms across an ample bosom. 'He's gone. Done a flit. Er, what's he to you? He hasn't sent you with the twenty-five bob he owes me?'

'Oh no! He took money from the dairy, you see . . . I wanted to have a word.'

'Owes you money too? Might have guessed! You won't get a halfpenny back. Don't suppose I shall either. Owes me for his lodgings, he does.'

Daisy felt both relief and disappointment. 'You don't know where he's gone then?'

'If I did, luv, I'd be after him. Set the police on him I would.'

Daisy stiffened. Wasn't that what she and Ellis had tried to do?

'But he's getting his comeuppance. Somebody else told the police about him. They came here and took him away. He's a bad lot, that one.'

Daisy swallowed hard. 'Took him away? You're sure it was the police?'

'Course I'm sure. They had him for three days and he didn't want to pay me for them. He came back and said the bobbies had made a mistake, got the wrong man. Mistaken identity, he was innocent.'

Daisy struggled to take that in. 'Was this a long time ago? Six or eight months?'

'No, he was only here for three weeks, came with good references too, he did. But after the police let him go he only stayed another week. He upped and went without paying for the last week, though he'd eaten like a horse. He was a bad lot. Good riddance, I'd say.'

Daisy felt defeated. She'd wasted time, not acted soon enough. 'He was Mr Corkill, wasn't he?'

'That's right.'

'Could you tell me what his full name was?'

'What was that? His Christian name? Bernard, I think. You stay away from him, luv. He won't do you any good.'

Daisy gulped and turned to her bike. 'Thanks.'

On the way back to the fish shop, she decided she'd have to forget about him. There didn't seem to be anything more she could do, she must find some other way to search for her relatives.

Daisy walked along Camden Street to Mr Fox's funeral

wearing Ruth's gaberdine and Brenda's hat. Already people were gathering outside their houses to pay their last respects as the cortege passed.

Because Brenda was now family, the Maddockses had been invited to the house first and told seats would be provided for them in the cortege.

She thought Ellis very protective towards his mother who seemed more bent than ever. She was cowering inside the big collar of her new black coat looking overwhelmed, a black-bordered handkerchief clutched in her black gloved hand.

For Daisy, it was the first funeral she'd been to. It had seemed miraculous during the war that her little circle was not touched by death. Now, the ending of a life, the departing of a loved member of the family was very sad. To see the grief of the Fox family was moving her to tears, too.

'He's had a good life,' people kept saying to each other. 'A full one, not like the young lads that died in France. But a great loss to the family all the same.'

The cortege gathered inside Camden Yard. Dolly, with black plumes on her head, waited patiently in the shafts of the little hearse, the top of which was laden with flowers and wreaths and the coffin in full view through the elegantly etched glass.

Daisy hardly recognised Charlie Chalker in his smart black coat and top hat holding open the carriage door to take Mrs Fox, her two sons and Brenda.

Another driver she didn't know was ushering her and Auntie Glad towards the best limousine. All six of the seats were filled. There was a line of other cars behind. As they drove at walking pace to the church through streets lined with friends, acquaintances and customers, the men removed their caps and stood bareheaded, silently saying their last goodbyes as the hearse passed.

Daisy found it a long and solemn service. When it was over, Gilbert pressed Uncle Ern to return to the house for refreshments.

'All of you, of course,' he said, though Daisy thought he looked coldly in her direction.

There was sherry to drink followed by a good sit-down tea of ham and pickles and currant cake in the downstairs dining room. Brenda took over the duties of hostess, as Mrs Fox seemed past doing anything like that. She pressed a glass of sherry into Daisy's hand.

It surprised her to find people were no longer talking about Albert Fox. She heard mention of the weather and the persistent shortage of meat. She would have liked to talk to Ellis but she'd been seated at the opposite end of the table where she knew nobody. She felt ill at ease, and when everybody had finished eating Daisy would have liked to busy herself helping Mrs Bagshott to clear the table. But Brenda shook her head and sat on at the top of the table, so Daisy stayed where she was until everybody else began to rise.

She wandered over to the window and looked out into Camden Yard, Ellis came to stand beside her.

'Life goes on for the rest of us,' he said sadly. 'It's all right for me and Gil, we have so much to look forward to, but Mam . . .'

She got round to telling him then that she'd tried to see the man who'd robbed his till.

'Daisy!' he was shocked. 'You shouldn't have gone alone, it wasn't safe. What did you want to do that for?'

'His name was Bernard Corkill,' she said awkwardly. 'I hoped your Corkill family might be related to mine. If he'd known my mother, I might have been able to find out more about her.'

'He was a rough character. You should have waited for me.'

'You've had more than enough to think about these last few days. Anyway, he wasn't there, so it didn't matter.'

'Bernard Corkill, you say?' Ellis shook his head. 'I bet Gil knew that all along. You were right when you said he knew the man.'

'Do you know him?'

'No.'

'It's no good asking Gil about my mother. He wouldn't tell me if he knew.'

'Our Corkills were carpenters. Cuthbert had only one child and that was Ralph. I don't remember them ever mentioning the name Rosa. Didn't you say her father was a vicar?'

'Uncle Ern said he was.' She sighed. 'It's not a common name.'

'Far more Foxes about.'

'How could I find out for sure whether I have any blood relatives or not?' Daisy couldn't rid herself of that yearning. 'I know so little about my roots.'

She thought of her mother's sad little history, and the treasured piece of paper she'd been given the day Brenda had taken her to the cemetery all those years ago.

'I was wondering, is it possible for me to get a copy of her birth certificate? Would that tell me more?'

'Yes.' Ellis seemed suddenly aflame with enthusiasm. 'Yes, I think it's possible. It would tell you the names of her parents and where they were living. I'll come with you. What about tomorrow?'

Daisy smiled. 'I'd like to, but Friday's our busiest day,

Auntie Glad doesn't like me taking time for myself on Fridays.'

'Monday then?'

'Yes, fine. A slack day because the fishing fleet doesn't go out on Sundays.' She smiled. 'That's what I like about you, you want to do things right away.'

'If you've got something burning you, Daisy, you should do something about it. Settle things one way or the other.'

'This has burned at me for as long as I can remember.'

'I know,' he said gently. 'Ask your Auntie Glad now if you can go straight after lunch on Monday.'

With Ellis standing beside her, Daisy thought Auntie Glad didn't have much choice but to agree.

On Saturday, Daisy went down to the market wearing her red coat and managed to find a red hat to go with it. It was very grown-up, with lots of red veiling and brown feathers and she thought it suited her.

But then she had second thoughts. Would it be all right for her to wear such a bright colour when she was going out with Ellis?

'No,' Auntie Glad told her. 'Too soon. Too soon for him to be gadding about with girls, too.'

'He said I was a comfort to him,' Daisy said uneasily.

'Give over, Glad,' Uncle Ern said. 'I wouldn't worry, Daisy. Not about the red coat, either. You're so young it won't matter. It won't upset Ellis, will it?'

Daisy was afraid it might upset his mother. She would have liked to put her bright clothes away for a month or two, but Ruth wanted her gaberdine back and Daisy had no other coat fit to be seen in.

On Monday, Ellis walked down to the fish shop to call

for Daisy as soon as he'd eaten his dinner. She was ready and waiting for him.

'Right, we'll go to the registrar of births, marriages and deaths.'

'It's alongside the town hall, isn't it?' Daisy was nervous. 'I want to hope but I'm afraid nothing will come of this either.'

She asked for a copy of her mother's birth certificate and slid the piece of paper she'd shown Ellis across the counter. It read: Rosa Mary Corkill, born May 25th, 1885, died June 17th, 1904.

The receptionist said, 'There'll be a charge, you realise that?'

She drew back.

'Yes, that's all right.' Ellis squeezed Daisy's hand and whispered, 'I'll see to it.'

'Will you wait? I'll have to search the registers, but as you have the date of birth, it shouldn't take too long.'

He could see Daisy standing first on one foot and then the other. Whatever the receptionist had said, it seemed to be taking her ages.

'Patience,' he whispered and started reading the notices pinned to a board.

At last the woman returned. 'Success – here we are.'

He could see Daisy's fingers shaking, she could hardly wait to get it out of the envelope to read. Ellis put his head alongside hers and looked over her shoulder.

Rosa's mother was called Violet May. Her father's name was given as James Edward Corkill, his occupation as Church of England Vicar. Their address was St Luke's Vicarage.

'There you are,' he told her triumphantly. 'You know a lot more now.'

'But we know her father left here years ago. Uncle Ern said he moved to Essex. We aren't any nearer finding him.'

He took Rosa's birth certificate from her fingers and took it back to the woman behind the counter.

'Could you tell me how we can find out more about James Corkill?'

'You want his birth certificate too? Was he born here in Birkenhead?'

'I don't know. What we really want to know is whether he's still alive and his present address.'

'Oh.' Her face cleared. 'He was a clergyman. There's such a thing as a clerical directory. Crockford's, I think they call it. Ask in the reference library, they might keep a copy there.'

He thanked her and took Daisy's arm. 'Round the corner to the free library,' he said. 'Let's see if we can find out more.'

He could see Daisy, all smiles, striding out quickly, as keen as mustard. He felt he was making a success of this.

In the reference library they looked up Daisy's grandfather in the current clerical directory, but failed to find his name. Ellis asked to see the directory for previous years. In 1904, James Edward Corkill was shown to be the vicar of a parish near Colchester. He'd died, they discovered, in 1910.

Daisy's eyes were glistening and over-bright.

'Sorry, another dead end. Just when I thought we were getting on so well.'

'At least I know definitely. It's better than not knowing.'

'Let's have a cup of tea. There's that new tea shop in Grange Road.'

'Auntie Glad said I must go straight back.' She seemed very disappointed as they began to walk to the fish shop. 'No living relatives for me after all. Silly to hope.'

He felt for her hand, wanting to comfort her. 'Never silly to hope. We all have to have that.' He felt so full of love for her, he was sure she was right for him. 'Would a husband do? Not exactly a blood relative . . . but a relative. Definitely a relative.'

It came out on impulse but it had been in his mind since he'd first seen her. She stopped walking and her blue eyes met his questioningly.

He took a deep breath. 'I'm asking you to marry me. What about it?'

'Oh! Oh!'

'Well? Will you? I really love you, Daisy. I've wanted to ask you for weeks, I was afraid you'd think we didn't know each other very well. It isn't all that long, I mean . . .'

'Yes.' She was smiling again, her eyes dancing with delight. 'Yes. Oh yes please. I'd love to marry you. A husband would be the very nicest sort of relation to have. Someone of my very own. You really mean it?'

'Of course. You don't feel it's too soon, I mean I'm not rushing you?'

'No.'

'You're not too young? To make up your mind about such things?'

'No. It's what I want. It's exactly what I want. For me, it's better than finding my grandfather. Honestly, Ellis. Much better. I didn't dare hope for this.'

'Right, we're engaged then. That gives me such a marvellous feeling; such a sense of security.'

'What's Auntie Glad going to say?' Daisy wondered.

Chapter Twelve

Ellis had asked Daisy if she'd like to go to the pictures with him the following evening; she'd been hesitant.

'Is it all right? For you to go to the pictures, I mean? Mourning . . . your dad . . .'

'Dad would know how bad I feel about his death – how his family feel. He'd want us to pick ourselves up and get on with life, not sit at home and mope.'

Daisy was ready and waiting when he rang the bell over the shop door at exactly the time he'd said he would. She shot downstairs to him. He tucked her arm firmly round his and set off at a great pace. She couldn't help but notice his air of repressed excitement.

'No pictures tonight. I want to talk to you. Where shall we go? I know, the station buffet again, we'll get a cup of tea.'

Daisy was surprised. He'd said he wanted to take her to see the Gish sisters in *Hearts of the World*.

'You're not disappointed? It's just that I've had a wonderful idea,' Ellis gulped. 'Utterly marvellous.'

'What is it?' Daisy asked.

'I've got to explain this properly. I hope you're going to agree. It's what I want anyway. I feel so . . .'

'Excited,' Daisy suggested.

'Thrilled, all of a jangle, I can't think straight.'

'You'll have to try,' she smiled. 'Or I won't know whether I agree or not.'

Ellis's brown eyes flashed fire. He couldn't keep still.

'Come on, let's go for that cup of tea. It'll calm you down.'

'I don't want to calm down. It's the most pleasing, tickling, delightful thing.' He swallowed. 'Daisy, I want us to get married.'

That made Daisy blink. 'You asked me that yesterday. I said yes. I really want to, Ellis. We're engaged, I haven't told anybody but I've thought of nothing else since.'

He turned her round to face him. 'I mean get married straightaway. What d'you think? Do you agree? We could do it if you're willing to come and live with me and Mam. Couldn't afford a place of our own right off, but if—'

'Right away?' Daisy felt ready to explode with joy.

'Why wait?'

'It's a wonderful idea.'

'You will? You'll do it?' He pulled her closer, into a bear hug.

'Yes, when?'

'A month or so. As soon as we can fix it up.'

'Yes, but what about your mother? Will she be willing to have me there?'

'More than willing, I'm sure. She's taken to you. Will your Auntie Glad be willing? That's more to the point. You'll need permission to get married. Will she and Uncle Ern let you?'

Daisy didn't know. 'Auntie Glad's always hinting she doesn't want me there, that I'm a burden to her.'

'Not now you've grown up. You work hard for them.'

'I could go on doing that. It would help a bit towards my keep.'

Ellis laughed. 'There's plenty you can do to earn your

keep with us. Since Dad had his stroke, Mam's pushed all responsibility for the housekeeping onto Ruby and I think it's getting too much for her. She'd be glad of help, and there's plenty to do in the office. Can you add up?'

'Yes, I'm good at that. Doing it all the time in the shop.'

'You'll have too much to do if you keep on working for your Auntie Glad too. I'd rather you didn't, but it's up to you.'

Daisy gave a little hiccup of pleasure. 'It seemed wishful thinking – to get away from fish. A sort of dream. I smell of fish all the time.'

'You don't!'

She laughed. 'I'll tell her I'll work until they can get someone to take my place. Now I understand why you were so excited. It's lovely, a whole new life starting soon.'

'Shall we go and tell them? I'll ask for their permission. It's only polite after all.'

'Now?'

'The sooner the better.'

'You are a man of action. Let's have that cup of tea first. Give me strength. I'm afraid . . . Well, what if she says no?'

'We'll have to persuade her, or your Uncle Ern.'

Daisy could feel herself shaking as she led Ellis up the stairs to the living room. Auntie Glad was dozing in her chair.

'Hello.' Uncle Ern put down his newspaper. 'You're home early.'

'We've come to tell you . . .' Ellis started again. 'It's like this, Daisy and I want to get married.'

'Goodness.' Uncle Ern pulled himself upright in his chair. 'It hasn't taken you long to make up your minds. You want to get engaged?'

'No, married,' Ellis said.

Daisy said softly, 'Will you give your permission?'

Auntie Glad was suddenly wide awake and said in a tone of finality, 'She's too young. Sixteen is much too young.'

Daisy's heart missed a beat. 'I'll be seventeen at Christmas, that's only four months or so.'

'I'll take good care of her,' Ellis put in. 'It's like this. Mother and I are rattling around in that big house and she likes Daisy.'

'But your father's hardly cold in his grave,' Auntie Glad thundered.

Ellis tried to explain. 'Because of his death we need . . . Dad wouldn't want to put a hold on my life. He'd want me to get on with it.'

'But your poor mother?'

'It'll be good for her to have Daisy there. She's too much on her own. Shutting herself away.'

'But the neighbours? What will they think? And what's the hurry?'

'It's what we both want.' Daisy felt desperate, the dream was beginning to fade. 'Please.'

'You hardly know each other. You should give yourselves time.'

'I know Daisy's right for me. I don't need time.'

'Well, we can't put on a big show, not like we did for our Brenda. Not for you. We can't go through that again, it cost a lot, you know.'

Daisy felt Ellis squeeze her fingers. 'We wouldn't ask you to, Mrs Maddocks.'

'It isn't as though you're really our daughter.'

'But you will give your permission, so I can get married?'

'Well, would I have to? We aren't really related.'

'I don't know.'

Ellis said, 'I'll find out what the legal position is tomorrow.'

'You've brought me up. I'd like you to agree, to have your blessing. Say you will. Uncle Ern?'

'I never thought you'd find a husband so quick. Would have laid bets on it taking you longer than our Brenda. Yet here you are, off at sixteen, who'd have thought that?'

Auntie Glad agreed. 'I never thought you'd marry young.'

'You didn't think I'd get married at all,' Daisy retorted. 'And that's why I don't want to give Ellis time to change his mind.'

'As if I would,' he laughed.

Daisy smiled. 'Brenda did three times. This is one way of making sure you don't.'

Auntie Glad said, 'You'll be waiting till you're seventeen?'

'We'd rather not,' Ellis said as he gave Daisy's hand another squeeze.

'Take your time, there's no desperate rush, is there? And what about our shop?' Auntie Glad demanded. 'We need you here.'

Daisy was amazed, it was the first time Auntie Glad had said she was needed for anything. She told her what she'd agreed with Ellis.

Uncle Ern said sadly, 'You seemed to take to it better than either Ruth or Brenda. I hoped you'd stay.'

Auntie Glad was off on another tack to Ellis.

'You'll be having the wedding breakfast at your place?'

'No, I can't give Ruby a lot of extra work.'

'We don't want a big party,' Daisy said.

'We aren't party people. Besides, Dad's just died, we aren't over that yet. Mam feels it. It wouldn't be right to have a party.'

'You'll have to arrange something,' Auntie Glad told him shortly.

'What we want is the state of marriage not the frills. We'll think about it.'

It was still only eight thirty, Daisy didn't want to part from Ellis this early in the evening, and she could see he didn't want to stay here now. They had told Uncle Ern and Auntie Glad and it seemed they wouldn't object to the marriage.

'Let's go for a walk,' she suggested and got him outside again. They strolled up towards the park.

'Shall I fix up for us to be married at the register office?' Ellis asked.

Daisy was churning inside. 'When?'

'I'd like to say next week, but everybody will say we're rushing into it. I'm impatient, aren't I? Perhaps if we waited three months – because of Dad. What about the first Thursday in December?'

'Auntie Glad will say that's still too soon,' Daisy giggled, 'but she'd say that if we waited a twelvemonth.'

'We'll invite just her and your Uncle Ern, Brenda and Gil and Mam.'

'There's Ruth.'

'I was forgetting. Ruth too, of course. Eight of us. I'll book a table at the Woodside Hotel. We'll all have a meal there afterwards. Will that be all right?'

'Lovely.'

'No white wedding, no orange blossom, no . . .'

Daisy smiled and clung more tightly to his arm. 'I'll have you, what would I do with orange blossom?'

He pulled her closer and kissed her cheek.

'I'll need a new outfit,' Daisy worried. 'Even for a quiet wedding.'

'That will be my wedding present to you,' he said with another kiss.

Gilbert felt he was being rushed to finish his tea the following evening. If they wanted to go to the pictures and see the full programme they needed to hurry but Brenda wanted to call in at the fish shop first.

'The navy dress I ordered for Mam came today. We can drop it in on the way.'

Gil was never keen to visit Brenda's parents and she knew it. He didn't care for her mother's sharp tongue.

'We won't have to stay. Good excuse not to.'

He drove down to save time and was all for waiting in the car while Brenda ran in with the dress.

'Come in and say hello,' she said. 'They'll think it strange if you don't.'

He followed behind and heard Brenda scream with excitement as he reached their living room. 'Getting married? You and Ellis?'

Daisy had that look on her face, like a cat that's been given a whole herring.

'Daisy! I didn't know you'd got that far! Did you, Gil?'

'He said nothing to me!'

For Gil it had come out of the blue and he didn't like the idea. Not Daisy! He felt as though a noose was tightening round his neck. He hadn't asked Bernard Corkill if he was related to Daisy although he'd drunk a pint with him in the Queen Vic several times recently. He was fairly certain in his own mind that she was. After thinking it over, Gil had decided that could set Bernard's mind working along dangerous lines and it was safer to keep his mouth shut.

'You've kept it very quiet.'

Daisy's blue eyes were on him. 'Didn't Ellis tell you?'

'Actually I've been out most of the day, I haven't seen Ellis or Mam.'

'Just fancy, us two marrying two brothers.'

'It's not as though you're really sisters,' Mrs Maddocks said in her usual sarcastic way. Daisy was the last person he'd choose to have in the family. Such a suspicious mind, even worse than Ellis.

'We'll be sisters-in-law,' Brenda crowed. 'I'll ask Mrs Fanshaw if you can borrow her dress.'

'No, no thanks. My wedding isn't going to be anything like yours. It's going to be very quiet, no fuss. That's what Ellis and I have agreed.'

'Your father's only just died,' Glad nodded to Gilbert. 'It's got to be quiet. Really, Daisy, you shouldn't be getting married now.'

The bell over the shop door rang through the building.

'That'll be Ellis now.' Daisy leapt to her feet. 'We're going to the pictures too.'

'Our Ellis hasn't wasted much time,' Gil said as Daisy headed for the stairs. 'What's the hurry?'

'It's what they want,' Glad said stiffly.

Daisy hurtled downstairs to greet Ellis and pulled him inside the door to kiss him. 'Auntie Glad's come round, I'm sure she'll sign the form so I can get married.'

Ellis was smiling down at her. 'I've got news for you. She doesn't need to. You don't need anybody's permission.'

'I don't?'

'So I was told at the register office. Because Auntie Glad and Uncle Ern aren't related to you and they haven't adopted you, you're free to marry even though you are under age.'

Daisy clung to him, shivering. It seemed even the law of the land saw her as without living relatives. She gulped. 'I've always felt alone, that I had nobody who really cared what I did. This drives it home.'

'You've got me now, Daisy. I care very much.'

'I've been thinking about that all day. You don't realise what a comfort it is.'

When Daisy settled into her seat at the Queen's Hall, she couldn't concentrate on the Mary Pickford film. Ellis's strong hand held hers in a warm clasp. For the first time, she felt her real life was more exciting than what was happening on the screen. She kept glancing at Ellis's profile in the semi-darkness and felt on top of the world.

The next day, Daisy had fish and vegetables to deliver to Brenda.

'They're doing themselves well,' Auntie Glad commented as she weighed the halibut out. 'I told her the whiting was good today and the herrings, but she wouldn't listen. Halibut indeed! She'll be wanting oysters and salmon next.'

When Daisy carried the bag into the clothes shop, there were no customers in and she found Brenda had had second thoughts about her marriage. As she took the money to pay for the food from her till, Brenda said, 'You're too young. Is this your way of escaping from the fish shop?'

'No!'

'If it is, you're going too far. Marriage is a big step. Far better to get yourself a different job.'

'I know, Brenda. I really do want to marry Ellis.'

Brenda sighed. 'Marriage is the one way you might make something of yourself. Your one chance. You don't want to throw it away.'

'I'm not. It's what I really want.'

'You could be jumping out of the frying pan into the fire.

His mother will keep you on the hop if you don't watch out.'

'She's nice to me.'

'I could still borrow the wedding gown – you want to look like a bride. It could be your only chance.'

'No thanks, Brenda.' Daisy didn't want her day to be a poor copy of Brenda's.

'Ellis is no great catch. Just a kid himself and an undertaker. Surely you'd rather have an antique dealer or a photographer or something?'

'I love him and he loves me.' For Daisy, that was all that mattered.

'Have you decided on the date?'

'The first Thursday in December.'

'I must say you two don't let the grass grow under your feet.'

Daisy felt she had to do something about her hair before her wedding. She was beginning to hate it. There was just too much of it and it was crinkly instead of shiny. Nothing but plaiting it as she'd done since she was ten was possible. To pile it on her head built it up high. It made her feel seven inches taller, and no hairpin was strong enough to keep it there.

She'd tried one single plait, thinking that would look more sophisticated, but it seemed as thick as a tree trunk and anything but sophisticated. She couldn't go on wearing it in two schoolgirl plaits much longer.

'I'll cut six or seven inches off for you,' Auntie Glad offered. 'It would be more manageable then and you'd be able to keep it up.'

Daisy didn't trust Auntie Glad and she wasn't sure she wanted to pin it up on the top of her head. That was old-fashioned now and would be a job she'd have to do when she got out of bed every morning. She didn't feel she had much talent for hairdressing.

She discussed it with Brenda when she delivered bloaters to her shop.

'Nobody young wears it up any more. That's for old bats.'

Brenda had had hers cut to shoulder length; she held it back with a big bow in the nape of her neck. 'This is so easy, I just comb it through and I've had the bow fixed on a hair slide.'

Daisy had tried to copy the style a few months ago, but it didn't work for her. No hair slide could control the abundance of her hair. She had to tie the ribbon into a bow every time, and the length of her hair flowed down her back beyond her waist. She thought it made her look less childish and liked it better than plaits, but Auntie Glad objected.

'I can't have all that loose hair flying around over my fish. The customers won't like it. You'll leave hairs on their cod steaks. You've either got to plait it or get it up out of the way.'

On Sunday afternoon, Daisy washed her hair. It was a big chore because it was very slow to dry. She rubbed and rubbed at it with a towel, but it still felt damp and cold when Gil and Brenda came round for their tea.

Brenda said, 'I'm thinking of having my hair cut really short. I'd do that if I were you. It's the very latest. Have it bobbed.'

Daisy twisted her fingers through it. 'How short?' She couldn't imagine not having a lot of hair.

'Just below your ear lobes.' Brenda pushed her fingers into it. 'Have it cut here. It'll be no trouble at all then. It would dry in no time and you'd just have to comb it in the mornings.'

Daisy knew she had to make up her mind one way or the other. 'Will you cut it for me?'

Brenda felt the thickness between her fingers and measured the length. 'It's lovely strong hair and there's such hanks of it. Why don't you go into Mayfairs in Grange Road and ask them if they'll buy it from you?'

'Will they?'

'I've heard they give a good price. It's used to make wigs. Even if they don't pay much, you'll get a professional haircut and that should make it look better.'

'I think I'll do that,' Daisy said. 'I want to look more grown up. Whoever heard of a bride with pigtails?'

Later that evening, when Ellis came to take her for a walk in the park, she pulled him towards a bench overlooking the duck pond and asked his opinion.

'You've got magnificent hair, Daisy, and I do love it.'

She was wearing it combed out and held back with an Alice band. But it was blowing about in the wind and it was only his hands that kept it from covering her face.

'Perhaps there is too much.'

All the same, it was a big step to take. She decided she'd have it cut to shoulder length like Brenda's. In the shop they offered her two pounds if they could cut it to get the maximum length.

'A short bob is much more fashionable than shoulder length these days, madam.'

'Right, do it.' First the hairdresser washed it. Seated in front of a mirror with a towel round her shoulders, Daisy closed her eyes and tensed herself for the touch of cold steel against her neck. The crunch of the scissors sounded ominous so close to her ears. The length and thickness of her hair looked prodigious tied at intervals and laid out across the counter.

Then the hairdresser snipped away at what was left on her head, set it into waves and put her under a drying hood.

As she combed it out later, the hairdresser said, 'I think it looks very smart. What do you think?'

Daisy opened her eyes cautiously to peep in the mirror. Her head felt light and free. She couldn't believe how different she looked. Her hair came forward over her forehead in waves. She was pleased.

'You've got naturally curly hair, but it was so long the weight made it hang straight but crinkly. I think this suits you much better.'

Daisy smiled at her reflection. At least she looked like a young woman now.

When Ellis saw it for the first time a smile lit up his face. 'It's lovely. I can't believe how well it suits you. You look beautiful, quite different.'

And she had two guineas to spend on clothes. Daisy really had very few things to wear apart from what she wore to work and she didn't want to take any of those with her to Camden Yard.

Ellis said she must go into Brenda's and choose a new outfit to be married in. She'd need new shoes, new dresses for everyday, and if she could run to it, new underwear too.

She bought a length of fine cambric and a yard of lace to make herself a nightdress. She'd finished it in two days and thought it had turned out reasonably well except that the lace round the top felt scratchy.

Dawn was a pale streak in the heavy black sky as Daisy laid out plaice in neat rows on an enamel tray. She then set it on the stone slab of a counter alongside the trays of halibut and hake. Behind her, Uncle Ern was chopping a large cod into steaks. His thick thatch of white hair was covered by a cap, his walrus moustache almost hidden behind his wool muffler.

'Blooming cold this morning,' he said, blowing on his hands as she moved the tray he'd filled to the counter. 'Very wintry. Are we done?'

'Fillets of cod next.' Daisy was sprinkling the ice remaining in the boxes over the fish she'd set out. Her hands were numb, but she was fizzing inside.

She found it almost impossible to believe that this was her wedding day and it would be the last time she'd help Uncle Ern set up the shop. It had come upon her almost before she felt ready.

To replace her, Auntie Glad had hired a sixteen-year-old lad called George who had been coming in this last week to learn what he'd have to do. He was jemmying open a box of kippers now. Daisy didn't mind setting out smoked fish, it wasn't so cold. Bloaters next, then smoked mackerel.

'You do a really good job, Daisy.' Uncle Ern was standing back, eyeing her work appreciatively. 'You make a good display. She'll be a hard act to follow.'

Daisy smiled at George. 'I put the herrings and the cod at the top of the counter. We sell more of those than anything else so they need to be near at hand. Shrimps and mussels go on this circular tray in the middle, and if you set lemons round it, it makes it looks pretty.'

Under the electric lights of the shop the fish gleamed and smelled like the ocean itself.

'You're going to miss doing this every morning,' old Willie told her.

The shop doors were closed and bolted until nine o'clock but the back door to the yard was open as Willie rolled in boxes of apples and oranges and Mrs Mack built them up into neat pyramids on the other side of the shop.

Daisy shook her head. 'I don't think so. I'll have other things to do.'

'Well, I'm certainly going to miss you, Daisy,' Uncle Ern said. 'It's time you went up to get breakfast.'

He got up at four to go to the wholesale market on three mornings of the week, and on these days Daisy cooked a breakfast of egg and bacon for him when they'd got the shop set up and ready to open.

'Cook the same for yourself today. It's your special day, after all. Ask your Auntie Glad if she'd like some too, let's all have a feast.'

Daisy felt different this morning, full of life. Like a firework about to explode into thousands of golden stars. She had no doubts about Ellis; no doubts that she was doing the right thing.

When the shop opened for business, George did the deliveries and Uncle Ern told all the customers it was Daisy's wedding day and they teased her about being starry-eyed and getting married so young.

'Look at you, hardly out of nappies yourself. It's not all a bed of roses you know. You'll have half a dozen kids before you know where you are.'

'Lovely,' Daisy laughed. 'A family is what I want.'

'Wait till you try it, luv. Babies are hard work, all those mouths to feed and clothes to wash. You'll soon have enough of it.'

'I don't think I will.' Daisy smiled. She was sure she wouldn't. A family of her own? It was what she'd always wanted. 'I'd like a big family.'

'No you wouldn't. A big family pulls you down. Never time or energy left for anything else. Never any money either, it's all gone on food and boots.'

The morning was over in no time. When the shop closed

and Daisy went upstairs after clearing up, she found Uncle Ern had fried salmon with fried potatoes and peas as a treat.

'After all, there's nothing else I'll have to cook today,' he smiled. 'This is a much easier wedding for us. Nothing to worry about.'

'No rush either,' Auntie Glad said, pouring out second cups of tea. The wedding had been arranged for four o'clock.

Afterwards, Daisy took a leisurely bath and put on her new outfit. Brenda had helped her choose a blue costume, a jacket and skirt with a paler blue georgette blouse. Then she'd taken her to the best hat shop in Grange Road and picked out a pert little feathered hat to put on her shorn curls. The outfit was Ellis's wedding gift to her.

Brenda had given her a blue plaid coat she could wear over the rest of her finery. Ruth had presented her with tan leather gloves and a handbag to match and Auntie Glad and Uncle Ern had put five gold sovereigns inside it. She thought the Maddocks family had been very generous to her.

Ellis had told her he'd drive the Austin down to call for her and the Maddocks family. Just as well, she thought as she waited for him, she could hear the rain running in the gutters. He arrived promptly and tooted outside. Daisy ran down with her overnight bag, while the family trooped down behind her, making a great clattering on the stairs.

Mrs Fox was already settled on the back seat. 'So you can sit beside Ellis in front,' she said to Daisy. But by the time Uncle Ern and Auntie Glad had climbed in, it was decided there'd be more room for Ruth in front with Daisy than with them.

'I shouldn't be squeezing you up like this,' she said. 'Not on your wedding day.'

'Ours is to be a different sort of wedding. What could be nicer than to have all my family tightly packed round me?'

Gilbert and Brenda were waiting for them outside the register office. Daisy mounted the steps holding hard on to Ellis's arm. Yes, she was very happy about getting married, but she had collywobbles in her stomach too.

'You'll be all right,' Brenda assured her, 'and you look beautiful today.'

Daisy felt her new hairstyle helped her to look her best, and she'd never had so many new clothes at once before. She couldn't help but notice they were all wearing the outfits they'd chosen for Brenda's wedding, and she was wearing her going away outfit.

They were shown to a waiting room. Daisy found that a shivery time. Uncle Ern was chatting away to Mrs Fox but Daisy felt she'd said everything that could be said.

At last they were called into a small wood-panelled room, and the registrar was standing in front of her and Ellis. Ellis made his responses in a firm voice and she promised to love, honour and obey him.

It seemed only moments before it was over and they were going back down the stairs and out into the wet street. Auntie Glad was heading towards the Austin.

Ellis said, 'I've asked Gil to take you all in the Dodge. You'll be more comfortable, there's so much more room.' To Daisy, he whispered, 'We'll have the Austin to ourselves.'

He'd arranged a special meal at the Woodside Hotel. They had sherry before sitting down to eat roast chicken. Daisy had never had a hotel meal before, but as they had a private room, it didn't seem very different except for the two waitresses bringing the food to the table, and the extra firm starch in the white tablecloth.

Shortly after they'd finished their coffee, Ellis went to pay for the meal. Daisy kissed everybody and said goodbye. Her overnight bag was strapped on the running board of the

Austin. They were to leave straightaway for a three-night honeymoon in Chester. Bowling along the New Chester Road, it seemed to Daisy a great luxury to have the use of a car like this.

'Gil uses the Dodge himself. Thinks nothing of it,' Ellis told her, 'so I decided I might as well take the old Austin. After all, it is our honeymoon.'

Daisy felt she'd never spent a more blissful few days. She'd had all Ellis's attention and found him loving and gentle. She was certain now that marrying him had been absolutely the right thing for her to do.

Chapter Thirteen

On Sunday morning, the bridal couple had a leisurely breakfast followed by a walk and then packed their bags to go home.

'It's been wonderful.' Daisy stretched with lazy satisfaction in the passenger seat of the Austin. 'A lovely rest in the lap of luxury.'

'It was only a boarding house, love.'

'All that time with nothing to do but enjoy ourselves. I've seen new places and done so many different things and I haven't lifted a finger. Such a change. I'm used to having jobs lined up in front of me. Usually too many to do in the time.'

'We all need a break once in a while.'

'This isn't just a break for me, I'm going to have a totally different life.' The thought niggled at Daisy's present state of contentment. She'd only been in Ellis's house a few times and she hardly knew his mother.

'There's no need to feel shy.' Ellis's hand left the steering wheel and groped for hers. 'Mam's planning to give you a welcome. She says the house needs new life breathing into it.'

'Sunday dinner.' Daisy nodded. That was why they were going back this morning.

'Gil and Brenda are invited. Ruby has been told to put on

a special spread. I hope we aren't going to be late. Mam said one o'clock.'

'It's only quarter past twelve,' Daisy assured him. 'It won't take long from here.' They were driving through Rock Ferry and she was beginning to feel uneasy.

'Mam will want to give us all a glass of sherry first. Drink to the future and all that.'

Ellis drove into Camden Yard and backed the Austin into its usual place in the garage. Daisy watched him take their two bags and head for the house. She followed, wanting to hold on to him, to stay close. He left her to shut the back door and when she turned, she could see from his face that things were not as he'd expected.

'What's the matter?'

'Don't know.' He was frowning. Daisy followed in his wake as he rushed up the passage to the kitchen. 'Ruby,' he called. 'Ruby?'

The kitchen felt cold, the grate in the range was full of grey ash and the sink full of unwashed dishes. There was no sign of Ruby.

'Where's Mam?' She could see fear on Ellis's face as he leapt for the stairs.

The living room was empty and the grate here had cold cinders in it too. Daisy felt stricken as she followed him to one of the bedrooms. She was quite relieved to see Mrs Fox sitting in a rocking chair in front of her gas fire. Ellis rushed over and tried to put his arms round her.

'What's happened, Mam? Are you sick?'

'I'm not too bad, but Ruby is. She's got the Spanish flu. Oh dear, everything's such a mess when I wanted it to be nice for you.'

His mother's grey hair was hanging in a lank curtain round her bent shoulders. Daisy had only ever seen it done up in a neat bun at the nape of her neck. It didn't look as though she'd bothered to comb it this morning and her cheeks looked sunken and pallid too.

'Don't worry about us,' Ellis said. 'Why aren't you dressed?' She was wearing her flannel nightgown with his father's old dressing gown on top.

His mother sniffed. 'I asked Gil to get the doctor to Ruby. He said we were both to keep warm, but there's nobody to light the fires. It's warmer in bed.'

'Gil could have lit the fires for you. Or Charlie . . . How is Ruby?' He turned to Daisy. 'Up another flight to her room. Would you see if she's . . . No, no, don't, I'll go. I don't want you to catch anything.'

Daisy swung him round as he was about to pass her. 'Of course I'll go. I've never had a day's illness in my life. Less likely to catch it than you.' So they both went up.

Ruby was lying back on her pillows. Daisy thought she was hardly recognisable as the woman who had presided over the kitchen. Her hair was in an even greater mess than her mistress's and her skin was white and clammy with perspiration.

'Ruby!' Ellis took her hand in his. 'How poorly you look.'

'I'm so sorry . . . Tried to get up. Fell on the landing, quite dizzy. Couldn't get downstairs,' she croaked. 'No dinner ready.'

'Don't worry.'

'Can we get you something?' Daisy asked. 'Have you had anything this morning?' There was a tumbler on her bed table with half an inch of water in it, but nothing else.

'No. Not hungry. Can't eat. Sore throat.'

'A hot drink? Some milk?'

'Tea. I'd love a cup of tea.' Ruby started to cough.

'You need more than that,' Ellis told her. 'You need

something to keep your strength up.'

On the way downstairs again, he drew Daisy to another room.

'I must show you where you're going to sleep. This has always been my room. Once I shared it with my brother Nick, now I'm going to share it with you. I made Gil help me bring the double bed back.'

'It looks very nice.' It was light and airy and overlooked Camden Yard.

'Brenda said I needed to get this,' he indicated the thick pink eiderdown, 'and new sheets and things.' The room had been thoroughly cleaned and dusted, nothing was out of place.

Down in the kitchen again, Ellis set about lighting the fire in the range. Daisy opened the meat safe. 'Here's the ribs of beef but it's a huge joint, it'll take hours to cook.'

'We'd better have dinner tonight.' He looked worried. 'Mam's opted out ever since Dad had his first stroke. She's out of the habit of doing things about the house, she's left everything to Ruby. Is there anything we can cook now? I'm hungry and goodness knows when these two ate last. There's another cold safe out on the yard wall.'

Daisy came back victorious. 'There's finnan haddock. I know how to cook that.'

'But when will it have been delivered?'

'It smells fresh. Nothing the matter with it. It's smoked anyway. But not enough for four of us.'

'We could have poached eggs on top. That's how Ruby does it.'

'I'm not used to cooking eggs. Where I lived it was easier to do double the fish . . .'

He smiled. 'I think I could do the eggs.'

'You've got the fire in the living room to light. What

about a lightly boiled egg for Ruby with some bread and butter and tea? I can do that. I'll cut the fish into three.'

Daisy took a tray to each of the invalids upstairs. She was dishing up their fish and laughing at Ellis's eggs. He was skimming bits of poached yolk from the pan when Gilbert pushed open the kitchen door. Brenda was right behind him carrying a bottle of sherry.

'Brrr, it's cold in here.' Gil gave a theatrical shiver. 'What's this then? No dinner?'

''Fraid not.' Ellis sat down beside Daisy and they started to eat. 'Change of plan, there'll be no dinner until tonight.' He told them what had happened.

Gil pulled a face. 'I'm hungry, I was looking forward to roast beef and Yorkshire.'

Ellis reached for another slice of bread. 'You should have done something about it. You knew Ruby was ill. Why didn't you pop upstairs to see if Mam was all right?'

'I did, yesterday,' he blustered. 'She was fine. Has she caught flu too?'

'No. You know what Mam's like, she's past looking after herself. Dad dying like that, it's knocked her for six. When did the doctor call?'

'Friday. He gave Ruby some cough mixture and said she was to take aspirin and stay in bed. I asked Enid to make hot drinks and that.'

'They'd need more than hot drinks in all that time.'

'Well, I think Enid did—'

'She doesn't work on Sundays.'

'She would have done if Mam had asked her.'

'You should have asked her! Mam doesn't think ahead.' To Daisy, Ellis sounded distinctly frosty. 'Surely you've noticed?'

'I keep telling you, Gil.' Brenda added her weight. 'And

I've told you too.' She turned on Daisy. 'Didn't I warn you? Now you've landed yourself with a lot more drudgery. A whole lot more.'

When Brenda and Gil had gone home to make themselves some sandwiches, Ellis took Daisy into his arms.

'What will you think of me? Brenda's right, I've brought you here to this. All the work of the house suddenly thrust on your shoulders.'

'And yours.'

'You'll think I was just out to get another pair of hands to work here.'

'No, Ellis. I'm not unhappy about it. In a way, it's broken me in, made things easier for me.'

'Easier? Can't be easier.'

'I thought we'd be sitting about making conversation. I'm not good at that.'

'You're shy, that's all.'

'But I'm used to work. I quite like it, it's what I'm used to. This way, I feel I'm needed. I'm being eased in.'

'You're a funny little thing, Daisy. I do love you. I can see now why Brenda refused to move in with us. She could see how things stood.'

'She did warn me. When I went to her shop to choose my outfit and – more than once. It didn't put me off.'

'Wouldn't you have thought Brenda would come over? If only to make sure they were all right. She could have got the dinner on.'

'It's more fun this way,' Daisy said and meant it. 'We'll have a good dinner tonight.' She was unpacking a big bag of fruit and vegetables that had been delivered from the fish shop. There was plenty of food in the house, it was just that nobody had got round to cooking any for some time.

The house gradually warmed up during the afternoon.

Daisy enjoyed brushing the hearth and setting the table with the best cloth and cutlery she could find, while Ellis opened a cookery book for advice on how to roast a joint of beef.

When Gilbert and Brenda came round, they had a drink together and then sat down to what turned out to be an excellent dinner. Daisy thought they were going to have a pleasant evening sitting round the fire, but it wasn't long before she could feel the tension rising between the brothers.

Ellis had felt relaxed and happy when he'd returned home. It had been a bit of a setback to find the domestic arrangements in chaos and Ruby ill in bed, but Daisy had coped with that. He was worried that Mam was so withdrawn. He didn't think it was good for her to be left alone to stare into space.

Once he'd got the water hot, he'd persuaded her to take a bath and get dressed. Daisy had suggested she do her hair and come and join them in the living room.

But Gilbert was riling him. Why hadn't he asked Enid to come in and help? If he didn't want that, he could have made sure Mam and Ruby had something to eat and were comfortable. If he'd wanted to, he himself could have kept things running to plan, or it wouldn't have hurt Brenda to get the dinner on for once.

Looking at Gil across the table, tucking into his dinner with gusto, Ellis felt renewed anger rising in his throat.

Gil had a piece of beef poised on his fork. 'Of course, Dad dying so suddenly makes it hard for us all, particularly for you, Mam, but Ellis and I are going to do our best to ease things for you.'

Ellis wondered where this was leading. 'Of course we are, Mam.'

'You and I must put our differences behind us, Ellis. We

221

all need peace and quiet to get over this, as much peace as we can get. We should let things tick over for a while.'

'Dad died over four months ago.' It had been on Ellis's conscience that he'd let things tick over for too long already. He'd come back full of energy to sort the business out.

'You and Daisy will be wanting to settle down. It'll be a new life for you both. A new life for us all.' Gil beamed round the table.

Ellis saw the look on their mother's face. For her, the new life could not bring the contentment of the old. She must think that unfeeling.

'Gilbert,' he choked, 'we left a lot of unfinished business when Dad died. We mustn't let things drag on.'

'There's no urgency.' Gil had a little runnel of gravy down his chin. 'Is there, Mam?'

Ellis felt the heat rush up his cheeks. Did Gil think he could distract him from their problems so easily? Brush everything out of sight? He couldn't let him get away with this. He wouldn't.

'Tomorrow morning, in the office. Nine o'clock. We'll get our problems sorted, Gil. All right?' It threw a real damper over the dinner.

In bed later that night Ellis clung to Daisy. That helped, having Daisy beside him would always help, but he was scared. Coping with his brother, making him take positive action to keep the business on an even keel wasn't going to be easy.

Ellis was down in the office early the next morning, screwing himself up to say the unthinkable to Gil. While he waited for him to come, he opened the ledger at the page showing the withdrawal of five hundred pounds. At nine o'clock there was no sign of him. Ellis could feel himself beginning to fume. He waited fifteen more minutes, then unable to stand it any longer he snatched up the ledger and strode over to the clothes shop. Brenda, elegant as ever, was wielding a feather duster in the shop; she had no customers.

'Where's Gil?' he asked. 'Upstairs? Not still in bed, I hope.'

She didn't look too friendly. 'He's just finishing his breakfast.'

Ellis took the stairs two at a time and burst in on him. Gil was sitting at the kitchen table munching toast. He lowered his newspaper.

Ellis couldn't help but show his irritation. 'I thought you were coming over at nine. There are things we have to sort out.'

Gil took his time studying the clock on his dresser. 'I was just coming. D'you want a cup of tea first?'

'No! How can you run anything this way? Starting work when you feel like it. Doing what you like, taking company funds for your personal use.' He stabbed at the offending entry. 'Like this. What have you done about it.'

'Hang on, Dad's just died—'

'Four months ago and it brought all this to a standstill, I know.'

'Because I've had to do other things.'

'I registered his death, Gil, and got all his personal accounts made over to Mam. I arranged his funeral and my own wedding. So what exactly is keeping you so busy?'

'It's no good sounding off and getting worked up like this, it isn't good for us. Dad's death – for me it was very emotional, I still feel raw inside. I'm sure it's left you—'

'Shut up Gil. I can't weep for you.' Ellis took a deep breath. 'An ultimatum. If you want this five hundred to be considered a loan you must ask our solicitor to draw up an agreement today. Commercial interest rates and we stop the cash from your salary.'

'Hold on a minute.'

'No! If you aren't prepared to sign such an agreement, then it's theft and I shall go to the police. Today.'

'Mam knows all about it. Dad knew, he agreed.'

'They did not. I saw what happened. No negotiation on this. I'll give you an hour to make up your mind whether we go to see Henman or I go straight to the police.'

'What's the matter?' Brenda had come up behind him. 'What are you two fighting about now?'

'Nothing, dear.' Gil closed the ledger. 'I'll be right over, Ellis. Give me five minutes.'

Ellis snatched the book from his brother's hands and went. Brenda's words followed him downstairs.

'What was all that about?'

Ellis waited in the office for another ten minutes; pacing round the desk, going out to the passage to see if Gil was coming and telling himself to stay calm. Stay calm? That was a laugh – he was anything but calm; he mustn't lose his temper altogether.

Should he have suggested having the title deeds of the property made over to the business? Gil could then pay rent. Ellis heard his step in the passage; hurriedly he sat down at the desk, he mustn't look as though he was frothing at the mouth over this.

Gil didn't look his usual puffed-up self. 'I'll sign a loan agreement. It was always going to be a loan anyway.'

'Right, you can ask Henman to draw it up.' Ellis unhooked the phone and asked the operator for the number.

As Gil waited to be put through, he said, 'I don't like your manner. You know I wouldn't do anything dishonest.'

Ellis got out the book that showed their daily cash intake, and pointed to the total taken on the day before their father had died. Gil had been out supposedly driving a client round all afternoon and Ellis had cashed up. He'd pencilled in the total lightly, expecting Gil to include another entry. Gil had added nothing for his afternoon's work and use of the Dodge. The same pencilled figure had been inked over, but could still be seen. Gil hadn't even bothered to rub it out first.

'I call that dishonest,' Ellis said. 'All the takings should be credited to the company. Not put in your pocket.'

He saw the colour rush up his brother's cheeks. 'Something went wrong. I didn't get that customer.'

'I suppose things often go wrong like that.'

Gil was saved from having to answer because their solicitor came on the line.

Ellis felt he'd won that round but things didn't get any easier. A week before Christmas, Charlie went off sick with flu. That meant he had to get up early himself to do the milk round on Wednesday and Thursday. When he suggested to Gil that he should take a turn he refused.

'Friday and Saturday? Customers pay for their milk on those days, it means the round takes twice as long. I'm only doing it on one of those days.'

There were more funerals too. Ellis was beginning to fear there would be another flu pandemic like they'd had last winter. He felt he had more work than he could cope with, he was being stretched beyond his capacity.

All the same, he was glad to go with his brother to their solicitor's office where the loan agreement was duly signed and the amount of interest to be deducted from Gil's earnings fixed.

Ruby had begun to feel better after a week. Every time he went up to her room, she told him how grateful she was to Daisy. She had run up and down stairs all day with hot drinks and hot-water bottles and nothing had seemed too much trouble. Just before Christmas, Ruby was down in the kitchen pottering round.

'I'll spend some time there too,' Daisy told him. 'Do some of the work, try and ease her in. She can't go back to doing everything, not straightaway.'

On Christmas Day itself, Daisy prepared the vegetables and stuffed the goose, while Ruby put the plum pudding on to boil and timed the cooking from her chair by the range.

'It's been a wonderful Christmas,' Daisy told Ellis as they walked home after having tea at the fish shop.

'It has, but only because you made it so.'

Ellis was worried about Charlie, he was now seventy-two and even in the New Year he wasn't picking up. Now Ellis was doing most of Charlie's work too, and he could see that they wouldn't be able to rely on Dolly the pony for much longer. She'd been pulling the float with the milk churns for over twenty years and, like Charlie, Ellis thought she was getting past doing it. He tried Black Bess with the float; the round took longer, she didn't know which houses to stop at.

He got into the habit of opening his account books on the end of the living-room table in the evenings because he didn't want to shut himself away from Daisy by staying in the office.

She said, 'I could help you with those if you show me what you do.' Within a week she was taking that job over, but it didn't solve all his problems.

'I'm worried,' he told her. 'The dairy's only just breaking even. Either we have to go for the bottled milk and a motorised milk cart, or we have to close it down.'

'Will Charlie be able to manage a motorised cart?'

'I doubt if he'll come back to work at all. I went to see him today, he sounded very chesty. I asked the doctor to call on him. His wife's afraid it could be pneumonia.'

Daisy frowned up at him. 'You treat your workers very well.'

'Can't remember a time when Charlie didn't work for us. He's been very loyal. Gil and I will have to decide one way or the other on this.'

'I wish there was more I could do to help you.'

'You wouldn't believe how much help you are. Just being able to talk things over, it clears my mind.'

The more Ellis saw of Daisy the more love he felt for her. His mother called her a little gem. Nobody could call her plain now. Tight waves and glossy curls fell forward over her forehead and suited her so much better than those two heavy plaits. He couldn't believe the difference. She always had a slight smile on her lips, and seemed to find pleasure in work. He was surprised at how much energy she had; she could be on her feet all day and still be full of bounce, whereas he felt spent by teatime.

Daisy was persuading his mother to dress and come down to have breakfast with them at nine o'clock, and she, too, seemed better.

'She cuts herself off,' Daisy said. 'She needs bringing out, more company.'

'She's grieving for Dad, but you're good for her, Daisy. Good for us all.'

'I must learn to cook. I've told Ruby I want her to teach me.'

'You aren't a bad cook. You kept us all fed.'

'I'm all right on fry-ups and fish, but I'd like to learn to make cakes and pastries and the sort of puddings you like.'

Ellis reflected that Ruby would like nothing better than

to teach Daisy, they were all learning to love her. She was turning the house back into a home, putting life back into them all. As far as he was concerned, he was brimming with love and admiration.

Daisy was thoroughly enjoying her new life. To have Ellis close by all day and every day was wonderful. He was always throwing his arms round her and planting kisses on her cheek and showing such affection.

She did her best to make a friend of her mother-in-law. She did it partly for Ellis, because he was concerned about her, but partly too because she'd never known her own mother and she'd not seen Auntie Glad as a mother figure. To have relatives had always seemed a wonderful blessing and she wanted to share Ellis's.

'Can I call you Mother?' she asked. 'I never had one of my own, you see.'

'Oh Daisy, I'd be so pleased – flattered – if you would.' Dora warmed to her and for the first time kissed her cheek.

Her mother-in-law touched Daisy's sympathies. While Daisy felt overflowing with happiness, Dora was depressed. Ellis said she'd been weepy and miserable since his father's funeral. She didn't look well.

Daisy made her join in as much as possible. She asked her what she liked to eat, and arranged with Ruby to make light meals and give her small helpings to tempt her bird-like appetite.

She tried to get her to take more interest in her appearance. She had a wardrobe full of hardly worn if somewhat old-fashioned clothes but she wore the same old dress and with a black shawl constantly round her shoulders.

Ellis whispered that he thought his mother was not taking as much care of her hair as she used to; that her bun was shrinking in size. Daisy thought the style too severe for her, and pointed to her own glossy mop, telling her how much easier it was to cope with short hair.

She made an appointment for Dora at Mayfair's in Grange Road where her own hair had been cut so successfully, and asked Gil to take them there, since Ellis was always out with the milk float.

When she came home, Dora was pleased with the way her thin hair was fluffed out round her face. Her face was white and soft and lax, giving her a look of fragility.

'I don't look such a washed-out mess now.' She smiled at Daisy for the first time. 'And that makes me feel better. I must do something about my clothes.'

She'd lost a lot of weight recently, and her clothes hung like sacks, too loose about the waist.

'Would Brenda do something about my dresses, if I asked her?' Daisy could hear the doubt in her voice.

'I could take them in for you,' she said. 'Well, this one certainly. I've got more time than Brenda.' She felt she had to make Brenda's excuses for her.

That started the afternoon sessions when they sat one each side the living-room fire. Dora had a way of sitting absolutely still in her Windsor chair with her hands clasped on her lap. Soon her black silk dresses fitted properly and Daisy was adding white lace at the throat to some.

'She looks so much better,' Ellis told Daisy. 'And she's taking more interest in things.' Dora had taken to wearing a large brooch made from a shimmering blue butterfly wing trapped between glass and marcasite.

'Your father bought me this on our honeymoon,' she told Ellis.

Daisy thought she still had a sad droop to her mouth as she talked mournfully of her recently dead husband and the sons she'd lost. Daisy tacked darts into more of her clothes and listened avidly.

Soon she knew the names of all Ellis's brothers, Esmond, Walter, Frank and Nicholas, and she could see the hurly-burly of family life twenty years ago through Dora's eyes. It awakened Dora's interest in the business and soon she was remembering more and could tell Ellis little anecdotes about it.

One day, Daisy looked up to find Dora's mild grey eyes watching her. 'I do have a sewing machine. I'm sure it would make the job easier for you. I should have thought of it before now, shouldn't I?'

She took Daisy to a cupboard and together they got it out and set it up on the table. It was an old Singer; Daisy was thrilled when she saw it. Ellis oiled it for her but it made a loud clicking hum as she turned the handle, and she found it took skill to keep the line of sewing straight. Daisy felt she could do neater stitching by hand, and besides, the noise of the machine came between her and Dora and prevented any further reminiscences. Daisy was very interested in those and she knew Ellis was too. There was so much he didn't know about his own family.

Occasionally, she practised on the machine using odd bits of cloth as she tried to get the hang of it, but more often she got her mother-in-law to talk about the old days as she stitched by hand. She felt they were getting on well together.

Chapter Fourteen

Ellis was feeling more confident in his dealings with his brother; after all, he'd won a major battle. But he knew there'd be many more battles to fight and he was overwhelmed by the amount of work he had to do.

He said to Gil, 'Come over at seven tonight. We've got to thrash out what we're going to do about the dairy.'

'At seven tonight?'

'I'm not back here until ten or eleven in the morning, and the rest of the day is squeezed tight with other work.'

'Brenda—'

'Bring her with you,' Ellis said impatiently. He wanted Daisy with him anyway.

He looked round the living-room table now; they were all here, including Mam. Daisy was cutting the sponge cake she'd made into neat slices and had made a pot of tea to go with it. He'd packed Ruby off to bed early tonight.

He pushed the sheets of figures towards Gil. They made dire reading. He'd already made up his mind that their only course was to close the dairy. Gil was frowning as he studied the figures, looking very hostile. He'd known for weeks what the situation was, he couldn't say this was coming as a shock.

His hostility worried Ellis. Daisy was in the habit of going over to have little chats with Brenda. She'd been pleased to be living close to her for that reason, but now she was saying Brenda was cooling towards her and she blamed Gil's attitude.

Ellis took a deep breath and started. 'The position is, we can't just carry on trading as we are.'

'Only because you're having to do the milk round,' Gil retorted. 'I told you to hire another man straightaway for that.'

'Not much point while its future hangs in the balance. Anyway, I thought Charlie might want to come back.'

'He's decided he's past doing it.'

'I wanted him to see it that way.' Ellis couldn't help sounding short. 'Not just put him out, not after all the years he's worked for us.'

'We could all see he was past it. Plain as the nose on your face.'

'Yes, Gil, but what else can you see clearly? It's decision time. I think we should stop the milk round.'

'Dad was against that,' Dora put in. 'There's been a dairy here since . . . Well, you know.'

'A small dairy, Mam. Conditions have changed; the big boys are taking over and bringing everything up to date. It would be pointless for us to spend on a motorised milk float and hire another man.'

'What about the shop?' she asked. 'It's still selling eggs and—'

'Barely breaking even. I wondered, Brenda, if you'd like to take the shop over? You could stock it with your gowns and—'

'No thank you, Ellis.' Her brown eyes shot up to meet his, so full of fight it shocked him.

'It was my idea,' Daisy was quick to say, 'that the shop

should be offered to you. I thought you wanted to expand.'

'I do, but my clothes shop has nothing to do with Zachary Fox and Sons. It's up to me what I do and I have my own ideas, thank you.'

Ellis suppressed his gasp. He wondered if Brenda knew her business was indebted to Zachary Fox for a loan. It didn't sound like it.

He said, 'The shop turnover isn't high enough to warrant keeping it open. We sell mostly milk and if the delivery round goes, there seems little point. Really, there's no alternative but to cease trading in dairy produce.'

'But we have to keep the shop open,' Gil protested, 'to take bookings for funerals and hire cars.'

'If you don't want to use the space, Brenda, then we could turn it into a reception area. Enid can act as receptionist cum booking clerk.'

'Blinds on the windows too, I suppose,' Brenda fumed. 'The sort of thing everybody expects in a funeral parlour?'

'I thought discreet etching on the glass. Sort of frosted . . .'

'Don't overdo it.'

'And I thought we should spend some of what capital remains on a motor hearse.'

'Trust you to want that,' Gil put in. 'And it would mean taking on another driver.'

'We've been doing three funerals a day. Most of our profit comes from undertaking.'

'There's profit in the hire cars too.'

'Of course there is. I'm not suggesting otherwise. But we don't know how much longer Dolly can go on.'

'There'll be plenty of mileage in Dolly if she doesn't have to do the milk round as well. When I do funerals, the elderly ask for horses rather than motor cars. Most have never ridden in a car in their lives and it's no time to start when they're dead.'

'Sooner or later we'll have to change to a motor hearse.' Ellis was adamant.

'That can be left till later. Another car for taxi hire is more important.'

Ellis gave up. 'Right. We carry on with hire cars and funerals. Really, we'll just be trimming down our activities to what we're finding profitable.'

'Right, have it your way. Let's do it. Close the dairy.' Gil was tight-lipped.

'I want us to agree.'

'I have agreed.'

Ellis sighed and reached for another slice of cake. 'There is one thing. I think I can salvage something from the milk round. The Co-op are interested in buying the goodwill for that. We just have to give them a list of our regular customers.'

'I suppose that's something.'

'Look,' Brenda said. 'You two aren't getting on very well, you're always fighting over one thing or another. Why don't you split it and each run your own show? Ellis could take responsibility for funerals, and Gil for weddings and hire cars.'

'It's always been a family business,' Dora protested. 'Are you sure you want to split—'

'Just the management,' Brenda flared testily. 'Ellis is always fighting to get the upper hand. This would put an end to it. The accounts can still be amalgamated at the end of the year and the profits split equally as they are now.'

Ellis thought about it. It would give him a free hand, get Gil off his back. Perhaps allow Daisy and Brenda to remain friends.

'A good idea. I agree. About the motor hearse . . .'

Gilbert sighed. 'What do you have in mind? Not the most expensive, I hope.'

'They'll all be expensive. You can't just go out and buy one. I inquired at that new garage – the big one on New Chester Road. The owner told me that some car makers will adapt their chassis to our specifications. We'd have to order it.'

'Oh! Couldn't the garage do it themselves? From an old van or something?'

'Yes, no doubt that would be cheaper, but I'd like the best and it will have to be reliable. I've asked for a few quotations.'

'We'll have to wait and see then.' Gil scraped his chair back and got to his feet.

'I won't rush into anything. It's going to need careful thought.' Ellis felt victorious, he'd got what he wanted. He smiled at Daisy.

A month later, Brenda was re-dressing her shop window with new stock that had just come in, lovely coats in royal purple which this year was the height of fashion. She was clothing her papier-mâché mannequins in blending shades of purple, lavender and pink.

She could see workmen taking down the sign over the dairy and it niggled. Work had been going on over there for some time to improve Ellis's empire. Gil could hardly keep a civil tongue in his head to anybody, he felt Ellis was taking control of the business from him.

Brenda was busy during the afternoon and it was only when she went to lock up for the night that she saw the finished sign in place. She stepped back, repelled.

The sign itself was bigger; the lettering leapt out at the

eye, twice as prominent as it had been. It read: 'Zachary Fox and Sons, Ltd., High-Class Undertakers.' New fancy glass had been put in the window. The etching on it was not unattractive but large letters curved right across, proclaiming it to be a funeral parlour. Nobody could avoid knowing that now. Another notice in the glass of the door said 'Funeral Directors and Specialists in Taxi Hire Cars For All Occasions'. Trust Ellis not to give the hire cars prominence!

Gil had been upstairs in their living room for the last hour. She raced up and urged him to the parlour window.

'Come and see what your brother's done now. Just look at the size of those letters saying funeral parlour.'

Gil came to stand beside her. 'It was your idea. Give Ellis a free hand with the funerals, you said. Let him get on with it.'

Brenda felt quite shocked. She had done that because she didn't want to think of Gilbert as an undertaker. When she'd got engaged to him, lots of people had asked her what he did for a living. She'd only to mention Fox's Dairy and they all added: 'Undertakers too, aren't they?' And before she knew where she was they were carrying on about coffins and embalming and such things. It set every nerve in her body jangling. She'd been squeamish and told Gil, 'It might have been all right for your Dad but the war's given us all a sickener. Nobody wants to think of funerals now. It's off-putting.'

She'd thought by encouraging him to concentrate on the car hire she'd avoid being known as the undertaker's wife. Brenda swallowed hard. She realised now she'd made a mistake. Truly a mistake she should have been able to avoid. It was only recently that she'd found out how much more profit there was in undertaking than in hire cars. She could have got over her repugnance if she'd known that. It was all adding to her dissatisfaction. Gil was grumbling at her, saying it had given Ellis the upper hand.

She was beginning to feel disappointed in Gilbert. In looking for a husband, she'd been aiming higher up the social scale, that was why she had broken engagements behind her. Like the others, Gil was turning out to be not quite good enough. Good-looking, quite handsome in fact, but not much business acumen and no push at all.

Things were not turning out as she'd expected; he was downright lazy. She felt let down; the first promise hadn't materialised. It was now quite clear to them both that she had the better business head. She was earning more from her shop than he was from his hire cars.

Fortunately, Ellis had agreed to amalgamate the profits and split them equally. They wouldn't lose out in cash terms.

Gilbert strode across the road to see Ellis. He was smarting after having words with Brenda. He'd always known she had a bee in her bonnet about him being an undertaker. It was getting him down.

'The man in black, a crow, a death's head,' she'd scoffed. 'How can I be proud of you? An undertaker!'

'It's a perfectly respectable trade. It's not as though I'm a hangman. We all have to earn a living.'

She flashed out, 'It's not as though you're making that much.'

Gilbert had clapped his hands to his face. Everything had changed in the months since they'd been engaged. She'd been an employee then, even if she had called herself a shop manager. He'd been running his family's business; she must have seen him as a catch. And damn it! It was money that had come from his family that had bought her business. He'd got himself into a dreadful mess over that and Ellis had made him eat crow. He hadn't told Brenda where it had come from, he wanted her to think he was well-heeled and could keep her in comfort. As of course he could.

Having spent his savings on the goodwill and the stock, he'd been a bit strapped for cash. But far worse, he'd been fool enough to be persuaded to put the dress business into Brenda's name. It had been a very generous wedding present to her.

And now she needled him by letting him know she was making more money than he was. It didn't help that she really enjoyed working in her dress shop and was very proud of it. It no longer satisfied her, though.

'I'd love to move to a better part of town,' she'd told him dreamily as they'd got ready for bed last night. 'A shop in Grange Road now, that really would be something. This one's too small, I can't keep a full range of sizes. Half the time I have to order clothes for my customers. I'd sell more if I could keep them in stock.'

Gilbert had no answer to that, except to decide that any extra money required would not be coming from him.

He found Ellis in their shop, which looked quite roomy now the counter and shelves had been stripped out.

'I'm glad we're not going to use this for anything else.' Ellis sounded pleased. 'Lowers the tone to be selling foodstuffs or ladies' dresses in front of a funeral parlour. I thought a desk here for Enid to sit at with a couple of comfortable chairs for clients, and silver-grey paint for the walls. It would be more in keeping, more dignified. What d'you think?'

'I don't like the sign saying this is a funeral parlour. It's too big.'

Ellis straightened up. 'It's the same size as the old sign saying it was a dairy.'

'Brenda says it's bigger, and look at that window, "Funeral Parlour" in huge black letters.'

'Black and gold. Ripping out the shop like this, I was afraid people would think we were closing down. I wanted to make it clear we're still doing funerals.'

'You have! Nobody could miss it.'

He heard Ellis's noisy sigh. 'I thought we'd all agreed – anything to do with funerals is up to me.'

'Of course, but my customers have to come here to book their hire cars too.'

'Yes, there's a notice on the door about that. Do you want another in the window? There's plenty of space, I thought down the side here. And we'll need something else or it'll look bare. I thought a couple of marble urns . . .'

Gil winced. 'Nothing too funereal.'

'It's got to look like a funeral parlour, Gil. People need to know where we are when they need us. For most families it doesn't happen often. It's not like selling milk where they come in every day.'

'We've got to advertise that we do car hire too,' Gil said. 'A large notice in the window with my name on it, saying weddings a speciality. I'll draw it up myself.'

'Right.'

'And no funeral urns or wreaths in the window, is that understood? Brenda won't like it.'

'OK. What about framed photographs of the cars?'

'That's a good idea. I'll arrange for a photographer to come.'

* * *

Within a few months, Daisy was thrilled to find she was pregnant. To have a child of her own seemed the ultimate gift.

'I couldn't ask for anything better,' she whispered to Ellis who couldn't stop smiling at the news. 'I'm over the moon.'

Her mother-in-law threw her arms round Daisy when she told her. 'A baby? I'm so pleased, though you're only a baby yourself. Delighted. My first grandchild. A new life to replace all those that have gone. Walter, I do miss him. Walter was so quick to pick things up. Understood everything in the wink of an eye. He had a good brain.'

'So has Ellis.'

'Yes of course, Ellis is quite his old self again. I thank you for that, Daisy. Ellis is fine, but so were Esmond and Frank. They died within five days of each other in France.'

'So hard for you, to lose so many sons.' Daisy could think of nothing worse. 'There was Nick too. I've heard Ellis talk of him.'

'Ellis misses Nick. Such bright red hair he had. The only one, the others were all brown.'

'Do you have any photographs? I'd love to see what they looked like. How closely they resemble Ellis.'

'Of course.' Dora looked pleased to be asked. Out came several leather-covered albums and out poured Dora's memories. Daisy turned the pages enthralled. Here was the family into which she'd married. She'd never tire of hearing anecdotes about Ellis's brothers, or of her new mother's early life. At last she had a family. She was a Fox now.

She stared at the formally posed pictures; none of Ellis's brothers looked like Gilbert, none were quite so handsome. She was pleased to find them much more like Ellis himself.

Ellis said when they were getting ready for bed, 'Talking about the family brings Mam back to life. You're doing her the world of good.'

Daisy sighed with pleasure, she felt she'd gained a good deal herself. 'She'll be knitting matinee coats soon, I'll bet.'

She'd been quite prepared to find Auntie Glad a bit sour about the coming baby. She was sour about most things.

'Babies are damned hard work. I hope you're prepared to be kept on the go morning, noon and night.'

Daisy couldn't suppress a chuckle. 'Thanks to you, I'm well trained to keep on the go.' These days she was more inclined to say what she thought to Auntie Glad.

It did surprise her, though, to hear Uncle Ern say sadly, 'You're so young! You haven't had much time to enjoy yourself.'

'I am enjoying myself.'

'I meant get out and about and have fun. Youth is the time to do that.'

She was even more surprised at Brenda's reaction. 'Poor kid! Just your rotten luck to fall for a baby so soon. I'm taking good care I don't.'

'Don't you want a family, Brenda? You said you did.'

'Course I do. But there are other things I want first.'

Daisy couldn't believe that because Brenda was ten years older than she was, and she'd been married longer.

'I want to build up trade in my shop. I haven't owned it very long, you see. I'm trying to save a little money to expand. I really want to do that. I'd love a high-class shop in Grange Road.' Brenda's brown eyes shone with ambition.

Daisy decided that although Brenda said she wanted a family, really she didn't.

As the months passed and her waistline went, Brenda was even more sympathetic. She didn't deal in maternity clothes, but she bought two dresses through the trade for Daisy.

'You've had rather a raw deal,' she commiserated. 'Having to run round after Ma-in-law, and now this before you've had a chance to settle down.'

'I do feel settled, Brenda. And I do want this baby. I'll have a real blood relation of my own at last.'

Brenda was growing more disillusioned with Gil. She felt she'd done what everybody advised; she'd got to know him before she'd committed herself to marriage. She'd thought hard about it and had been sure – well, as sure as anyone could be – that Gil would make a good husband.

It depressed her to find how wrong she'd been. Ellis had more about him. He might be much younger but he was quick to see what ought to be done and to get down to doing it. Even if Gil could see these things, he'd never do them. If he could put something off for another day, he would.

On top of his other faults, Gil was tight with his money, he turned over very little of what he earned to her. She'd had to nag to get him to give her any housekeeping. This surprised her because before they were married she'd thought him generous; always the best seats at cinemas and theatres, always a box of chocolates and a programme. He'd loved to take her for meals and drinks and little drives into the country. He'd never let her pay for anything.

When she complained he wasn't paying his fair share of the household expenses, he said it was her fault he didn't earn much because she'd stopped him taking over the undertaking. Brenda knew he'd never wanted to do the undertaking, driving round town was more his sort of thing. And anyway, if as Ellis had suggested the profits of both enterprises were to be amalgamated before being shared, it wouldn't make the slightest difference.

That aroused her suspicions. One Friday morning, she waited until she saw Gil drive off in the Dodge, and then went across to the office where she knew Daisy would be making up the books. She wanted to know exactly what Ellis and Gil drew by way of wages, but it wasn't the easiest thing to ask. Daisy would expect her to know how much Gil drew. Brenda was afraid he wasn't telling her the truth. She positioned herself behind Daisy where she could read the entries in the ledger.

She said, 'Gil's finding it hard to manage on his wages. He says finding the housekeeping money for me can be difficult some weeks. He's quite mean with it. Are you managing all right?'

'Yes, fine, but it's different for us, Mother pays her share too. You know she owns the business now, but it's held in trust for Gil and Ellis. They each draw their weekly wage and at the end of the year the profit is split three ways, an equal share for each.'

Brenda swallowed her pride. 'Gil says he's not paid as much as Ellis. That can't be right, can it?'

Daisy shook her head. 'They draw exactly the same amount. That was Mother's suggestion, she thought it the fairest way.'

Daisy's finger pointed to this week's payments. 'It adds up to three hundred a year each.'

Brenda felt a little sick. As she'd suspected, Gil had lied, he'd told her it was much less. Why, when she could so easily find out? She felt let down. The figures danced before her eyes.

'But look,' she said, 'Gil is getting less than Ellis. He's right.'

'No, I know what that is,' Daisy told her. 'Once a month he repays part of his loan.' She turned back a page. 'Here's last week's, you can see he gets the same.'

'Loan? What loan?'

'For your shop premises.'

Brenda felt cold inside. 'He's repaying a loan for that?'

'Yes, to the business.'

Gil had told her he'd bought the clothes shop from his own money. 'Why?'

'Didn't you know?' Daisy seemed shocked. 'Ellis was upset when he found Gil had paid for the freehold of your building from company funds. He insisted on Gil making repayments. We all thought you must know.'

Daisy leaned back in the chair and groaned. Brenda looked livid. For the first time since she'd been married she let all her dissatisfactions pour out.

'He said nothing about a loan to me. The shop was supposed to be my wedding present. "My gift to you," he said. So how much is outstanding?'

Daisy did her best to calm her. 'It's just on the property. There's no loan on your business.' She said nothing about the row Ellis had had over it. She was upset, too, to find just how unhappy Brenda was. She'd always wanted the best for her. But it didn't surprise Daisy, she'd never trusted Gilbert, she knew he told lies. Ellis called him a twister and a fraud. She'd heard the ins and outs of all the difficulties he'd had with his brother.

'I should have listened to you,' Brenda moaned. 'You told me he was a rotter. I didn't believe you. How could you see through him when I couldn't?'

'You were in love with him,' Daisy said. 'Rose-tinted spectacles and all that.'

'Oh hell! I'm going to give him what for when he comes home.' Brenda slammed out of the office.

Daisy pushed the ledgers into the drawer. She was past being able to concentrate on figures now. Gilbert was the one thing about her new life she did not like. He was a source of trouble to all of them and as a family member there was no way she could avoid him.

Chapter Fifteen

As the date on which her baby was due drew nearer, Daisy bought some flannelette and started to sew baby gowns.

Dora picked one up and said, 'We must go up to the attics. There's all sorts of things up there you might find useful, cots and prams I used for my children. On second thoughts, the pram had a lot of wear, it's probably too shabby.'

Daisy was thrilled. She felt her financial position had altered radically. Not only did Ellis insist on paying her for the work she did on the accounts, but she had only to mention that she needed something for the money to buy it to be forthcoming. But the list of things she'd need for the baby seemed endless.

'I'd love to see what you've got.'

'We'll go up after dinner.'

Up on the top floor of the house, Daisy trailed behind her mother-in-law as she opened each door in turn. The attics here were not the dusty crammed places the fish shop attics had been. Ruby kept one as a bedroom, but the others were not used any more. The furniture was still in place, everything was neat and tidy if a little dusty.

'This room was . . .' Dora seemed to choke with anguish. 'Esmond and Frank's bedroom.'

Daisy looked round with a lump in her throat; there was a big brass bedstead, its mattress covered with a dustsheet and a washstand with matching jug and basin.

'They came down to the bathroom of course,' Dora said when she saw Daisy looking at it. 'The washstand's been here for generations.'

This was making Daisy see Ellis's brothers more clearly. She opened the old-fashioned wardrobe. Their clothes still hung inside.

'Their Sunday suits.' Dora closed the door quickly, her eyes were bright with unshed tears. Daisy found herself out on the landing again and heading for another door.

'The nursery stuff is in here. Once, before my time, this was a real nursery, presided over by a nanny.'

'Didn't you have help with your large family?'

'A girl, yes, just to help. Mostly I looked after the boys myself. Never had much to do with the business, you see. I didn't help in the office like you do. Though Albert always told me what was going on. Talked about it, you know.

'Here we are. The night nursery. This is the full-sized cot. There were two, but this is the better one, I think. I also had a smaller cradle on rockers I used for the first few weeks. Ah, there it is.' She lifted off the sheet that covered it. 'Enoch Corkill made it for one of his own babies and I thought it so pretty that he gave it to me when Nicholas was born.'

'It is pretty,' Daisy said. 'I'd love to use it.'

'Perhaps a new mattress,' Dora murmured. 'A new mattress for a new generation. You should get a new one for the large cot too.'

There were boxes tidily stacked up. 'These two are toys, but many are wooden toys made in the carpentry shop, they never go out of date.'

Dora opened up another box. 'Baby clothes, cot blankets and suchlike.' The boxes were neatly packed and Dora was careful to keep them that way. She held up a frilly dress. 'This was Gilbert's Sunday best, and I think Esmond and Frank wore it too.'

Daisy wanted to giggle at the thought of Gilbert wearing pink frills. 'They were dressed like girls?'

'Yes, it was the fashion then for little boys to wear skirts until they were shortened.'

'At what age would that be?'

'When they'd learned to use their potty and could be relied upon to stay dry. Then they were allowed to wear trousers.'

'A sort of reward?'

'Easier to wash girl's knickers than wool worsted trousers. I think that's why it was done. Here's a little sailor suit, this was Ellis's. He'd have worn this when he was about three.'

'If I have a boy, he'll certainly wear that.'

'You must sort through everything.' Dora smiled. 'Come up by yourself and decide what you want to use.'

Daisy was delighted at the thought. 'It's wonderful to think all these things have been used by Ellis and his brothers . . .'

'And by generations of Foxes. Some of these small tables and chairs were here when I came. That high chair was. And some were used by Corkill babies too.'

Daisy felt a warm glow. She was no longer alone in the world, without relatives. Dora was making her feel at the very centre of a large family.

'I remember that little rocking chair. Enoch made that for his own children, Cuthbert gave it to me when I had Esmond. He loved it and the younger ones too.'

Daisy had always been very interested in the Fox and Corkill families, but all this was sharpening her curiosity, she wanted to delve deeper into their history.

'I know the Foxes and Corkills were partners and friends

as well as being related. I'd love to know exactly how they were related,' she said when they were back by the living-room fire. 'I'm hooked now on finding out all I can about both families.'

She asked to see the photograph albums again and to have pictures of the Corkills pointed out to her.

Dora opened them up eagerly. 'This was Gilbert's christening party. Here's Cuthbert and his wife Alice with little Ralph. He'd be about three there.'

Daisy gazed at their sepia features, seeking a likeness to herself. She couldn't say there was one. The old-fashioned clothes and huge hats seemed to dominate everything else.

'It'll be good to have children in the house again. Soon we could be a real family here.'

Daisy breathed a sigh of satisfaction. The children would be hers.

Ellis thought she was doing too much and wanted to cut down the time she spent working in the office, but Daisy laughed at him and said she felt fine. He tried to persuade her to rest on her bed in the afternoons but she preferred to spend the time with Dora in front of the living-room fire. Her mother-in-law shared her interest in the Corkill and Fox families and was only too willing to share her memories.

'Tell me about your husband,' Daisy urged.

'He loved this house. Of course, he grew up here. Never lived anywhere else and never wanted to.'

'Ellis feels the same.'

'It's because of the business, you see.' Dora Fox smiled. 'It means everything to the Foxes. The difference between a comfortable life and one where they'd have to seek paid employment. Albert's father drummed that into him.

'We all had big families in the old days. I had six boys and two girls, though my poor daughters never grew up. I was lucky to rear six and I'd have them still if it wasn't for the war. If all six had lived, the business wouldn't have supported them all. In the past, some of the family always had to seek their living elsewhere.'

'Was it the youngest who had to do that?'

'Not always. All my sons wanted to work in the business, it was held up as an honour to carry on the name of Zachary Fox. With just Gil and Ellis left, at least they can both work in it and make a good living. For just two, it should be easy.'

Daisy had her doubts about that. Gil and Ellis didn't get on. The business was giving them something to fight over.

'I wish you'd tell me . . . all about it.'

'What d'you want to know?'

'Who started the business and when. And how the Corkills fit into the picture. And all about it. I've read through a lot of old papers and looked at the accounts drawn up years and years ago. It's all fascinating and to see how little was paid in wages . . .'

'Everything was cheaper in the old days.'

'If I knew more about the people and what each of them did, it would be even more interesting.'

'Zachary Fox started the dairy.'

'In eighteen forty-two, it says so outside. Established eighteen forty-two. In Queen Victoria's heyday.'

'Yes, Albert told me his family were farmers and had the milk. Zachary was the fourth son and it was the usual story, the farm couldn't support them all. That was how he came to start his milk round. Soon he was collecting milk from other farms as well.'

'What happened to their farm?'

'I think it was sold off for housing eventually. Albert never knew what happened to his relatives. They moved away and he lost touch.

'The dairy did well from the start. Zachary bought this house and the shop that goes with it. At the same time he set up the dairy in the yard behind.'

'And the stable?'

'Yes, a stable for his horses, a cart shed and a loft to keep hay.'

'You ought to write down all you know about the business, Mother.'

'Who'd want to know all this?'

'I do, and Ellis, and perhaps my children when they're grown up. It'll all be forgotten if you don't write it down.'

Dora sighed. 'Perhaps if you'd help me. Do the writing of it, I mean. I don't know if I'm up to that.'

'Of course I will. It would be a labour of love. Let me get a pen and some paper. We could start now. Ellis will be thrilled.'

Daisy put her sewing on one side and ran down to the office for pen and paper and then, as Dora told her more, she started to write.

'When Zachary's sons were growing up he needed to expand and they started doing a bit of undertaking. They had the horses, you see. Two horses to pull the milk floats but they needed more work for them to do. No point in keeping horses eating their heads off and earning nothing.

'After eleven in the mornings, one horse could pull the milk float duly covered with a black cloth for the occasion, and the other a carriage for the main mourners. It was the fashion in those days for the rich to have very extravagant funerals. Zachary did his best to provide as much show as possible.'

'Do you know if the Corkills were living here then, right at the beginning?'

'Yes, Enoch Corkill had already set up his carpentry shop

out there in Camden Yard and lived over it. He made coffins to order as well as tables and chairs. In those days, there were lots of small undertaking businesses.

'Albert said Enoch was a very religious man, that he started arranging funerals for his neighbours partly to help those who could not afford the service from anybody else. He was making the coffins anyway; he had relatives in the church and they first put the idea into his head.

'Most of the funerals Enoch arranged were walking funerals. Poor families hadn't much money to spend when there was a death. He and Zachary were providing funerals for different levels of society. But if a client of Enoch's wanted horses, he'd arrange to have that service from Zachary, and Zachary ordered the coffins he needed from him.

'Eventually the undertaking side of the business built up and earned more than either the dairy or Enoch's carpentry. It made sense for them to join forces, though each continued to do other work to provide a better living.

'To start with, Zachary provided much of the expertise about the undertaking business and earned the most, but business built up, sometimes they had more than one funeral running at once. They were friends and eventually they decided to pool their resources and become partners.'

'When would that be? What year? I'd like to get a clear picture.'

'I don't know. I don't think I ever heard anybody say.' Dora's pale eyes stared over Daisy's head and seemed to see only the past.

'D'you know, Cuthbert had a son whose wife wrote an account of the business. I'd forgotten all about it until now. Albert really prized that book.'

'Really! Do you still have it?'

'Somewhere, dear. It's not an account exactly.'

'A diary? She kept a diary?'

'Yes, that's it. She kept a diary.'

'Where is it, Mother? I'd very much like to read it.'

'It wasn't easy to decipher . . .'

'I'll manage. Oh, I do hope you can find it.'

That started a hunt through all the boxes in the attics, much of it done by Daisy herself.

'A big leather-covered book,' Dora said. 'Brown leather.'

Daisy needed more rest now her baby was due to be born within the next few days but that didn't stop her searching in every possible place. Though she didn't find the diary, Daisy didn't count it time wasted; she found other treasures, a Christening gown of silk and lace, and a truly beautiful shawl of finely crocheted silk, spun as light as air.

'I know Albert had it. He found it difficult to read and I deciphered some of it.'

Ellis was intrigued when he heard of it and he helped her search through the deep cupboards in the office.

'It might just have been put amongst the ledgers and account books. Some of them go back beyond the turn of the century.'

But it wasn't there either. Daisy felt exhausted as well as frustrated when it was time to go to bed.

That night Daisy's baby, a strong healthy boy of eight pounds, was born in the double bed in which he had been conceived. It was one week before her eighteenth birthday and three weeks before Christmas. When she first held him in her arms, she felt such a tug of mother love it left her breathless. As Ellis lifted him from her arms, she saw real tears in his eyes and knew he felt the same pull of love.

Throughout her pregnancy they had deliberated over what

name to choose and had decided that if it should be a boy, it would be Nicholas. Of Ellis's four brothers who had lost their lives in the war, Nick was the one he missed most.

Whatever Brenda and Auntie Glad thought about babies, Daisy knew that, for her, nothing could spoil the thrill of holding her son in her arms.

Brenda was down in her shop when she saw Ellis running across to her, his face all smiles.

'Daisy's had a son in the night.'

She felt a surge of excitement. 'It's all over? He's here safe and sound? And Daisy?'

'Yes.' Ellis was giving her the details when Gil came heavily downstairs and he had to repeat them all.

Brenda said, 'I'd love to see the baby. Is it all right if I come now?'

'Yes, it's a good moment. Daisy's just finishing her breakfast. Both she and Nicholas will need a sleep after that. He's been bathed and fed and the midwife's just gone.'

'Gil? Keep an eye on the shop for me, I won't be long. You can see him later.'

'You must be thrilled,' Brenda said as Ellis took her up to the bedroom.

'I am. Hardly know what I'm doing. Still can't believe I'm a father.'

'Daisy? How are you? Congratulations – a son. I can't wait to see him.' She bent to kiss Daisy's cheek, then went to the little cradle and stood staring down at the new baby.

'Isn't he lovely? You must be totally beguiled. Could I hold him, just for a minute?'

Daisy pulled herself up the bed. 'He's not asleep yet, I've just put him down.'

Brenda picked him up gingerly. 'I'm not used to babies,

I didn't realise . . .' She carried him to the window to see him better.

'Such round blue eyes and he's looking straight up at me,' she marvelled. 'Hello, Nick, I'm your Auntie Brenda.' She half laughed at Daisy. 'You are lucky! So perfect, such tiny fragile hands, yet he's got a good grasp on my finger. Oh, I think you're beautiful.'

Brenda knew she was staying too long. Ellis had removed Daisy's tray and her eyes were closing.

'You must be thrilled with him, I know I would be.'

Daisy yawned. 'You? I thought you wanted to put off all this.'

'Not any more. I'd love to have a babe like yours.'

Nothing was turning out as Gil had expected. He'd hoped for so many things, satisfaction and status from running a thriving business as well as the cash rewards to enjoy a few luxuries. The business was thriving but he wasn't getting what he wanted.

Gil felt Ellis had elbowed his way in and taken the power that once had been his. There were times when he could feel his brother's contempt, and that was belittling. Ellis was doing him down; he made him feel a failure and he'd turned Mam against him too.

It made Gil feel an outcast. The situation was making him moody and irritable. His gut reaction was to put up his fists and fight Ellis, but common sense told him that would make the family despise him more.

It was bad enough that he'd been pushed onto the sidelines in the business, but his home life was not bringing him contentment either. Life with Brenda had promised so much but now he didn't know what to make of her.

She was always complaining. Since she'd found out about

the loan he'd taken to buy the freehold of the clothes shop and flat, there was no shutting her up. She'd been quite unreasonable about that. After all, she'd refused to live with his mother and nagged for a place of their own. He'd provided that and the clothes shop she'd so much wanted, so he couldn't see what she had to complain about. He'd given her everything she'd asked for, but there was no satisfying Brenda.

Now she'd seen Daisy with a baby, she was saying she wanted one too. Once he'd sired a child by mistake and he'd seen that as a major disaster. Of course, it made a difference that he and Brenda were married, but Gil hadn't really changed his opinion about babies. A child would only complicate their lives and create a good deal of unnecessary work and expense. When, over their breakfast, Brenda kept on about how much she was longing for a baby, he turned on her.

'It's only a couple of months since you were telling me you had ambition. That you wanted to expand your business and get a better shop.'

'I want that too.'

'How d'you think you're going to do that and look after a baby?'

'Daisy manages to work as well, she's still doing the books in the morning.'

'She's got Mam to keep an eye on her baby, and Ruby to do the cooking. You refused all that.'

'I could get someone to help me in the shop.'

'What's the hurry? Much better if we each try to expand our businesses first. Try to push our joint income up. Then you'll be able to afford the help.'

When Brenda discovered Daisy was pregnant again after only two months and apparently pleased about it, she was overcome by the urgent need to get pregnant too. She talked about it morning, noon and night and Gil was driven into giving in.

'Right,' he told her. 'If you want a baby that badly, we will.' It was the only way he could hope to have any peace. He didn't feel ready to support a child as well as a wife, but it seemed he had no choice. He thought luck was on his side as the months passed and the baby didn't come.

He was getting fed up with Brenda. Once the novelty of married life had worn off, she'd been mean with her favours.

'Once a week is plenty,' she'd told him, and blamed headaches or feeling tired as an excuse to put him off. She soon began to fuss about not getting pregnant and things improved once he'd pointed out that she never would unless he had his full marital rights. In that direction things were better, but Brenda expected the earth from him, he could never do enough to please her. She was always carping about something and she had a way of letting him know he wasn't coming up to scratch as a husband.

Within a year of being married, Gilbert knew he'd made a big mistake. She'd driven him into chatting up Violet who worked as a barmaid in the Queen Vic. She was a good bit older than he was and had been abandoned by a no-good husband. But she had a room to herself and welcomed him there. The trouble with Vi was that she was rarely free in the evenings until late, and going home after midnight put him in bad odour with Brenda.

There was Edna too. At first, he'd thought her more to his taste. She was a schoolteacher he'd met at the table tennis club and very sporty, she could give him a good game, he often played with her. But he'd come to the conclusion he was never going to get more than a game of table tennis out of her. She was looking for a husband and keeping herself pure for him.

Brenda kept on longing for a child. It seemed to Gil that the world was divided into couples who craved a baby and couldn't conceive, and couples who produced a baby every year and ended up with huge families. He'd always thought the Foxes belonged to the latter. It certainly looked as though Ellis had the same fecundity, and Gil hadn't been at all surprised when his former girl friend Stella had found herself with child. Nowadays, he thought often of the child he'd sired so easily.

He'd done the right thing by Stella, he'd offered marriage as soon as she'd told him. He'd been very fond of her. He thought of her now, a small girl with white-blonde fly-away hair; she'd been one for a laugh and a bit of fun. Quite the opposite to Brenda. He'd have had a much better life with Stella.

When he'd met her, she'd been engaged to another man who'd already gone to America to make his fortune. She'd told Gil he was doing all right there, though working virtually day and night. The plan was that he'd send for Stella once he was established.

Stella had dithered, unable to make up her mind whether she wanted to go to Chicago to join Clarence Booth or stay in Birkenhead and marry Gilbert. Gilbert had played along with that for months, expecting her to settle for him in the end.

But then she'd shown him a letter. Clarence Booth had written that it wouldn't be long before she could come over and they'd get married. He was looking for some nice rooms to rent, then he'd send her the fare.

'Write back,' Gil had told her, 'and let him know you're going to marry me.'

But Stella had decided she preferred the excitement of going to America and Clarence Booth.

'I'll have the baby first and get it adopted. I'll tell him I need a few more months here because Mam is ill.'

Her mother truly was ill with cancer. Stella had the baby and left it with the sisters in the convent. Gil knew she was at her mother's bedside when she died. He'd comforted her and escorted her to the funeral. Two weeks later she'd sailed for New York.

Gil had never seen his son. He wasn't sure he wanted to but he was thinking of him more these days and wondering how he was turning out.

Over the following months, Gil felt his life was falling apart. Not only was he having to pacify Brenda if he wanted any comfort at home, he was also having to swallow his anger and appease Ellis at work. He knew he had to get on better terms with his family. For weeks on end, he schooled himself not to retaliate when Ellis complained about something he'd done, or more likely something he'd omitted to do. He made a point of being disarming, of never rubbing Ellis the wrong way. He took to buying little gifts each week, flowers or chocolate, both for his mother and his wife. He felt, in time, that relationships were beginning to improve.

Once Gil felt he'd allayed Ellis's distrust and suspicion of him, he started on a programme of persuasion. He was determined to have his own way on what he considered to be important.

He wanted to expand the car hire side of the business. If he was to prove to his mother and to Ellis that he knew what he was doing, it was the only way. Their capital account was growing but not fast enough; he knew they hadn't enough to buy the hearse Ellis wanted as well as new hire cars.

'We ought to replace the old Austin,' he kept telling Ellis. 'It's nine years old and no longer smart or reliable. It doesn't look good at weddings and funerals. And most other undertaking firms are still using horse-drawn vehicles. It adds to the pomp and ceremony of the occasion and you said yourself the elderly like horses. There's no real need for you to get the first motor hearse in Birkenhead.'

Ellis finally agreed when the Austin broke down at Woodside. Gil had met passengers off the London train, loaded them and their luggage and then been unable to start it.

'I swung and swung on the starting handle until I was in a lather of sweat. My shoulder still aches. Had to find a taxi for my passengers. It would have to be the Websters from Claughton, frequent regulars. I told you the Austin was past it.'

'Right, we replace it. What d'you have in mind? What make of car?'

Only that morning Gilbert had seen the most wonderful racing car, a Bentley, and he hungered to have one himself. He also fancied a bull-nosed Morris 12 sports car, but he knew he couldn't hope to own either. The trade made a sedate saloon the only choice.

He sighed with longing. 'There are some wonderful American cars on the road now.'

'Austins are cheaper. That big garage on the New Chester Road sells them and it's handy for us. They've got new ones on show. We've been satisfied with this one.'

'You have.'

'Haven't you? It's lasted a long time.'

'I fancy the Ford. The Model T.'

'That's American.'

'It's assembled in Manchester. And really we need more than one. It would look good to have two or three all the same. We could find work for at least four cars. We're having to turn clients away.' Ellis knew that, Gil had told Enid to keep pointing it out to him. 'It stands to reason, the more work we take on, the more we'll earn.'

'We'd need another driver.'

'Another two drivers,' Gil told him. 'Got to have them if we're going to build the business up.'

Ellis sighed. 'Why don't you go and look at the cars? Find out exactly how much they'd cost. If we buy two we should get discount.'

Gil smiled. He'd already done that. Model T Fords could be bought new for £125. The garage had quoted £240 for two.

He'd have a word with Bernard about it tonight if he happened to be in the Queen Vic. Gil wanted to get three matching vehicles. Then with the Dodge as well, he'd feel he had a real fleet of hire cars.

Since Brenda had had a home of her own, she had encouraged Ruth to visit her whenever she had an evening off. She'd make a pot of tea, build up the living-room fire, push the big armchairs close to it and they'd settle down for a long heart-to-heart talk. Ruth came more and more often.

Brenda had always needed a confidante and now Daisy no longer was, she needed her sister more than before. In the old days, she'd pitied Ruth because she seemed uninterested in men or in going out to have fun. Ruth's life was spent working in Grange Mount Maternity Hospital and visiting her family. Once or twice a month she went to a theatre or cinema with one of the other midwives. It had seemed a drab existence.

But now Brenda was beginning to think Ruth's life was

well-ordered, well-organised and stable. Ruth was content with what she had.

Gilbert was usually out when Ruth visited and Brenda couldn't stop herself complaining about what he was doing; she knew she must seem anything but happy to her sister.

Ruth asked, 'Does Gil go out because he knows I'm coming? He's rarely in.'

'He often works in the evenings. It's when everybody else wants to be taken to theatres and dances.' That's how Gil explained it to her and how at first she put it to Ruth. But as time went on she admitted that Gil still played a lot of table tennis in the evenings and he made no secret of going to the pub. He rarely wanted to take her out.

And often, more and more often these days, Brenda confided her need for a child. This was something Ruth understood as a midwife. She was ever ready with advice on what Brenda must do to give herself the best chance of conceiving.

'You must persuade Gil to do his bit.'

'He doesn't need persuading. He's ready and willing to do it any time. All the time. It's not that.'

'That's the wrong thing for you, Brenda. You mustn't let him do it every night. Keeping him waiting for a week, he'll have more seed then. That will give you a better chance of getting pregnant. We'll work out the best time of the month for you.'

Ruth had done so and Brenda had followed her directions to the letter for many months now. She sighed; even that wasn't doing the trick.

Bernard Corkill sat looking at the pint of beer on the table before him. Gilbert had fetched him from the public bar to have this drink in the lounge and steered him to this quiet corner at the far end. It was quite some time since he'd last spoken to Gil, but occasionally he'd heard his voice here in the lounge. Gil never drank in the public bar, he considered that beneath him.

Tonight, Bernard could hear sounds of merriment and singing out there. The public bar was much the jollier place but he was glad to sit down and take the weight off his legs and have the free beer too.

He studied Gilbert's back as he stood at the bar. He was wearing a smart jacket and looked prosperous. Gil was rather inclined to push his prosperity down the throats of others. Although he was vaguely related, a distant cousin, and they'd seen quite a lot of each other at one time, Bernard disliked him.

He'd gone right off Gil when he'd refused to give him a pound or two to keep Alf's wife and family from starving. Gil had known how important it was that Alf was kept sweet. Gil was not the sort you could rely on. Not trustworthy.

Gil returned and put a packet of Players down beside Bernard's beer. Such generosity must mean he wanted something. Bernard wasn't going to ask. He mustn't look keen to have Gil's business, that would give Gil a handle to drive down the price. Gil had beaten him down to rock bottom when he'd found the Dodge for him.

'How are you keeping?' Gil asked. 'Haven't seen you for ages.'

'I'm in the public most nights.' Bernard took a long draught of his beer.

'Are you still in business?'

'That's a nice way of putting it.' Bernard smiled, he was going to play hard to get though he needed the work. It was the only way with a twister like Gil. 'I don't do much now. I've got a steady job.' This was an out and out lie, but Gil had that effect on him. 'Bus conductor.'

'Oh! I was hoping you'd find me another car. Actually, I need two. Is it on?'

Bernard sighed with pleasure that Gil had asked. 'Depends what you want,' he said carefully.

'Fords, Model T.'

'Plenty of them about. Might be possible. I'm not promising, mind.'

'No, of course not. A matching pair. Possibly four all the same, that's what I'd really like, but two to start with. New or nearly new, the least possible mileage.'

Bernard put his tankard down heavily. A practised gesture that drew attention to the fact that it was empty.

'Another pint?'

'I don't mind if I do. He watched Gil go to the bar to get it and made up his mind to play him along as far as he could. He'd need to be tough when they talked money. This time, he was going to pin Gil down to a price before he did anything.

When they settled down to their second pint and Gil mentioned his figure, he was shocked.

'Sixty pounds each? No, for that I'm not prepared to take the risk. It's not on.'

'What did you have in mind?'

'A hundred each.'

'What?' Gil banged his tankard down on the table. There was no mistaking the irritation he was feeling.

'New paperwork provided. No sign of a previous owner if there's been one.'

'No, I'm not paying that. I can buy them all legal and above board from a garage for a hundred and twenty-five.'

After some haggling, they agreed to split the difference and settled on eighty. Bernard was content with that.

Chapter Sixteen

December 1925

Ellis couldn't take his eyes off Daisy, she was leaning forward in her chair talking to his mother, her arms round their third son Peter, now nine months old.

'A tea party, that's the best. Get us into the right mood for Christmas.'

'A children's tea party? For Nick's birthday?'

Daisy smiled. 'No, until Nick starts school he won't know enough children. I mean a family tea party, a celebration for us both.'

'When?' Ellis asked cautiously.

'Next Sunday – that falls between Nick's birthday and mine.' He'd be four this Friday and Daisy's twenty-second birthday fell the following week.

'What about me?' wailed Martin, their second son; he'd just turned three.

'You've had your birthday,' Nick told him bluntly. 'Not long ago. Don't be greedy.'

'I didn't have a party.'

'You had a special cake and we sang for you. And we had jelly and blancmange for tea.'

'Not a real party.'

Ellis pulled Martin up on his knee. 'This party is for all

of us,' he told him, trying to keep the peace.

Martin was indignant. 'Not for Peter. Not his birthday. Not his turn.'

Peter was asleep in Daisy's arms. She kissed his forehead; he didn't stir. 'Just for you and me and Nick,' she laughed.

Enjoyment was shining out of her. Ellis thought she was growing more attractive as she grew older. Daisy's face had a serene expression when at rest, but it was rarely at rest. At the moment her lips were parted in a smile and her eyes gleamed. She radiated happiness and inner strength. He'd known, as soon as he'd put his arms round Daisy, that it would be like this. It had felt so right.

He looked at his three sons; they'd arrived in quick succession, all with plump rounded limbs and light brown hair. All beautiful babies and Daisy was delighted with them. She was that rare woman who did not find a large family too much work. Energy continued to spark out of her. Ellis felt very bound up with his young family and the house seemed alive in the way it had when he'd been young. It always seemed comfortable and welcoming.

They'd had to make changes to suit their growing family. Daisy had opened up the old nurseries on the top floor, and employed Olive, a girl of eighteen, the eldest of a big family, to help with them.

'So I can go on helping you in the office,' she'd said. 'And your mother can get away from them when she wants to. They can be a bit boisterous.'

Daisy had been so pleased with the way Olive fitted in that she'd taken on her younger sister Elsie to help Ruby in the kitchen.

Ellis counted himself a very lucky man. He had everything in life he could wish for. He worked hard and he was pleased with what he was achieving; he wanted to continue increasing the profit.

He'd acquired his first motor hearse only last month. In order to keep costs low he'd chosen to get a local garage to build a body to his specifications on the chassis of a crashed Morris van. It was made mainly of wood and everybody said it looked smart. To order a specially designed body from a manufacturer would have been very expensive. He was still one of the first undertakers in Birkenhead to have a motor hearse. Better still, people were asking for it. It seemed at last that horse-drawn carriages had had their day. He'd sold Black Bess and got a good price for her from a rag and bone man. Dolly was getting too fat for anything heavy but she could still pull the little hearse if anybody ordered it.

His mother had been much better over recent years. She spent a lot of time with the children and had put on a bit of weight. She told him often that Daisy and the children had brought her back to life. She had what she wanted, a home with her family and her grandchildren all around her.

Ellis knew he'd taken on the greater share of the work, but he tried not to mind. Now Gil had five hire cars, their turnover was much increased. Sometimes it irked him to find Gilbert playing table tennis with one of the drivers, and he was never sure that when Gil drove off he was going to pick up a fare. Ellis suspected that he went on quite a lot of personal outings. Enid was doing most of his routine book-keeping.

If there was one thing Ellis was not happy about, it was his brother. At one time he'd thought Gil's behaviour had improved but now he was aggressive and overbearing. They were barely civil to each other these days.

He asked Daisy, 'Are you going to ask Gil and Brenda to this party?'

'We can't not ask them if it's a family do.'

He pulled a face.

'We won't need to ask them over Christmas if we do it now.'

Daisy and her two older boys had a fine time decorating the Christmas tree and putting swathes of holly and ivy round the living room for the party. She wanted it to look festive because by then Christmas would be just over a week away.

The day before the party, Daisy took the morning off from her book-keeping and instead set about icing her own birthday cake, a traditional rich fruit cake which Ellis loved. She decided then that Victoria sponge cake would better suit the stomachs of the very young and very old in the family – that phrase delighted her, *in the family*. She set about making two, a large one for Nick and a smaller one for Martin so he wouldn't feel left out.

It was mid-morning by then and Daisy left Ruby to take the cakes out of the oven when they were cooked, and took a pot of tea up to the living room to have with Dora. She found her mother-in-law slumped in her chair with her eyes closed.

'Are you all right, Mother?'

Dora stirred. 'I don't feel very well, a headache and a bit of a sore throat.'

'Oh dear, just before Christmas too. You'd like a cup of tea?'

'I'm parched. I'd love one.'

'Shall I get you some aspirins?'

'Yes, dear, if you wouldn't mind.' She sounded weary. 'I'm probably getting a head cold or something.'

'I hope that's all it is.'

After Dora had drunk her tea, she said she'd like to lie

down on her bed for an hour. It was almost dinner time when Daisy went to see how she was.

'No better. I feel shivery.'

'You should have got into bed instead of lying on top. It's quite cold in here. Come on, get yourself undressed and get into bed.' Daisy helped her up and turned the bed back.

'I'll get you a hot-water bottle and ask Elsie to make a fire for you. You'll be better having your dinner on a tray up here.'

'I think so. You're very kind, Daisy, when I'm not well.'

When Daisy went up ten minutes later with two hot-water bottles, Elsie was lighting a fire in the small grate but she could see Dora was shivering.

'You're still cold, what about a bed jacket over that nightie?'

'A good idea. I don't often wear a bed jacket. I've got a blue one, it'll be in the wardrobe.'

It was an enormous piece of mahogany furniture with a mirror in the centre door; each side was a separate compartment.

'Whereabouts?' Daisy opened one of the side doors. Inside were fitted shelves and drawers. All she could see were hat boxes and a book covered in brown leather.

'That was Albert's side. Try the other door.'

'Here we are. It's pink but it's a nice one.' Daisy took the bed jacket to the fire to warm before helping Dora into it.

'Thank you, that's better.'

'You should feel warmer now. It's cod and parsley sauce for dinner, you'll try a little?'

Daisy had left one of the wardrobe doors open. She went back to close it and the leatherbound book caught her eye again.

'What's this book?' She put her head on one side but it

didn't seem to have writing on its spine.

'Is it something of Albert's? I keep my hats there now.'

'Do you mind if I look?' Daisy took it out. 'D'you know, I think . . . Mother! This is it!'

'What?'

'D'you remember telling me years ago about a diary that one of the Corkill family had kept? We hunted and hunted . . .'

'Let me see. Yes, I do believe you're right.'

Daisy took the book to Dora's bed and opened it with awe. It smelled old and fusty. The first page had lettering in faded gilt. It read: 'This is the diary of –' and the name Polly Corkill had been added in ink, together with the year, 1865.

'Let me think.' Dora was frowning. 'Yes, Polly was Enoch Corkill's daughter-in-law.'

'Oh, this is wonderful! Such a find!'

Dora was contrite. 'I should have thought to look in the wardrobe. I'm sorry, Daisy.'

'I can't wait to read it. You don't mind if I have first go?'

'Go ahead. I couldn't read now.'

It was a cold, wet afternoon, not fit for any of them to go out for a walk. Daisy left Olive to amuse the children, she couldn't wait to read the diary. Coming across it so unexpectedly had been a staggering stroke of luck. The writing was tiny and rather cramped. Dora had been right about it being difficult to decipher.

Daisy discovered immediately that the diary had been a twenty-fifth birthday gift from Polly's mother-in-law Mrs Prudence Corkill, and that Polly's husband Prosper had received an identical diary on his twenty-ninth birthday ten days later.

Polly had written: 'Prosper writes little and I'm sure he'll never use it, though he promises to record something every day. I told his mother that I'd use it next year if he did not, but she was not mightily pleased with me.

'"He can use it next year himself," she retorted. "And the year after that if need be. He can use as little or as much of the page as he wants, it isn't dated or divided in any way. And neither is your own, Polly. I'm surprised you haven't noticed that."'

Polly seemed contrite; she'd written: 'In future, I really must think before I open my mouth.'

Polly declared it was her intention to make an entry every day and to unburden her heart. Daisy warmed to her as she found that Polly had a son of three years and another of nine months and was very proud of the cottage in Camden Yard in which they lived. It had one room down and two up. Daisy felt she was getting a picture of what life had been like in those far-off days.

Entries in the diary soon fell off. Sometimes weeks would go by without any. Polly complained that her life was humdrum.

In March she wrote that her baby was teething and had given her a very broken night. Henry Fox had been worried about his pony called Flash and when he got up to see to him in the night, he'd seen Polly's candle lit and knocked to ask for Prosper's help to give the pony a turpentine enema. Flash was suffering from bloat and colic and moaning piteously and the two men stayed with him for the best part of the night. Polly complained she'd been left to deal with the baby herself.

The following week Enoch had had to repair the shaft on the milk float for the second time. It wasn't until Daisy reached the entries for May that she began to learn more about the Fox forebears and became thoroughly absorbed.

May 12th, 1865. Such a tragedy, Henrietta Fox was laid to rest today. I called her Auntie Hetty, she has been my good friend and mentor ever since I married and came to live in Camden Yard. Prosper's mother is devastated. They were truly best friends for twenty years and have made the Yard a very pleasant place to live, with all their children happy here together. We are all numb that Auntie Hetty has gone. She had a cough first but then the pleurisy caught her. It all happened so quickly.

July 12th. I am shocked to find I have another baby on the way and Aaron only ten months old. I am still feeding him and feel it is too soon, but Prosper said he was pleased and hoped for a daughter this time.

October 21st. Such a shock for all of us. Camden Yard is plunged into turmoil at the news. Zachary Fox has announced he is to marry again. So soon after poor Auntie Hetty was laid to rest too. He is sixty-six and in his dotage, a silly old fool because his bride is to be Effie Wells, the serving maid working in his dairy, aged only nineteen. A pert-nosed, yellow-haired hussy if ever there was one.

The name Fox will suit Effie well. A real vixen and sly with it. He seeks marriage with her but she schemes to better herself. For her, there can be no reason other than to gain financial advantage. Up from serving maid to mistress of his big house.

November 2nd. The deed was done yesterday. Such a smart wedding, Effie tried hard to look like a lady. We were all invited and ate royally at the wedding breakfast. I am too near my time to feast. I suffered badly from the colic all night.

All my family feel such sympathy for Zachary's sons. Henry, George and Daniel. Their father has asked them to leave their rooms in the big house. Dan and George have been found rooms in the yard. Henry, being married, has been given the cottage next door to ours, which once housed their milk roundsman. His wife is incensed and a very unhappy neighbour.

January 18th, 1866. I was delivered of another boy child three days ago. We would both have preferred a daughter but he is strong and healthy.

I think my confinement encouraged Mrs Euphemia Fox to announce she is with child. She has not been slow to conceive. Hetty's sons are overcome with such bad news. They are sore afraid they'll be disinherited by their father's new family.

June 1st. A son has been born to Effie Fox and Zachary. To be named Zac junior. Strong and healthy by all accounts. I have not been invited to see the child and won't go. Effie knows how to please old men. Zachary is puffed up and Hetty's sons very cast down. We all sympathise with them, an upstart of a stepmother ten years younger than they are and a new family starting. The inheritance they envisaged for themselves is now in jeopardy. Effie will have to be kept in comfort for the rest of their lives, and she no more than a jumped-up serving wench. She now says more might be made from their business so that they could all be fed and housed in greater comfort and she's going to set about doing it.

*June 2nd. We of the Corkill family are cast down with
our own troubles. My mother-in-law Prudence drew
her last breath in the early hours of the morning. Only
51, that's no age at all. She's not been well for some
time though. They say one life is given and another
taken.*

*May 18th 1867. A most miserable year for us all. Henry
Fox told me today that he lives in dread of Effie
producing a son every year for the next decade but no
sign of another yet, and Zachary no longer feels well.
I fear Effie wears him out.*

*No such luck for me. We'll have another mouth to
feed soon. Prosper wants to have more say in the
carpentry shop and more wages for doing it. He says
he is paid little more than a hired carpenter.*

*October 10th. Poor Zachary. The end came for him
very quickly. Kicked by his own horse Dobbin ten days
ago. His leg broken and turned septic.*

*October 24th. Zachary willed everything he owned to
his wife. Mrs Euphemia Fox puts herself in charge of
their business and says she'll run it from now on.
Henry and his brother are mightily upset and fear they
may be put out of the Yard altogether. How can they
possibly rely on Effie? She's only out for herself and
little Zac.*

*November 8th. George and Daniel Fox have gone to
join the army. They say they want to get right away.
Effie will not allow them to play their part in the
family business. She orders them to do the menial jobs*

and is very strict with them.

Prosper's father tells us that Henry and his family need not worry too much, he will see to it that the business continues to thrive. Corkill family fortunes depend on that too. He thinks Effie works hard on their behalf. I think she twists him round her little finger.

November 10th. Mrs Euphemia Fox is to be seen about the Yard more and more. Yesterday, she took it upon herself to come round on Enoch's arm, saying they propose to weld all the businesses more tightly into one; the dairy from Fox's and the carpenter's shop from Corkill's and, most of all, the funeral undertaking.

She says greater profits will result. The horses Tallyrand and Dobbin, both dapple greys, can pull both the milk float and the hearse.

Old Zac bought both of them on her recommendation. He wanted to buy the famous black horses from Belgium to pull the hearse, but she told him it was too expensive to get the stallions and the mares turn brown with age and no longer look smart for a funeral. Only a Gypsy woman would know such things. She shows her low origins. Especially the undertaking business booms because there are always epidemics sweeping through Liverpool. They spread here across the river making life precarious for all but leaving us many to bury.

Christmas 1867. I laboured through the night of Christmas Eve and was delivered of a healthy daughter on Christmas Day. She is to be called Alice. Prosper *tells me he's delighted. I feel very tired; exhausted, in fact.*

February 4th, 1868. I find it unbelievable. Enoch Corkill, my much respected father-in-law, is to marry Euphemia Fox! He has four grown sons and three daughters-in-law to take care of him and is in no need of a wife. Especially one such as Effie Fox. We are mortified and outraged. Prosper says his father will not listen to reason.

It has caused such strife in the family, setting sons against their father. For Effie to have done it once, causing trouble in the Yard, was bad enough, but to set out to do it again having seen poor Zachary into his grave within two years of marrying him and bearing him a child – though who is to say Zac really is the old man's child? Prosper says not, he looks nothing like the other Foxes.

Effie Fox has caused nothing but trouble from the day she married into the business, for it is only too obvious it was the business she wanted and not old Mr Fox.

March 2nd. Effie is now the second wife of Enoch Corkill and we are supposed to celebrate the fact. The one good thing is that Enoch has vacated his quarters over the carpentry shop to move into the big house with her. I am glad to move into my father-in-law's rooms for my family is in need of the extra space. He has left them in a sad state.

The Corkill family should have remained independent and carried on their own business. It was a terrible mistake for Enoch and Zachary to become partners. Effie Wells has taken over both businesses. Now this hussy comes to tell my husband what to do. He tells us all he's been misnamed.

'I'll never be able to prosper. Not now.'

He can barely keep a civil tongue in his head to anyone – a stepmother of twenty-three, telling him how to run what should be his to control! Prosper continues to make coffins and the trollop allows him to arrange the cheaper funerals, but everything is to be as she wants it, he is allowed no say in anything.

My poor Prosper and his brothers feel disinherited. The scheming bitch will want it all for her baby Zac. I read the sign outside the shop, which says, Zachary Fox and Sons, and weep. There has never been any mention there of us Corkills and I fear both Corkill and Fox sons will be pushed out and I will starve in my old age.

May 10th. Effie has bought a brougham for her own use. Such a grand carriage, meant for town driving, closed with glass windows and doors. She likes nothing better than to drive round the town showing off to all how high she has risen in the world. She says it isn't an extravagance because they can hire it out, and often at funerals it will be needed for the elderly of the family. Now, of course, another horse is needed to draw it. Prosper counts it fortunate she didn't choose a vehicle that needs two horses to pull it. Effie can spend money like water. She has her big house on Camden Street, having turned out the Fox boys. She wants to live like a queen and can convince herself and her doting husband it is all for the good of the business. She makes out she knows everything.

June 4th. Effie is showing signs that she is with child, though nothing has been said to any of us. She still goes about ordering the business, taking a much more active part than my father-in-law. Prosper is in despair that she starts a second family of Corkills. We fear we will be vanquished like the Foxes. Henry and his growing family remain but he does little work. He complains so hard he has little energy for anything else.

August 13th. Effie delivered of another son after less than six months of marriage. Now we can all see how she gets her husbands. She sets herself up over all of us, but is little more than a whore. Enoch is very much puffed up. The boy weighed nine pounds and is to be called Cuthbert.

August 20th 1869. Effie has done it again after just one year. Another son, to be called James. Enoch thrives too and she has a clasp of iron on all business matters. She handed out increased dividends to all sons this year. Henry feels disposed to be less critical of her, but it takes more to please Prosper. He is very cast down and feels he's had his birthright stolen from him.

Polly had written very little after that, but she'd recorded the birth of two daughters to Effie and Enoch, one in 1871 and another two years later. The last few pages remained blank.

It was mid-afternoon when Daisy closed the diary. She felt all of a flutter at having learned so much and shot down to the office to find Ellis.

'It's wonderful,' she laughed. 'A revelation. You've got to read it yourself,' but she outlined what she'd discovered. 'Gil was right when he said the Corkills were blood relatives. Zac Fox was a half brother to Cuthbert Corkill, they had the same mother.'

Ellis was affected too and could do no more work. He got down on his hands and knees in front of the big cupboard, and combed through the records kept there.

'Many of these documents are in Effie's handwriting. The accounts bear her signature year after year.'

'We now know she was in charge of both sides of the business.' Daisy felt almost intoxicated. 'We must find out for how many years that went on, and who ran the company afterwards. And what happened to Polly and Prosper, and Effie's children.'

Ellis spread the account books across his desk and tried to work out the exact dates. Between them, they worked out that Effie had been in charge until 1898. Then little Zac took over.

Daisy looked up, her cheeks flushed. 'It's time I went to see how Mother's getting on. She'll be ready for another cup of tea.' Ellis went with her to carry the tray.

'I've had a sleep,' Dora told them. 'I feel a bit better. It is a head cold. Nothing worse.'

'Thank goodness for that.' Ellis seemed excited too. 'It would be awful to be sick over Christmas.'

'I'll get up for the party tomorrow.'

Daisy then had to relate what she'd read in the diary.

'Did you know Dad's father?' Ellis asked her. 'My grandfather.'

'Yes, he was living here when I first knew Albert. An old man, but he still did some of the work.'

'Can you remember his given name?'

'I called him Mr Fox.' Dora had to think for a minute. 'Zac. That was it, Zac. Another Zachary. He hadn't been running the business for very long, about six years, I think.'

'That's because Effie carried on until she was quite old.'

'When did Dad take over?'

'The old man died in . . . it would be nineteen hundred and four.'

Daisy said, 'What about the Corkills? You knew Cuthbert?'

'Yes, I seem to remember him running the carpentry shop while Dad looked after the dairy.'

'So was responsibility for the business split up again?'

'I don't really know . . .'

'It should be in the records,' Ellis said. 'It's just a matter of searching through them.'

'There's so many.'

'Yes, but I'll start at the beginning and work through.'

Daisy was thoroughly worked up. 'I think I could draw up family trees from what we know now. I'll do it this evening after we've put the children to bed. I'd better go up and see them. I'm neglecting them today.'

The sky had cleared just before dusk. Because they'd been cooped up indoors all afternoon, Daisy took Nick and Martin out into the last rays of pale wintry sun in Camden Yard. They kicked a brightly coloured beach ball about and ran around after it, calling it football. It was a wonderful way to tire them out before bedtime.

'Daisy.' Ellis came out waving a newspaper at her. 'Mam's just pointed this out to me. There's something here you'll want to see.'

The *Liverpool Echo* was delivered every evening but it was Dora who was most interested in it. 'Come on, Nick, have a game with me.'

Daisy read: 'At Liverpool Crown Court today, Bernard Oliver Corkill, age 38, was found guilty of stealing a Rolls-Royce motor car on June 4th. It had been parked in Bold Street at three o'clock on that date and when the owners returned at four thirty it had gone. He has been convicted twice previously for the same offence and was sentenced to two years' imprisonment.'

Daisy felt in a whirl. 'Stealing cars?'

'We knew he was a thief. Didn't he steal money from our till?'

'But cars?' That was making Daisy think. Gil knew this man though he'd denied it at first. Later he'd changed his story and said the thief had pretended to be Ralph Corkill. Gil had certainly gone to a lot of trouble to keep the police away from him.

'If only we could talk to this man, I'm sure he could tell us why Gil protected him.' Daisy was frowning.

Ellis kicked out at the ball, sending both boys chasing hard after it. 'Not a savoury character.'

He turned to smile at Daisy. 'D'you know what I think? Gil knows this Bernard Corkill is related to the Corkills who lived here, and he doesn't want us to know.'

She laughed. 'Hope he isn't related to me. Not now he's a convicted thief.'

Chapter Seventeen

Daisy felt really worked up by the revelations in Polly's diary and the newspaper report about Bernard Corkill. She ate her tea, fed and washed baby Peter, and read a story to the older boys, but her thoughts were firmly fixed in the past.

When she'd been growing up, she'd been determined to find her family roots and yet she'd let it all drop. She couldn't believe it was four years since she'd thought much about it. It had all come to a dead end. When she'd found that the man who'd stolen from the till had done a runner from his lodgings, she'd thought she'd lost the trail and made no further effort to find him. She should have done. She'd given up looking for Polly's diary too, yet it had been here all the time. She'd been too wrapped up in looking after babies and having more.

Of course, once she had the family for which she'd craved, she didn't need the other so badly, but all the same . . .

Now she was thoroughly roused again. Daisy opened the diary and set about drawing up family trees for both the Foxes and the Corkills. She became completely absorbed in the task and the time flew. Ellis was sitting at the other end of the living room table sorting through mounds of old documents.

'What have you found out?' she asked him.

'We knew that Effie amalgamated the two firms. Her first accounts were for the year eighteen sixty-seven, and the Foxes and the Corkills appear to have been in business together ever since. The work was divided up, of course, just as it is today. The Corkills did the carpentry.' Ellis was putting the papers together. 'It's bedtime.'

Daisy yawned. 'Do you know what happened to Prosper?'

'I think he spent his life working in the carpentry shop, but Effie's signature appears on the carpentry records up to the time of her death. Only then does Prosper sign.'

'So Effie did push him out? Polly was right?'

'Yes, but she wouldn't have starved in her old age.'

'I'm going to take the diary up to bed with me, to read again.'

It was very late when she put her light out. By then it was all clear in her mind. Enoch Corkill and Effie had had two sons and two daughters. Cuthbert Corkill lived in the yard. For the first time she asked herself what had happened to James Corkill, the second son, who had been born on 20 August 1869, and the daughters born in 1871 and 1873.

Dora was right, there were other branches of the Corkill family with whom they'd lost touch. Daisy was almost sure she was related to them. It was not impossible, they were living in the same town. She settled down to sleep but sleep wouldn't come. It was two o'clock when she got up to look at her mother's birth certificate. That had given her the name of Rosa's father. She was almost sure it was James, but was her mind playing tricks on her?

She slid quietly out of bed, not wanting to wake Ellis. She kept all the things that had belonged to her mother in a tin in her wardrobe. She'd put Rosa's birth certificate in there too.

The door creaked as she opened it. She felt inside and

found the cold square metal box and was creeping out to the landing where she could put on the light. She heard Ellis turn over.

'Whatsthematter?' He raised himself up on his arm. 'Are you all right, Daisy?'

By that time she'd snapped the light on and off again. Rosa's father's name was definitely James! James was Cuthbert's brother and Enoch's son by Effie Fox.

Daisy was tingling all over. 'I am related to your Corkills.' She threw herself back on the bed and laughed aloud. 'Can you believe it? Related to your Corkills! The proof was here all the time, I just didn't work it out. How could I have missed that this evening? What a nitwit I am.'

Ellis hugged her close. 'Then you and I must be related. You're loaded with blood relatives now, Daisy.'

'At last, I've found them.'

The next day, Dora got up for Sunday dinner and said she felt well enough to stay up for the party. In the afternoon, Ruth arrived with Auntie Glad and Uncle Ern, and brought a soft ball each for the boys. Uncle Ern presented Daisy with a jar of his potted shrimps.

Daisy was still excited by what she'd found out and the family trees she'd drawn up.

'I must show you. It's the most wonderful birthday present I've ever had.' She laughed.

The Maddockses, too, were enthralled by Polly's diary and what Daisy had found out.

'That's right.' Glad pored over Daisy's workings. 'Rosa Corkill and her brother are here.' They could talk of nothing else.

'Uncle Ern, do you remember the name of Rosa's brother?'

He had to think for a moment. 'Bernard, that was it.'

'It all fits in.' Daisy gurgled with pleasure.

She'd arranged a few games for the children to play, hunt the slipper and put a tail on the donkey, and eventually they got round to playing them. Nick and Martin ran about boisterously making plenty of noise. Peter had learned to crawl and there was no stopping him demonstrating his new skill. They all enjoyed it for a while.

Daisy was waiting for Brenda and Gil to come. They were late and the children were getting hungry. She was beginning to wonder whether she should run across the road to chivvy them up when the doorbell rang as a signal that they were coming up the stairs.

Brenda came in wearing a new beige dress, of eye-catching design.

'This is the very latest.' She did a twirl on the hearth rug. 'Do you like it, Daisy?' It was very short. 'Wonderfully comfortable to wear, so light and loose.'

To show just how loose, she hitched it momentarily at the unmarked waist, revealing elegant legs as high as mid-thigh.

Behind Brenda's seemingly friendly words was a touch of hostility that Daisy didn't understand. These days, Brenda was never welcoming when she went over to see her. Once she'd been the most important person in Daisy's life and she found this new attitude hurtful.

Daisy could see both her mother-in-law and Auntie Glad disapproved. They couldn't take their eyes from Brenda's hemline. Brenda sat down on the settee, with her knees in full view.

'Good lord, Brenda, you're hardly decent,' Auntie Glad gasped. 'You showed your stocking tops and suspenders! I thought skirts were short last year – didn't think they could get any shorter, but by Jove!'

'Everybody will be wearing their skirts this length soon.'

'I won't,' her mother thundered. 'You don't go out in the street like that, do you? I wouldn't dare.'

'You're old-fashioned, Mam.'

Daisy tried to cover the moment of discord by taking them down to the dining room for tea. There was a row of birthday cakes set out on the sideboard.

She thought Uncle Ern was looking tired. He said, 'Lovely to see you settled and happy with the family you wanted, Daisy.'

'I hope you aren't going to overdo it.' Auntie Glad pulled a face. 'Three little ones are quite a handful, but the way you're going on . . . Ellis?'

He laughed. 'I've told Daisy we'll have to draw a line somewhere. She doesn't think three are enough.'

'Ellis, you said you wanted a daughter!'

'Yes, but there's no guarantee that's what we'll get.'

'I really would love to have a daughter,' Daisy said with longing in her voice. 'Then perhaps I'd be content.'

'You don't know what's good for you,' Auntie Glad told her.

'I think she does,' Dora said gently. 'She's made this a happy home for us all.'

Daisy was glad she had Peter next to her in his high chair, she could fill the uncomfortable moment by cutting up his meal.

Auntie Glad was tucking into the cold beef. 'We thought you'd be staying to help us run the shop in our old age, Daisy. We're thinking of selling up.' It was the first time such a thing had been mentioned.

Brenda looked a little shocked. 'You'll sell it as a going concern?'

'If we can,' Uncle Ern said. 'Getting too much for us, time we retired.'

They discussed the pros and cons of selling the shop for a long time. When the meal was finished, Daisy took them back to the living-room fire.

Auntie Glad said, 'What's the point of us struggling on? You don't want it and neither does Ruth. No family to hand it on to. Ellis, I don't suppose you know of anyone looking for a sound business? It's always made a profit.'

He shook his head.

'In a way I'll be sorry to see it go to a stranger,' Auntie Glad mourned. 'The shop's been in my family for two generations. Just not enough Maddockses to carry on.'

'There always seemed a lot of Maddockses to me,' Daisy chuckled. 'And more than likely you've lost touch with a whole lot more.'

'Everybody had much bigger families in the old days.' Dora delicately patted her nose with an embroidered handkerchief. 'Like the Corkills.' She smiled at Daisy. 'They'll still be around.'

Gil said irritably, 'Those Corkills died out, Mam, I told you.'

Dora had re-read the diary and wanted to talk of Daisy's newfound connections.

'No, they didn't die out, Gil. In every generation, Corkill children grew up in the yard and then had to go elsewhere to earn their living. We lost touch with the other branches of the family, that's what happened.'

'No.' Gil was trying to contradict that as usual.

'You haven't heard my news.' Daisy laughed out loud and leapt to her feet. 'I'm related to the Corkill family that lived here. Let me show you the family tree I've drawn up. Ralph was a cousin to me.'

Gil looked shocked. 'He can't be.'

It gave Daisy great pleasure to put the evidence in front of him. 'So you see, it's no good trying to convince us otherwise.'

He stared down at the page of the diary on which Polly had written of the birth of Enoch Corkill's children.

Brenda looked over his shoulder and chatted on. 'I'm amazed. We thought our Daisy had no one of her own.'

Daisy was watching Gil, he looked deflated. She took a deep breath. 'You knew all the time, didn't you, Gil?'

'No, I'm amazed too.'

'You knew the day we first came here to have tea when you and Brenda were engaged. I know you did.' She could feel herself bristling with anger. 'You tried to stop your mother talking about my family. You knew how keen I was to find my relatives. Any relative would have done, I felt so alone in the world. It would have given me a great deal of satisfaction to know just where I fitted into a real family. You denied me that.'

'I didn't know, Daisy . . .'

'Of course you did. Just as you knew five minutes ago when you said the Corkills had all died out. And I know why. The Corkills were partners in the business, weren't they? You didn't want anyone else to claim that inheritance. You wanted to keep it for yourself.'

'Daisy!' Uncle Ern was shocked.

Gil had got himself together. 'I gained nothing personally. It was the business.'

She could see he'd never admit anything. It was his way.

'You're being silly, Daisy. We asked our solicitors to seek out Corkill relatives. We did our best to find you.'

'Not that it matters now,' Daisy said. 'I married into the family anyway.'

Auntie Glad straightened up in her chair. 'It does matter, Daisy. You've been done down. You'd own a share of this business in your own right. If only we'd known.'

'Nobody knew,' Gil spat out. 'Nobody knew, I tell you.'

'Henman did advertise,' Ellis said. 'That's true.'

'He failed to find anyone,' Gil insisted. 'Nobody put in a claim. We all thought the family had died out.'

Daisy looked at Ellis. They both thought otherwise.

Brenda felt very much on edge as she got up to leave. Gil was already on his feet. As soon as Ellis closed the front door behind them she burst out, 'Some birthday party, I must say.' She rushed ahead of Gil, across the road to her clothes shop.

'Daisy can be ferocious. She's a right pain in the neck.'

Brenda turned to face Gil. 'What she said was right though, wasn't it? You're always trying to pull a fast one on someone. Always going on about the Corkills dying out.'

'No, I tell you, I believed they had. I wish we hadn't gone. I don't know why she asks us. She hates me.'

'I wish we hadn't gone too. I hate going.'

'I thought you wanted to, that you enjoyed it.'

'You and Ellis always row.'

'This time it was Daisy. In front of your family too.'

'You shouldn't have kept on so. You protested too much.'

'I didn't know, I tell you.'

'All right, but it was awful anyway. All those children, they get on my nerves.'

'Brenda! You keep going on about how much you like children.' He was taking his time to unlock their door.

'Not *hers*. Everyone makes such a fuss of them.' She pushed past him into the shop.

'So what? I ignore them. Why can't you?'

Brenda came to a dramatic halt in the middle of the shop. 'I thought you loved children. I thought you wanted us to have a family.'

'For Christ's sake, Brenda,' he burst out. 'We should have known. Seeing Daisy with her brood, it's the worst thing you could do. She's always brimming with delight over them. It makes you feel you're missing out.'

'I am missing out.' Hadn't she been longing for a baby of her own for years? Hadn't she ached and hankered for one, until she'd become obsessed with the need for a child?

'We'll think of some reason not to go next time we're asked.'

'Gil! I'm talking about us having a family. You do want it, don't you?' She was pleading now.

'You know I do.'

The trouble was, Brenda thought bitterly, for them babies didn't come. Gil was making haste to get to bed, she knew he was in no mood to talk about it tonight but she couldn't stop.

'Did you hear Daisy say she'd like to have a daughter? You'd have thought she had enough, wouldn't you? There's no satisfying her.'

'For God's sake, Brenda, don't start that again. Not tonight, I'm tired.'

'Go to sleep then,' she retorted crossly.

Brenda clung to her side of the mattress, wanting to cry with frustration. She wanted a more sympathetic husband and she wanted a baby. The need for a child had become a persistent hunger that nagged and wouldn't go away. It was always in her mind, colouring everything else, and she was getting older. She was thirty-two, no longer young for a first baby. She was haunted by the feeling that she'd left it too late.

Brenda knew the only way to rid herself of this longing was to have a baby of her own. A daughter was what she really wanted, a pretty little girl with curly hair who would call her Mummy, climb on her knee and throw her arms round her.

Each month she hoped to find herself pregnant and each month she had proof that she wasn't. There seemed to be no end to the waiting. She was beginning to fear it would never happen. Gil said he wanted a family but it was only to keep her quiet, really he didn't care one way or the other. When she turned to him for support, he laughed and said he was doing all he could.

Gil tugged on the bedclothes and turned over, taking more than his share. Brenda pulled viciously until she retrieved them.

He'd even accused her of being jealous of Daisy. That had hurt. Daisy was so proud of her family, how could she not be envious? Brenda now counted it her biggest mistake to think owning her own business and making a go of that was more important to her. She hadn't been desperate for a baby to start with, and it had seemed the natural thing to avoid it for a little while by using French letters. Gil had hated them but he'd agreed because he'd been in no hurry to face the added expense of a family.

All her life, Brenda had felt sorry for Daisy, the little waif who'd been so grateful for anything she was given, even well-worn clothes. She'd been such a plain, pathetic girl, so eager to fetch and carry for everybody. Who could help feeling sorry for her?

Brenda had been so sure Daisy was making a mistake in marrying Ellis. She'd done it straight off without giving it the slightest thought. By any logic it ought to have been a disaster, but tonight, again, she'd seen the way Ellis looked at his wife. He adored her, couldn't do enough for her, couldn't stop himself reaching out to touch her.

Daisy had landed on her feet. Brenda had told her so and she'd laughed and agreed, but it wasn't fair that Daisy should have three babies while she couldn't have even one.

Brenda wiped away a tear on the sheet. She'd made so many mistakes she no longer trusted her own judgement. She'd stood out against living with Gil's mother, she'd even warned Daisy against doing it. Daisy had ignored her advice and gone to live in the Foxes' family home without a second thought and seemed very happy there. Brenda knew Daisy had a much better house than she had, it had more style. She'd even had Ruby to do all the cooking for her right from the start, while she'd had to work all day in the shop and then go upstairs to cook and clean.

Brenda had found she had far too much to do, and Gil wouldn't lift a finger. He'd been brought up to sit back and be waited on in the house. He was no help to her at all and could be quite nasty if pressed to do a household job. He expected meals to be put on the table in front of him and he'd complain if they were late. He went out to the pub several evenings each week, leaving her to clean up on her own. This wasn't how she'd envisaged marriage.

She'd had to hire Sally to help her in the shop, otherwise she was pinned down there between nine and five every day. Brenda felt she was able to cope now with a woman to clean in the mornings. The problem was that by paying out wages from her profit, she could no longer save much towards expanding the business.

On top of that, she'd been over-optimistic about the extra profit she'd be able to squeeze out of her shop. Her clothes were too upmarket and high fashion for her position in Camden Street. She'd sell more if she were in the centre of the town. And closing the dairy had reduced her sales; women used to come up every day for milk and saw her fashions displayed; now they no longer came.

Gilbert got up the next morning feeling out of sorts. He felt he'd made himself look a bit of a fool in front of both his own family and Brenda's. He should have kept his mouth shut about the Corkill family having died out instead of harping on and on. Daisy had taken great pleasure in proving him wrong. He hoped that would be the last he'd hear of it, but it had left him uneasy and somehow full of foreboding.

And then Brenda had gone on about having a baby again. He knew how much she wanted a child but it was pointless moaning about not getting pregnant. That didn't help, it just repelled him. She was jealous of Daisy, though she wouldn't admit it.

Gil knew he was late for work again, but he had to have more tea to get himself going. Brenda was down in the shop, he could hear the bell ping as customers came in. He opened yesterday's newspaper. He hadn't had time to read it properly.

He heard the sudden pounding of feet on the stairs and pushed his paper under the table out of sight. It infuriated Brenda to find him reading. She thought he should be up and chasing round like her.

'D'you know what I've just heard?' Brenda was already infuriated. 'Customers in the shop talking together about a barren woman.'

'Talking about you?'

'No, about someone they worked for. They said she was a barren—'

'Why should that bother you?'

'I hate the word.'

'Brenda, it's in the dictionary.' He thought it unhealthy

that she should be like this. He made an effort to soothe her. 'I suppose they had a trail of kids behind them.'

'They left two prams outside. They're on the way home after taking their older ones to school.'

'That's what I mean. They're jealous of women like you who aren't hung about with kids and who have time to do other things in life.'

Brenda burst into tears. 'But others will be using that term about me, don't you see? I hate it.'

Gil got to his feet and pushed his handkerchief into her hand. When that didn't help, he put his arms round her and gave her a hug. Oh boy, was he sick of this.

Brenda wailed, 'I don't feel a real woman.'

'What about seeing the doctor?' He'd said that a few times already in similar situations.

'I've been to see him.'

That surprised him, she hadn't said anything to him.

'What did he say?'

Brenda sniffed into the handkerchief. 'He can see no reason why I shouldn't conceive. He said, if I'd just relax, it could happen.'

'There you are then.'

'But it isn't happening.' Brenda's voice rose on a note of anguish. 'I wish I could get pregnant.'

Gil wished so too. He couldn't stand much more of this. 'Look, we've had great fun trying, haven't we?'

'You've had great fun but you've failed. I can't believe you could fail, not when your brother and Daisy are breeding like rabbits.'

'It's not my fault,' he retorted, then he hurriedly corrected himself. 'It's not necessarily my fault.'

Brenda broke down in tears again. 'You're blaming me.'

Gil knew very well it wasn't his fault. Nobody could

accuse him of being infertile. He had a son now aged ten, the result of his affair with Stella Thorpe, but he must be careful not to upset Brenda any further or his life wouldn't be worth living. She knew nothing of that and this wasn't the time to tell her.

'I've got to run somebody down to Woodside for the train,' he said, taking his half-eaten round of toast from his plate. 'Must go.'

Gil had hardly crossed the road before Brenda heard another step on the stairs. This was the time Mrs Mudgely, the woman who cleaned for her, arrived. She wiped her eyes and opened the door.

'Come in.' Keeping her face averted, she retreated to the bathroom where she splashed cold water on her eyes and dabbed them dry on a towel. They felt better but she hardly dared look in the mirror, tears always made her look awful. Her worst fears were confirmed, her face was blotchy and her eyes red. She couldn't possibly show herself in the shop like this. Besides, she felt on an emotional knife edge. She couldn't bear it if Sally asked what was the matter.

Neither could she stay here in the flat while Mrs Mudgely cleaned. Brenda rubbed cold cream into her complexion and powdered liberally round her eyes. She put on lipstick and didn't look quite so bad. She'd go out for a while and pull herself together. It was a dark and drizzly morning; she pulled on her hat, a deep cloche that fitted low on her forehead and half shaded her eyes from view.

She ran downstairs and went quickly through the shop. There was only one customer in.

'Sally, I have to go out for an hour. Back as soon as I can.'

Outside on the pavement the keen wind was heavy with

drizzle. With her umbrella held in front of her, nobody need notice she'd been crying.

She was angry with herself for breaking down again like that in front of Gil. He thought she was a nutcase for taking it to heart. She walked rapidly, not caring where she went. She found herself in Grange Road, the busy shopping centre. Once she'd been ambitious enough to think she might own a business here. It was all pie in the sky. Now she knew what Gil was really like, she didn't think she'd ever manage it.

She stopped to look in shop windows. It took her mind away from her own problems. She'd go into Robb's, the big department store; they kept the best ladies' fashion department in town. She needed to study their stock and compare it and their prices with her own.

It cheered her a little. Her customers were getting excellent value for money. Her clothes were of equal quality. Her steps took her almost without any conscious decision into the baby linen department. There she fingered the baby gowns much as she had the ladies' fashions.

If only she'd come in here to buy. They had such lovely nightgowns in soft flannelette and tiny vests, Brenda wanted to drool over them. She came to a christening gown, all pin tucks, ribbons and lace. She'd never seen anything quite so beautiful before. She could almost see her own baby wearing that. She'd dress her daughter beautifully on all occasions, but for her christening this was it. She'd never find anything she liked better than this.

Brenda took out her purse and bought it. It seemed the most natural thing to do at the time. She felt a little better as she walked briskly home. Mrs Mudgely was polishing in the living room, her bed had been made and the room dusted and polished.

Brenda closed the door and unwrapped her purchase, eager to see it again. Tissue paper had been folded into it. The lacework was more delicate and even more beautiful than it had seemed in the shop. She spread it out across the bed, marvelling at the workmanship. It had been very expensive.

It wasn't fair that the baby she craved didn't come. To have a child was a desperate inner need she couldn't satisfy, and the longer she was denied it, the more desperate the need became. Brenda took off her coat and hat. Her tears were barely under control but she mustn't cry now. There was a lump in her throat, but nobody could tell from her eyes that she'd been crying.

She went down to her shop, she ought to keep an eye on what Sally was doing there. She didn't really trust her.

Gilbert took his newspaper to his bedroom at two o'clock. He had a fare to take out this evening and he thought he'd have an hour on his bed now while things were quiet. It took his breath away to see the white satin baby dress spread out on the coverlet.

Oh God! Whatever was Brenda thinking of? She was always talking of having a baby, but to go this far? It was downright unhealthy. He ran down to the shop.

'Can I have a word with you?' he said to Brenda.

'What about?' There were several customers in, but Sally was still there.

'In private.'

She followed him upstairs reluctantly. 'What is it?'

Damn it, she must know what concerned him. If she didn't, then . . . He led her into their bedroom.

'What's this baby dress on the bed? You haven't bought it for the baby you hope to have?'

She was blinking at it as though she'd never seen it before. 'No, I bought it for Daisy's baby.'

Gilbert was shocked. 'Daisy's baby wouldn't fit into that. He's nine months old. I'm not a fool!' Brenda knew all about clothes and how they were sized, she'd never make such a mistake. It had to be for the baby she wanted so much. She just wouldn't admit it.

'This . . .' He looked again at the white satin confection. It wasn't just any baby dress. 'Isn't it a christening robe? Peter's been christened in the family gown like the rest of them. What's coming over you?'

He was scared. This wasn't natural. He should never have married her, she wasn't right in the head. She'd always been a bit strange, and was for ever demanding something from him. Always it had been what she could get out of him, never what she could give. He'd been too hasty by half when he'd married her. He was fed up with Brenda.

He scooped up the christening gown and threw it at her. 'It's stupid to buy things like this when you aren't even pregnant.'

He saw her anger flare up at him. 'I thought you wanted a baby too.'

'I do.' Anything to stop her going on like this. 'You know I'd like a son to follow me in the business.' Gil kept his ire in check to make one last effort. 'Why don't we adopt?'

'Adopt? That isn't what I want.'

'Nor me, but—'

'It would be second best.'

He couldn't prevent his eyes rolling up to the ceiling in despair. 'Wouldn't second best be better than nothing? Surely it would get the need for a baby out of your system.'

'That's not what I want, Gil. I want my own baby, not somebody else's.'

Chapter Eighteen

January 1927

Brenda wouldn't let herself hope; wouldn't even let herself think she could be pregnant, but she felt all of a fizz inside. She should have started her monthlies yesterday and she hadn't. Useless to tell herself she might just be a little late, that it might all come to nothing. For the first time she had real hope. Far greater than the hope that had sustained her these last few years.

Gil laughed cruelly. 'Don't bank on it yet,' he told her. 'It might never happen for you.'

Two more days passed before Ruth popped into the shop to see her.

'I've just come from home, it's my day off today. Spent last night there. Mam thinks she's got a buyer for the fish shop at last. I'm taking her to look at houses this afternoon. Isn't it wonderful news? They've been waiting so long.'

'Wonderful, high time they were able to take things easy.' Brenda was pleased for her parents, but she had news that was even more thrilling. She rushed her sister upstairs and put on the kettle.

'Three days overdue. What d'you think? Is it going to happen for me? It feels like I've been waiting for ever too.'

Ruth was cautious. 'Could be. Three days? A bit soon – you could just be late.'

'I know, I know.'

'Any other signs or symptoms?'

'Such as what?'

'Tingling in your breasts?'

Had she? Brenda shook her head, she wanted to say yes but she hadn't noticed anything like that. 'But I'm hoping.'

'I hope so too.' Ruth kissed her cheek. 'I'll keep my fingers crossed for you.'

An hour later they were down in the shop. Ruth was looking for a new outfit. One of her colleagues was getting married and she was invited to the wedding. Brenda felt almost sure, she spent the day eddying round half dazed with hope.

A few days more and she really did feel tingling in her breasts. She was over the moon. At last it looked as though she was going to get her dearest wish.

'It's a relief,' Gil said. 'I'm glad. At least now you'll be happy.'

Brenda had expected him to show some pleasure on his own account. 'I'll not be truly happy until September the tenth when my baby will be born.'

'You know the exact date?'

'It's the expected date.' Brenda beamed at him. 'Ruth's worked it out for me.'

She hadn't meant to spread the news immediately, not until the first few months were safely over. She was half fearful she'd made a mistake with her dates, or that something would happen to deprive her of this baby. But another month or so went by and she couldn't keep such stupendous news to herself any longer.

Brenda heard from Ruth that their parents had found

themselves a house and would soon be moving in. At a time when she knew she'd find Daisy working on the books in the office, she went across to tell her, and then she couldn't stop herself going straight on to her own good news. Daisy leapt to her feet and threw her arms round her.

'I'm so pleased for you.' She was laughing with delight. 'Guess what? I think I'm off again too. For the fourth time.'

Brenda laughed too, but she knew she'd have been mortified to hear this if she hadn't started her own baby. They compared dates and Brenda found that Daisy's fourth baby was due five weeks before her own.

'I do hope I'll have a daughter this time.' Daisy's face was shining with delight.

'So do I. I definitely want a daughter.'

'I daren't build my hope up too high. Boys seem to be what I get.'

'I'm hoping with all my might.' Brenda giggled. 'It's a miracle for me to be pregnant at all and I'm going for exactly what I want. The full works, it's got to be a little girl.'

'I expect you'll be pleased with whatever you get,' Daisy said. 'I always am.'

'I may not get a second chance so it's got to be a daughter for me.' Brenda was adamant. 'In fact, Gil doesn't really believe it's happening now, even though I've been down to see the doctor and he says so. Sometimes, I can't believe it either.'

For Brenda, there were soon plenty more signs that she was indeed pregnant. She was sick every morning as soon as she got out of bed and felt so nauseous for the rest of the day that she was finding it very hard to continue working. She managed to find another part-time assistant to help Sally in the shop. Sally worked in the mornings and Ida in the afternoons. The two girls were managing the shop reasonably well between them. Brenda had only the ordering and the accounts to do. She decided she'd keep them both on after the baby came, so she could spend more time upstairs with her daughter.

Brenda didn't feel well throughout her pregnancy. It didn't help her to see Daisy sailing through her fourth without any trouble at all. Daisy continued to work in the office during the mornings and run round after her little boys during the rest of the day. She took them to the park and she played with them out in the yard at the back. Brenda couldn't believe Daisy had so much more energy than she had. She worried that she was too old for this; she'd be thirty-four before the baby was born.

She was down at her doctor's surgery frequently, wanting a tonic to make her feel more on top of things. She consumed several bottles of physic but none of it did her any good.

Ruth came more often to see her. She palpated her expanding abdomen and told her all was proceeding exactly as it should be. She took her out for walks in the fresh air and advised her on diet. Nothing seemed to help.

'I feel so low and I look terrible.'

'You don't.' But Brenda knew even Ruth didn't think she had the bloom that Daisy had.

'I wish all this was over, and I had my body back to myself. I hope it comes early.'

'Your baby needs to stay where it is for the full forty weeks.' Her sister was quite severe. 'It won't do it any good to come early, believe me.'

By the latter months of pregnancy Brenda felt worse and her blood pressure was higher than it should be.

'Rest more,' Ruth advised.

'How can I? I've still got Gil's meals to cook.' She knew

Ruth was only trying to help and that she sounded thoroughly irritable and out of sorts.

It didn't help when Ruth had a word with Gil about helping more in the house. He flew into a rage with Brenda when the best she could produce for his dinner was egg on toast. 'Get a woman in to do the work if you can't,' he told her.

She went across the road to Daisy with her tears only half under control, she couldn't help it. Daisy was in the kitchen having a cup of tea with Ruby and Elsie Lane, one of the sisters she employed. She was full of sympathy and immediately asked Elsie if she knew of anybody who would suit Brenda.

Elsie said, 'I've another sister about to leave school. She's looking for a first place. She helps me mam at home and can do a bit of cooking and cleaning.'

Daisy told Brenda, 'You know we've been very pleased with Elsie and Olive.'

'Our Flo's only just fourteen. She's very willing but you might have to show her things. I mean, this will be her first job. Would you want her to live in or out?'

Olive, the nursery maid, slept in the night nursery with the boys, but Elsie went home every evening after they'd had tea.

Brenda tried to think. 'I've only got two bedrooms, and I need one for the baby.'

She'd had a lot of pleasure from fitting it out with nursery motifs on the wallpaper and curtains, and buying a lovely cot and a nursing chair. Her daughter was going to want for nothing. The room wasn't very big and it would spoil the whole effect if she were to put a bed in it too. Besides, Gil was in the habit of walking about half naked from the bathroom. 'She'd have to live out. Is that all right?'

Elsie said, 'There's a lot of us at home, I think Mam would like her to get a live-in job, but Flo, she'd just as soon stay where she is. I think she'd like to try working for you, you being related like. And she'd be near us.'

'I'll give her a good training,' Brenda promised. 'Show her everything. Will you send her round to see me?'

When Flo came shyly into the shop, she looked little more than a child. Brenda doubted that she'd please Gil with her cooking but she said she could do breakfasts and make stews and she was prepared to work all day for what Brenda paid her morning cleaning woman. She sacked Mrs Mudgely and took Flo on. She didn't want to pay out any more on wages.

Flo was always ready to make Gil a cup of tea and was capable of following recipes from a cookery book. She seemed to enjoy cooking. If she had a downside, it was that she didn't seem to notice untidiness and dirt. Brenda felt it gave her more cleaning to do herself, but her presence in the flat meant Gil's complaints stopped.

In the nurses' home, Ruth sat at her dressing table and fluffed a powder puff over her nose. She'd always thought her nose too big but now that she was growing older it no longer seemed to dwarf her other features as once it had. It was all in the mind of course, she'd come to accept now that she'd never be beautiful.

Her serious grey eyes stared back at her. She was wearing well considering she'd be thirty-seven this year. No lines yet, not even the faintest sign of them, but then she had the sort of skin that showed nothing, no lines and certainly no colour. She was afraid her cheeks were rather pasty.

She was getting ready to go out. A visit to the theatre or music hall was a monthly treat she took with her friends

Marjorie and Jean, other midwifery sisters. She was looking forward to it.

Ruth was not dissatisfied with her life, she enjoyed bringing babies into the world. She was good at it, and she liked the independence of having her own salary and her own room on the sisters' corridor.

She saw herself as being on the periphery of life; her involvement was her job, her role was to help others cope with their real-life traumas. She didn't want children of her own and she'd schooled herself not to want a husband because she wasn't the sort of woman who was likely to attract one.

Ruth felt she'd had a difficult childhood and adolescence, living over the fish shop, subject to her mother's acid tongue and with a younger sister who outshone her. It had probably been her own fault but everything had seemed to get on top of her following a crisis in the family when she'd been twelve. It had been an awful upset for them all. Dad had put his arms round her and said, 'Don't talk about Rosa. If anybody asks you, say you don't know. Don't tell them you found her. Most important of all, don't tell our Brenda, she doesn't know how to keep her mouth shut. We daren't trust her. Luckily she was at school at the time. This is between you and me and Mam. Don't even think about Rosa.'

'But I can't stop thinking about her, not when her baby's still here.'

'Think of Daisy as your little sister and put her mother right out of your mind. Our livelihood depends on your doing that. Promise me, Ruth. You're a big girl now, old enough to understand the importance of this.'

She'd promised, of course, and never spoken of that terrible happening to anyone, but she hadn't been able to put it out of her mind. It had haunted her, given her an occasional nightmare; it still could. Ruth shivered, it had made the family close ranks against the world.

Ruth peered into her mirror as she combed out her hair. She wore it up under her cap while she was on duty, so it made sense to keep it long, but in this day and age when everyone else was having it bobbed she wondered if she was too set in her ways. She thought about it often, but always put off making any decision. Now she fashioned it expertly into a French pleat up the back of her head. Brenda told her she was old for her years, but nursing turned girls into responsible beings at an early age.

Nursing was a great improvement on the fish shop. She and Brenda had both been brought up to help in the shop while they were at school. Mam had expected them to make it their life's work and had promised to leave the business to them in her will.

'Heaven forbid,' Brenda had spat at her. 'You can leave the lot to Ruth. I'm having nothing to do with the fish shop.'

Ruth had been talked into working there when she'd left school, though she hadn't wanted to. The prospect of doing it for the rest of her life had been daunting. It had been Brenda who had led the revolt against it, even though she was three years younger.

Ruth had admired Brenda's courage; they spent a lot of time together and were close, but at the same time she felt very ambivalent about her sister. Everything came more easily to Brenda. She had a fine, delicate complexion and small, well-balanced features; she was a very good-looking girl and knew it. Brenda couldn't avoid attracting attention, sometimes she made Ruth feel invisible. If they were standing side by side behind the fish counter the customers always approached Brenda. Everybody favoured her, she was popular with young and old. Ruth had even accused her parents of favouring Brenda and after that outburst had gone to weep on the bed they shared. Dad had come in and put an arm round her shoulders.

'We love you too, Ruth,' he'd said. 'We do try to treat you both the same, but now you've pointed it out, perhaps . . . That's the advantage beautiful people have over people like you and me, but if Brenda's got the beauty, you've got the brains. You'll always have a good brain while beauty fades with age. Just remember that when you're feeling envious.'

She thought now of how Brenda's delicate skin was already showing fine lines round her eyes.

'You must use the talents you've been given, Ruth, to get what you want from life,' Dad went on. 'You stick at things, I think you could do almost anything. I'll do my best never to favour Brenda again.'

'Dad, you do it all the time. So do I. There's something about Brenda that makes us all want to please her.'

'You must kick me if you see me overstepping the mark. I do it without realising.'

'I'm as bad as you are. It's a mystery to me why we all do it. It must be inbred.'

As a teenager Ruth had not been happy to see the boys she knew partnering off with her girl friends without giving her a second glance. It was even harder to bear when Brenda blossomed into a real beauty who could take her pick of any in the neighbourhood.

Ruth had been seventeen when Alec Jones had approached her, the first and only boyfriend she'd ever had. He'd been twenty at the time and told her she was the first girl he'd ever asked out. He'd not been handsome and, according to Brenda, no great catch either. She looked down on him because he was a railway ticket collector.

Ruth had enjoyed his company and they'd got on well together. Having a boyfriend of her own had given her confidence.

Alec had been a very serious young man and was attending night school classes to better himself. It had been his ambition to get into the railway offices, and she hadn't doubted that he'd do it one day. But in 1914 Alec had joined the army as a Kitchener volunteer and been killed within a month of going to France. She'd never found anyone to take his place although it was thirteen years now since he'd been killed.

Alec had persuaded Ruth to go to night school with him. She'd carried on after he'd been killed and at twenty years of age she'd taken her School Certificate. Even Mam had agreed she was too well-educated to work in a fish shop after that and this had made it easy for her to train as a nurse.

She'd spent four years at the Borough Hospital before coming to Grange Mount Maternity Hospital to do midwifery. She'd taken to nursing; it had been a delight to escape from the fish shop, wonderful to get away from trade of any sort. Ruth loved the middle-class atmosphere of Grange Mount. It had been a rather grand private house until 1846; a lovely Georgian building with a magnificent black and white stone floor in the large entrance hall. She felt settled and content here.

Ruth stood up and smoothed down her satin slip. She'd wear her blue costume tonight. It always made her feel smart to get out of uniform and her clothes never became shabby because they didn't get much wear.

She took the lipstick she'd bought herself from the drawer and then hesitated. Somehow lipstick didn't seem right on her lips; Mam had brought her up to think only fast women wore it. Brenda wore it, of course, and it made her look very pretty.

She heard a tap on her door. 'Come in, Marjorie.'

'Are you ready?'

Ruth was taking her mackintosh from the wardrobe. 'Almost.' She picked up her gloves.

'You haven't put your lipstick on yet.' Marjorie was wearing a deep plum shade, but she was almost a decade younger than Ruth.

Ruth turned back to her mirror, and slid the lipstick lightly over her lips. She hoped she was getting it on straight, she needed more practise. When she glanced at her reflection she wished she'd bought a paler colour, this looked a bit garish.

'That's more like it.' Marjorie smiled at her. 'Got to have a bit of glamour when we go out. Let's see if Jean's ready.'

It was a pleasant stroll from Grange Mount down to the Hippodrome in Grange Road. Ruth loved the air of excitement in the theatre. They were early and could watch the seats fill up. They liked the rear stalls and if they booked early enough they could be in the row immediately behind the most expensive seats in the theatre.

They always did themselves well, taking chocolate to eat during the performance and having coffee in the interval. Ruth watched people arriving in full evening dress, there was often somebody they recognised. A tall blonde caught her eye as she settled into her seat and slid her shoulders out of her furs to reveal a dark blue satin dress beneath.

'Mrs Foster.' Jean nudged her.

'She had twins last summer,' Marjorie added.

'Identical boy twins, I remember them.' Ruth smiled. The man three seats from that woman looked familiar too. From the back he resembled Gilbert. She watched as he turned sideways to speak to his companion. It might almost be Gilbert.

At that moment, the lights were lowered, and a hush fell upon the auditorium. Ruth sighed with pleasure as the performance began.

Brenda continued to feel tired and generally unwell as her pregnancy progressed.

'I think it would be better if you had a hospital delivery,' Ruth told her. 'Much the best place for you, and I'll be able to look after you.'

Brenda's doctor agreed, and as her blood pressure was continuing to rise, she found herself sent there five weeks before her baby was due.

'For bed rest,' they told her. 'You're doing too much at home.'

Daisy had always booked the district midwife and had her babies at home without any complications. She was making the same arrangements for this baby and looking forward to having her usual easy time. But when the midwife came to see her, she found her baby was lying in the transverse position.

'Is that bad?' Daisy asked.

'The baby's lying across your abdomen this way. The head is here when it should be down in your pelvis ready to be born by now.' She sent her to the clinic being held at Grange Mount Hospital.

'Can you do anything about it?' Daisy asked the doctor who examined her.

'Yes, I'll try and turn it round.' He tried to turn it by external manipulation and sent her home feeling rather bruised. A week later, the day before her baby was due, the midwife called again to see her and told her the baby had reverted to its original position. She sent her back to the hospital clinic which was being held that afternoon. An X-ray was ordered.

Then, because she was at term, Daisy was sent up to the antenatal ward where she was to rest overnight.

Brenda was already there and pleased to see her. Their beds were moved together when she told the sister on duty of their relationship. Gil and Ellis came visiting that evening and they had quite a jolly time. Ruth was on nights and at eight o'clock she came on duty and took charge of the hospital.

The next morning, Brenda felt distinctly under the weather. She had backache and couldn't eat her breakfast. Daisy was as lively as usual and was talking of being allowed back home when the doctor did his mid-morning round. But he told her that the placenta was in the wrong place and would prevent the baby being born normally. She'd need a Caesarean section and it would be done tomorrow morning.

'Under the circumstances, it's the safest method of delivery for both you and the baby.'

Brenda could see Daisy was downcast. 'Tomorrow isn't long to wait,' she told her. She was envious of that.

'But a Caesar . . . I'm not looking forward to that. I'm scared.'

'It's better than having to wait another five weeks like me. And I'll probably have to spend all that time here in this hospital bed. And I feel really ill. Worse than ever today. I wish it was all behind me and I had my daughter in my arms.'

Dinnertime came and Brenda toyed with the mutton stew she'd been given. She was waiting for her plate of rice pudding and prunes when she felt a twinge in her abdomen. She lay back against her pillows and wondered if she was starting in labour. She called one of the nurses over, hopeful that she, too, would soon have her ordeal behind her.

'Could be early labour but probably not,' was the verdict. Brenda was disappointed. 'You aren't due yet, anyway. Better for your baby if it stays where it is a bit longer.'

Brenda told herself she'd have to be patient, but being confined to bed and the regime of medication and four-hourly blood pressure readings was getting her down. She didn't feel well and the twinges were coming quite often and getting more painful. The midwife came to time them but said the pains had not settled into a regular pattern. She advised Brenda to try and go to sleep! As if she could.

Daisy had settled down to read a book. It was almost suppertime when she said she thought she was feeling her first labour pains. That brought the midwife to her bedside and speedy confirmation she was in labour. The obstetrician was summoned and he decided that the Caesarean section couldn't wait until tomorrow. Arrangements to do it would have to go ahead immediately. When the flurry round Daisy's bed died down and the trolley arrived to take her to theatre, Brenda felt envious.

She said, 'Good luck, hope you get a daughter this time.'

Daisy looked terrified as she was being wheeled away.

When Brenda doubled up with a really searing pain, the midwives at last agreed that she really was in labour too. She thought everything was going more easily for Daisy, for her it would all be over very soon.

Brenda counted that day as by far the worst in her life. Soon she was racked with terrible pains, and although the midwives gave her pethidine, it only dulled them a little. Gil came to sit by her bed in the visiting half-hour, but he looked acutely uncomfortable and didn't know what to say.

Her pains were so bad she could hardly speak to him, it was all she could do not to cry out.

She willed the hours to pass, wanting it to be eight o'clock so Ruth would come on duty and help her. She'd be more sympathetic than the day staff, Brenda knew she could count on her. At last she saw her coming round the beds, talking to each patient looking calm and collected.

'I can't stand much more of this,' she panted. 'I hope it isn't going to last much longer.'

Chapter Nineteen

Ruth listened to the day staff's report and was surprised to learn Daisy was in theatre undergoing a Caesarean section and Brenda was in labour. Such a coincidence that both should give birth on the same night, and particularly when she was in charge of the hospital. The staff were concerned about Brenda. She'd been in labour a long time and was making very slow progress.

Ruth did her routine round of the hospital. At the moment it appeared that only Daisy and Brenda would give birth during the night, though new admissions could come at any moment and alter the whole picture.

She could hear Brenda's cries from the ward door. When she saw her, she was clearly agitated. She'd known Brenda was not the sort who suffered pain in stoic silence. Ruth told the ward staff to take her to the labour ward so the other antenatal patients could be settled down for the night.

She organised the drug round and took the prescribed sleeping pills to each ward. Then went along to the labour ward to sit with Brenda for a little while in an attempt to calm her, but she had other duties to attend to and had to ask a junior to stay with her.

Back in her office, Ruth felt on edge. She'd delivered countless babies and felt very confident about doing it, but this time it was her own sister and that made a difference.

She knew just how much Brenda wanted this baby. Nothing must go wrong for her.

The phone rang. 'It's Gilbert, Ruth. How's Brenda?'

'No news yet, I'm afraid.' She could hear a babble of voices in the background. He wasn't sweating this out on his own.

'She was in quite a state when I came in at visiting time.'

'She's in the best place, Gil. We'll take good care of her.'

'It'll be born tonight?'

'Probably, but not for a while yet.'

'I do hope for Brenda's sake it's a girl. She's set her heart on a girl.'

Ruth shivered. 'Nothing we can do about it if it isn't.'

'You try telling Brenda that. If she wants something, she expects to get it. I don't know what she'll be like if it's a boy. Will you ring me, when there's news?'

'Yes, I'll let you know.'

'Whatever time of night it is. Don't worry about waking me up.'

Ruth shivered again as she put the phone down. Gil was right. Brenda was setting too much store on having a girl. It was hardly normal behaviour. She must know that nobody had any control over choosing the sex of their child. It wasn't reasonable to build her hopes up so high. Reasonable or not, she knew Gil was right, Brenda would be devastated if she didn't get what she wanted.

Ruth went down to the theatre and looked in through the glass in the door. Daisy was a mound under green sheets. She was just in time to see the baby being lifted out and handed to the midwife who wrapped her in a bath towel and lowered her into the special cot on wheels that was always taken into theatre when a Caesarean section was being performed. One of the doctors went over to assess the baby. The midwife had attached name tags and was pushing the cot out.

Ruth opened the door for her. 'Is it a girl?' She thought so but wasn't sure.

'A lovely little girl. Strong and healthy.'

'That'll please her mother, it's what she wanted.'

They were heading towards the nursery at breakneck speed.

'You are in a hurry.'

'My cousins are coming over to see me tonight and I'm late.'

Because Daisy had been taken down to theatre just before eight o'clock, one of the midwives on day duty had had to stay with her.

'You go, I'll take over now.'

'What about the register?'

'I'll fill that in after I've weighed her.'

'Thanks a lot, Sister.'

'How's the mother?'

'OK, no problems. They're just closing her up. She said the baby was to be called Jane if a girl. Here are the notes, such as they are. I've filled in the time of birth and the house officer said he'd be up later to write his bit in.'

'Right.'

Nurse Jolly, the midwife in charge of the nursery, was seeing that the babies had their ten o'clock feeds. She came to look at the new arrival. 'I'll bath her later.'

'Leave her for me,' Ruth told her. 'Her mother was brought up in my family, I think of her . . . Well, she's almost a sister and this handsome babe is almost a niece. I want to get to know her.'

When she'd got things ready, Ruth unwrapped the towel, admiring the baby's good colour and plump rounded limbs. Jane let out a lusty cry.

Daisy would have been disappointed if it had been another boy. Ruth placed her carefully on the nursery scales. Jane weighed in at seven pounds, four ounces. A perfect baby, lean and long, neither too small nor too big. Round blue eyes stared up into Ruth's face as she bathed her. Daisy should be very pleased.

Ruth was delighted for Daisy and glad she had only Brenda to worry about now. She looked in on the labour ward. Brenda was making heavy weather of it. She was making a lot of noise when the pains came and her blood pressure had shot up even higher.

'Help me,' she panted when she saw Ruth.

'You're doing fine,' Ruth told her gently. Brenda was frightened, her face was wet with sweat. She mustn't let her sister see she was worried.

Ruth had seen Max Harris the registrar obstetrician working in theatre; she'd worked with him for the last three years and found him easy to get on with. She picked up the internal phone and asked him to look at Brenda before he went home.

Now that her routine work for the early part of the night was over, Ruth could stay with her. She sent the midwife down for her supper and took her place. She did her best, encouraging Brenda to take the gas and air. She found her sister wasn't the easiest of patients.

Max Harris came then, still in his theatre greens. He looked hot and tired.

'Another Mrs Fox? Did I hear someone say she and the Caesar I've just done are sisters-in-law?'

'They are, but not only that, I'm related to them.' Ruth smiled at him as she explained. 'Brenda is my sister and the Caesar – she's almost a sister too.'

'Family night tonight, eh?'

'Yes, and somehow much more of a worry.' Ruth laughed wryly.

'You're emotionally involved, that's why.'

'Involved in every way. I've almost gone through this pregnancy with Brenda. I know just how much she wants this baby, she's desperate for it. You will do your best for her?'

'I do my best for them all, you know that.' He studied the charts they were keeping and then looked up at Ruth. 'But for your sister, since you ask, I'll do my very very best. I'll examine her to see how she's getting on.'

Brenda gasped, 'You've got to give me something for these pains.'

'I'm afraid the birth's too close to give you more pethidine now, Mrs Fox.' Max was at his most formal with her but rolled his eyes heavenwards at Ruth. 'It could harm your baby.'

'I've got to have it. Can't stand . . . any more. Ruth, you've got to . . .'

'Gas and air will help.' Ruth put the mask in her hand. 'Use it when you feel the next pain coming.'

'Oh my God, it's coming now.'

'Come on.' Ruth put the mask over her nose and mouth. 'Big breaths.' Brenda writhed in agony before collapsing back exhausted.

'Baby's well on its way, shouldn't take much longer,' Max Harris told her cheerfully.

Ruth left her with a midwife and led him back to the office.

'I can't stand much more of this either,' she said. 'You wouldn't believe how much more wound up I feel.'

'I can see you are.' He was smiling sympathetically.

'Is it my imagination or are the baby's heart sounds growing weaker?'

'They are. I was considering a Caesar for her too, but she's too far on to do it now.'

'She's never going to push this baby out without help.'

'No, she'll need forceps, probably high forceps. You get things ready. I'm going to see if they've kept some supper for me, I'm starving. I'll be back.'

'You won't be long, will you?'

He laughed. 'Half an hour at the most.'

Ruth bustled round making the necessary preparations, feeling quite nervous. Brenda's cries were going through her. She wanted to go away and leave it to the other midwife, and why not? The girl was perfectly capable, she too had delivered hundreds of babies.

Ruth hurried to the postnatal ward to see how Daisy was and then to her office to ring Ellis.

'Congratulations,' she said. 'You've got a lovely daughter this time.'

'A daughter? Daisy will be over the moon.'

'She's just back from theatre but not yet round from the anaesthetic. She's all right.'

'I can't believe it, a daughter at last. Daisy will be thrilled. I'm thrilled. When she wakes up, tell her I can't wait to see them both tomorrow.'

Ruth couldn't stay away from the labour ward. She ended up sitting by Brenda, holding her hand and murmuring words of encouragement. An hour later, the child was finally delivered by Max Harris using high forceps.

'It's a girl.' Ruth felt hot with relief that Brenda had delivered the daughter she so very much wanted, but the next second she saw that the baby was dusky blue and wasn't breathing.

'Help!' Ruth said as she gave the tiny bottom a sharp

slap. The shock made the baby take her first long juddering gulp of air.

Max Harris was beside her in an instant. 'Good, you've fixed it.'

'Oh God,' Brenda groaned, 'that was awful. Never, ever again!'

'You say that now,' he told her. It was his set piece, Ruth had heard it several times before. 'But you'll feel very different in a year or so.'

Ruth beckoned him back to the newborn infant lying on a warm towel. She'd cleared the air passages but Brenda's baby was not breathing well. He carried her to the resuscitation table where he aspirated her stomach contents and listened to her heart.

Ruth swallowed hard; the baby was a weakling, five weeks early and puny, she was afraid it wouldn't survive. She popped her quickly on the scales; four pounds seven ounces.

'Oxygen,' the doctor mouthed at her.

Ruth spent much of the night in the nursery, agonising over Brenda's baby, doing all she could for it. The two cots were side by side. Jane Fox, Daisy's child, strong and healthy, and Lorna Fox, a weakling struggling for breath. Ruth felt like crying. Brenda would compare the two children and weep too.

She lifted Brenda's baby out of her cot; she felt floppy and light. She'd been put to the breast but neither mother nor child had had the strength or inclination to achieve a feed. Ruth tried to get her to suck a few mouthfuls of boiled water but she was having none of it. This baby would have to be tube fed if she was going to get enough inside her to thrive.

Ruth's stomach muscles tightened with pity. She was

afraid, so very much afraid that Brenda's child would not survive. Brenda would be heartbroken. Ruth had tried so hard to help her conceive this child, and help her through a difficult pregnancy, and now . . . How would Brenda feel if it was all to be for nothing?

Mam and Dad too. They were looking forward so much to their first grandchild. They made much of Daisy's boys but Mam had never thought of Daisy as her own. It wasn't the same thing at all for them. Tenderly, Ruth put Brenda's baby back in her cot and lifted Daisy's out.

The difference in weight was marked. The difference in colour too. Daisy's baby was pink and healthy with lovely rounded limbs, while Brenda's had a red and wrinkled face and her skin looked loose on the tiny frame.

Ruth gulped. It didn't seem fair; if Brenda's child were to die . . . After such a difficult pregnancy and birth, she'd fear for Brenda's health.

Nothing seemed to go well for Brenda though she'd tried so hard. She was very unhappy, her husband was a continual disappointment. She couldn't rely on him for anything. Brenda really did need this daughter; she'd longed for her all these years and gone through so much to get her. If Brenda lost her it would be more than she could bear.

All her life, Ruth had watched her family do their best to give Brenda exactly what she wanted. The thought came to her unbidden. If only she could give Daisy's beautiful baby to her now . . .

Daisy was in a very different position. Everything had worked out miraculously well for her. She was happy with her three boys and a husband who doted on her. Daisy was well-balanced, she'd be better able to cope with a sickly baby and survive if the worst happened. One disappointment wouldn't put her back too far.

Ruth was fond of Daisy too, but Daisy would have no trouble getting pregnant again if she wanted to. She probably would in any case.

Ruth pushed her fingers under her starched headdress and scratched her head. Was it practical? Could it be done? Neither Daisy nor Ellis had seen their baby yet. Brenda had shown little interest in hers, but she would as soon as she recovered from the harrowing birth. Gilbert didn't yet know he was a father.

It so happened that she'd looked after both babies since they'd been born, no other midwife had been involved. Nurse Jolly was in charge here in the nursery, but she was looking after the other forty or so newborns in their canvas cribs. Most snuffled and mewed throughout the night but some demanded proper feeds. She'd nursed them and settled them down with drinks of water or gone to the wards to see if their mothers were awake and could feed them. Nurse Jolly's mind had not been on the Fox babies; she'd told Ruth about her visit to the cinema last night, every detail, including the entire plot of the film. Ruth could make sure she had no reason to do anything for the Fox babies for the rest of the shift.

She could feel her heart pounding. Could she? Dare she exchange the babies? It would mean so much to Brenda. Ruth hadn't yet filled in the birth register with the time of births and the babies' weight and condition, so that would be no problem, but she'd have to alter their case notes.

She laid them out on her desk to see what she'd have to do, and could hardly believe her good fortune. Jane's given name was not on her notes at all, she was called Baby Fox. She herself had written Lorna Fox on the cover of the other set, but she could easily replace the folder with a new one. As far as the records were concerned, it wouldn't be too difficult. But would she dare?

She hovered over the cot in which Brenda's baby was struggling for life; moved it under a light to see better. She was holding her own, her colour had improved and she was breathing a little more easily. She might just pull through, but Ruth knew she'd have to exchange them now or the opportunity would be gone. She inserted a tube into the tiny stomach and gave the baby an ounce of breast milk from their stock.

Max Harris had delivered both. Would he remember? Brenda was the fifth he'd delivered by forceps in the last twenty-four hours, he'd told her that when they'd got mother and child settled. He'd not seen the babies again. In the morning the paediatrician would take over their case. Would anybody remember under circumstances like that?

She felt sure it was perfectly possible.

Ruth looked round the nursery. It was a familiar sight, always a little creepy when the black of night pressed against the bare windows. With the lights turned down, the room was full of shadows and the soft mewling of the newborn. All she'd have to do was . . .

The nursery door was on a rod that closed it automatically after use. It was squeaking open. Ruth jerked back as Nurse Jolly swept in with another canvas cot.

'I thought I'd better bring Hector back. He was yelling his head off and I didn't want him to set the rest of them off. I put him in the linen room by himself but he's gone to sleep now. Hector, what a name to give a poor child, though he's living up to it already.' Nurse Jolly rarely stopped chatting. 'It's time for first tea.'

It was half past four in the morning, everybody had a half-hour break in the dining room before the routine rush started of morning tea, washes, medicines for the mothers and six o'clock feeds for the babies.

'You go, I'll relieve you here.' It was what Ruth needed above everything else. Half an hour alone here.

Nurse Jolly was peering down at Brenda's baby. 'How are the two Fox babies? Both born on the same night, that's a turn-up for the books isn't it?' She turned to look at Daisy's baby. 'Was this the forceps delivery?'

It encouraged Ruth that she'd got them mixed up. Nurse Jolly had come closer to them than anyone else but she hadn't registered the details.

'Yes, that's right.' Ruth tried to smile.

'She's a little beauty. Right, I'll be off for tea.'

As the door squeaked shut, Ruth crept across the nursery to the drawer where the name tags were kept. She wrote out a duplicate set for each baby.

Her hands were shaking slightly as she cut off the originals and fixed on the new. Jane Fox, Daisy's baby, was now Lorna. Brenda would have the lovely baby girl for which she'd craved. Her hopes and dreams would come true.

Ruth cut the old name tags to bits and flushed them down the staff toilet. She didn't want any incriminating evidence like that left about. She filled in a new file cover for Brenda's baby, cut the old one into pieces and didn't know what to do with them. They were far too big to go down the toilet. She pushed them into the bag she had brought over with her – she always brought her comb and powder puff and a novel to read, in case they were quiet.

Very carefully she wrote her notes on both babies, with the exchange in mind. Then she filled in the birth registers. The deed was done.

When Nurse Jolly came back from tea, Ruth went to see Daisy.

Daisy could hear a voice. Somebody was talking to her, but

she sounded a long way away. She struggled to open her eyes.

'Hello, Daisy. How d'you feel?'

It was Ruth, her face smiling down at her from between its folds of starched muslin.

'Drink . . .' Daisy felt her head being raised and cold clean water took some of the fur off her tongue. She felt more awake. 'Where am I?'

Ruth's smile widened. 'You've had a little girl. Just what you wanted.'

Of course! She half remembered. 'Did you tell me this before?'

'Yes, you were hardly round from the anaesthetic.'

'A girl?' Daisy felt better already. 'Lovely.'

'What are you going to call her?'

'Jane Myrtle Fox.'

'That's nice. I've told Ellis. He says to tell you he's delighted and can't wait to see you both at visiting tomorrow.'

It was only then that Daisy noticed it was still dark, and that her arm was strapped to a splint with a bottle of water or something dripping into her vein. It was very uncomfortable but, worse, she had a thick pad of wadding on her abdomen and that was very sore.

'You've had a Caesarean birth.'

'Awful. It hurts.'

'I'll get you something for the pain.'

'Can I see my baby?'

'She isn't very well, Daisy, I'm afraid. She weighs only four pounds seven ounces.'

Daisy felt a stabbing concern. 'She's going to be all right?'

'I hope so, but she's very frail. She's having oxygen to help her breathe at the moment, but I'll bring her up to see you in the morning.'

Daisy lay back on her pillows feeling dreadful. She'd thought this baby was going to be as big as the boys had been. The doctors had told her she was developing normally and would be perfectly all right. The only problem had been that the placenta was in the wrong place and blocking a normal birth. They'd told her a Caesar would solve everything, but it seemed it hadn't. She felt a tear roll down her cheek. She was still woozy, she could feel herself drifting off again.

Ruth went down to the dining room for tea but she couldn't eat. She was back in the office within ten minutes. She still had plenty to do.

She had her first misgivings when she remembered telling Ellis that he was the father of a beautiful little girl. She hadn't mentioned any problems with her breathing. And she hadn't got round to ringing Gilbert as she'd promised.

She lifted the phone and asked the operator to put her through to the clothes shop. It rang and rang but nobody answered it.

'Keep trying,' she told the operator, so it went on ringing, but the phone was in the back room behind the shop. Either Gilbert was sleeping like a log or he hadn't come home at all. From her point of view, it wasn't a bad thing.

Ruth felt a glow of achievement, this was going to work. There was only the midwife who'd handled Daisy's baby in theatre. She'd been very keen to get off duty and hadn't stayed around long enough to know the birth weight. The chances of her remembering that Jane Fox had been a big healthy baby were slight. It was unlikely that anybody would know the difference.

Her phone rang, it was Ellis. 'I haven't been able to sleep. Has Daisy come round from the anaesthetic all right?'

'She's doing fine, Ellis. I gave her your message. The baby, though, she's had breathing difficulties, she's not too well.' Ruth felt panic rising in her throat. Had she told Ellis his baby weighed seven pounds four ounces when he'd rung last night? She couldn't remember, but the birth weight was something everybody wanted to know.

'She's poorly?'

'Yes, she is rather.'

'Daisy's upset about it, isn't she?'

'Yes, though she's still drowsy from the anaesthetic, still drifting in and out.'

'Oh dear! What did the baby weigh?'

Ruth swallowed hard and closed her eyes. She prided herself on being truthful and honest; telling lies didn't come easily. 'Four pounds seven ounces.'

'Oh! Small then.'

'Very small. She's a bit frail, Ellis, I'm afraid, but she's held her own overnight.'

'Tell Daisy I've rung again, will you? And I do hope the baby—'

'She'll be well looked after.' Ruth was used to offering words of comfort to anxious parents. 'By the way, Brenda's had her baby too. Another girl and they're both fine. Would you give the news to Gilbert? Tell him I tried to ring him in the night but he didn't answer his phone.'

Daisy was not feeling too good. It was ten o'clock in the morning by the time she felt fully awake, and all along the ward new mothers were feeding their babies.

'Can I see my baby?' she asked a passing nurse. She couldn't wait to hold her new daughter. Always before she'd held the baby within minutes of the birth, and being at home and surrounded by her family she'd been able to do that as often as she'd wanted to. It wasn't good to be in hospital like this, recovering from an operation.

The nurse was returning with her baby at long last. Daisy craned forward to catch her first glimpse and held out her arms. Such a lightweight. She couldn't believe how tiny she was.

'How much does she weigh?'

'Haven't they told you?'

'I can't remember.'

'She was four pounds seven ounces.'

'Is that all?' Daisy was shocked.

She listened as the midwife explained that it was possible to rear babies of low birth weight these days and that her daughter could grow up to be a perfectly normal child and a healthy adult. It was just that Jane might be a delicate child and would need great care and attention over the first year or so.

Daisy felt cold inside and found that hard to believe. She'd been so sure this baby would be a healthy seven or eight pounds like the others. It had felt the same to her. She'd done nothing different. She stared down at the scrap of humanity lying in her arms and felt moved with pity that she was having such a poor start in life. She hugged her closer, stroked her head of soft down.

The midwife came back to her bed. 'Come on, aren't you going to try feeding her? This one will need feeding up. Let's have you sitting up straighter. You fed your other babies yourself?'

Daisy felt herself being pulled higher up her bed.

'That's better. I gave baby some boiled water but she wasn't keen on the bottle. Come on now, my little love, you get going on this.'

Daisy tried to suckle baby Jane but she wasn't interested, she kept falling asleep in her arms.

'We might have to tube feed her for a day or two,' the midwife said. 'But it's better to try.' She clamped the baby back on the breast and sat over them for a while but even she couldn't get the baby to suck.

'Neither of you is strong enough yet.' She picked up Jane to take her back to the nursery. 'So you can rest,' she told Daisy.

The other mothers had their babies in the swinging canvas cots at the foot of their beds. Daisy would have liked to have had hers there too.

Chapter Twenty

Ruth got into bed that morning feeling overwhelmed by what she'd done. Had she really had the nerve to change those babies over? She'd been on permanent night duty for seven months now and had thought she'd mastered the art of sleeping during the day. This morning she couldn't, her mind raced.

What had seemed so easy and right in the dark hours of the night, now in the harsh light of morning seemed an outrageous thing to do. She'd had no right. She'd acted like God.

Impossible now to believe she'd get away with it. Baby Jane looked a typical premature baby, she had breathing difficulties, the normal assumption would surely be that her lungs weren't mature enough for normal respiration. Yet Daisy had had a normal full-term pregnancy.

And Brenda's baby born five weeks premature had weighed in at a healthy weight for a full-term child. Lorna looked and acted like a full-term baby. Surely somebody would notice and assume the two Fox babies had been mixed up by accident? Possibly blood tests could prove it.

Ruth shivered. If questions were asked about the possibility of a mistake being made, the blame must fall upon her. She had signed the register for both births; she'd looked after both babies, keeping Nurse Jolly jealously at a distance. When she went on duty tonight, surely Matron would ask questions.

Ruth turned her face into her pillow. Useless to tell herself she'd been programmed to put Brenda's needs ahead of those of other people, certainly above her own. She always had, the whole family had. It had been a fact of life at the fish shop.

Her bedroom curtains glowed pink; shafts of sunlight were coming round them, lighting up her room. It was useless to tell herself that Daisy would understand. She'd been brought up to put Brenda's needs before her own too, but this was asking too much. Ruth could see now that she'd deprived Daisy of her own child, and condemned her to a long struggle to bring up Brenda's weakling, possibly to watch that child die in infancy.

She comforted herself with the thought that Daisy would do a better job than Brenda. She was motherly by nature and had had plenty of experience. If the baby could be reared, Daisy would do it, and she would have a wonderful home with Daisy. And Brenda would be happy; she'd been given a pretty and healthy baby, exactly what she'd craved for all these years.

Perhaps she shouldn't have done it. It was certainly not good for her own peace of mind, but both babies were still within their own families. Gilbert and Ellis were brothers and Brenda and Daisy almost sisters. The two families had tight bonds, the babies would each know their natural parents. Anyway, what she'd done could not be undone now. Not by her. Daisy must never know.

Daisy felt she'd dozed away most of the day. She'd been half asleep when Ellis had come to her bedside and kissed her at visiting time that evening.

'All these drips and things.' He looked quite shocked as he stared at the needle running into a vein in her elbow and the metal splint behind it. 'I didn't know you'd have to have all this.'

'I'm all right. Ruth said it would all come down tomorrow. Nothing to worry about, not as far as I'm concerned. It's the baby.' She tightened her lips in distress.

Ellis felt for her hand. 'Where is she? I expected to find her here with you.'

'They're keeping her in the nursery.'

'I haven't seen her yet. Ruth said she was frail. How has she been today?'

'I get the feeling they're worried about her, but they say they're keeping her in the nursery until I've recovered enough to look after her. I'll be glad when Ruth comes back on duty tonight, she'll tell me honestly. Why don't you ask the nurse if you can see her now? Perhaps she'll tell you how she's getting on.'

Daisy looked round the ward as she waited for him to come back. There were ten beds in it and at each one, doting parents were engrossed in their new babies. She could see Brenda and Gil down at the bottom end. When Ellis came back he looked very serious.

'Poor little mite.' His eyes were bright with unshed tears. 'Perhaps I've let the babies come too quickly one after the other.'

'No, it isn't that, there's two years between Peter and Jane, much longer than—'

'I know, but why did this happen? They told me they were having to feed her by tube.'

'It's my milk they're giving her. She isn't strong enough to suck, she won't take as much as she should.'

'The nurse said she's lost a bit of weight. She isn't even four pounds seven now.'

'That's awful!'

'Not as bad as it sounds. She said all babies lose weight when they're first born and little Jane will soon start gaining on what they're putting into her.'

'I'm bothered that her chest rattles and bubbles. They seem to see that as more of a problem.'

'Such a worry.' Ellis squeezed her hand.

'She's lovely though, isn't she? And we did so want a daughter.'

When the bell rang to signal the end of the half-hour and the visitors had reluctantly gone, Brenda came down to talk to Daisy.

'I had a terrible time,' she confided. 'I can hardly walk now.'

'At least they let you try,' Daisy sighed. 'I'm all hooked up to this contraption, they won't let me out of bed.'

'I don't know how you can face having babies; four of them in such quick succession. It's an awful process.'

'This might cure me of wanting more.' Daisy pulled herself painfully up the bed. 'I wish they'd let me have mine with me. Is yours asleep? I'd love to see her.'

'At least you're spared the hassle of nappy changing.'

Daisy smiled. 'You'll soon get used to that.'

'I'll fetch her to show you. She's easily the prettiest baby here.'

Brenda came back proudly displaying her infant. 'I'm made up with my Lorna,' she said. 'The nurses keep telling me to put her down in her cot, that I mustn't nurse her so much. They say I'll spoil her and she'll expect it all the time.'

'Can I hold her?'

Daisy thought she felt solid, her movements were strong. 'The weight of her!'

'Seven pounds four.'

Daisy smiled down at her, bemused. 'She's absolutely gorgeous.' The sort of baby she'd expected to have herself. Not unlike Peter when he was first born.

'She's greedy, a real guzzler, and she doesn't cry much.'

Daisy sighed. 'She'll be much easier to look after than my poor little Jane.'

Ruth had tossed and turned for most of the day, her mind fluttered round and round the enormity of what she'd done to Daisy. She felt a bag of nerves and was scared of going back on duty. When faced with it, she couldn't eat her breakfast of sausage and tomato.

She had to force herself to knock on the door of Matron's office that night and her stomach felt as though it was full of crawling crabs. She fully expected to be told that somebody was suggesting a mix-up between the Fox babies.

She was so tense she hardly took in what she was being told, knowing only that what she'd dreaded wasn't happening. Ruth did her routine round of the hospital feeling light-headed, hardly knowing what she was saying to the patients.

Brenda was filled with delight that she had such a pretty daughter. Ruth tried to take comfort from that. She had to force herself to pause for a few moments at Daisy's bed. She'd think it odd if she didn't, but it was one of the hardest things she'd ever had to do.

She heard her name being called as she went down the corridor, and when she turned and saw the house officer who'd been on duty last night hurrying to catch up with her, she began to shake. He'd seen both the Fox babies and their mothers last night and had a continuing responsibility for their care.

'About that baby, Jane Fox,' he said.

It made Ruth stop breathing, but he went on to mention some slight change in her treatment. Ruth was struggling to pull herself together when he went on to talk about another baby.

She was sweating when she got back to the office. Twenty minutes passed before she felt capable of putting out the sleeping tablets. There were no patients about to give birth tonight and Max Harris wasn't in the hospital, but she wasn't looking forward to seeing him again. Surely he'd notice.

She didn't know how she got through the next two days and nights. So far there'd been no trouble, but the thought of seeing Max Harris again was still hanging over her. She was scared he'd question her about the Fox babies.

When she went on duty on the third night, she found the theatre was being set up for another Caesarean section and he'd been called in to do it. Ruth stayed well away but just before midnight he came to the office to see her.

'Straightforward case, should be no complications.' He flung himself down in the chair opposite her desk and smiled at her. She sensed he'd got the business part said and something different was coming. Ruth felt herself freeze up inside. She could almost see the question on his lips.

'I was thinking, the other night . . .' She gripped the edge of the desk with stiff fingers.

'You said you enjoyed ballet. I've got two tickets for *Swan Lake* at the Royal Court in Liverpool. It's not until next month. I was going to take my mother for her birthday but Dad got in first, he's booked to take her on holiday. Would you be offended if I asked you to come instead? Will you be able to get that night off?'

Ruth couldn't speak, the office was spinning round her.

'How about it? Will you come with me?' He was looking at her with dark eager eyes.

'No,' she gasped. 'No.' She couldn't! Couldn't possibly. Not with Max Harris. 'No, I'm sorry, terribly sorry, I've agreed to do something else. So sorry.'

She knew she was flustered and not saying the right things.

He was looking at her more closely. 'It's not until the twenty-eighth of next month. It's a touring company . . .'

Ruth was paralysed with terror. 'No, no.'

'I thought you said you liked ballet. Didn't you tell me you went to see *Nutcracker* last year?'

'Did I? Yes, of course I did. I loved it.'

'Then it's me? You couldn't spend a whole evening in my company?'

'No, no. It isn't like that, I like you.'

'Is something the matter, Ruth?'

'No.' She let out a long juddering sigh. 'I'll be all right in a moment. I'm sorry.'

He was getting to his feet. 'Nothing I can help with?'

She shook her head and swallowed hard. 'Just leave me alone for five minutes.'

Ruth covered her face with her hands and continued to shake.

Oh God! She'd thought he was asking about the Fox babies. She'd thought the axe was about to fall on her neck. It had never occurred to her that he might ask her out.

What had she done? He must think her very strange. Totally round the bend. How was she ever going to face him again?

Daisy felt it was taking her much longer to recover from the birth this time. Brenda was discharged with her baby a week before Daisy was allowed to go, but even then baby Jane was not well enough to go with her.

Daisy was glad to be home and have her family round her, but every day she went back to the hospital to see her daughter, taking a supply of her own milk. She was pleased that Jane was making progress and was now able to take feeds from a bottle. Every day, she tried to teach her to take the breast.

Jane was five weeks old when she reached five pounds in weight and was deemed strong enough for Daisy to manage. She was excited about having her home at last, but a bit anxious too.

'You've been wonderful to me,' she told Ruth. 'I don't know how to thank you.'

Daisy thought Ruth seemed quite embarrassed by her praise, but she really had found her helpful.

'Will you pop in to see us from time to time? I might need more help, you know all about babies.'

'Only the newborn,' Ruth said quickly. 'You probably know more about older ones. This is your fourth, you're an experienced mum.'

'Jane's so frail, what if she gets ill?' Daisy pleaded. 'It didn't matter what I did with the boys, they thrived and were healthy. They hardly needed looking after.'

'If you want me to,' Ruth said.

'You know I do.'

So Ruth got into the habit of calling in regularly on her nights off. Daisy was always pleased to see her and they'd sit drinking tea and talking, not only about baby care but everything else that interested them. Daisy found her mother-in-law was a great help too.

'I'm so thrilled to have a granddaughter. Boys seem to run in this family, girls have always been scarce.'

'You had two daughters,' Daisy said.

'Yes, little Jane reminds me of them. The boys were all as strong as oxes but the girls . . .'

Daisy didn't want to think of what had happened to Ellis's sisters, it made her feel even less confident about the future.

Between them, Daisy and Dora nurtured baby Jane. She didn't sleep well and Daisy was up several times every night with her. She was difficult to feed and often chesty through the first months. When Jane caught croup, Daisy telephoned Ruth and asked her to come. Ruth was on the doorstep early the next morning as soon as she came off duty. Daisy found her very supportive and felt closer to her than she'd ever been before.

To Brenda, Lorna was exactly the daughter she'd envisaged having, even down to the fair curly hair and blue eyes. She thought her very pretty and spent a good deal of time and energy on finding beautiful clothes for her to wear. She bought a handsome baby carriage to take her out so others could admire her too.

Brenda found quite soon that Lorna was hard work. She put her on the bottle as soon as she got her home but that turned out to be even more work than breast-feeding had been.

That Lorna woke up for feeds in the night hadn't seemed a big problem while she was in hospital and could spend all day in bed, but now Brenda was home she felt the broken nights were making her tired and grumpy the next day.

'It wouldn't hurt you to take a turn,' she told Gilbert. 'You could get up and give her a bottle.'

But Gilbert disliked getting out of bed in the night. He pretended to be asleep when the baby cried. Brenda had always thought him lazy.

'You leave everything to me,' she complained when Lorna's cries finally drove her out of her warm bed. 'You're bone idle, that's your trouble.'

'You wanted the baby, not me,' he grunted. 'This was your idea.'

Brenda began to wonder if it had been such a good idea after all. Her life had changed completely, she didn't feel entirely in control of things now.

Ruth had helped to move their parents into a smart, newly built semi-detached house in St David's Road. It was close to the park and in a real residential district with not a shop in sight. It was exactly the sort of house Brenda would have liked for herself.

It was near enough for her to push the pram so she took Lorna up several times a week. She always went if she knew Ruth would be there on her nights off. Her sister loved to feed and change the baby and that gave her a little break. Her mother was missing the shop and feeling she needed more to do. She made a big fuss of Lorna too.

'Our first grandchild,' she said, bouncing her up and down on her knee.

'Daisy has four,' Ern protested, 'and she's always brought them for us to see.'

'Lovely children,' Glad agreed. 'But this is our first real grandchild.' She held her up to look more closely at her.

'A beautiful baby, Brenda. Funny though, now her hair's growing, it's more like Daisy's. Really tight curls. Where did they come from? Not from either you or Gilbert.'

'Must be a throwback.'

Ruth got to her feet with a jerk and said, 'I'll put the kettle on for tea.'

'What's the matter with her?' Glad wanted to know.

'She'd like to have a daughter like mine,' Brenda smirked

with satisfaction. 'I expect she feels life is passing her by.'

Ruth knew there'd be no way she could avoid Max Harris. A week later, he was still working in the labour ward when she went on duty. She'd had time to work out what she needed to say to him.

'You must think me very rude, it was very kind of you to ask me out and I turned you down with such awful emphasis.'

'You wouldn't change your mind?' His eyes were pleading now. 'You weren't planning another night out with the girls? I saw you at the Argyle with a couple of sisters not so long ago.'

Ruth had been taken aback at being invited. Now she was surprised that he'd noticed her at the Argyle when she hadn't seen him.

'I go out every month with Croft and Marshall.' But she'd arranged to go with them on a different night, and anyway, she'd much prefer to go out with Max Harris. He was attracting a good deal of attention from the nursing staff.

'They can go without you for once. Take pity on a lonely man and come with me?'

Ruth swallowed hard. Her smile wavered.

'Come on, Brenda.' Gilbert was out of bed and getting dressed. 'It's nearly nine o'clock. The girls will be on the doorstep at any minute.'

Brenda turned over, feeling heavy with sleep. She'd been up twice in the night giving Lorna her bottles and had fallen into a deep sleep at half past six.

'You let them in,' she gasped.

'Get up, you can't stay in bed now, the baby's awake.'

Brenda could hear her billing and cooing happily to herself.

'She's all right.'

'But for how long? I want some breakfast, I've got to go to work.'

Brenda settled back on her pillows. 'Get your own breakfast, I'm whacked. You could bring me a cup of tea for a change.'

The next moment she felt the bedclothes being ripped off her. She howled with annoyance and tried to grab at them but missed.

'Come on, get yourself dressed.' Gilbert sounded irritable.

'I have to sleep when the baby sleeps. I'd never get my rest if I didn't.'

'Screaming like that, I'm surprised you haven't set the baby off.' The door slammed behind him.

With the bedclothes in a heap on the lino, Brenda decided she might as well get up. Slowly, she set about making herself ready for the day. She fastened on her watch; it was nearly ten past nine. She pulled a face. Sally was late this morning, she was getting lax. At that moment the doorbell rang through the building, and the baby made a more plaintive sound, somewhere between a moan and a cry.

Brenda hastened to fasten her blouse. She'd hoped to have had her breakfast before Lorna needed feeding again. She let out another stronger cry, she'd be going full blast in a moment.

Gilbert was coming back upstairs; she could hear two lots of footsteps and voices too. It was Flo who'd come not Sally. Brenda felt a surge of irritation that Sally was late. The shop ought to open on time. The bedroom door crashed back as the baby opened her mouth to let the world know she wanted more food.

Gilbert said, 'Flo's brought a message from Sally. She isn't coming in today, she's got a cold.'

'Oh hell!'

'If you want to sell anything in that shop of yours, you'd better get down and open it up.'

He slammed the door shut as Lorna wailed for her bottle. Brenda hurriedly combed her hair and applied a powder puff to her nose.

'You're not due for more milk until ten,' she told Lorna irritably. 'You'll just have to wait.' The baby didn't like being kept waiting, her face was becoming scarlet and damp. Her cries followed Brenda to the kitchen. She poured herself a cup of tea. Flo had the breakfast bacon sizzling in the pan and the scent was making her feel hungry.

'Do what you can for the baby,' she told her fourteen-year-old maid.

'Shall I give her a bottle?'

'Can you make one up?'

'I think so. Me mam fed all hers herself but our Kennie was never satisfied. He used to have bottles as well.'

'Half and half cow's milk and boiled water with two teaspoons of sugar,' Brenda told her before shooting downstairs. It was twenty past nine, there were two women waiting on the step.

'Yer late opening,' one complained. 'I wouldn't have waited except I've got to have a new dress. That green one in the window. Can I try it on?'

Flo was close behind her in the shop. 'How much milk does she take?'

'As much as possible, or she'll be yelling again before you can turn round.'

Brenda was beginning to think that having a baby to look after was less fun than she'd supposed. The pretty dresses she bought her had soon become soiled and the ribbons were not easy to iron. Lorna made more work than she'd ever thought possible. She was so demanding, wouldn't wait a moment for her milk, and there were all her smelly napkins to wash when she did settle down. Brenda could hear her crying from down here. After about ten minutes there was a merciful silence. Flo must have managed to make her a bottle. Thank goodness for Flo.

Brenda found the morning strangely soothing. She much preferred to run the shop than look after a baby. It was quiet and orderly and she loved showing the smart clothes she'd chosen to her customers.

Sally was off work for a week, and no sooner did she come back than Ida, the afternoon girl, went off with what appeared to be a similar cold. Brenda felt peeved. Here she was paying for help in the shop and then having to do the work herself. When a week or two later Sally stayed off again and sent a message with Flo that she had a sore throat, Brenda lost her temper. She sent Flo back with a message telling Sally that if she wasn't in the shop within the hour she'd give her the sack. A worried Flo returned alone.

Flo seemed to have a way with babies and loved sitting down to feed Lorna. Brenda decided Flo could be nanny to the baby and she'd run the shop herself in the mornings. Flo had plenty of energy and was willing to make bacon sandwiches and cups of tea as well. She was turning out to be a reasonable cook and was good at stews and casseroles. Brenda took care of the baby in the afternoons while Flo cooked a hot dinner for them and tidied up.

In the shop, the afternoons tended to be busier than the mornings Although Brenda had Ivy to help, it meant she had to spend a lot of time there herself. Usually, Lorna seemed quite happy to sleep in her cradle in the back room, and if she cried while Brenda was busy, a customer would sometimes pick her up to comfort her.

Once a rather overbearing customer had told her it was wrong to keep the child in the shop and she was neglecting her. She'd stalked out without buying the expensive outfit she'd chosen. It had infuriated Brenda that she'd found out the hard way that a crying baby could put customers off.

Lorna was letting fly one afternoon and Brenda was doing her best to quieten her when Daisy called in.

'Mother wants to know if the dress she asked you to order has come in yet.'

'No, not yet.'

Suddenly the shop seemed to fill with customers who needed her attention. Daisy took the baby into her own arms and whispered, 'Shall I take her for a while? We're going to the park. It's a fine afternoon, an outing would do her good.'

Brenda could see Olive through the window waiting with Daisy's boys and a pushchair. She was keeping an eye on the big pram that had served Fox babies a generation ago.

'Oh, if you would. Lorna's pram is out in the shed at the back.'

'I'll put her head to toe with Jane. Room for two in ours, one of the good things about an old-fashioned pram.'

Brenda sighed with relief when she saw the cavalcade of pram, pushchair and two toddlers move off. She didn't know how Daisy could cope with so many children.

Ruth had not felt on an even keel since she'd switched the babies. It was always on her mind. She was edgy and irritable with her patients and the contentment she'd always felt was gone.

At last her four nights off had come round and she'd slept all day. She was looking forward to her outing with Max Harris but tonight she was changing into her green dress and coat to go out with her friends. She'd told Brenda she was going to the Hippodrome again tonight and she'd seemed envious.

'I never go anywhere these days,' she'd complained.

'Get Gil to take you,' Ruth had advised. She noticed her sister was looking miserable. 'You could take the baby across to Daisy's for once, she'll look after her.'

Brenda pulled a face. 'It wouldn't be for once. Daisy takes her out most afternoons now.'

Ruth caught her breath; it made her knot up inside to hear Brenda admit she was regularly handing the baby back to her real mother, after she'd gone to such lengths to give Lorna to her.

'You should have told me how much work babies make,' Brenda complained. 'With one to look after, it's almost impossible to do anything else.'

Ruth couldn't stop herself retorting, 'Daisy makes light of it and she has four.'

Little snippets of conversation like this were driving home to Ruth that although Brenda had said she was longing for a baby, she hadn't much mothering instinct.

Ruth felt the walk down to the Hippodrome had cleared her head. She told herself she must put Brenda and the babies out of her mind or she'd go mad. Tonight she'd try. Nothing was required of her but that she enjoy herself. They were a party of four. Her usual companions Jean and Marjorie, and Marjorie's sister who worked at the Children's Hospital was coming with them as well.

Once inside the theatre where she could watch the audience finding their way to their seats, Ruth felt herself beginning to unwind. She let her gaze travel down the rows to the seats in the front circle. The man she'd thought resembled Gilbert was here again in almost the same seat.

But if it was Gilbert, it certainly wasn't Brenda he was with. Probably just a trick of the light. There was the usual expectant hush in the auditorium as the lights were dimmed and Ruth sat back to enjoy the show. It was a dramatic play that engrossed her from the start.

When the interval came, Ruth's mind was still in the fictional world. Marjorie led her off to get their customary coffee. Ruth was carrying two cups back when she came face to face with Gilbert on his way to the bar.

It was so unexpected that a wave of coffee slopped into both saucers. Her first feeling was of disbelief, but it really was Gilbert! He was laughing down at the girl on his arm. A pretty dark-haired girl she didn't know. Ruth pulled herself together.

'Hello, Gilbert.' She watched his mouth drop open. He was horrified that she'd seen him here. The guilt was plain on his face. He pushed past her without saying a word.

She was shaking when she sat down. She had more coffee in the saucers than she had in the cups. Jean laughed at her clumsiness and carefully poured hers back. Ruth felt numb with shock. It must have been Gilbert she'd seen the last time they'd come here. No wonder Brenda had looked unhappy and was complaining he never took her out. He had another woman!

She felt as though she'd been kicked, and if she felt like this, how would Brenda feel? Another terrible thought came: did Brenda know? Ruth didn't think so, surely she'd have confided in her if she did.

When the next act started, Ruth couldn't concentrate. What did stories matter when real life had taken such a twist? She felt heavy with guilt herself. She'd been worried about switching the babies before this. And now? Clearly baby Lorna would have been better off left with her own mother.

Ruth felt she'd robbed her of doting parents and a happy family life, and for what?

She'd thought of it as doing her best for Brenda, but Brenda's marriage no longer looked safe and she wasn't looking after the baby properly. She preferred to spend her time in the shop, she wasn't really interested in babies. She'd changed her mind about them just as she'd changed her mind so often in the past about other things. Brenda wasn't cut out for motherhood.

When the play finished, Ruth clapped like an automaton with the rest of the audience and pretended an enthusiasm she didn't feel. She went with the other sisters to have a ham sandwich and a cup of tea at the Copper Kettle because that was what they usually did. She knew she wasn't herself, she had to say she had a headache when Marjorie asked her if something was the matter. She was glad when it was time to walk back to the hospital. She wanted to be alone in her room, but once in bed she couldn't sleep. Her head was going round with the wrong she'd done.

Ruth shuddered, she'd half expected baby Jane to die, as she'd seen so many other sick babies do. But Daisy had managed to bring her through the first dangerous months and she was beginning to thrive. Perhaps what she'd done wasn't such a bad thing for Jane.

All the same, Ruth felt she'd give anything to have the babies back in their rightful homes. What would Daisy think of her if she knew the truth?

The horror of what she'd done was threatening to overwhelm her.

Chapter Twenty-one

Ruth had to drag herself out of bed the next morning: she felt sleep sodden and sick. This was the day Max Harris was to take her to the ballet. She didn't feel up to it and wished she'd never agreed to go.

She thought about ringing him to say she wasn't well, but she hadn't the energy to go down to the phone. Her parents were expecting her to spend the next few days with them. It was lunchtime before she got there.

'Where've you been till now?' her mother demanded. 'Another minute and we'd have started without you.'

Ruth had no appetite and found it a struggle to eat. Her mind swirled with worry about the babies she'd switched and Brenda's marriage. Afterwards, she went out in the garden and felt she'd wasted a rare day off by falling asleep in a deck chair.

'It's time you came off night duty,' her mother said. 'You don't know whether it's day or night.'

By evening, she felt like a zombie but she had to get herself ready to go out. Her face looked pale and strained as she put on her lipstick. She thought it made her look like a painted clown and wiped it off again. She'd arranged that Max Harris would pick her up here, so she had to go.

He came in his car so he could drive them to the station. He seemed more of a stranger without his white coat, but

Mam was very impressed. Ruth found him in a jolly mood, which made her own misery seem worse.

She was faced with another meal in a restaurant, and could only get a little of it down.

'You've got a bird-like appetite,' Max told her. Fortunately, he had plenty to say, though Ruth could not have said what he talked about. She was nervous and on edge and unusually silent.

Once the theatre lights were dimmed, she felt a little better. The beautiful music touched her. On the way home she was able to talk about it. She told him she'd enjoyed it and thanked him prettily.

But she'd been stiff and silent, and she didn't think Max would want to repeat the outing.

As the months rolled on, Ruth was finding it harder to concentrate on her work. She was forgetting the most obvious things and was not as efficient as she used to be. She felt she was losing control. Matron told her she didn't look well and asked if she was able to sleep during the day.

'No,' Ruth admitted; she was finding it very difficult.

'Mr Harris thinks you may have been on night duty too long. He said you don't seem yourself.'

'I'm all right.' She had been on permanent night duty now for almost a year.

'Perhaps you've done long enough,' Matron said. 'We have to think of your health.'

Ruth found day duty no easier. Her mind was going round in circles and she was tortured with guilt. She was in a downward spiral from which she couldn't pull out. She hadn't been sleeping during the day but she wasn't able to sleep at night either. She was still lying awake, scared that sooner or later the truth would come out. Always, she wondered what she could do to put things right.

She could tell Brenda and Daisy, of course, but the very thought of doing that made her go cold all over. She couldn't see Brenda accepting her own child now. Jane wasn't nearly as attractive or as rewarding as the baby she had, and Brenda was paying scant attention to Lorna's needs. Ruth had expected Brenda to be a loving mother and she wasn't.

And as for Daisy, Ruth wanted to cry when she thought of the harm she'd done to her and her baby. Daisy had every right to be furious with her. More than furious. What she'd done was unforgivable.

Yet she'd done it with the best of intentions. She'd done it for Brenda's sake; she'd always loved her and been close to her. Ruth had wanted to help her, but she hadn't helped Daisy and she loved her too.

Ruth couldn't stay away from either of them now. She had an uncontrollable urge to visit to offer advice of any sort. As if help with the everyday matters of baby care could cancel out the harm she'd done.

Everything was going wrong. She'd felt sick since the night she'd seen Gil out with another woman. Poor Brenda, Ruth was full of pity for her and for the baby, who couldn't possibly be in a happy home now.

It took Ruth some time to get round to the idea of talking to Gilbert. He knew she'd seen him. It was only right she should protest on Brenda's behalf after seeing him behaving so wantonly. She could threaten to tell her sister. She needn't be ham-handed over it, she could point out that Brenda needed his support now she had a baby to bring up as well as the shop to run.

The thought of doing it frightened Ruth. She'd never found Gilbert an easy person to get on with. But this was something she could do in her role as helper and she was never one to baulk at doing her duty. She'd need to get him on his own, of course, but that needn't be difficult.

She'd called to see Daisy so often she knew she'd find her working in the office during the morning. She'd seen enough of Gil to know he was often about the yard or the office at that time. Ruth decided she'd go when she had a morning off duty. She'd leave it until shortly after midday when Daisy went upstairs to her children. She'd have a word with Gil first and then pop in on Daisy.

When it came to the point, Ruth had crawling crabs in her stomach again. She spent most of her off duty that morning trailing round Robb's department store looking at the clothes they had for sale, though she was in no mood to buy anything. She was watching the time carefully as she walked down to Camden Street. Shortly after midday she was in the undertaker's reception area.

'Mrs Fox might have gone upstairs by now,' Enid told her. She recognised Ruth as family.

'I'll find her,' Ruth said and went on down the passage. She was in luck, the office door was ajar and she could see Gilbert sitting at his desk. She'd known he might be out driving, in which case she'd have had to do this over again.

She needed all her willpower to go on. She felt she had to for the sake of Brenda and the baby. She saw this as going some way to offset the harm of switching the babies. She tapped on the door and pushed it open. Gil had a newspaper spread out on the desk before him; he straightened up in the chair. He was not pleased to see her.

'Daisy's gone upstairs,' he said, pulling a ledger in front of him.

'It's you I want to talk to. About the other night when I saw you at the Hippodrome.'

The muscles in his face tightened. He said aggressively, 'What about it?'

'Who was that woman you had on your arm?' As soon as the words were out, Ruth knew she was going about this the wrong way.

'That's none of your business. I don't want to talk about my affairs. Not to you.'

'It is my business.' She had to go on now. 'Brenda's my sister and I don't want to see her hurt.'

'Bloody hell! Stop interfering, woman. This has nothing to do with you.'

'I've come to ask you to think of Brenda. Things aren't easy for her.' Ruth's heart was pounding like a wild thing in her chest. 'I want you to promise . . .'

His pale green eyes stared into hers. 'Promise what?'

'Not to see that woman again. If you don't, I'll tell Brenda.'

Ruth couldn't believe her eyes, a smile was lifting the corners of Gilbert's lips. She heard him chuckle. He couldn't control his mirth and the next moment he was laughing outright.

'What's so funny about that? Brenda will be terribly upset.'

'Get out of here, Ruth.' He took out his handkerchief to mop his eyes. 'Do your damnedest and see if I care.'

Ruth fled. Her head had felt in a whirl before, now it was spinning. She was having the most awful palpitations. She found herself outside in the yard; she wanted to head for the gate and escape. She had to be on duty by one o'clock but she was in no fit state to walk back down the street. She stood for a few moments with her eyes closed leaning against the wall, fighting for self-control. She didn't see Ellis approach.

'Hello, Ruth, are you looking for Daisy?' He made her jump. 'Come on, she'll be upstairs with the baby. She gave us another wakeful night, I'm afraid.'

He'd passed her, she knew he expected her to follow. What would he think, finding her like this? Ruth felt she was being whisked upstairs to their living room. She could hardly breathe when she got there. Daisy was sitting on a low chair with a baby on each arm.

'I've got both of them here.' She smiled up at her. 'Flo's got a streaming cold and was afraid she'd give it to Lorna. Isn't she lovely? I can't resist babies. Just look at them, in age they're twins. Lorna's just gulped down a full bottle. She's really putting on weight and she can almost sit up. She's much more forward than my poor little Jane.'

Ruth took Jane from her and instantly resumed her role of mentor.

'Jane's coming on too.' She sank onto a chair. Jane was her niece and Ruth wanted to do her best for her. 'She'll catch up eventually.' The usual supportive words came easily. She'd read up on baby feeding and baby development in order to do this.

'Are we giving Lorna too much?'

Ruth was able to discuss the pros and cons of diet in the first year of life, until gradually her jitters went and she began to feel more normal. Although Daisy was the one she'd harmed most, she seemed happy and content and was coping well. When Dora joined them and she could smell their dinner being put out downstairs, Ruth was able to escape without making a complete fool of herself.

Gilbert sat back in his chair, staring out of the office window, then he blew his nose and put his handkerchief back in his pocket. He didn't know why he'd laughed at Ruth, but if he hadn't laughed, he'd have cried. The nerve of her to come and nail him in his office and threaten to tell Brenda!

Everything had suddenly turned sour for him. He was having a bad time. Nobody gave him any respect.

Brenda had gone berserk when she'd caught him in the café with Moira Stanford. He'd never before seen her in such a rage, screaming and shouting. He'd done his best to play it down, but Brenda wasn't having it. She'd cottoned on very quickly that he had a regular weekly arrangement with Moira.

It had seemed a good idea to book some time with her and pretend she was a customer. He'd had to, otherwise Enid could have booked him to drive a genuine customer and he wouldn't have been able to keep his date with her.

He'd known he'd be in trouble if Brenda found out, but he'd not expected problems from Moira. For the last six months he'd been picking her up on Wednesdays at the end of the road where she lived. Usually he picked her up before twelve and took her to a nice hotel for lunch. She had a caravan on a farm out Heswall way, and they went there afterwards.

Yesterday, he'd gone directly to Moira's house to make sure all was well for next Wednesday since they'd parted in such a hurry. She'd come to the door with her red hair flying round her face. 'Don't come here ringing my doorbell.' She'd dragged him into the hall and half closed the door so he wouldn't be seen. It had upset him to find her as angry as Brenda. He couldn't see what she had to complain about.

'I've never been so embarrassed in my life. To be accosted in a public place like that. Making a spectacle of us, letting everybody in the place know she'd caught us doing something we shouldn't.'

'We don't have to go back there.'

'Too right. I won't be going anywhere with you again. There could have been neighbours of mine in that café, acquaintances, people who'd tell my husband. I can't be doing with that. You'll land me in trouble.'

'Moira! I'm the one in trouble. It was a chance in a hundred that Brenda saw us. It won't happen again.'

'You told me you weren't married. It came as a shock to have your wife descend on me full of fury. Calling me all the names under the sun.'

'So what? You're married too.'

'But I don't try to hide it by telling lies. That's what I don't like. It gets up my nose. I've had enough.'

'Moira! Come on, your husband is none the wiser. You're all right.'

'No thanks to you. She was like a mad thing, even pursued me out onto the pavement. Get lost, Gil. For me it's not worth taking risks. I've had enough. It's over.' She'd pushed him out on the step. 'Don't dare come to my house again.'

The door slammed in his face. He'd spent a lot on Moira, giving her a good time, and this was the thanks he got. He turned away boiling with frustration, and slunk back to his car, which he'd left in the next road so he wouldn't be noticed by her neighbours. He couldn't stand it, Brenda and Moira fighting him off at the same time.

Nobody cared about him, it was total rejection. He felt a right failure.

And it wasn't just his social life, or his love life or whatever Brenda wanted to call it. He'd had yet another barny with Ellis about money, and that always upset him. Ellis no longer bothered to hide the contempt he felt for him. It was there on his face plain enough for everyone to see. That had made him feel small too.

If he were to be honest he'd have to admit that his brother was a more successful businessman. He knew how to make money from anything. Everything went right for Ellis.

Today, even his mother had told him not to be silly. He felt exposed, insecure. He was no longer holding his own with anyone.

Gilbert felt cold, he'd been sitting behind the wheel of his car for ages on this windy corner. He was fighting a losing battle. Everything he tried seemed to misfire. He'd go and have a beer to cheer himself up. No good going back home, that would only allow Brenda to vent her temper on him again. Everybody thought he was a loser. But he wasn't, not entirely, his taxi business was doing all right. He wasn't making any fortune, who was? But he was making a profit, no need to run himself down about that.

At the pub door he came face to face with Bernard Corkill who was on his way out. Gil cheered up. Bernard's eyes showed no disrespect, in fact they were shining with pleasure at meeting him. 'How about a pint on me?' Gil invited.

'Love to, but I can't, not now. I'm supposed to be meeting someone in Liverpool in ten minutes. Late already.'

'I was hoping to see you. I'd like you to get me another . . .' He lowered his voice. 'Another car, you know.' Actually he'd only thought of it at that moment.

'Oh, right.' There was interest on Bernard's face. 'Shall I pop into your place some time?'

'Yes, do that.' Gil was all sunniness. Bernard was the one person who still looked up to him. He believed in him and thought he was making a success of his taxis. Bernard didn't even suspect that he'd cheated him out of his share of the business. He could still hold his head high and feel that with Bernard he had the upper hand.

That's what he'd do. He'd build on his strengths. Put

another car in his fleet. Damn Brenda, damn Moira and damn Ellis too.

Ruth spent the rest of the day on duty. She oversaw a student midwife deliver a baby in the afternoon and a different student deliver another in the early evening. Both were normal births without complications and the students were reasonably competent, which was just as well because her mind had been anywhere but on the job.

She'd been trying to decide whether she should carry out her threat and tell Brenda she'd seen her husband in the Hippodrome with another woman. She'd meant to, but now she was afraid it would hurt Brenda more than it would Gil. He'd laughed at her and didn't seem to care if she did, though Ruth could see nothing amusing about it. He'd called her an interfering woman and he'd been right about that.

When she came off duty at eight o'clock that night, she still hadn't made up her mind. She sat on her bed for fifteen minutes before deciding to go to see Brenda. She felt edgy and knew she wouldn't sleep if she didn't.

Ruth had been going to Brenda's quite a lot but usually she went earlier in the evening than this. In front of the clothes shop she hesitated again, she didn't want Gilbert to be here; she wouldn't know what to say to him now. But usually if Gilbert was in when she arrived, it was a signal for him to go out.

When Brenda came down to let her in, Ruth could see she'd been crying. 'I'm glad you've come,' she said; her voice sounded flat.

Ruth followed her upstairs to the kitchen and watched her fill the kettle. 'How's the baby?'

Brenda gave a little sob and started to feel for her

handkerchief. 'It's not the baby, it's Gil.'

Ruth guessed what was coming and why Gilbert had laughed at her. Brenda already knew.

She said tearfully, 'He's got somebody else. He's always out with her.'

Ruth told her then, that she'd seen him in the Hippodrome. 'How did you find out? About the other woman?'

'It was only yesterday. Daisy had taken Lorna for a walk and the shop was unusually quiet. Ivy was here and I hadn't been out for ages, I just had to go. I walked down Grange Road to see the latest styles in the big shops. You know I have to keep abreast of fashion.' Brenda mopped her eyes. 'I saw them having tea in the Copper Kettle Tea Rooms, right in the window as bold as brass. With his new Ford parked outside.'

Ruth swallowed. 'What did you do?'

'I went straight in, pulled out another chair at their table and sat down. Oh Ruth, I've suspected for a long time . . .'

Ruth put her arms round her and gave her a hug.

'Anyway, it threw Gil. He didn't know what to do with himself. Couldn't get the bill paid and out of the place quick enough.'

'He admitted it?'

'No, not exactly.'

'What did he say?'

'You can't believe a word he says. He gave me a story . . . Said she was a photographer and he was making arrangements with her to take pictures of his hire cars. To advertise his fleet, as he calls it.'

'Perhaps she was.'

'If so, she'd already taken the pictures. He must think I'm half blind if I haven't seen them. They were in the office last week when I went over to see Daisy about something.'

The kettle was boiling hard and sending clouds of steam up to the ceiling. Ruth found the teapot and made the tea; Brenda was no longer up to it. She led her into the living room and sat her down on the couch.

'The woman was off like a racehorse as soon as we reached the pavement. Gil brought me back here still protesting, but I went into the office with him and found he'd booked himself out to drive a Mrs Stanford to Chester. I don't trust him, not an inch. To think of all the men I turned down. I could have had almost anybody when I was young. Why did I have to pick him?'

The baby gave a half cry from the bedroom.

'Shush.' Brenda looked up with agonised eyes. 'I hope we haven't woken her. I couldn't stand any more of Lorna's yowling tonight. It took me ages to get her off, she can't be due for another feed yet.'

Ruth said, 'She might go back to sleep if we're quiet,' but there was another little cry and a moan. After a moment or two's silence, Lorna opened her mouth and let forth a lusty wail.

Brenda burst into tears. 'I can't put up with this. She's a little terror.'

Ruth couldn't believe her ears. She couldn't stop the tears running down her own cheeks as she went to the cot and lifted baby Lorna out. She needed a clean napkin. Ruth changed her and carried her back on her shoulder.

'What time is her feed due?'

'She doesn't care what the time is. She's always ready for more. I can't stand it.'

Ruth swallowed back her agony. 'What time was it when you last fed her?'

'About . . . Oh Lord, I can't remember. Flo fed her. It would be about five, I think.'

'That's over four hours ago, Brenda. Have you made up a bottle for her?'

'No, I was too tired and I'm so bothered about Gil. There's too much on my mind.'

'You have to see to a baby, however tired you are,' Ruth couldn't help but snap. She pushed the crying child into her sister's arms and went to the kitchen to make up a bottle. She found three feeding bottles on the draining board not even rinsed out.

'Brenda! How many times have I been through what you must do to sterilise—'

'Give over, for God's sake. She's over four months old now and fit as a fiddle. She doesn't need all that sterilising.'

'She does. When the weather gets warmer she could catch gastro—'

'Oh, shut up. I'm not in the mood for a lecture tonight.'

Ruth scrubbed at one of the bottles and wanted to cry. What a terrible thing she'd done! Brenda didn't want the baby at all. It was just the thought of having one that had appealed to her, and dressing it up in frills to wheel round town. What a fool she'd been not to realise that.

Ruth's forehead was throbbing, she rested it for a moment against the cold glass of the window before taking the bottle she'd filled to Brenda.

'You feed her. It's like being on a treadmill. Day and night, over and over.'

Ruth took the baby and sat down. 'I told you it would be more work than breast-feeding.'

'That was horrible, I hated it,' Brenda pouted. 'And I hate Gil, he doesn't play fair with anyone. I wish I'd never married him. He never thinks of me, only of himself, he's downright selfish.'

'You have to think of the baby . . .'

Brenda wailed. 'If he's got another woman, Ruth, I have to think of myself.'

The baby's wide blue eyes stared up at Ruth. She was sucking vigorously, a lovely adorable baby. It was wringing her out to hear Brenda talk like this.

'I wish I'd never had a baby. I'll be looking after her for the rest of my days.'

'No, only for—'

'Fourteen years until she leaves school. Twenty before she's off my back. That's a twenty-year sentence, whichever way you look at it. I don't know how I'll get through it.'

Ruth felt she was being swamped by a tidal wave of fury and reproach.

'You and Gilbert, you're both selfish. Neither of you is giving any thought to the baby you said you wanted so much.'

All her life she'd loved Brenda and bent over backwards to give her what she wanted. Dad had too, and Daisy, and no doubt the countless boyfriends who'd clamoured for her favours. Brenda cast them all in the role of acolyte and wanted them to look after her. They'd all gone along with that. Brenda could charm the sun out from behind the clouds when she put her mind to it, but when she was in a mood like this, she was horrible.

Ruth was consumed with envy. She'd never quite mastered the longing to have more of what came so easily to her sister. She spat out at her, 'You're behaving like a spoilt bitch.'

Brenda jerked up, her beautiful face ravaged by tears. 'I'm upset.'

'I'm upset too. After all I've done for you . . .'

'What's so difficult about coming here to hand out glib advice? You say, do this, Brenda, or do that, and you'll find it easy. You think everything's easy, but it isn't. What do you know about being stuck here on your own? Being woken in the middle of the night and having to get up?'

Ruth could see Brenda quivering with rage and self-pity; her self-control snapped.

'Do you know what I did for you? I gave you this lovely baby and let you think she was yours. I expected you to think she was wonderful, everybody else does. I expected you to love her and cherish her. To enjoy looking after her, and to—'

'You let me think she was mine?' Brenda was stunned, the colour was ebbing from her face. 'What d'you mean?'

Ruth felt frenzied. 'This is Daisy's baby. You wanted a perfect daughter and I gave her to you.'

'What?'

Ruth could see savage rage in every line of her sister's body. She went on in a whisper, 'Your baby is Jane, I let Daisy believe she'd given birth to her. Jane was a weakling, I didn't think she'd live this long and I didn't want you to be without a baby. Not when you wanted one so badly and you'd found the pregnancy so hard.'

'Oh my God! Does Daisy know?'

'Of course not.'

'Ruth! Oh my God! What an awful thing to do!'

Ruth could no longer think straight, she felt sick with foreboding. She cuddled Lorna more closely and burst into tears. Brenda was on her feet, her face working with indignation, her voice scathing.

'I can't believe what you've done. You don't understand what being a mother means, do you? I couldn't bring up a baby that wasn't mine. I'm not doing it. We'll have to tell Daisy and get her to take it back. I want my own flesh and blood. What have you done with Lorna's shawl? We'll take her over with us.'

'What, now?' Ruth had cold cramps in her stomach. She should never have told Brenda! What had possessed her?

'Straightaway. I want my own child.'

When the doorbell rang, Dora had already gone to bed and Daisy was feeding Jane beside the dying embers of the living-room fire. Ellis was yawning as he waited for her to finish.

'Who can that be now?' He got up to answer the door.

They'd been listening to a programme of late-night dance music. Daisy switched off the wireless and strained her ears. Above the slurp slurp noises Jane was making she could hear voices and more than one pair of footsteps coming upstairs. She tightened her blouse round herself in a prickle of unease. Ellis wouldn't normally bring anybody up when he knew she was breast-feeding. He came in carrying baby Lorna.

'Brenda? What brings you over at this hour? Is it the baby?'

'She's all right, love. They've something to tell you.'

Daisy could see it was something important, something dreadful by the look on Brenda's face. It was only then she realised Ruth was with them. Her heart turned over, she'd never seen Ruth in tears before. Ellis pulled two more chairs to the fire, his face was grim.

'What is it?' Daisy could feel the tension between the sisters and knew she was stiffening too.

Daisy listened to what seemed an extraordinary tale and yet it did not. She was only too familiar with the effect Brenda had on people, but to find she'd not given birth to sweet little Jane who tugged at everybody's heartstrings, that she was not hers at all? She couldn't take it in, didn't want to.

She tried to blink back her own tears. With baby Jane

tugging at her nipple, how could she not think of her as her own? Her bond with Jane was cement hard. It had to be when she'd mothered her, cared for her every need all these months. She couldn't part with her now, it would be like tearing herself in two.

Brenda, too, seemed harrowed by the news. 'So you see, Jane is really my baby. I've brought Lorna back to you.'

Daisy's arms tightened round Jane. She couldn't possibly hand her over to Brenda. Brenda wouldn't look after her properly. Jane was delicate, she needed to stay here with her.

'A terrible mix-up you've caused, Ruth,' Brenda burst out. 'Why? For heaven's sake, why?'

Daisy could feel herself trembling with reproach. There was no reason that made sense to her. Impossible to believe Ruth would do such a thing; Ruth loved her, Daisy would have trusted her anywhere. It was hurtful to find Ruth put Brenda's needs so far above her own. But of course Ruth was closer to Brenda, always had been, they were real sisters. Ruth had been afraid Jane wouldn't survive and she wanted to make sure Brenda had a baby. Daisy understood all right, but for her it was raw agony. Ruth must have known how cruel this would seem to her.

'I'm so sorry, so sorry, Daisy.'

To see Ruth weeping and in a near hysterical state was unbelievable too. She was the most controlled person Daisy knew. They went on and on talking over the same wounding facts. It was making Daisy fall apart, her head was spinning. The door opened and Ellis's mother came in wearing a flowing dressing gown.

'Is something the matter? I could hear . . .'

Ellis had no sooner told her than Olive came downstairs with Peter in her arms and she had to be told there had been a mix-up with the babies. 'Get Peter a drink of milk, he'll soon go back to sleep,' Daisy suggested.

'We're waking the whole house,' Ellis said. 'Look, it's getting late and we've talked everything over twice. We're just arguing now and it's getting us no further. I think we should go to bed.'

Ruth was shaking her head. 'I'm so sorry.'

Brenda jerked to her feet. 'I can't stand any more of this. I knew Lorna wasn't mine. I've never felt close to her. Deep down inside me, something told me she wasn't mine. I'm going home, I'll take Jane with me.' She held out her arms in front of Daisy.

Daisy felt close to panic. 'No,' she said. 'No! I can't give Jane up now.'

Ellis stood up. 'Leave her here, Brenda. You need a decent night's sleep after this, and Jane will wake up for a breast-feed about two.' His gaze swung to Daisy. 'Take Jane up to our room and put her down in her cot.' Never had she felt more grateful for his support.

'She's mine,' Brenda shouted, trying to take her.

'Better if we leave any decisions until tomorrow,' Ellis said firmly, while Daisy hurried off with her precious bundle. It took only a moment to put Jane down and tuck the blankets round her.

She could hear Ellis's voice, tight with desperation. 'Brenda, we'll sort things out in the morning. Go home, you'll feel better after a night's sleep. We need to think things out.'

Daisy heard them clattering downstairs and then the front door slammed. She took a deep breath. Thank God, Brenda had gone! Ruth was still sobbing audibly in the living room. Dora's low voice offered words of comfort. Slowly, Daisy went back.

'Forgive me. Forgive me, I didn't realise what I was doing. Didn't think it through.' Ruth had worked herself up into an explosive pother now.

Ellis came back still holding Lorna, she'd fallen asleep in his arms. The fire had gone out, he stood on the hearth rug with his back to it. His face was paper-white, Daisy could see he was exhausted.

'I'd better get a car out and run Ruth back to the hospital.'

Daisy felt as though her world had turned upside down, she wanted Ruth out of here too, but . . .

'She's in no state . . .'

Ruth raised red eyes to meet hers. 'I didn't realise what it would do to you, Daisy. Forgive me, say you forgive me.'

'We're trying, Ruth,' Ellis told her. 'Shall I ring the hospital and say you aren't well? It's gone midnight, you'll be in no state to work tomorrow. We could find you a bed here for the night.'

'Yes,' Daisy agreed. 'That's the best thing.'

'We'll have to make one up,' Dora said. 'I'll get some sheets from the airing cupboard.'

'This little one will need a bed for the night too.' Ellis put Lorna into Daisy's arms.

She caught her breath as she stared down at her. This was her own daughter. She'd had to stifle the envy she'd felt when Brenda had first shown Lorna to her when she was newly born. Now? Lorna was strong and beautiful but Daisy wasn't drawn to her in the way she was to Jane. She'd always thought blood ties were the tightest of bonds but she'd been wrong. In this world you made your own relationships and formed your own bonds.

Olive was taking Peter back to bed. 'Where can we put Lorna?'

'The pram?'

'Yes.' Ellis helped Olive carry it up to the night nursery, where Olive put the sleeping child down.

When she finally got into bed that night, Daisy held on tight to Ellis. She thought neither of them could hope to sleep.

'I can't believe Lorna is really ours.'

'I can,' Ellis sighed. 'I've looked at her several times and thought how like you she is. She's got your hair, all tight curls, she's white-blonde but babies often are, their hair gets darker as they grow older.'

'I can't give Jane up now. I'm breast-feeding her. I can't let Brenda take her.'

'We can't refuse, love. Jane's her child, she has every right to take her.'

'What are we going to do?'

'We'll have to think about it . . . In the morning.'

Chapter Twenty-two

Daisy knew some sound had broken her sleep. She lifted her head from the pillow to listen. Ellis was breathing deeply beside her, and baby Jane in her cot near the bed seemed sound asleep too. The room was in darkness, the night silent except for the tick of the alarm clock.

It came again, a moan of pain, an eerie lament in the night. It came from the next room. They'd moved Nick down there because Jane would need his space in the nursery soon, but it wasn't Nick. Daisy remembered then that last night they'd made up the other bed in the room for Ruth.

Ruth cried out again like a soul in torment. Shivering with nerves, Daisy slid out of bed and pulled on her dressing gown; she was wide awake now, well used to being woken in the night. She crept out of her room and closed the door quietly so Ellis and Jane wouldn't be disturbed.

'Ruth? Are you all right? Are you having a bad dream?'

The moaning ended in a gulp of distress. 'If only it was a dream. Something I could wake up from. Something that hasn't happened. It's a terrible thing I've done to you.'

In the dim glow of Nick's nightlight Ruth's face was screwing in agony, her eyes were swollen and red. She had done a terrible thing. Daisy didn't know what to say to her.

'I'm so sorry, Daisy.' Her voice was a stage whisper. She

turned towards Nick's bed. 'I hope we aren't going to wake him up.'

'Nothing will wake Nick. He'll sleep like a log until morning. Always does.'

'I've got such a bad conscience. I wish I could make amends.'

'I feel very churned up myself. I still can't accept that Jane isn't my own flesh and blood. I'll always love her. I can't bear the thought of parting with her, and yet poor Lorna, it'll take me time to love her as I should.'

'I've done a terrible thing.' Ruth was weeping and making no attempt to stem the flow. 'I wish I could turn the clock back.'

'Can't be done.'

'No. It was always you we cut out at home, wasn't it? Always you. How unfair.'

'It felt unfair when I was young, but now . . .' Daisy knew that since her marriage she'd had everything she wanted in abundance. She had nothing to complain about but losing Jane.

'When you were young,' a moist hand came out to grip hers, 'I felt so sorry for you, we all did. Left high and dry like that. Even more sorry for your poor mother and so guilty that we didn't do more to help her.'

Daisy felt suddenly stiff with tension. She sat down on Ruth's bed.

'What could you have done for my mother?'

'We could have made her feel more welcome in our house.'

'Uncle Ern would have done his best.'

'He did, but Mam resented her presence and I suppose Brenda – and me too – we followed her lead. The customers were gossiping about her. Even at school the girls asked about her in that way . . . Salaciously. Our teacher said she was a scarlet woman. I didn't like that. I'm sure we made Rosa feel we didn't want her. When Uncle Harry was drowned, she must have felt so alone.'

Daisy couldn't move. She felt she'd been turned to stone.

'This is the very first time . . . that anybody has volunteered a memory of my mother. A personal memory. I wanted to know about her, what she was like and everything. I pleaded and pleaded for information, but I got so little. I remember asking you, but . . . Why didn't you tell me this then?' It was a cry from Daisy's heart.

'How could we tell you we'd been so hateful to your mother?'

'She wouldn't feel that. You gave her a home.'

'Of course she felt it. Why else would she kill herself?'

Daisy felt her head spin. 'Kill herself?'

Ruth slowly sat up, her face stark. 'Didn't you know? Oh God! Didn't you know?'

Daisy couldn't move. Her mouth was suddenly dry.

'You didn't! Of course you didn't.'

Daisy shuddered. 'Uncle Ern said it was an accident. That she banged her head.' She felt dreadful. Her mother had killed herself? 'She had me, she wasn't alone. Why would she kill herself?'

'She'd heard that Uncle Harry's ship had gone down with all hands.'

'How?' Daisy could hardly get the word out. 'How did she kill herself?' Uncle Ern had said she'd fallen and banged her head on the ice box in the yard. But he'd been very vague, she'd had her suspicions then, hadn't she?

'We found two empty aspirin bottles beside her.'

'Just aspirin? Would that kill?'

'She'd taken a lot. Enough . . .'

'But Uncle Ern said she'd banged her head.'

'She let the sash window . . . that one in the attic, fall on her head.'

'Oh no! She couldn't have done that! The cord snapped, Uncle Ern was right, it was an accident.'

'Mam thought the cord had been cut, Daisy. That Rosa might have been afraid she hadn't taken enough and wanted to make sure. You know . . .'

Daisy moistened her lips. 'But the window, might have been an accident?'

'Perhaps by then she didn't know what she was doing. Perhaps she panicked. Perhaps she wanted someone to take care of you and was trying to call down to someone in the yard. We don't know.'

'How awful!'

'You were crying, really letting rip. Screaming your head off. I went up to see why she wasn't soothing you.'

'You found her?' Daisy gulped. 'I thought you were at school, that she'd been taken to hospital by the time you came home.'

'I didn't go that day, I had an upset stomach. Mam gave out that I was at school so people wouldn't ask me . . . question me. I was terrified, I couldn't cope. Mam and Dad were drumming into me that I mustn't give the game away.'

'What game?'

'Not a game at all, I'm sorry. What must you think of us? We were trying to save our own skins by then. Trying to cover it up.'

'But why?'

'It's a criminal offence to commit suicide or aid and abet anyone else to do it. Your mam was already the talk of the town. We had to pretend it was an accident. They wouldn't have let her be buried in hallowed ground. There would have been renewed scandal. We would have got into more trouble and the business . . . Well, you know how much that business meant to our family, it had to be profitable or we'd have had nothing to live on.'

'What did you do? What did Auntie Glad do?'

'She threw out the aspirin bottles and teased out the ends of the cord. When the police came round asking questions, they said the cord had looked frayed for some time; that they'd been intending to get a new one for it.'

'You got the new cord.' Daisy was hurting inside as she remembered. 'When I moved into the attic just before Brenda got married. You were a bag of nerves that day.'

'Yes.'

'You could have told me then. Uncle Ern could have told me the truth. I was grown up by then. I wanted to know, to understand.'

'No,' Ruth said softly. 'They didn't want you to know. Not ever, and now I've gone and let the cat out of the bag. So sorry for myself I could no longer think of you. Why do I always harm you?'

'You don't,' Daisy choked, but she was afraid she couldn't forgive Ruth.

'Mam and Dad, they were trying to protect you, Daisy, that's all. They thought it better for your peace of mind that you shouldn't know. Dad felt very guilty, Mam too. They had your best interests at heart, though I know Mam doesn't always seem to.'

It had gone three when Daisy finally crept back to her own bed. She found it hard to believe Ellis and Jane had slept through all that. Daisy expected Jane to wake soon for her feed. She edged close to Ellis and put her cold feet on his. He stirred and put an arm round her, pulling her closer though he was hardly conscious. He was the source of warmth she needed.

What a night it had been! She felt at fever pitch and miles away from sleep. How could she relax after revelations such as these? She understood many things that had puzzled her before. That Auntie Glad had altered evidence to keep the truth from scandal mongers and to avoid hurt to her made her see Auntie Glad in a kinder light. It had been her way of protecting her family and her business. That her poor mother had killed herself was a terrible weight on her chest. Why hadn't somebody pointed out how much her baby needed her and how much she would love her?

But that was all past history. Daisy told herself she mustn't let herself be upset by it now. A more immediate problem was that Brenda wanted to take Jane from her.

It was after six when the alarm clock woke Daisy. As usual, Ellis was out of bed quickly and getting dressed. He lifted Jane from her cot and changed her nappy.

Daisy felt woolly with sleep, she couldn't wake herself up. Her frenzy had gone, leaving her feeling drained. Ellis lowered the baby into her arms.

Daisy yawned. 'She didn't have a two o'clock feed. She slept through for the first time.'

'Didn't I hear you get up?'

'To Ruth not to Jane.'

'What are we going to do about Ruth?'

She told him then what Ruth had told her in the night. 'She's in a terrible state, I think she needs to see her doctor. I'll suggest it.'

'Ruth didn't choose the best time to tell you about your mother. That was bad news on top of bad news.'

Daisy lay back on her pillows feeling exhausted, but it

pleased her to find Jane feeding vigorously. She held her close.

'I dread having to give her up, that's the worst part.' The future seemed black.

Ellis sighed. 'I was thinking about it in the night. Should we report this mix-up to the hospital?'

'No, Ellis, think what that would do to Ruth. Better if we keep it to ourselves.'

'Brenda expects us to hand Jane back now.'

'She's demanding it.'

'It's her right, love. If we try to hold on to her, it will only get Brenda's back up and make her more determined. She sees how much you love Jane and want to keep her, and that makes Jane more desirable to her. Besides, Jane is Brenda's child, she's doing what everybody expects a mother to do.'

'It's going to take me some time to accept.'

'Daisy, Brenda gets tired of things once the novelty wears off. She hasn't shown much mothering to Lorna. She handed her back to us like a shot, didn't she? She soon got fed up with her. With a bit of luck she'll get tired of Jane even more quickly. Jane's a lot more demanding.'

Daisy let herself be persuaded. She had to hope.

When she took a cup of tea in to Ruth, she had her face partly hidden by bedclothes. What she could see was ravaged with tears, her eyes swollen.

'Did Nick wake you up?'

'He climbed all over me before running off to find Olive.'

'Breakfast in fifteen minutes. We all eat in the kitchen these days.'

'I couldn't eat, Daisy.'

'Come on, get dressed and try. Ellis is going to run you down to see your doctor afterwards. We think that's the best thing for you. You need a break to get over this.'

It took Ruth more than half an hour to come downstairs. Daisy thought they were all unusually silent at breakfast. It was a relief when Ellis took Ruth away. She felt very restless, and it seemed no time at all before Ellis was back and bringing Brenda upstairs.

'I thought I'd come for my baby now. I'll be able to get her settled before I open the shop.'

Daisy felt bereft. She was nursing Jane on her knee in the living room. She'd finished washing and dressing her but felt reluctant even to put her down in her cot. She wanted to protest.

Ellis said quietly, 'Let her go, Daisy.'

She tightened her arms round the baby. She couldn't!

'It'll be for the best. She is Brenda's baby.'

Daisy relaxed her grasp, held out the child to Brenda.

'A shawl,' Brenda said. 'She'll need that.'

Ellis found one. 'Do you want to take her cradle?'

'I can put her in the pram when she's down in the shop.'

He said, 'She slept through the night for the first time.'

'I fed her at six.' Daisy couldn't believe Jane was being taken from her. 'I'll come and feed her at ten.'

'No.' Brenda drew herself back. 'Flo can give her a bottle. She's old enough for that now.' She was heading for the stairs.

'Can I take her out this afternoon? For a walk? Like I've been taking Lorna?'

'Just for a walk.'

Brenda had gone and Daisy was fighting back a sense of loss.

Ellis put his arms round her. 'This is the only way, love.'

'Jane's not used to bottle feeds.' It was a cry from the heart.

Daisy ran up to the nursery to find solace with Lorna.

Olive had made up a bottle and Daisy sat down to feed her, feeling pangs of conscience. Poor little thing, she didn't feel for Lorna as a mother should, she hadn't chosen her name. But Ellis was right, Lorna was going to have hair exactly like hers, already there was a lot of it. Why hadn't she noticed the likeness before?

The baby was kicking on her lap. Daisy couldn't help but smile at her, and she was rewarded with a lovely smile in return and a chuckle of contentment. It brought tears to her eyes; how could she not love such a beautifully rounded and healthy baby like this?

The morning seemed unreal to Daisy. She couldn't get herself going. She drifted down to the office but she couldn't settle to work.

Ellis said, 'Give the accounts a miss this morning. You're well up to date with them.'

'I can't concentrate.'

'Neither can I, love. Can't think of anything but little Jane.'

Daisy abandoned her usual routine and drifted back to the nursery. She couldn't stay away from her children today.

'Lorna could do with some more clothes,' Olive told her. 'I found a dress that Jane hasn't grown into yet, but we need her feeding bottles and teats.'

From the living-room window Daisy could see Brenda working in her shop. For her, it was business as usual. Daisy needed to pop across to get Lorna's things, but she couldn't face it. Jane would be there and she'd want to pick her up. She set about teaching Peter and Mark their letters.

At dinner, Ellis looked very down. 'I can't get myself going today.'

Daisy knew he was as upset as she was about the babies. Outside, it was sunny and blustery, just the day to let the boys run off their energy in the park.

'Come out for a walk with us,' she said. 'It'll blow your cobwebs away.'

'I think I will. We could call at your Auntie Glad's to see if Ruth's been put off work.'

'I'll have both babies . . .'

'Just for the walk, Daisy. Brenda won't give up that quickly.'

'How long do you think it'll take her?'

He shook his head in silent misery.

After dinner was over, Olive reminded her they had no outdoor clothes for Lorna.

Daisy put on her coat and since Nick had been made ready for the outing she took him across the road with her.

Brenda had several customers in the shop and a pile of new gowns across her arm. She looked more her usual self than Ruth had this morning, and better than Daisy felt now.

'Jane's been fine. Took a bottle at ten and another just now. Absolutely no trouble at all,' she told her.

Daisy's spirits sank. 'I've come to fetch her for a walk. I'm thinking of going to Auntie Glad's. Ruth went home this morning.'

'I told Flo to get her ready.'

'And I need some clothes for Lorna and her bottles and—'

'I chose nice clothes for my baby, they'll come in for Jane soon,' Brenda told her frostily. 'And she's already using the bottles, you'll need to get your own.'

'Right.' Daisy felt put in her place. 'Perhaps I could borrow a bonnet and woolly coat for Lorna to wear now. Until we can sort some things out for her.'

Taking Nick by the hand, Daisy climbed the stairs, feeling tight-lipped. She'd been afraid Brenda would take it like this.

The rooms all opened off the landing, and the living-room door was half open. She'd almost reached it when she heard men's voices.

'I like the Ford, it's nice to drive.'

'Economical to run.' Gilbert was there but it wasn't Flo he was talking to.

Daisy tapped and pushed the door to open it wider. 'I've come to get Jane, Gil. I'm going to take her to the park. I've . . .' She stopped, taken aback. Sitting on the green velvet couch was a man of about forty, gaunt and ungainly with brown hair combed forward.

Daisy knew she'd seen him before, she was searching her mind as to where . . . He half smiled, showing bad teeth, and it came to her in a rush. It was Bernard Corkill, the man who'd stolen money from the till in the dairy all those years ago!

How she'd wanted to talk to him then. She'd even gone to his home to look for him. There'd been so much she'd wanted to ask, but now she knew.

Gil leapt to his feet with unusual haste and ushered her out of the room. 'This way. Jane will be in the bedroom.'

He hadn't introduced them. Yet he must know they were related. It seemed he wanted to keep them apart. Daisy felt she was being hurried away from Bernard Corkill.

Gilbert called, 'Flo? Are you there?'

She was tying a bonnet on Jane that Daisy hadn't seen before. A very smart affair trimmed with angora wool.

'I wish you'd tidy up the living room, Flo. There's hardly room to sit down for shawls and feeders, they're spreading everywhere.'

'Yes, Mr Gilbert.'

'I need a coat and bonnet for Lorna,' Daisy said. Lorna's clothes, washed and ironed, were folded into neat piles in her bedroom.

'These are what she usually wears, aren't they? And I could do with another shawl. You carry them for me, Nick.'

The fact that Lorna's cot had been made up with clean sheets brought a needling of fear. Clearly it had been made ready for Jane.

Daisy was retreating with Jane in her arms. The living-room door had been shut tight. Gilbert obviously wanted her to have no further contact. That annoyed her, made her march up to the door and throw it open with a flourish.

'Thanks, Gil. I'm taking Jane now and I've also taken a few garments to keep Lorna warm.'

Bernard Corkill was looking straight at her. She said to him, 'Hello, I'm Daisy Fox but I used to be Daisy Corkill. I'm Rosa's daughter. You're her brother, aren't you? So you're my uncle. What d'you think of that then?'

There was a look of utter incredulity on his face.

Daisy felt hysterical. 'Why didn't you introduce us, Gil? I thought I'd convinced you of the relationship. Aren't you ready to accept it even now?'

'Get out,' he shouted. 'Get out of here. It's all lies. You're always trying to stir up trouble.'

She turned and ran down the stairs.

'Who's that, Mam?' Nicky piped behind her. 'If he's our uncle why don't we know him?'

The encounter left Daisy feeling flustered and out of sorts. Ellis was putting his coat on when she got back; he took Jane from her.

'Mother's decided to come too, it's going to be quite a family outing.'

'Brenda says Jane's been no trouble.'

Daisy put all her weight behind the big pram with the two babies in it and it fairly flew along the pavements. Ellis strode along with her, his lips set in a straight line.

He and Daisy were leaving Olive behind. Although Peter in the pushchair was lighter to push, Olive had to go at the pace that Mrs Fox and the toddlers Nick and Martin could manage.

'Had we better wait for them?' Ellis asked. 'And I could do with getting my breath back. Let's sit here for a moment.' Daisy flopped down beside him on the park bench. There was only one thing they could talk about and they were soon going over the same ground about the babies again. The movement of the pram had lulled both of them to sleep. Nick was the first to reach her.

'Olive's taking us to feed the ducks, Mam. Are you coming?'

Olive and the pushchair drew level. Dora said, 'Elsie gave us some stale bread for the ducks.'

It was still a good walk to the duck pond which was at the other end of the park.

Ellis said, 'We'll not come with you, Mam. We want to call at Auntie Glad's house to see if Ruth's any better. We'll see you when we get home.'

Daisy watched the backs of the other half of the family retreating along the path. Peter's piping treble wafted back to them.

'It's peaceful sitting here.' Ellis felt for her hand. There were few people about. With the warmth of the sun on her face, Daisy felt drowsy after her broken night. She leaned back and closed her eyes.

She knew she must have dozed off when she heard Ellis's voice and woke to find Bernard Corkill looking down at her. She yawned, feeling heavy and sluggish, and tried to pull herself upright on the seat.

He said, 'I heard you say you were coming to the park

. . . I remember you, of course.' He sat on the bench beside her.

'You do?'

'When you were a baby, a year or so old.'

'I was nineteen months when my mother . . . when she died.'

'That would be the time. You were just a toddler. I couldn't take you in.'

'What d'you mean?'

'Gladys Maddocks expected me to take you off her hands when Rosa died – to bring you up. Tried to persuade me, said it was my duty, but I couldn't. I was married at that time but my wife wouldn't agree. She threw me out the following year and I've lived in lodgings ever since. What could I do, a man on my own? Anyway, you were better off with them, they had a permanent home.'

Ellis spoke across her. 'You knew Glad and Ern?'

'Only because they took Rosa in. I used to go and see her. Mrs Maddocks used to go on at me about the disgrace Rosa was bringing to her family.' Bernard was gazing into the far distance where a horse and trap were bowling along Park Road North.

Daisy said, 'I wish you'd stayed in touch. When I was growing up, it seemed I hadn't a living relative. I felt so alone. But you know Gilbert. You know him well. Have you always—?'

'Yes, he's a sort of distant cousin.'

'He's my brother,' Ellis said, 'but I don't know you, neither does my mother.'

'My father cut me and Rosa off from all our respectable relatives years ago. They didn't want anything to do with either of us. They thought us a couple of black sheep, nothing but trouble.'

Ellis was leaning forward. 'Cuthbert Corkill, you knew him?'

'My uncle, yes, but as I said, we weren't welcome at his place.'

'But you stayed in touch with Gilbert.'

Bernard pulled a face. 'Perhaps he's not so fussy about the company he keeps. I can give him a good game of table tennis, or I could. We enjoy the same things.'

'Your father was Cuthbert's brother? Was his name James?'

'You seem to know all about my family. My father was a vicar but he was quite inhuman to Rosa when she found herself in the family way. Too saintly to care about us sinners. He felt we were dragging him down.'

'Our family too. We spent a lot of time searching things out.'

'Why?'

Ellis and Daisy both started talking at once. Ellis smiled. 'You first, Daisy.'

'I wanted to find my relatives. I was sure I must have some somewhere. Everybody has.'

Ellis said, 'And I was looking for Cuthbert Corkill's family. Gilbert told us they'd all died out.'

'He knew I was still in the land of the living.' Bernard was frowning.

'Did you never see the notice our solicitor put in the *Liverpool Echo*?'

Bernard's deep overhanging forehead was furrowed in thought.

Ellis went on, 'It said something like: Anyone related to the Corkill family, one time of Camden Yard and more recently of Clifton Crescent, may hear something to their advantage if they contact Messrs. Henman and Gibbs.'

'Somebody showed that to me.'

'But you didn't make contact.'

'No, Cuthbert Corkill wasn't likely to leave anything to me in his will. He and Ralph never wanted anything to do with me.'

Ellis said slowly, 'I understand Cuthbert left everything to his son Ralph, but he was killed and didn't leave a will. Did you know about that?'

'I found out quite recently that Ralph had been killed in France.'

'Only recently?'

'I saw his name on the war memorial. That was the first I knew.'

'Gil didn't tell you?'

'I told him.'

'I think he knew.' Ellis pondered. 'He's known for a long time. The army would have notified Ralph's relatives of his death. It's you who didn't hear of it at the time. Gilbert applied for letters of administration and his estate was distributed to Ralph's kith and kin in accordance with the law of the land. We Foxes inherited it.'

Bernard was leaning across Daisy. 'Why the Foxes?' he demanded.

Ellis said, 'We were related. You said Gilbert was your cousin.'

'A distant cousin.'

'Nobody else came forward. No closer relatives.'

'Gil knew about me. We've always been in touch. He knows he'll find me at the Queen Vic most nights, we often meet there. He knew exactly what my relationship to Ralph Corkill was. It was closer than his.'

Bernard turned to look at Daisy in a very queer way. She

thought he was about to say something, but he checked himself.

'Did he leave much?'

Ellis shrugged. 'Cuthbert was Albert Fox's partner. He owned the carpentry shop.'

Daisy could see Bernard's face puckering with anger.

'The dirty twister, he's done me down.' His gaze met Daisy's. 'Done us both down.'

Ellis had a triumphant gleam in his eyes. 'I knew Gilbert was fiddling something as soon as I started looking at the business accounts. It's going to be very difficult to sort out now.'

But Bernard wasn't listening. He leapt to his feet and rushed off.

Chapter Twenty-three

Bernard set off up the broad walk of the park at a furious rate. He was boiling over, blind with temper. He tripped over a toddler pushing a stuffed dog on wheels and stumbled. It made him lash out at the toy with his foot.

'What d'ya do that for?' the harridan of a mother bellowed after him. 'You leave my lad alone. You bad-tempered old buffer.'

'You should keep your child under control.'

'You got to look where yer going.'

Oh God! His legs moved faster and faster, he was striding on with his shoulders hunched and head bent low. He'd thought of Gilbert as a friend and an ally, but he'd robbed him of his inheritance and done it so slyly he hadn't even noticed. He'd had to have it pointed out to him!

And he was still doing Gilbert favours, still finding him cars, still taking all the risks, and Gil was still negotiating down what he asked him to pay, even though it was more than fair.

Bernard knew exactly when it had happened. Gilbert had had him over a barrel. It was when he'd sought him out in Camden Yard after he and Alf had been seen trying to nick a car outside the Gaiety Theatre. He'd been almost out of his mind with fear. He'd been sprayed with blood when he'd fought off that wild woman. He'd had to avoid being picked up in that state at all costs. He'd gone to Gilbert begging for help. He'd been desperate for a bath, clean clothes and an alibi. Gil had given him what he needed but he'd wanted payment for the favour. Gil always wanted to be paid for what he did. Damn it, he'd offered him money, been willing to pay him even though he'd been short at the time.

He'd had to ask him to wait and Gilbert never wanted to wait for his money. Instead he'd asked him not to claim on his uncle's estate. He had said uncle, not cousin. He hadn't known then that Ralph had been killed or that he'd left no will. Bernard wasn't expecting to inherit anything from his uncle. Gilbert had made him promise not to claim and it was a promise he'd kept. More fool him.

Gilbert always drove a hard bargain but Bernard hadn't realised just how hard that one was. He'd really done him down.

What made it more painful was that Gil had known how much in need of money he was. He had just come out after serving his first stretch in prison and he hadn't had a penny to his name. He'd had to live hand to mouth in grotty lodgings ever since his wife had thrown him out. Some of them were terrible places and he couldn't always pay the rent. And all the time, Gilbert was living in comfort. He had a comely wife working her guts out in the shop for him while he rested on a plush velvet couch upstairs. He was living on income that by rights was partly Bernard's and he was driving round in the shiny new cars he found for him.

Bernard's rage had made him walk so briskly he was sweating. He couldn't slow down, couldn't keep still. He'd expected Gilbert to treat him fairly, but Gilbert didn't treat anybody fairly. Well, he wasn't going to get away with this. Gilbert had used him, had been using him for his own ends all these years.

His mind was spinning through a hundred ways to wreak vengeance on Gilbert Fox. He could go to the clothes shop and tell his pretty wife what a cad her husband was. He could get her worked up and angry in the hope she'd throw him out to fend for himself. Serve him right if she did.

He should have explained things more clearly to Gilbert's brother. And Rosa's girl – she'd been done down too. He should get them all on Gil's back, but none of these things were bad enough. Bernard wanted to squeeze him; pressurise him till he screamed for mercy. He'd find him, he'd give him what was coming to him.

The urgency to get even drove Bernard to the clothes shop and made him look through the window. He could see Gil's missus inside, dolled up to the nines, a good-looking wench. She had a customer inside. Bernard waited while she interleaved a dress with tissue paper and placed it reverently in a bag. It was a bit embarrassing going into a place that sold only women's wear but he wasn't going to let that put him off.

The doorbell pinged as he went in and she turned with her sales lady's smile. It froze on her lips.

'Is Gilbert home?' Now he was close he could see that Brenda looked drained. She was no longer as beautiful as he remembered.

'No, he's at work.'

'What time will he be back?'

'Your guess is as good as mine.' She sounded irritable.

Bernard retreated. 'Tell him I called. Tell him I'll see him in the Queen Vic tonight.'

Daisy watched Bernard Corkill rush off at breakneck speed in what to her had seemed the middle of a conversation.

'He's a very strange man. I'm thankful he didn't bring me up.'

Ellis smiled. 'The things we're learning! You could well have had a worse time with your real relatives than you had with Auntie Glad and Uncle Ern.'

'If only I'd known I was related to Ralph Corkill!'

'Gilbert knew all along.'

'Yes, and did his best to hide the fact from me.'

'From us all, Daisy. I knew I was right about Gil taking over the Corkill assets illegally. I suspected it from the start when he tried to stop me seeing the company accounts. When I accused him of doing it he biffed me on the nose. Then somehow he managed to convince me I was making a mistake.'

'Because your father thought it was all above board.'

'Dad didn't know of Bernard's existence.'

'He must have done, Ellis. His own brother's child?'

'Well, yes, he knew he'd been born but he'd had no contact for years and so many men were killed in the war. D'you know, I think Gilbert thought I'd be killed in the war too and he'd be the sole beneficiary.'

'He knew all the time you weren't Ralph's closest relatives.'

'Yes, well, we found that out when we worked out the Corkill family tree.'

'He did his best to stop us finding out.'

Ellis was thoughtful. 'And even then I didn't think it was Gil's intention to defraud. We didn't know where Bernard Corkill was, I didn't expect Gil to know either.'

'But he did. Bernard says they were in touch the whole time.'

'Our Gil's a fool. He tells such lies, even though he knows he could be found out.'

'He got away with it, didn't he?'

'At the time. But the truth's coming out now.'

Daisy knew she'd have been thirteen or so at the time of Ralph's death. Uncle Ern would surely have claimed on her behalf if only he'd known she was related. What a difference that would have made to her when she'd been growing up.

Ellis said, 'It'll be hard to unravel what's owed to you and Bernard after all this time, but no doubt we'll have to come to some arrangement now.'

The sun had gone behind a cloud; she shivered and got to her feet. 'If we're going to Auntie Glad's it's time we were on our way.'

'I'll walk part of the way with you, Daisy, but I won't come in. I've plenty to do back in the office and my head's in a whirl with all this.'

Auntie Glad had moved to a stylish newly-built house in a smart new road. She opened the door to Daisy. There was a strong aroma of recently cooked kippers coming from the kitchen.

'Our Ruth's here,' she told her. 'Came this morning, she's very upset. I think something must have happened at the hospital but she doesn't want to talk about it. The doctor's put her off work for a week. Told her to rest and he's given her some tablets to help her sleep. She's flat out in bed now.'

This was what Daisy had come to find out. Under the circumstances, she decided to let Ruth tell them what had happened in her own time. It wouldn't do for her to go into long explanations about what Ruth had done.

The pram had to be left in the porch in case its wheels marked the new carpet runner in the hall. Jane had woken up so Daisy carried her in. Auntie Glad wanted to make a fuss of Lorna and woke her as she lifted her in. She had a new three-piece suite in brown velvet and a matching set of dining table and chairs to go with the best pieces from the fish shop. She was very proud of her new home.

'Our Brenda's got her troubles too. Has she told you? I never did think that much of Gilbert. Fancies himself too much, always oiling and trimming that moustache. Is everything all right with you?'

Daisy was taken unawares by that. She couldn't answer truthfully. She managed, 'If Brenda and Ruth are in difficulties, then I feel it too.'

Auntie Glad started on the long list of Gil's failings as a husband, most of which Daisy had already heard from Brenda herself. She found it hard to sit and listen and keep her mouth shut.

Through the French window of the living room she could see Uncle Ern working in his new garden. She carried Jane out and went to talk to him. He was thinking of the future, trying to convey how bright and colourful his garden would be in a few more months, when the flower seeds he was planting were in full bloom. Daisy didn't stay long. Her mind was filled with very different things.

Ellis was hanging his coat on the bentwood stand in his office when through the window he saw Bernard Corkill walking up the yard to talk to one of Gil's drivers. He was waving his arms about and seemed angry.

Ellis hadn't expected to see him again so soon but it wasn't hard to guess what he wanted. He went out to speak to him. When Bernard turned round, Ellis could see his face was white and he was crackling with tension.

'I'm looking for Gilbert,' he said. 'His wife said he was working. Is he in his office?'

'No, he's out driving. Can I help?'

'You know what I want with him. Will you tell him I'll be in the Queen Vic tonight?'

'Yes, all right.'

As he watched Bernard stride away, Ellis thought again about what he'd told him in the park and felt uneasy. He was glad to see Daisy pushing the big pram up the passage.

'I've taken Jane back to Brenda. It seems so strange without her.'

'How's Ruth?'

She told him and had more to say about Auntie Glad's new brown velvet suite.

'Daisy, Bernard Corkill's been round here.'

She looked disconcerted. 'What did he want?'

He shook his head. 'He was looking for Gilbert. He's going to have it out with him.'

'I should think he's looking for recompense.'

'Yes, Gil's going to be furious with me. He'll say I opened my mouth too wide.'

'He's brought all this on himself. What he did was fraud. He claimed assets for your business he knew you weren't entitled to.'

'I know, but I wish I hadn't said anything to Bernard. He's going to blow this up and have a mammoth row with Gil.'

'Serve him right. It's what he deserves.'

'Gil thinks he's so clever and the rest of us are so stupid we won't notice what he's up to.'

Daisy pushed her tight curls off her forehead. 'What did you make of him? Of my Uncle Bernard?'

'He's bitter and twisted. About his father and now about our Gil too.'

Daisy sighed. 'I don't like Bernard very much even if he is my uncle. I'm glad we've made contact. It's success of a sort because once I tried very hard to find him, but . . .'

Ellis laughed at her. 'Haven't I been telling you? You can't choose your relatives, you're landed with them, so there's no guarantee you'll love them. Except a spouse, of course.' He kissed her cheek. 'The rest you have to accept.'

'Bernard's been in prison, he's a convicted car thief. What d'you think will happen now?'

'He'll demand compensation. But Dad asked the solicitor to advertise, there was nothing stopping Bernard putting his claim in.'

Daisy shivered. 'If there's trouble coming to Gil, he's asked for it. But he can look after himself, he's twice the size of Bernard and much younger.'

'All the same,' Ellis said, 'I wish I'd never mentioned it in the park.'

Lorna was waking up and giving little cries. Daisy lifted her from the pram. 'I'd better get her upstairs She's due for a feed.'

Ellis said heatedly, 'Gilbert's a lazy fool who doesn't know which way his bread's buttered and he doesn't play fair with anybody. Me, Brenda, anybody.'

'And, it seems, not Uncle Bernard either.'

'Or you.'

As soon as Daisy had gone, a new and horrible suspicion filled Ellis's mind. Daisy had reminded him that Bernard had been to prison, he was a convicted car thief and he and Gil had always been in touch. Could Gil's fleet of cars be stolen property?

Ellis used his keys to open Gil's files and searched through them for the documents relating to the cars. Gil had told him he'd bought the cars from the garage in Rock Ferry because they were prepared to give greater discount than the garage they usually dealt with. He knew better than to believe anything Gil told him was gospel truth.

The paperwork looked all right. The bills were receipted, nothing at all to arouse suspicion. All the same, Bernard had spoken of cars, half inferred . . .

Gilbert felt hungry. He'd been out driving most of the day and was glad to be heading back through the gates of Camden Yard. With a flourish, he backed his Ford into its place under cover. There was only one other car here; it pleased him to think the other two were still out working.

He ought to be happy with the way his taxi hire business was developing. He now had four Fords, all very similar; a smart fleet of cars. He'd had smart maroon uniforms made for his drivers. He employed two full-time and one part-time and there was plenty of work coming in to keep them all busy. He felt his business ought to be making more profit than it was. There was more money coming in, of course, but the outgoings were much greater too. Another car and driver would help.

He did a lot of his paperwork at home on the kitchen table. He'd agreed with Ellis that Dad's big desk in the office should be his, and Ellis and Daisy should use only the smaller one, but he always had the feeling that Ellis was looking over his shoulder when he tried to work in there.

He saw Ellis come out into the yard and wave to him. 'Gilbert?' It was almost as though he was watching what time he started work and what time he finished. 'Have you got a minute?'

Gil would have liked to say no; he sauntered over to his brother reluctantly. 'What's the matter now?'

'Bernard Corkill's been here looking for you.'

That tightened Gil's nerves. Ellis's attitude told him he was in trouble. He'd told Bernard to keep away from here.

He didn't want Ellis finding out where the cars had come from.

There was contempt in Ellis's voice. 'I knew you were working a fast one when you took over Cuthbert Corkill's property. I knew when you tried to stop me seeing the accounts.'

Gilbert froze. Because so many years had passed he'd felt safe about this secret. He'd thought it buried and forgotten. But if Bernard had found out, the result would be worse than anything he'd so far imagined. And Ellis knew it.

'It was deliberate theft, wasn't it, Gil? Or do they call that fraud? Either way, I'm afraid I've enlightened your friend Bernard.'

Gilbert could feel the sweat breaking out on his forehead as anger gushed through him. 'You've enlightened him? You bloody fool!'

'You're the bloody fool. Bernard wants to talk to you about it, he said he'd be in the Queen Vic tonight.'

Gilbert's head was thumping. He didn't see Ellis go back to the office but suddenly found he was standing alone in the yard. He took deep breaths to steady himself. He'd have to work out some story to tell Bernard. It wouldn't be impossible if he put his mind to it. If Bernard knew he'd cheated him . . . At the time, it had been like taking sweeties from a baby. It had been Ellis who'd caused the trouble over this.

Gilbert strode across Camden Street to the shop. Brenda had re-dressed the window with new and elegant outfits. The shop looked prosperous, though she was getting more secretive about how much profit she was making. He crossed the floor to the stairs at the back, getting inquisitive glances from the lady customers round the rails of clothes.

It had just gone five o'clock; Brenda didn't close until half past and then she had to cash up and tidy the shop before coming upstairs.

Once on the landing, he could hear the baby mewling plaintively. He went to her bedroom door and slammed it shut.

'What's for tea, Flo?' She was chopping cabbage in the kitchen and there was a good smell coming from the oven.

'Casseroled mutton chops with baked potatoes followed by cabinet pudding.'

'Good, I'm hungry.'

He sat down. She'd already set two places at the table. 'I'll have mine now.'

Her eyes went to the clock. 'It isn't ready yet. Mrs Fox's orders were to have it on the table by six o'clock.'

He could still hear the baby, it was getting on his nerves. 'Can't you shut the baby up?'

She shot off to the bedroom and came back with it in her arms. 'She's been sick.'

Gil felt impatient. He was going to the Table Tennis Club in Dacre Street to meet a girl called Mavis. He'd played with her a couple of nights ago, and she'd been as quick and eager as a terrier. They'd have another game tonight and then he'd take her for a drive and stop somewhere for a drink. It could turn out to be a good evening.

He asked, 'How long have the chops been in?'

'About two hours.'

'That should be long enough, shouldn't it? They smell done.'

'The book says three hours, and the taters need that too.'

Gil felt empty. 'I'll have mine now. I want to go out again.'

'It won't taste right, Mr Gilbert, and I haven't put the cabbage on yet.'

'I don't like cabbage. Come on, don't mess about.'

Flo pushed the crying baby into his arms and fled to the oven. He looked at it in surprise. Wasn't this Ellis's baby? A right little runt if ever there was one. Really puny, but she could bawl loud enough to rouse the dead. A few moments later a plate with two mutton chops and a baked potato slid in front of him.

'Here, you have her back. I can't do anything with her and she smells horrible.'

'I'll let Mrs Fox's dinner cook some more, shall I?'

'Of course. What's that baby doing here? Where's our Lorna?'

'Over the road, I think.'

Flo quietened the baby and Gil lost interest. He started to eat.

'I've done too much cabbage now.'

He ignored that too. Flo was right, the chops were tough and the potato hard. He mashed it up with his fork and added butter. It helped a little but it wasn't the best dinner she'd cooked.

He was finishing off a large portion of the cabinet pudding when Brenda came up from the shop. The pudding wasn't bad except Flo hadn't got round to making the custard.

'You've eaten already?' Her face was twisting with irritation.

'I'm in a hurry, I want to go out again.'

'It's a pity you don't stay out,' she retorted.

He didn't like that, she wasn't usually sharp with him while Flo was about.

Brenda said more calmly, 'A friend of yours has been here looking for you. The one who went to prison for stealing cars. He said he'd see you in the Queen Vic tonight.'

That gave Gil's nerves another prod and made him snap,

'Bernard Corkill? He won't if I can help it.'

'Fallen out with your friend, have you? Double-crossed him too?'

Brenda was too close for comfort. All his good plans were collapsing, making him feel a failure. But all was not lost. He could handle Bernard. He'd work on a story to placate him.

He said, 'I'll have a cup of tea, Flo. Before I go.'

Flo was giving the baby a bottle. She got up and put the child in Brenda's arms while she filled the kettle. The baby was beginning to wail again. Brenda tried to push the teat into her mouth to keep her quiet. Her tongue kept trying to push it out.

'She doesn't like the bottle,' Flo said from the sink. 'She's not used to it.'

'She's had some, hasn't she?'

'About half.'

'She'll have to get used to it now.'

'Why?' asked Gil. 'What's that little pipsqueak doing here?'

Brenda said stiffly, 'You can go home, Flo,' before launching into a long tirade about how upset she was because of what Ruth had done.

Gil found it hard to believe. 'You mean that's my child?'

'Yours and mine.'

'Good God! The other was better. Ellis knows?' He'd said nothing about it when they'd come face to face in the yard.

'Of course. He and Daisy have got Lorna.'

'So I'm the only one who didn't know?' Gil felt he was being sidelined. 'Why keep this from me?'

'Keep it from you? Don't be daft. You were out with your fancy woman, how could we tell you?'

Talk like this made him cringe. 'I was here for breakfast.'

'By then I was opening the shop. I needed you last night. Ruth and I had a big confab over at Ellis's place. Everybody was there except you. Even your mother was.'

Gilbert felt his stomach churn with fear. He couldn't handle all this trouble. Whichever way he turned, there was more. 'What about my cup of tea?'

'For heaven's sake, it's made. You can pour it, can't you?'

He knew Brenda was losing patience with both him and the baby. He saw her give the child a little shake.

'She's not sucking at all.'

The teat was on her tongue but she was drifting off to sleep.

He lifted his teacup to his lips. 'Perhaps she's had enough. What a plain little thing she is.'

'These awful clothes don't help. Daisy has no idea how to choose clothes to make a baby look nice.' Brenda groaned with irritation. 'I want my dinner, I've been on my feet all day. Babies take up so much time. Will you get her wind up?'

'Lord love us, I'm having my tea. No, I don't like babies.'

Brenda pursed her lips as she lifted Jane up on her shoulder and patted her back. The baby gave what sounded like a hiccup and Gilbert saw a stream of milky fluid eject from her mouth and trickle down the back of Brenda's elegant fawn blouse.

She screamed. 'Hell! She's been sick. You have her for a minute while I get this off. I'll have to wash it now, what a nuisance.'

Gil found she'd dumped the baby on his knee. Jane opened her mouth and yelled.

'I don't want her. What if she's sick over me?' He followed Brenda to their bedroom, holding the howling baby in outstretched arms. 'Where shall I put her? I don't want her to be sick on my bed.'

'Hold her a minute.'

'I want to go out.'

Brenda turned round in her underslip and snatched Jane back. 'Go out then. And for God's sake don't come back.'

It scared him to hear her saying such things, with such dislike of him on her face. He changed into his new Fair Isle pullover.

'I mean it, Gil. Go and live with your fancy woman. She'll enjoy putting meals on the table for you so you can hurry out to enjoy yourself with someone else.'

'I can't, don't be silly.'

'She doesn't want you to live with her? She doesn't want a permanent arrangement?'

Moira didn't want anything more to do with him, but he wasn't going to admit that to Brenda, not when she was in a mood like this. And not when everything else in his life was turning sour on him.

He said, 'I married you. You're my wife.'

'I thought you'd forgotten. You chase off after every bit of skirt that crosses your path and expect me to wait on you as though you're royalty. I'm sick of being your wife. I've had enough. I can support myself with the shop, I don't need you and I don't want you. Get out.'

'I've nowhere else to go.'

'How about home to mother?'

'Live with Ellis and Daisy?' he snarled. 'No fear. I'm not leaving here. My name's on the freehold. I'm paying off the loan I took to buy it. If you don't want to live with me, you get out.' Gil picked up his coat and rushed for the stairs. 'Goddamn you, Brenda!'

She was a witch, what had he ever seen in her? This on

top of all his other troubles. He climbed into his Ford and drove off to the Table Tennis Club. Thank goodness he'd met Mavis. There was always another woman who was interested. This evening, he needed a bit of fun to buoy himself up. He'd work out how to bring Brenda round later on; Bernard too. As he changed into his kit at the club, he was looking forward to seeing his new girlfriend.

There was no sign of her when he went into the club room. He didn't let it upset him, he assumed she'd be a few minutes late. There was a cafeteria at one end , and he ordered himself a cup of coffee.

'Not many people in tonight,' he said to the girl behind the counter. Only two of the five tables were in use.

'It's early yet. It gets busy later,' she said, pushing his coffee across to him. Gilbert sat down to wait.

He was jumpy already and the repeated ping of bat against ball was making him worse. Waiting wasn't good for him. Ten minutes went by and he went to check what time Mavis had booked the table for them. She'd suggested six thirty, so they could have a game and there'd be plenty of time for other things afterwards.

It came as a shock to find she hadn't booked for six thirty. His eye went down the page. She hadn't booked at all. She'd definitely said she would. He felt a stirring of unease. Had she forgotten, or . . .

Gilbert bought another cup of coffee and sat down again. A young gawky lad on his own sitting two tables away was making the usual remarks about the club and the weather. After another ten minutes, the lad suggested they have a game while there was still a table available.

'Why not?' Gilbert stood up. It would loosen him up and help pass the time. He had the dragging feeling that Mavis had stood him up.

'I haven't seen you here before, have I?' he asked the lad.

'I'm a new member. Only been once before.'

He wasn't much of a player. A real beginner, who couldn't give him a decent game. Still no sign of Mavis. Gilbert lost patience. It hadn't occurred to him that she mightn't come. She'd seemed keen to see him again. He felt she was kicking him while he was down. He couldn't stand much more. He slammed into the changing room and got dressed.

Where now? Not the Queen Vic, but he needed a proper drink. He'd seen a pub just round the corner from here called the Grapes. He walked instead of moving his car, with his chin hunched into the lapels of his coat. The lounge bar was rather dark and shabby. He felt brassed off, nothing was going right tonight.

With a double whisky in front of him, he tried to think of how he could get back on good terms with Brenda. That was the first problem he had to solve. He'd say he was sorry, of course. Then he'd say he wanted them both to turn over a new leaf, he'd blame overwork for his shortness of temper, and make a fuss of that squawking baby. He didn't fully understand why Brenda had given the better baby to Daisy. He ought to talk to Ellis about that when he had a moment.

Then there was Bernard. He'd keep out of his way for a few days until he'd worked out some softener.

Gilbert ordered more whisky as the bar became more crowded and the babble of voice grew louder. The atmosphere was blue and smoky, and he seemed to be the only man drinking alone. But he sat on over yet another drink, afraid an apology wasn't going to be enough to bring Brenda round. A present? It would have to be something very expensive.

Gilbert sighed, he couldn't face her until he'd thought this through. Everything he tried was ending in failure. Surely it was time his luck changed.

Bernard was feeling low. When he'd left Ellis Fox's office, he'd gone back to his lodgings to get his tea and put his feet up for a bit. He knew he'd find Gilbert Fox sooner or later, he wasn't going to give up. He'd go down to the Queen Vic later on and have a pint there.

Bernard had now drunk four pints and he'd walked round the lounge several times before retreating to the public bar. He'd seen no sign of Gilbert. When the landlord called time, he was growing impatient. It began to look as though Ellis had warned his brother and he was staying out of his way.

When the pub emptied, Bernard went slouching up Market Street with his shoulders more bent than ever. He was tired and the night was cold and dark. He was tempted to go home to bed but he'd have one last try at finding Gil. If he wasn't home now, he soon would be.

He'd just turned into Camden Street when the Ford T drove in behind him, slowing to swing into the entry leading to Camden Yard. To see Gil driving round in a fine car while he was on foot brought another rush of resentment.

Bernard followed silently, he felt his luck had changed. Once he'd left the street, there was no light except that on the car. He watched Gil get out to open the big gates then drive through and straight on to park his vehicle. Good, he'd got him now. Bernard slipped through the gates just as he'd done on that other night so long ago and waited in the shadows until Gil came back to close them.

'Hello,' he said, stepping forward to show himself.

* * *

Gilbert was startled, it made him jump and his heart jolted into sudden overdrive.

'Bernard! What are you doing here?' He knew only too well and he had no excuses worked out. He said, trying to sound as though he was joking, 'Not in trouble again, I hope?'

Bernard's tone was aggressive. 'I'm not, but you are.'

Gil felt his muscles tighten. He'd been rehearsing what he'd say to Brenda, he knew she was still awake because he'd seen their bedroom light on as he'd turned into the entry. He'd been dreading facing her, but this was worse. He didn't know how he was going to get out of this. He mustn't let Bernard see how nervous he was.

'Me?' he said as lightly as he could. 'What sort of trouble?'

Bernard was swaggering, clearly he felt he had the upper hand now. 'Think back to the night you gave me clean clothes and a bath.'

It was the last thing Gil wanted to do. It showed that Bernard understood only too well that he'd done him down. He had to stand his ground. 'You asked me for help and I gave it.'

'Not out of the goodness of your heart.' Bernard came closer and Gil could see black hatred on his face. He felt a swirl of fear. He was used to seeing contempt on Ellis's face and on Brenda's, but this was different, Bernard had always looked up to him.

'You expect payment for everything you do. I was willing to pay, but you did me down. You took Cuthbert Corkill's assets when you knew they were legally mine. Mine and Daisy's.'

'She's just a troublemaker.' Gil couldn't stop himself

shaking. This was a tougher Bernard, there was a ruthless glint in his eyes.

'You're the troublemaker. But I want my inheritance, Gil. You're going to give it back to me.'

How could he? It had been worked through their accounts over the last few years. He'd taken out a bit of extra capital under the pretext of paying for the new cars, there wasn't much left. Ellis was going to be on his back with a vengeance if they had to shell out to Bernard. He felt in a cold sweat, panic-stricken. He needed to think. Should he admit it and apologise? Or should he deny any wrongdoing, say it was all a mistake?

Gil said, 'Look, it's cold out here. Let's get out of this wind where we can talk.'

He closed the gate and led Bernard down the yard to the building where he kept his table tennis equipment. It felt a little warmer inside. They both blinked in the sudden light when he switched it on.

The building was half derelict now, he kept a couple of old bedsheets covering the table to protect it from dust and bits of dropping plaster. He didn't know how to appease Bernard now he'd got him here. If he turned nasty he could always give him a right hook to the chin. If it came to a fight, Gil knew he'd win, but for once he was afraid it would make matters worse. He started folding the sheets back.

'We're not here to play ping pong,' Bernard spat at him. 'You conned me into not claiming what was legally mine. How much did you get?'

'I perjured myself on your behalf.' Gil was clicking the celluloid balls together in his hand. 'You'd have been found guilty of murder if I hadn't given you an alibi. You were known to be a car thief. You'd been close enough to the woman who was killed to get drenched with blood.'

'I didn't kill her.'

'OK, but even though it was your accomplice who did the killing, you'd still have hung. You were in it together. No price is too high for what I did for you. I swore you'd been here with me, exactly on this spot, when the woman was being killed in town. Not many would do that for their friends. The police couldn't shake me, I stood up and did my best for you and it saved you.'

Bernard came closer, there was a leer on his lips. He propped his bottom against the corner of the table.

'I counted you my friend as well as my cousin. I knew you drove a hard bargain but I trusted you. I bet you've got papers over there in your office that set out exactly what you got. I want to see them.'

'It happened years ago, they won't—'

'Your brother will show them to me if you won't. Or Daisy. You cheated her too. We must point that out to her, see what she says.'

Gilbert swallowed. He'd not expected to be scared of Bernard, but this was rattling him. This on top of everything else.

Bernard's lip curled. 'There's nothing worse than a man who preys on his friends, sets out to make money from them. You knew I had no idea how much you were taking from me.'

Gil edged back, feeling threatened.

'It's payback time now. I want what you owe me.'

'All right.' Gil opened his wallet and took out the few pounds he had there, pushing them along the edge of the table.

'That's no use. I'm not talking petty cash.' Bernard was raising his voice. It was a good job they were too far from the house for anyone to hear. 'I'll take a couple of hundred now, a cheque will do But it will mean regular payments.'

Gil felt a cold chill run down his spine. That sounded like blackmail. 'I don't have that sort of money.'

'You do. Your business is earning, isn't it? You've been living on the fat of the land all these years while I haven't known where to turn for the next penny. I want what's rightfully mine.'

Gil felt desperate, he had to get rid of him. 'The business belongs to my mother—'

'Not the taxis. You made a point of telling me they were yours.'

'I can't possibly . . . There's Ellis too. Look, we'll talk about it in the morning. Discuss it properly.'

'What's the point in putting it off?' Bernard was full of menace now. He'd raised his voice another octave. The man was like a wild thing, he'd never had any self-control.

'For God's sake.' Gil had come out in a cold sweat. 'Calm down.' He felt his fists curling up. He'd have to hit him to get out of here.

'Don't raise your fists to me,' Bernard snarled. 'You won't fight your way out of this.'

Bernard was staring at him, his eyes bulging. Gil could see a nerve throbbing in his temple. He'd never seen him so full of confidence before. Bernard really believed he could blackmail him, that he'd got him cornered.

Gil shivered and clenched his fists tighter.

'Don't try that, you'll be sorry if you do.' There was an authoritative ring to Bernard's voice.

It was the only way. Gil knew he had brute strength on his side. Bernard was nothing but a runt.

Suddenly Bernard leapt at him. The split second before his weight crashed against Gil was one of paralysing terror. He fell back as he felt cold steel rip through his belly; saw his own blood on the wicked blade shining under the bare electric bulb. There was more spurting out, blood everywhere. He gasped: 'That woman . . . you were her killer?'

'Come on, Gil, you must have known I wasn't the accomplice.'

Gil's hands groped for the edge of the table but he was sliding down. Oh my God! He'd never have believed Bernard could kill!

Chapter Twenty-four

Brenda was woken by a whimper from the cot. She turned over, pulled the blankets round her ears and tried to shut it out. Daisy and Ellis had told her that Jane had slept through the whole of last night, they seemed to expect her to do it again. Brenda listened, willing her to go back to sleep. Another whimper came followed by a thin mewl, then Jane was settling into a steady grizzle.

Brenda was about to slide reluctantly out of the double bed when she sensed she had it to herself. She put out an exploratory arm. She had! She sat up, put the light on and looked again at the clock. It was one thirty in the morning! Gil was always in bed by this time. He must have taken her at her word, he wasn't coming home. Thank goodness, she hoped he never would. She felt cheered as she got up to see to the baby.

Jane was soaking wet. Brenda had to change her nightgown as well as her nappy and by that time the baby had worked herself up and was crying with lusty impatience.

Brenda had boiled water ready for what she'd hoped would be her six o clock feed. She diluted the cow's milk as Ruth had taught her to do for Lorna, then she had to warm it a little, by which time Jane was screaming.

The bedroom felt freezing in the middle of the night and Brenda hadn't put a dressing gown on. She got back into bed and took Jane there to feed. She was a very slow feeder. Lorna could empty her bottles in no time but Jane kept pushing the teat out of her mouth and whining. She was used to breast-feeding and clearly preferred it, but she would have to get used to this.

Daisy hadn't been able to tell her how much milk Jane took at each feed, so she made up the same amount Lorna had been taking. It seemed to take ages to get the bottle down her, but Brenda knew she had to do it or the baby would be howling for more in a couple of hours. She could feel herself beginning to doze off.

She was brought back to full wakefulness with a jerk. She felt the baby tense in her arms and seconds later the milk was spurting back. Jane had vomited all over herself, her mother and the bed.

'Damn, damn, damn!' Brenda leapt out with angry tears scalding her eyes. Jane was crying again, and she'd need another clean nightie. What could she do to soothe her now? She wished Ruth were here, or Daisy, they'd know. Even Flo would be able to nurse her back to sleep.

She washed and changed Jane and put her back in her cot. She needed to wash and change herself, the smell of vomit was turning her own stomach. Jane was howling with surprising lustiness for one so puny. Brenda gave her a drink of boiled water which seemed to do the trick. Wearily she crept into bed on Gil's side and hoped she'd be allowed to sleep for the rest of the night.

Fifteen minutes later she was up dragging the soiled sheet off the bed. The smell was horrible. She dumped it in the bath and ran cold water on it. Then she opened her bedroom window and got back into bed. She was cold to the core and wide awake, the blanket next to her skin felt scratchy.

She hadn't actually gone back to sleep when Jane's ticking

whimper started again. Brenda put on the light; it was a quarter to three. She felt bone weary and wanted only to be left alone. What was she going to do for this baby now? She had to get her off to sleep.

Condensed milk, that was it. Fresh milk didn't suit her. Brenda put her dressing gown on this time and went to make up another bottle. She wished she'd thought to boil the kettle again when she was up last time. Now she had to wait for it to boil and for the water to cool afterwards. She made herself a cup of tea. Oh God! What a night this was and Jane was working herself up into a frenzy once more.

In case she was sick again, Brenda sat on a hard chair to feed her. She watched with distaste as this time the tiny mouth worked purposefully on the teat. Jane was perfectly capable of drinking from a bottle if she wanted to. The baby's eyes were closed but wet with tears and her nose was running. Brenda wondered how she and Gil could have produced such a plain child, but there was a podginess about her features as though she was going to take after the Maddocks side of the family. Half the bottle went down with reasonable speed before Jane stopped sucking. That would do, she wouldn't chance overfilling her tiny stomach and risk having it all come back again.

Brenda got back into bed. The baby was mercifully quiet and slept but at five thirty she had to go through the whole performance again. The only good thing was that Gil hadn't come home.

Brenda was in a deep sleep when the alarm clock went off and she had to get up. She felt sleep sodden and exhausted.

She was dragging herself round the kitchen when Jane started to cry again. She'd have to wait until Flo came, Brenda couldn't touch her now she was decently dressed for work. It wouldn't do if she smelled of baby sick down in the shop. She'd done all she could for her.

She made herself a cup of tea and sat down to drink it, watching the hands of the clock cover the last ten minutes to eight o'clock.

Such a relief to hear Flo ring the doorbell. She directed her straight to the cot and was able to relax once the fretful clamouring stopped. Brenda felt she couldn't cope with this baby. It was driving her mad. She didn't even like it. It was all Ruth's fault; if she'd had it from the beginning she'd have loved it.

It was ten o'clock and she had customers in the shop when Ellis came over. She wasn't sure whether he was cross or anxious.

'Where's Gil? Has he overslept? Enid says he meets the London train every Tuesday for a regular customer. He has to be there by half ten.'

Brenda was disconcerted and drew him into the back room.

'He didn't come home last night.'

'Well, where is he?'

'Spent the night with his fancy woman, I suppose. I told him to get out and he has. I'm not having him back here after this.'

Ellis looked taken aback. 'His car's here. He can't be far. I'd better tell Enid to send one of the others.'

Brenda felt uneasy as she watched him run back across the road.

During the morning, Daisy tried to work as usual on the accounts in the office but everybody was on edge because Gil seemed to have disappeared. He'd never done anything like this before. He didn't like Ellis interfering in any way with the taxis and though he was often late in the morning, he was always much in evidence during the day.

The other drivers had come to work and having cleaned their cars were standing about in the yard waiting for jobs. Business was being carried on much as usual, Enid was taking telephone requests for taxis out to them.

Dora came down to see if they'd had any news of Gil.

'No,' Daisy told her. 'It seems he and Brenda had a row last night and she told him to get out.'

'He's a very silly boy,' his mother sighed. 'Not like the others. He's always been such a worry.'

After dinner had been eaten and cleared away, Daisy fed Lorna while Olive got the older children ready for their afternoon walk. Her breasts felt painfully hard and full, she tried to get Lorna to suck on them but she wouldn't. Lorna was used to the bottle and wasn't prepared to accept any alternative. She drained the bottle in moments and then gave her mother a wavering smile which made Daisy hug her. The baby gave an audible chuckle which delighted her further; she felt a surge of mother love for Lorna.

She was a lovely baby and hardly any trouble. Brenda had reported proudly that mostly she slept through the night, and had done so since she was six weeks old. Now at nearly six months she was sleeping less during the day, but she was so good-tempered, she billed and cooed to herself and didn't demand the attention that baby Jane did. Daisy had had to get the playpen out because she could roll and push herself about the floor if she put her down.

But she couldn't stop thinking about Jane. She longed to know how she'd fared with Brenda during the night.

'Leave her be,' Ellis advised. 'Until it's time to take her for the usual walk.'

It was half past two when Daisy went to collect her.

Brenda looked quite haggard, she had customers in the shop.

'Yes,' she whispered, 'I'd be glad if you'd take her out. It'll give Flo a chance to catch up with the work. Jane's been tetchy all morning.'

'Did she sleep through the night again?'

'She did not. She was terrible; sick all over my bed, had me awake half the night. I feel awful.'

This was what Daisy had expected to happen. She'd hoped Brenda would want to give Jane back to her. Now she didn't know what she wanted. Lorna was worming her way into her affections and she was her own flesh and blood. She didn't want to give her up either.

She moved to the bottom of the stairs, feeling full of sympathy for Jane.

'I'll go up and get her. By the way, Ellis is asking if you've seen Gil. He hasn't come to work yet.'

'No, and I don't want to either.'

'But his car's in the back, Brenda. He can't be far away or he'd have taken it.'

Brenda frowned. 'Who knows what he gets up to.'

Upstairs, Flo reported that Jane wasn't taking much of the diluted condensed milk. She'd cried most of the morning and taken only an ounce or so each time she tried to feed her. She'd gone to sleep about midday and not woken since.

Daisy carried Jane over to her own nursery. Partly to give her a proper feed and partly to ease her own discomfort, she put her to the breast. The poor little mite seemed half starved. Then she put her in the pram with Lorna and they all went for a walk. It was a pleasant sunny day, and Dora for once went with them.

While Olive played ball with the boys, Dora and Daisy sat on a bench with the pram parked close by. Dora was upset.

'How could Gil go off with another woman like this? It's not as though he's been married that long. I feel sorry for Brenda.'

'You needn't be,' Daisy sighed. 'She told me she'd rather he never came back.'

They talked round and round their problems, Gil's disappearance and the consequences of what Ruth had done.

'Gil's made such a mess of his life, done so many silly things . . .'

It was an early summer day and the sun was warm. They stayed out most of the afternoon. It was nearly five when Daisy wheeled the big pram round the corner into Camden Street. She didn't want to hand Jane back to Brenda but she was steeling herself to do it when she saw Enid run across the road from the clothes shop. When Daisy went in with the child in her arms, there were no customers and she was surprised to find Flo in charge. She'd never served in the shop before.

'Where's Brenda gone?' She expected to hear she was upstairs having a rest.

Flo turned round, her young face twisting with anxiety.

'The drivers have found Mr Gilbert,' she gulped and her voice dropped an octave. 'Awful, absolutely awful.'

'Where is he?'

'Under the ping-pong table. Two of the drivers . . . They were waiting for jobs and went for a game to pass the time. He's been stabbed.'

Daisy's mouth was suddenly dry. 'Is he badly hurt?'

'He's dead.'

It was a few seconds before Daisy could move, then still hugging the baby she shot back across the road after her mother-in-law who was taking Peter in through the funeral parlour.

Although the house had its own front door the family rarely used it when the door was open for business because the internal passages behind led into one another. It saved getting keys out. There were two policemen inside.

Ellis rushed to meet his mother. 'What's happened?' she asked.

'Let's go upstairs, Mam.' He put an arm round her. 'You come too, Daisy. I need you.'

Three hours later, Daisy was sitting by the fire with her mother-in-law. For a long time, they'd stood at the living-room window looking down on Camden Yard. It had never been so busy, even now policemen were going about their business. Daisy had drawn the curtains on them and switched on the lights, though daylight was not quite gone.

She felt there was an unreal quality about everything though they'd tried to follow their usual early evening routine. For the children's sake, the adults had struggled to eat their tea and talk of anything but the horror that was filling their minds. The children had been washed and Dora had read them a story before they'd all been put to bed.

Daisy was glad to have Jane safely up there too, but she couldn't help but think of Brenda. Ellis had told them she'd been absolutely hysterical when she'd heard what had happened. He'd had to stop her rushing over to the building.

'It was a dreadful sight, I'm glad she didn't see it. Gil had been stabbed over and over again. It was a frenzied attack, there was blood everywhere.'

'Where is Brenda?'

'I drove her round to her mother's house. I thought she'd be the best person to look after her.'

Daisy had shivered. 'Is Gil still over there?'

'I don't think so, they told me they'd take him to the morgue when they'd finished taking photographs and that. Thank goodness you'd taken Mam and the boys out.'

'Who could have done it? Do they know?'

'I think they thought it might be me. They certainly kept on at me. Such questions.'

'No!' Daisy was feeling a little hysterical herself. That was ridiculous, Ellis was the last person to hurt anyone.

'I told them about Bernard Corkill. That he'd been round yesterday asking for Gilbert. Apparently he went to see Brenda in the shop too.'

'Oh my goodness!'

'He's never come near me before.'

'Do you think . . . ?'

He shook his head. 'I don't know.'

Ellis was down in the office now. After he'd taken Brenda to her mother's, he'd had to go down to the police station to make a statement. He was finishing work that normally he'd have done in the afternoon.

Daisy sighed. It was impossible not to feel fluttery with shock and thrown thoroughly out of kilter by these events. Dora had been so well recently, she had even put on a little weight. Despite her new hairstyle she still clung to her long black dresses and black shawl and now her eyes were red and her hands were trembling slightly as they lay on her lap.

'Such a terrible end for poor Gilbert. Whoever would have thought it could happen here on our own premises? I don't feel safe here any more.'

'It's safe for us, perfectly safe.' Daisy tried to find words of comfort. But what did one say to a mother whose son has been murdered?

Dora was remembering times past, recounting anecdotes of Gilbert's childhood, some of which Daisy had heard before. She made soothing noises whenever her mother-in-law stopped, and wished she could think of something good to say about him.

Dora's dark, intense gaze met hers. 'Gil was such a one for getting into trouble.'

'Not like Ellis.'

'Not like any of the others. He was one on his own.' She gave a little sob. 'I've never told anyone before, Daisy. It was my secret. Albert thought it better to make it so . . . He was a very good man and his sons took after him.'

Daisy straightened up. Dora was stiff with tension, she could see by her manner that some new confidence was coming.

'Gilbert was not his child.'

That made Daisy gasp.

'I was five months gone when I married Albert. Does that shock you?'

'No,' Daisy denied. 'No.' But all the same . . . 'Rosa, my mother . . . She was not the only one then?'

'It happened to many, I fear. I was luckier than most. Albert knew, of course. Said it would be better if nobody else did. He didn't want any scandal, you see. He was a very kind man, I'd known him for years.'

'Who was Gil's father?' Daisy had to ask.

'A ne'er-do-well. A handsome womaniser who abandoned me as soon as I told him there was a baby on the way. Gil was like his father. Albert tried to treat him as his own son but Gil was always disappointing us. He tried our patience sorely. Always up to mischief. Never wanted to work. All the others were like Albert, upright and honest. If only Walter had lived . . .'

Daisy kissed her cheek. 'Thank you for telling me. It helps me to understand things better.'

'Tell Ellis for me. He might like to know there's no bad blood in his veins.'

Daisy told him when they were in bed that night. 'There's bad blood in my veins though,' she said sadly. 'Bernard Corkill and my mother . . .'

'No,' he told her, 'it's the last thing you have. Don't you worry about your relatives.'

Ernest Maddocks climbed the stairs with a tray of morning tea for his womenfolk. He was glad to have his girls at home but wished it wasn't trouble that had brought them.

Ruth was wide awake when he took her cup in. 'Tea in bed. Thanks, Dad, this is a lovely treat.'

His second daughter was still comatose. He said, 'I've brought you a cup of tea, Brenda.' She gave a little grunt in response. 'Your mother says you should wear this today.'

Brenda's head lifted from her pillow and she looked at him bleary-eyed. 'What's that?'

'A black blouse.'

'Don't want it.'

'Better had, love.' He left it on a chair for her and went to his own room with tea for himself and Glad.

'Breakfast in twenty minutes,' he heard Glad calling as she went downstairs later. The rest of them had finished eating when Brenda appeared. She was wearing the scarlet blouse she'd had on when Ellis had brought her round yesterday.

'You can't dress yourself up like that, Brenda,' her mother fumed. 'Another scandal for the family, that's what this is going to be, and you're going to make things worse. Why didn't you put on that black blouse of mine?'

'It's horribly old, Mam, and it's too big for me.'

'You can't be seen wearing red. You've got to show you're grieving.'

'But I'm not, Mam. I wanted to be rid of Gil and now I am. I'm over the awful shock. There's nothing to grieve about. Quite the opposite. What is there to eat?'

'We've had egg and bacon. Your bacon's still in the pan. You'll have to do your own egg.'

'Toast is all I want.'

Ruth got up. 'I'll do it for you, Brenda.'

'I'm not going to wear your old clothes, Mam. You aren't turning me into a frump.'

'Thank you very much, I must say.' Glad was indignant.

'I'll go round to your place and pick up some clothes for you,' Ruth offered. 'You've got a black blouse?'

'I've got a nice grey one . . .'

'You've got blouses of every colour,' her mother thundered. 'You'll wear black if you've any sense.'

'I'll bring you two or three outfits.'

'I could go myself . . .'

Ern had to stop this carping. 'Your mother's right, Brenda. Your husband's been murdered, you've got to look as though you care. It's all right saying things like that to us but your customers will be shocked. Everybody knows the Foxes . . .'

'Mam shouldn't have bragged that we'd married into the family.'

'That's as maybe,' Glad put in. 'But you can't wear that red blouse. Even white would be better. You always used to wear white blouses.'

'A sign of serfdom. I was an employee then. Since I've owned the shop I wear smart clothes of any sort.'

Ern could see Glad bristling with ire. 'Everybody will be talking about you,' she said. 'You've got to look as though you're missing him. People will be sorry for you then and possibly buy from you instead of going elsewhere. If you play it right it could be good for your shop. Play it wrong and it won't. I know, Brenda. I've been in business all my life. Been through a scandal too, and I know just what that can do.'

Ern said gently, 'If customers mention Gil to you, love, you've got to say the right thing.'

'Play the bereaved wife, overcome with grief,' Glad added. 'Even if you aren't.'

Ruth went out and later in the morning Brenda was glad to see her mother getting ready to go out shopping. It meant she'd have a rest from her sharp tongue. Her father was weeding the flowerbeds in the garden. Brenda went to help him and decided that one day she must have a garden of her own.

It seemed next to no time before her mother was back, dumping her bags on the kitchen table.

'I knew there'd be a scandal,' she said, filling the kettle to make a cup of tea. 'It's all over town already. Mrs Smith next door stopped me as I was coming in, to ask how you are, and to tell me that Bernard Corkill's been arrested for the murder.'

Brenda gasped. 'That fellow who steals cars?'

'I don't know what he does, but I'd heard already. I met one of our old customers in town. She said he was in police custody and was helping them with their inquiries.'

'Good,' Brenda said, but she felt jittery. 'The sooner they charge him and have him in court, the sooner it will all die down.'

She felt in limbo. She wanted to start her new life but Mam wouldn't let her break free from the coils of the old. 'I think I'll go home, I want to see to the shop.'

'It's much too soon for that. Gil hasn't even been buried.' Mam kept nagging at her.

'That mightn't happen for a long time,' she sighed. 'He didn't die in his bed, after all.'

'Better if you stay here with us for a couple of days to get over it. Anyway, you can't be seen in the shop yet. It ought to be shut, as a mark of respect.'

'It's my living. I want to be there.'

'I thought Ellis said he'd ask Ivy to work full-time for you this week.'

'He did, but I don't know definitely that she is, do I?'

'Ellis will see that everything's all right.'

'Ivy needs an eye keeping on her. I'll have to go, I want to go, Mam. It's my home too. I can't sit here shut off from everything. I want to get on with my life. I'm going to have a bit more fun from now on.'

'You'll be staying here for another day or two,' Glad ordered. 'You hardly know what you're doing.'

Chapter Twenty-five

Gil's macabre murder sent a shock wave through the family. They all felt on edge. Daisy wanted to shield her little boys from it but found it almost impossible. They'd seen the police on their premises and were asking questions. She told them as much of the truth as she could without frightening them, and thought it best to stick as closely as she could to their usual routine. She saw them off to the park with Olive after dinner. Dora couldn't be persuaded to go with them.

'I don't feel like it. I didn't sleep last night, I think I'll go and lie on my bed.'

Daisy set out with the two babies in the big pram to visit Auntie Glad's house. On top of everything else, she was worried about Brenda and hated the uncertainty of not knowing what her plans were for Jane.

She found all the family sitting outside in the sunny back garden. They were having a spell of warm weather which was a rare treat so early in the summer. Uncle Ern came to open the gate so she could wheel the pram across the grass to them and Ruth found another chair for her.

Brenda had been interviewed by the police and was looking white and drawn, but she bombarded Daisy with questions. There was little Daisy could tell her that she didn't already know.

Auntie Glad said, 'You've heard Bernard Corkill's been

arrested and is helping them with their inquiries?'

'No!' That gave Daisy another jolt. She quaked inwardly and wondered if things would have been different if he hadn't found out what Gilbert had done.

'Such a shock for Gil's mother, she'll be upset,' Uncle Ern said.

'She is, very.'

'I don't suppose Ellis is,' Brenda put in. 'He never seemed to like Gil. They were always arguing about something.'

'He's shocked. Sickened by it.' Daisy knew just how much Ellis was feeling it. Jane give a little whimper. She was working herself up for a good cry. Daisy knew the signs only too well.

'I'm better off without him,' Brenda said defiantly. 'I know I am, we've been having terrible rows. Well, you all know how things were. I should never have married him.'

'Brenda, you shouldn't say such things!' her mother said. 'It isn't nice now he's dead.'

'I wouldn't dare if he wasn't.'

Daisy felt more than a little surprised at Brenda's outspokenness. 'All the same, it was a horrible end for Gil. It makes my skin crawl to think of it.'

'Troubles never come singly,' Auntie Glad sighed. 'Our Brenda's not the only one with difficulties. Ruth's told us about exchanging the babies.' Daisy was relieved to hear it.

There was a plaintive wail from Jane. Daisy picked her up to comfort her before she woke Lorna too. She was convinced now that her best chance of keeping Jane was to appear ready and willing to hand her over, in the hope that Brenda would tire of looking after her.

'I've brought Jane to see you,' she told her now and put the child in Brenda's arms. Brenda stared down at her daughter with some distaste.

'Poor thing, she's hardly good-looking, is she?' Jane continued to grizzle.

'Thank you for taking it so well, Daisy.' Ruth was quieter than usual.

'Are you better?'

'Yes, I'm trying to put it behind me. I'm going back to work next week. I do hope you forgive me.'

Daisy tried to smile. 'You're forgiven, Ruth,' she said. 'It's just that what's done isn't easy to undo. I'd like to put it behind me too but I can't stop thinking of Jane as mine. I've sort of bonded with her.'

She looked across at the way Brenda was holding Jane; she was not hugging her closely, nor was there any show of affection. Daisy understood the reason, but it grieved her.

'It's altered the way we think of our babies, hasn't it, Brenda?'

'Yes. It was an awful thing to do, Ruth. Utterly terrible.'

Daisy felt quite misty-eyed. 'Yet now I know Lorna is my flesh and blood . . . mine and Ellis's, then it does make a difference. I'm beginning to feel more motherly towards her. She's a beautiful child.'

'And not so troublesome.' Brenda sighed. 'This one doesn't give anybody much peace.' Jane was snivelling. 'Is she due for a feed or something?'

'No, I fed her before setting out. What do you want to do now?'

Daisy meant did she want to keep Jane here with her. She hated this uncertainty and wanted a decision. If Brenda insisted on keeping her, now while they were staying with Auntie Glad might be a good time for them to settle down together.

'Shush, shush.' Brenda began to jog the baby up and down to soothe her. 'I'm going to expand my business. I mean,

I've got to look towards a future on my own now, haven't I? I'd like to get better premises in Grange Road. Running my own shop is much more my sort of thing than marriage. I shall quite enjoy being single again and—'

Jane gave a loud hiccup and a stream of half-digested milk shot over Brenda.

'Oh hell! She's always puking over me! Yuk!'

Daisy's arms closed round Jane as she was thrust back at her.

'I'll have to go and change, it always smells disgusting. Makes such a lot of unnecessary washing too.' Brenda's face was twisting with irritation as she set off towards the house. 'Good job you went round to get some more clothes for me this morning, Ruth.'

Daisy felt an upsurge of hope. It sounded as though Brenda wouldn't have time for babies in the new way of life she planned for herself, though she hadn't actually said so. She reached for the bottle of boiled water she'd brought with her. Jane's little frame was still shuddering with sobs but she was quietening down. Ruth was watching her.

'Brenda's right about the smell and the washing,' Daisy said. 'She is always being sick.'

'It's just regurgitation.' Ruth was handing out advice as she'd always done. 'Nothing to worry about.'

'I'll have to change her, all the same.' Daisy had brought some of Jane's clothes with her because she'd been half afraid she'd have to leave her here.

Because Brenda was still locked in the bathroom, she removed the offending bib and dress and sponged Jane down with water from the kitchen sink. While she was doing it she saw Uncle Ern walk across the lawn with another man who sat down next to Ruth in the chair Brenda had vacated.

After a few moments, Auntie Glad got up and came to the kitchen.

'Who's that?' Daisy asked as she prepared to take Jane back.

'A friend of Ruth's, would you believe? A doctor, no less.'

'He looks nice.' Daisy examined him from a distance.

'This is the second time he's called to see how she is. I'm going to make a cup of tea. What a good job I made scones this morning.'

'I'll put Jane back in her pram, she'll go off again now. Then I'll give you a hand.'

'Daisy,' Ruth said when she went over, 'this is Dr Max Harris.' Ruth looked quite different. Her cheeks were pink and there was a new sparkle about her. 'Daisy Fox, d'you remember her?'

He crushed Daisy's hand in his. 'Of course, your sister, the one with a big family.'

'That's me.'

'The Caesarean section,' Ruth added.

Daisy giggled. 'I hope that label isn't going to follow me round for the rest of my life.'

Brenda came back looking bandbox fresh in a new black outfit.

'Ah, the second Mrs Fox. Your other sister. And these are the two babies?' Daisy held her breath while he gave the pram a cursory glance. 'Doing well, I see.'

'Very well,' she said, wondering whether Ruth had told him what she'd done. Ruth changed the subject quickly.

'Max is going to run me and my suitcase back to the nurses' home in his car. Then we're going out tonight.'

'Auntie Glad's making a cup of tea for you,' Daisy told her. 'I said I'd give her a hand.'

In the kitchen Daisy saw the best china was being brought out, together with the best embroidered tray cloths.

She said, 'A bit over the top for tea in the garden, isn't it?'

'Nonsense,' Auntie Glad said. 'Not for our Ruth and a young man like that, they're professional people. Butter the scones for me.'

Daisy smiled as she set about it. 'Brenda won't be able to say she pities Ruth any more.'

'Why would she say such a thing?'

'She's always said Ruth has nothing in her life but work. The boot will be on the other foot from now on.'

Afternoon tea in the garden turned out to be quite a jolly affair. Her family all seemed in a buoyant mood; there was no mention of Gilbert's violent death, for the moment, he was forgotten. The two babies slept right through it, and no further mention was made of them.

Then Ruth fetched her suitcase and her friend carried it out to his car which he'd parked at the front gate. They all followed to see her off and Ruth kissed them all.

Daisy said, 'I don't think I've ever seen Ruth look so happy.'

'It's all right for her,' Brenda said. 'She can walk away from what she did, but what about me?'

'We're going to have to sort things out between us,' Daisy said with a soft sigh. 'It's time I went home.' This was the moment she was dreading, leaving Jane here. Walking away from her. She waited for Brenda's response but she had to ask, 'What are we going to do about Jane?'

Brenda was looking down at her sleeping daughter. 'She still smells a bit of sick, Daisy.'

'Shall I take her or leave her here with you?'

She could see Brenda's beautiful face puckering with

distaste. 'I could do with a decent night's sleep. I need to get over Gil . . .'

'Of course you do.' Daisy felt a jerk of pure joy. 'I'll take her home.'

'I don't think I could cope with her.'

Daisy felt every muscle in her body relax as relief flooded through her. Brenda didn't want to keep Jane!

'Well, not just yet, anyway.'

That dampened Daisy's spirits a little. It sounded as though Brenda would want her back as soon as she recovered from the shock of Gil's death.

Within days, everybody in Birkenhead knew that Bernard Corkill had been charged with the murder of Gilbert Fox, and Brenda was notified that Gil's body would be released for burial.

Ellis arranged the most lavish funeral possible, it was what his mother wanted. It was to be held on a Thursday afternoon, half-day closing, as many of their friends and customers were in the retail trade. Both Brenda's business and their own closed for the whole day as a mark of respect and so all their employees could attend the burial. The entire fleet of hire cars followed the hearse.

The manner of Gil's death meant his funeral brought the biggest turnout Ellis had ever seen. Hordes of men with their caps in their hands lined the streets and paid their last respects to Gil as the cortege passed.

Daisy provided the funeral tea in her formal dining room. Brenda sat at the table in her widow's weeds looking pitiful and stayed on until after Ellis had shown the last guest out.

He came back and slumped into his chair again. Dora's eyes were closing, she looked exhausted. Daisy was glad it was over, she felt bone weary. She got up. 'I'll make us a fresh pot of tea.'

Brenda said, 'I want you to know that I'll pay the loan that's outstanding on my premises. I want to stand on my own feet, be independent from now on. I can earn my own living.'

Ellis said, 'Brenda, you'll be entitled to a share of this business. Gil will have left it to you. Mam told him to make a will when he got married, didn't you, Mam?'

'I don't know whether he did,' Brenda's voice was heavy with doubt. 'I can't find one. Are you sure it isn't in the office?'

'Even if he didn't, it will come to you. It's only right his estate should support his wife and child.'

Brenda sighed. 'Ellis, I'd like you to take all Gil's belongings out of my house. His clothes, everything.' Then she looked at his mother. 'I can't bear to be reminded . . .'

'Of course not, dear.' Dora mopped at her eyes. 'Such a sad day. One doesn't expect one's children . . .' She pulled herself to her feet. 'I think I'd like to lie down for a while.'

Daisy said, 'I'll come up and see you in a little while.' Then she turned to Brenda. 'We've got to decide what's to be done about Jane. Do you want to take her home with you now?'

There was repugnance on Brenda's face. 'No, I don't think I could, she'd remind me of Gil more than anything else. She's his daughter. She'd be better off with you, Daisy. I haven't got the knack of looking after babies, I don't know why I ever thought I had. You always seem so happy with your children. I suppose . . . I wanted to have what you had.' The beautiful melting eyes lifted to meet Daisy's. 'Will you keep her?'

Daisy knew she'd never need to ask anything more of

life. 'Of course we'll have Jane. Nothing would suit me better.' The moment of triumph went, she stiffened. Did Brenda expect to keep . . . ?

Ellis asked, 'What about Lorna?'

Daisy held her breath.

'Well, she's yours, isn't she?'

Daisy felt such a surge of joy she hardly took in what Ellis was saying.

'If we keep Jane now, Brenda, we'll want to keep her for good. It won't suit either her or Daisy if you decide in five or ten years' time that you want her back.'

'I won't! I'll pay you to look after her.'

'We don't want to be paid,' Ellis said seriously. 'Daisy and I would like to adopt her – to make sure she is ours for good. You think about it carefully for a few weeks.'

'I already have.' Brenda's beautiful face was puckering with pain. 'I want the single life. How can I work in the shop if I don't get a decent night's sleep? I don't think I could look after her. I don't want the responsibility.'

Ellis said gravely, 'Then it looks as though we'll all get what we want.'

'I mean, I'll be able to see her regularly. She'll be growing up just across the road. I shall be a most devoted aunt. I want you to take all the baby things away too, Daisy. All the clothes and prams and napkins . . .'

'Tomorrow,' Daisy told her happily.

As she and Ellis were getting ready for bed that night, Daisy said, 'I couldn't have borne it if Brenda had decided she wanted Jane back.'

'I didn't think she would, love. If she couldn't cope with Lorna, I was sure she'd never cope with Jane.' He chuckled. 'It looks as though we've got ourselves another daughter.

How d'you feel about being mother to five?'

'You know I'll love it. We'll bring the two girls up as twins,' Daisy said happily. 'That gives us the perfect family.'

Echoes Across the Mersey

Anne Baker

It's August 1914 and the threat of war is weighing heavily on the people of Liverpool, but not on Sarah Hoxton. For Toby Percival, the dashing son of the owner of the factory where she and her mother work, has told her he loves her. Her mother is afraid they will both lose their jobs but Sarah is prepared to risk everything for Toby's love.

Maurice Percival is furious when he discovers his son is involved with a factory girl and they become locked in a fierce battle. Fired with the fever of patriotism and determined to defy his father, Toby volunteers to fight in the trenches. Sarah is left facing what seem to be insurmountable obstacles but with the help of her friends, family and a strength she never knew she possessed she struggles on while the escalating tragedy of the Great War unfolds. It's not until the fighting is over that she finds peace, and even then it's not where she expected it.

Don's miss Anne Baker's previous Merseyside sagas:

'A heartwarming saga' *Woman's Weekly*

'A delightful tale of love and family' *Woman's Realm*

'Another nostalgic story oozing with atmosphere and charm' *Liverpool Echo*

'Truly compelling . . . rich in language and descriptive prose' *Newcastle Upon Tyne Evening Chronicle*

0 7472 6437 6

headline

With a Little Luck

Anne Baker

Alice Luckett is only a child when her father, Len, commits suicide. Her mother disappeared several months before, so Alice goes to live with her grandparents who have little time for the poor girl. Her only real happiness comes from the hours she spends next door with Nell Ainslie and her handsome son Eric.

Slowly but surely, Alice comes to terms with her loss. But when her uncle gets involved in the bakery business where she works, a chilling memory from the night of Len's death comes back to haunt her. And a shocking revelation changes life for the whole family . . .

Praise for Anne Baker's previous bestselling Merseyside sagas:

'A stirring tale of romance and passion, poverty and ambition' *Liverpool Echo*

'Highly observant writing style . . . a compelling book that you just don't want to put down' *Southport Visiter*

'A gentle tale with all the right ingredients for a heartwarming novel' *Huddersfield Daily Examiner*

'Another nostalgic story oozing with atmosphere and charm' *Liverpool Echo*

0 7472 6139 3

headline

Now you can buy any of these other bestselling books by **Anne Baker** from your bookshop or *direct from her publisher*.

FREE P&P AND UK DELIVERY
(Overseas and Ireland £3.50 per book)

Nobody's Child	£5.99
Legacy of Sins	£5.99
Liverpool Lies	£5.99
The Price of Love	£5.99
With a Little Luck	£5.99
A Liverpool Lullaby	£6.99
Mersey Maids	£5.99
A Mersey Duet	£6.99
Moonlight on the Mersey	£6.99
Merseyside Girls	£5.99
Paradise Parade	£5.99
Like Father Like Daughter	£5.99

TO ORDER SIMPLY CALL THIS NUMBER

01235 400 414

or e-mail orders@bookpoint.co.uk

Prices and availability subject to change without notice.